SIMPLY
FORBIDDEN

Books by Kate Pearce

SIMPLY SEXUAL

SIMPLY SINFUL

SIMPLY SHAMELESS

SIMPLY WICKED

SIMPLY INSATIABLE

SIMPLY FORBIDDEN

Published by Kensington Publishing Corp.

SIMPLY FORBIDDEN

KATE PEARCE

APHRODISIA

KENSINGTON BOOKS
http://www.kensingtonbooks.com

APHRODISIA BOOKS are published by

Kensington Publishing Corp.
119 West 40th Street
New York, NY 10018

All Kensington Titles, Imprints, and Distributed Lines are available at special quantity discounts for bulk purchases for sales promotions, premiums, fund-raising, and educational or institutional use.

Special book excerpts or customized printings can also be created to fit specific needs. For details, write or phone the office of the Kensington special sales manager: Kensington Publishing Corp., 119 West 40th Street, New York, NY 10018, attn: Special Sales Department, Phone: 1-800-221-2647.

Aphrodisia and the A logo Reg. U.S. Pat. & TM Off.

ISBN-13: 978-0-7582-4139-9
ISBN-10: 0-7582-4139-9

First Kensington Trade Paperback Printing: February 2011

10 9 8 7 6 5 4 3 2 1

Printed in the United States of America

SIMPLY
FORBIDDEN

1

Knowles Hall, England, 1822

"Why on earth did you invite him, Christian?" Lisette Delornay-Ross nudged her twin's arm and nodded at the corner of the sunny breakfast room where Major Lord Gabriel Swanfield read the newspaper and continued to ignore everyone around him.

"I didn't invite him." Christian poured himself more coffee. "Philip did."

Lisette leaned her elbows on the table and contemplated her brother. "But he's nowhere near Father's age, so how do they know each other?"

"I've no idea. Why don't you stop bothering me and go and ask Lord Swanfield himself?"

"Because he'll stare at me as if I'm a worm and then give me a one-word answer that tells me nothing."

"I take it you've already met him then?" Christian smiled. "Is he really that unforthcoming?"

"When I was introduced to him the other night he barely bothered to say a word to me." Lisette stood up. "Perhaps I'll go and ask Father. He'll probably tell me the truth."

Christian leaned back in his chair to study her, his blond hair catching the light, his long, elegant body shown to advantage in his brown coat and black breeches. "The real question is, why are you so interested in Lord Swanfield?"

"Because I hate being ignored?"

"That's certainly true, but there are plenty of other gentlemen here this week eager to flirt with you. Why not go and bother one of them?"

Lisette frowned. "Are you warning me off?"

"As if you would pay any attention to me if I did." Christian shrugged. "As far as I know, he doesn't mix much in society."

"But what you do know of him, you don't like?"

"Don't start, Lis." He sighed. "As I said, if you really want to pry, go and talk to the poor man."

"Perhaps I will."

Determined not to be shown up by her brother, Lisette marched across to where Lord Swanfield sat hidden behind his newspaper and cleared her throat. He lowered the paper the merest inch and studied her over the top of it.

"Yes?"

Lisette gave him her sweetest smile. "I just wanted to wish you good morning, my lord. We've scarcely had a chance to speak since your arrival."

The paper came down another three inches, allowing her to look into his eyes. Up close, they were a very dark blue and fringed with long lashes.

"And you are?"

Good Lord, the man didn't even remember being introduced to her! Lisette kept smiling. "I'm Miss Ross, Lord Knowles's eldest daughter. I'm acting as my father's hostess this weekend."

"Ah. A pleasure, ma'am." His fingers twitched on the newspaper as if he intended to flip it back up and dismiss her, but

Lisette was quicker. If he intended to be so dismissive of her, she could definitely be a little forward.

"I was wondering what brought you here to Knowles Hall during this particular week. I don't remember your name being on the guest list." She smiled graciously. "Not that you aren't welcome, of course."

His dark brows drew together. "I'm looking for some horses. Your father told me to come down anytime I liked. I didn't realize all this nonsense would be going on."

"Or else you wouldn't have come."

He met her gaze properly for the first time, a hint of wary surprise in his. "Exactly."

Beneath the careful upper-class cadences of his voice there was a slight northern burr, which deepened his tone and made it rougher and far more interesting.

"Well, I'm sorry that we are spoiling your quiet week in the countryside."

"Thank you."

She couldn't decide whether he was incapable of detecting her sarcasm or really quite rude. She suspected the latter. "You think us frivolous and unworthy of your interest then, my lord?"

He started to fold the paper and she caught sight of the deep parallel scars on his left cheek that disappeared below his high collar. "I didn't say that."

"But you obviously think so. I don't believe you've spoken a single word to anyone since you walked into this room."

He raised his eyebrows. "I've spoken to you."

She stared at him for a long moment as she struggled to control her tongue. "Are you going out with the shooting party this morning?"

A shudder of something that looked like revulsion passed over his face. "No, Miss Ross, I'm not."

"Then would you like to join me and some of the other

ladies for a walk around the estate?" She wasn't quite sure why she made the offer when he was being so objectionable, but she refused to be defeated by any man.

"Unfortunately, I'm already engaged. Your father has found someone to show me around the stables."

"Which is why you came here in the first place."

"Indeed."

He stood up and dropped the newspaper onto the table. She found she had to look up at him, which was unnerving. She'd only viewed him from above last night when her father had brought him into the great hall. At five foot eight, she was tall for a woman, but he topped her by at least five inches. He was as lean and elegant as a greyhound, his shoulders accentuated by the confines of his black coat and his long thighs encased in clinging buckskin. He inclined his head the barest inch.

"Good morning, Miss Ross."

She dropped him a quick curtsey. "Good morning, my lord."

He nodded and strolled away, stopped to talk to one of the footmen positioned by the door, and was directed on his way.

"Well," Lisette huffed as her half sister, Emily, and her friends came up beside her. "What an incredibly rude man."

"What did he say to you?" Emily inquired, her face flushed and her blue eyes eager.

"He said that he didn't want to be here, and that he'd only come to look at a horse."

"He didn't!"

Lisette smiled at her younger sister's indignant expression. "He most certainly did. I suspect he wishes us all to the devil."

Emily's two friends giggled and whispered at Lisette's language and she reminded herself to be more careful. At eighteen, Emily's prospects for an excellent marriage were much on her mind. Lisette didn't want to spoil anything for Emily by drawing the ton's attention to her less than reputable half sister.

"I wonder if he will attend the ball on Friday."

Lisette sighed at the hopeful gleam in Emily's eyes. What was it about dark-haired brooding men that sent all young girls into a flutter? In her experience, good-looking men did not make good husbands or lovers, being far too concerned with their own appearance to care about a woman's feelings.

"I'm not sure if he'll be staying the full week, Emily. Once he's decided on a horse, he'll probably be off."

"Oh." There was a wealth of regret in Emily's response that Lisette tried to ignore. She was very fond of her sister, but frequently amazed at the differences between them. Emily had been protected by their father all her life, whereas Lisette had only met him three years ago. Emily's safe, romantic view of the world had never been Lisette's and never would.

"If he does stay, I'm sure he'll dance with you." Lisette patted Emily's shoulder. "He can hardly say no." She paused to consider her words. "Well, he probably could, but I'm sure Papa can persuade him to change his mind."

Emily pouted. "But I don't want him to ask me out of duty. I want him to ask me because he can't *bear* not to dance with me. He is an *earl*, Lisette!"

Lisette struggled not to smile. "Then make yourself pleasant to him over the next few days, and I'm sure he'll come around and ask you to dance. Why wouldn't he?"

"He'd probably rather ask you. What man wouldn't?" Emily looked glum.

Lisette chuckled, remembering the complete lack of interest in Lord Swanfield's rather fine eyes. "After the way he just spoke to me, I doubt that."

Emily grabbed her hand. "Oh, shall we have a wager to see who can get him to ask us to dance first? Wouldn't that be fun, Lisette?"

"But I don't want him to dance with me."

"Then you'll let me win, won't you?" Emily smiled at her companions and the three of them disappeared in the direction of the gardens, still whispering and giggling.

Lisette smiled lovingly at Emily and went to talk to the other guests. The house party wasn't large and was mainly for Emily's benefit as she was going up to London for the Season later in the month. Philip had decided to introduce Emily to some of the other girls who were making their curtsey to the Polite World so that she would feel more comfortable during her debut.

"Well?"

Lisette stopped at the table to look at Christian who was grinning up at her. "Well, what?"

"Did Lord Swanfield tell you why he was here?" Christian asked.

"He did, thank you." She made as to go past him and he caught her hand.

"Don't tell me: he's looking for a wife."

"How amusing, Christian. However did you guess?"

His hazel eyes narrowed. "He's not after Emily, is he?"

Lisette disengaged herself from his grasp. "Of course not, although she seems to have developed quite a tendre for him."

"But he's only been here for a few hours!"

"That's all it takes, brother mine—think of Romeo and Juliet."

Christian laughed and rose to his feet. "And think how happily that ended." He reclaimed Lisette's hand and tucked it into the crook of his arm. They walked to the door and into the shadowed hallway beyond. "You weren't as silly as Emily when you were eighteen."

"Thank goodness. But there was scarcely an opportunity for me to be silly in a convent-run orphanage, was there?"

"That's true, but since we moved to live with *Maman* you've certainly made up for it."

There was an edge to Christian's words that made Lisette pause. "What's that supposed to mean?"

"You've gained a reputation, sister mine, a reputation that won't help Emily at all."

Lisette stopped walking completely. "Are you suggesting I'm too 'fast' to associate with my own half sister?"

He regarded her steadily, his long body aligned with hers as he leaned in close. "Yes, I think I am."

"And since when did Emily's well-being and comfort become more important to you than my own?" Lisette was surprised at how much Christian's defection hurt. They'd always had each other. Were things about to change?

Christian sighed. "Lis, that's not what I meant, and you know it. I'll always put you first."

"Obviously not, and, for what it's worth, your reputation is far worse than mine."

He shrugged. "And I'm a man, so it doesn't matter as much. You might not like it, but that's the way of the world."

Lisette realized she was a breath away from losing her temper. Dealing with obstinate males one after the other was extremely trying. "What do you think I should do? Find a husband and make myself respectable enough to please everyone?"

His smile was wicked. "You could always start with Lord Swanfield. I believe I said he was looking for a wife."

Before Lisette could retaliate, Christian was gone, his laughter echoing down the long hallway to the back of the house. She stared after him, her lower lip caught between her teeth. How dare he suggest that she was somehow at fault? She'd been more than polite to Lord Swanfield, endlessly kind to Emily, and was being the perfect hostess for her father. What more could she do to ensure the house party went off well? Remove herself from it?

But Christian had implied she should do just that and distance herself from Emily. Lisette set off to the kitchens to meet with the cook, her thoughts in turmoil. Perhaps she shouldn't have volunteered to help out this week and should've stayed in London with her mother. Philip had already found an elderly relative to chaperone Emily through her first London Season. Helene, Lisette's mother, was hardly a suitable candidate for the job, being the proprietor of a pleasure house.

Lisette sighed as she fixed a smile on her face. It was too late to change anything now. She would make sure Emily was protected from any hint of scandal, even if it meant staying in the background for once and behaving herself. Perhaps she should simply sit beside Lord Swanfield and be ignored. She could scarcely get into any trouble with him.

Gabriel Swanfield admired the twenty-stall stables and the large barn beside them and wished he had something half as grand at his property in Cheshire. Not that he ever went there, not that he cared whether the place thrived or rotted to the ground . . .

"My lord?"

He turned to attend to the head coachman who had been assigned to be his guide. "I do apologize, Mr. Green, what were you saying?"

"I was just mentioning that the current Lord Knowles has spent the last few years improving the stables, the facilities, and the breeding stock, sir. We have several very promising colts to show you."

"Excellent. I'm also looking for at least one four-year-old to ride now, and a couple of youngsters to bring on."

"Well, we'll be happy to help you, sir. Would you care to walk down to the main paddock?"

Gabriel followed behind the older man and admired the greenness of the fields, the wilderness areas, and the maze spreading out around the mellow Elizabethan manor house. In the near-distance he could just see the colorful skirts of the young ladies on the terrace, no doubt getting ready to go for their walk.

He imagined Miss Ross taking charge of them and knew that like a good sergeant at arms, she would have no trouble controlling her troops. She'd startled him that morning with her directness, the way she'd taken him on and left him in the dust. Despite himself, he'd also admired her hazel eyes and light brown hair, the high arch of her eyebrows, and the determined angle of her chin.

For a chit not long out of the schoolroom, she was indeed a formidable opponent. She seemed more assured than most of her contemporaries and far more aware of her effect on a man. It had been difficult not to stare at her as she flitted back and forth between all the gentlemen, her smile bright, her eyes far too knowing.

He glanced back at the huddle of ladies and realized they were meandering down toward the stables. He quickened his step and caught up with Mr. Green and enjoyed the sight of the young foals kicking up their heels in the pasture. He pointed at a young black horse.

"That's the one I'd pick."

"You have a good eye, sir. That's Thunderbolt, his lordship's pride and joy."

"Then I doubt he'll be selling him." Gabriel searched the other horses. "What about the gray?"

"That's Shadow. He's a three-year-old and also very promising. I'm sure his lordship would be more than happy to tell you all about him."

"Good." With one eye on the rapidly approaching ladies, Gabriel gestured back at the stables. "Shall we go and look at the older horses?"

"Yes, sir."

Gabriel managed to avoid the chattering women and took his time peering into all the stalls as Mr. Green told him about each horse. At the end of the second row, he found a horse he liked, a big chestnut-colored gelding. He nodded his approval at Mr. Green.

"Is it all right if I go into his stall and take a good look at him?"

"Of course, sir. That's Wellington. He's got a nice temperament, that one; he's not scared of much." Mr. Green unlocked the door. "Take your time, sir, and if you want me to get him saddled up for you, just give me a shout." He gave a heavy sigh. "I need to go and be civil to the ladies and stop them scaring my horses with all that squeaking they like to do."

Gabriel went into the small stall and put one hand on Wellington's rump so that the horse knew he was there and hopefully wouldn't kick out. He walked around the flank of the horse, noticed the way its ears flicked toward him with interest but without fear. He ran his hand along the horse's withers and up his long neck until he reached his face.

"You're a nice lad, Wellington, aren't you?" The horse whickered back and appeared to nod his head. Gabriel scratched under the horse's chin, produced a carrot top Mr. Green had given him, and held it out on his palm. "Here you go, boy."

Nice manners, a soft mouth, and an intelligent face. Gabriel slid his hand down the horse's front leg and checked his tendons, and finally his hoof. Then he repeated the process on the three other legs. As he crouched down in the straw, he heard girlish laughter and stayed where he was. Hopefully the ladies would pass by without noticing him.

To his dismay, they seemed to stop right outside the stall door.

"I'm sure Mr. Green said Lord Swanfield was around here somewhere. I wonder where he has gotten to?"

"If he has any sense, he's probably running back to the

house as fast as he can. No man wishes to encounter a large group of ladies while he's talking horseflesh."

Ah, Gabriel recognized that second voice, the slight hint of a French accent, the sharp intelligence behind every word. It was Miss Ross, but who was she talking to?

"Well, I'm disappointed. I wanted to begin my campaign to get him to ask me to dance at the ball."

"As I said, he probably won't still be here by then. He doesn't strike me as a particularly sociable man."

"But I *want* to dance with him. He is an earl and he is so tall and handsome." Emily sighed. "I wish I'd gotten to see him in his uniform."

Gabriel grimaced as the unknown voice described him. She epitomized exactly what he disliked about the women of the *ton*. All she cared about was his title and his looks. And God knows, he had no illusions about his scarred appearance, and his title was a sham.

"Lord Swanfield is also far too old for you."

"He's not. Father says he's only just turned thirty."

"And you are only eighteen, Emily." Miss Ross laughed, but there was no malice in it. "Think how old he'll be when you are twenty-five, positively ancient!"

There was a slight pause. "I hadn't thought of that."

"And five years after that, you'll have to push him around in a bath chair and take him to Tunbridge Wells for the waters."

Despite himself, Gabriel grinned. How clever of Miss Ross to point out all his potential failings as a husband rather than outright forbid the younger girl to think of him.

The girl named Emily sighed. "Well, I suppose we should go back. The others will be waiting for us."

"Yes, indeed, we should. Maybe you can capture Lord Swanfield's interest at the dinner table with your sparkling wit and conversation."

"What an excellent idea. I'm sure I can win our wager and get him to promise to dance with me before you can."

"Perhaps you will."

Gabriel's smile disappeared as the two women made their way back along the row of stalls to the exit. Miss Ross had entered into a wager, had she? He discounted the younger girl, knew he would have no problem disappointing her in short order. But Miss Ross? Watching her try to exert herself to win his favor might be amusing.

Gabriel stood up and brushed the hay from his breeches. Perhaps he would stay on until the Hunt Ball after all.

2

So far Miss Ross had disappointed him. She had made no effort to ingratiate herself with him at dinner at all. In truth, she'd sat as far away from him as possible, and allowed the gushingly youthful and chatty Miss Emily to claim all his attention. He reckoned she had hardly spared him a glance but to laugh at his efforts to deflect the younger girl's incessant questions about his life in the military.

He drank one obligatory glass of brandy, discussed horses with his host, which was no hardship at all, and excused himself from joining the ladies. He had no desire to sit between the debutantes and listen to them giggle all night. After his incarceration in Spain, he hated being shut in and hated the thought that he had to do anything to please anyone else at all. He'd rather be with the horses and breathe the clean, quiet air of the English countryside.

As he walked away from the house, he turned his face upward and inhaled. His cravat seemed too tight and he pulled at the carefully arranged folds until it came loose. The evening light was golden, the sky tipped with pink-edged clouds, and the horizon a hazy blurring of light and impending darkness. Gabriel lit one of his narrow Spanish cigarillos and headed down to the stables. The smell of warm oat mash and manure didn't bother him half as much as the overperfumed and often underwashed bodies of his fellow guests.

"Now, please be a good horse and stand still."

He halted by the stable, drawn to the sound of a now familiar French accent. What the devil was Miss Ross doing back here? He walked as quietly as he could up to the stall and peered over the door. She stood with her back against the wall, one hand reaching out toward the horse's neck. She'd discarded the low-necked gown she'd worn to dinner, in favor of a simple blue dress and stout boots. Her hair was drawn back from her arresting face in a single long braid.

"May I help you, Miss Ross?"

She jumped so violently that the horse followed suit and almost knocked her over. Instantly, Gabriel joined her in the stall and used his voice to calm the frightened animal, his hands to soothe and placate.

"You frightened me."

He glanced over at her, but kept his hand on the horse's rope halter, his attention on the high-spirited mare. "You frightened the horse. Don't you know any better?"

"The horse was perfectly fine until you came along."

"I'm not so sure about that." He wanted to smile at the indignity of her tone, but kept his expression bland. "You could've been trampled or kicked."

"I know." She swallowed hard, and he noticed the pallor on her face, the terrified look in her hazel eyes.

"Miss Ross, if you are afraid of horses, why are you here?"

She looked directly at him then, as if trying to convince him that her fear meant nothing. "Because I am determined not to be."

"So you wander into any stall and scare the living daylights out of the poor animal?"

"I didn't scare her! You did."

Gabriel gave the mare one last reassuring pat. "Perhaps we should continue this discussion outside." He opened the stall door and waited for Miss Ross to move past him before checking the latch was secure. She lingered in the narrow cobbled passageway between the stalls, her arms folded across her chest and her cheeks flushed. She looked far younger in her plain clothes than in her dinner finery, and far more vulnerable. He found himself intrigued by the contrast.

"Well?" he asked.

"Well, what?" She glared at him and he was reminded anew of her ability to disconcert him. "I do not have to explain myself to you."

He closed in on her and deliberately blocked her exit. "That is true."

She sighed. "But you will not let me pass until I do."

He nodded and settled his shoulder more comfortably against the cold stones behind him. Eventually she looked at him.

"My father loves horses."

"Aye, he does."

"And I'm afraid of them."

Gabriel frowned. "Did you have a fall recently? Have you lost your nerve?"

"Lost my nerve? I've never had it." Her smile was derisive. "I'm simply an appalling rider."

He studied her from the tips of her boots to the top of her head. "I find it hard to believe your father would have allowed that. He must have set you on a horse as soon as you were able to stand."

"I've only been riding for three years." She took a deep breath. "I didn't grow up here with my father. I grew up in France."

It was none of his business where she had grown up or how she had been raised, but Gabriel found himself wanting to ask anyway. It seemed they had more in common than he had imagined: both displaced as children, both trying to overcome unusual circumstances in their lives. He curbed the unusual impulse and concentrated on the problem at hand.

"I could teach you."

"Why would you do that?"

He shrugged. "Because the idea that anyone is too scared to ride appalls me. And it will give me something to do with my time rather than hiding in my room avoiding the other guests." He motioned back at the stalls. "Is that the horse you normally ride?"

"Yes, that's Sugarplum. I was trying to reacquaint myself with her before the hunt at the weekend."

"Then meet me here tomorrow morning at five, and we'll begin."

She stared at him for a long moment and he stared right back, felt his body tighten and respond to the surprise in her hazel eyes.

She nodded. "All right, I will."

He bowed and started to turn away and then remembered something important. "Borrow some breeches. I'll teach you how to ride astride first." He didn't wait to see if she protested. If he was to teach her properly, he needed to see her legs. He smiled into the darkness and imagined those legs wrapped around his hips as he fucked her.

It was a long time since he'd been inspired to fantasize about sex, and his cock responded far too enthusiastically. Miss Ross was an unusual woman. Beneath her charm and ability to appear as empty-headed as all society women obviously lurked a keen mind and a sharp tongue. He found himself excited by the contradictions she presented and far too ready to take her on.

Unfortunately, as a protected upper-class virgin, Miss Ross was unlikely to share his lusty enthusiasm for a quick roll in the hay. He sighed as his shaft started to throb. Tonight he'd simply have to make do with his imagination and his hand.

Lisette glared after Lord Swanfield's retreating figure. Why on earth had she agreed to meet him on the morrow or believe that he would help her? Something about the way he had calmed the horse and his softly spoken words had lulled her into a state of security. He seemed far more at ease with Sugarplum than he was with her, or with any of the other guests.

She sighed and started back up the slight slope to the house after him. He could at least have waited and escorted her inside, but that might have caused comment, and he avoided notice like the plague. She'd watched him surreptitiously over dinner, how he'd flinched at every loud noise and every slight brush of Emily's hand.

Had he suffered during the war? He was certainly physically scarred by it. Perhaps beneath his silence lay unimaginably awful experiences. When she got back to Town, she would inquire of her army friends as to exactly what Major Lord Gabriel Swanfield had gotten up to in the recent conflict. Perhaps that would help her understand him better.

She'd always enjoyed a puzzle and Lord Swanfield was certainly a challenge. Having caught her at a disadvantage, he'd seen her at her most vulnerable, stripped of artifice, and he hadn't seemed to mind. In truth, something in his brusque manner encouraged her to be just as blunt, which was almost refreshing.

The house, ablaze with light, welcomed her, but she avoided the main entrance and turned toward the kitchen door. She didn't want Christian to know she'd been out or guess whom she'd met; he was far too astute not to notice her interest in the enigmatic Lord Swanfield. And she was interested. She could no longer fool herself that she wasn't. His unexpected appearance in the barn, and his surprising offer, had intrigued her.

Was he worth taking up Emily's wager for? Lisette smiled at the direction of her thoughts. Surely not. All *she* had to do was get up early the next morning and see if he really was a man of his word.

Gabriel checked his pocket watch and muttered a curse as he looked up at the house. There was no sign of Miss Ross, and it was now two minutes past five. She'd probably played him for a fool and was sleeping happily in her bed, laughing at him in her dreams. He stuffed his battered watch back into his pocket and turned toward the elegant lines of the impeccably kept stables.

His stupid impulse to help her had been exactly that: stupid. He should know by now that society ladies were far too shallow and frivolous to actually keep their promises. More fool him for imagining that Miss Ross was somehow different. He let out his breath and started toward the stables. Since he was up, he might as well take Wellington out and try his paces.

"Good morning, my lord."

Gabriel stopped walking and looked back over his shoulder. Miss Ross had appeared on the path, her cheeks flushed as if she had been running. He took out his watch and checked it again.

"You're late."

Her eyes widened at his tone and her chin went up. "Hardly."

"Almost five minutes late."

"And it makes a difference because?"

He scowled at her. "Because I don't like to be kept waiting."

She kept walking until her boots were lined up in the gravel with his and poked him in the chest. "I'm not one of your men and this isn't the army. If you have other things to do, I'll wish you good morning and go back to bed."

He looked down at her for a long moment and grudgingly admired the lack of fear in her eyes and the way she stood up to him. "Don't be late next time."

"Yes, sir." She pretended to salute him. "Now, are you going to teach me how to ride properly or not?"

"Aye. Your horse is already saddled and I've spoken to Mr. Green."

"Good, then shall we cease wrangling and be off?"

He bowed and gestured to the mounting block by the old red-brick wall. "Wait here."

She did as he asked and climbed up the three steps to stand on the top of the old stone step. From this angle Gabriel had the perfect view of her long, shapely legs encased in tight buckskin. She looked well, dressed as a man. He immediately wondered whose clothes she had borrowed, imagined her wearing just his shirt instead, her legs riding his hips. . . .

"My lord?" A young voice interrupted him and he found himself staring down at the gap-toothed stable boy.

"Thank you, lad." He took Sugarplum's reins from the stable boy and led the horse over toward Miss Ross. "I want to see you mount up."

She paused, one hand on the horse's saddle. "Why? I can manage this part."

"I'm sure you can, but I want to see your seat and check your stirrup position." He waited until she swung herself into the small saddle and pushed her booted feet into the stirrups. "Ah, the stirrups are too long. Let me fix them for you."

He slid his hand under Miss Ross's knee to release her foot from the stirrup. She jumped and the horse sidestepped and threw back its head. He realized her calm demeanor was a sham. "It's all right, lass." Instinctively he smoothed his hand down her shin and back up over her knee in an endless caress until she stopped shaking.

"Are you talking to me or the horse?"

Her tremulous question made him look up from her boot to her pale face. He stared into her eyes and couldn't look away. The mixture of courage and fear in them was one he was so familiar with, he could almost taste it. "Both of you." He squeezed her ankle. "You both need to relax."

She sighed and he felt the vibrations all the way through his fingers. "I *was* thrown recently. I was very lucky not to be trampled to death."

"That's enough to scare anyone." He patted her knee and let go of her ankle. "I've changed the stirrups. I'll mount up now. Will you be all right?"

"Yes, of course."

He admired the lilt of her voice even as he doubted its validity. "Perhaps you can show me a nice level field or piece of ground away from the house where we can practice undisturbed."

She nodded and gathered the reins the stable boy held out to her. She pointed down the hedge-lined row to the right of them. "There is a field down by the stream we can use."

He clicked at Wellington, enjoying the way the big horse responded so easily to his commands, and backed him up to join Miss Ross. "We'll walk the horses down there. I want you to concentrate on relaxing in the saddle and keeping your balance."

Without repeating himself or checking to see that Miss Ross was attending to him, he squeezed the reins lightly and set off. Wellington's long, even stride was a pleasure of effortless ease compared to some of the horses he'd been forced to ride in the treacherous mountain campaigns in Spain. He remembered his last desperate ride, his fear as the mule lost its footing and slithered down the rock pile, the pain and blackness descending over him.

"My lord?"

He forced his thoughts back to the present. "Yes, Miss Ross?"

"Do you want me to get down and open the gate?"

"I'll do it." He sounded far too blunt, but during his captivity he'd gotten out of the habit of speaking. Speaking led to punishment and he'd had enough of that to almost kill him. Much better to stay silent and endure. It had also infuriated his captors immensely.

He opened the gate and led Wellington through, waited for Miss Ross to join him, and then shut it again. Once remounted, he turned to face her.

"Let's start from the beginning, shall we? Take your feet out of the stirrups; tie your reins onto the saddle and cross your arms over your chest."

By the time the stable clock struck six times, Lisette was halfway between wanting to kill Lord Swanfield and kiss him. He'd made her perform endless tasks to perfect her balance and help her regain her confidence. In truth, she felt much more secure on the horse than she ever had before. But she also felt sore and close to tears as he ordered her around like a scullery maid, his moments of approval so rare she found herself trying hard to earn the slightest hint of a smile.

She cleared her throat. "I need to go back. I have to be at the breakfast table to greet my father's guests."

He frowned and glanced at the distant stable clock. "We've only been here an hour."

"And an hour is all I have to spare." Lisette headed toward the gate and waited for him to follow. "If you wish to keep riding, I'm sure I can find my way back to the stable alone."

"No, I'll accompany you. But can you wait a moment while I try out this horse?"

"Of course." Lisette summoned a gracious smile. He didn't bother to reply, just swept by her into a fast posting trot, a canter, and then into a full gallop. She could do nothing but admire his prowess. He moved as if his body was part of the horse, his hands relaxed on the reins, his hips rolling with each motion. She also knew he wasn't doing it to impress her; his focus was totally on the horse.

After a few minutes, he drew to a thundering stop an inch from her horse and grinned at her. His smile was so dazzling she blinked, and then it was gone.

"I think I'll buy this horse."

"I'm sure my father will be delighted."

Gabriel jumped down to open the gate and then remounted.

"You ride as if you were born on a horse. Did your father put you up there as a baby?"

"By the time I knew of him, my father was too old to do anything with me." His mouth twisted. "I spent most of my early life in the stables annoying the coachmen, until they took me in hand and made sure I learned, not only how to behave, but how to ride and care for my horses."

"At least you learned. I grew up in a French convent."

He turned to look at her, his black hair disordered by the wind, his cheeks flushed with color. "Not many horses there, then."

"No, none at all." She wondered if he'd inquire further about her unusual upbringing, almost hoped he would, but wasn't entirely surprised that his interest lay in the lack of horses at the nunnery rather than her plight. The stable yard came into sight, and Lisette saw the small stable boy perched on the fence waiting for them.

"Thank you for your help."

He shrugged. "You did well."

The horses stopped and the boy ran to their heads to hold

the reins. Lisette turned to find Lord Swanfield waiting to lift her down. She managed to swing her leg over the saddle, but when she tried to kick her other foot free she found the strength in her knees gone and clutched at his solid form.

"Put your hands on my shoulders."

She obeyed, simply because she had no choice, and felt the warmth of his body and the flex of his muscles beneath the fine wool of his coat. His hands closed around her waist and he slowly brought her down to the ground, her body aligned with his. Behind her, she heard the stable boy whistling to the horses as he walked them away. Lord Swanfield didn't release her and she made the mistake of looking up at him. He bent his head and kissed her, nipped at her lower lip until she opened her mouth to his tongue.

With a groan he backed her up against the shadows of the stable wall where no one could see them. His kiss was as hot and possessive as she had hoped—had she hoped for this? This torrent of unexpected emotion, this desire to open herself to him and for him?

She wrenched her mouth away from his. "I didn't say you could kiss me."

"I didn't ask." He lowered his head again and kissed her harder and she forgot to argue, just luxuriated in the sensation of being engulfed, devoured, and possessed. . . . His hands roamed over her body, kneaded her buttocks, and pressed her closer and closer to the thickness of his buckskin-covered erection. She stood on tiptoe and threaded her hand through his black hair, tried to fit herself against his heat and the promise of his muscular frame.

When he finally lifted his head, her lips were swollen, her breath coming in pants.

"Was there something you wanted to ask me, Miss Ross?"

"What?" Confused, she sought his eyes and saw lust and

something far more watchful in his dark gaze. "What was I supposed to ask you?"

He stepped back and bowed. "It's of no matter. I'll see you here tomorrow at five."

Lisette brought a trembling hand to her lips, suddenly conscious of where they were and of the possibility of prying eyes. Despite what Christian believed, she was usually very careful to behave in an appropriately ladylike manner when she was at her father's house. But she didn't feel ladylike. For the first time in a long while she wanted to experience the sexual joys her mother always hinted at, joys Lisette had begun to believe were not meant for her.

"Miss Ross?"

There was a hint of impatience in Lord Swanfield's voice, as though he'd never kissed her, or as if she had disappointed him in some way. She studied his face, saw the desire he couldn't conceal, and dropped her gaze lower to the shape of his hard shaft rising from his breeches. Had he felt anything, or was this just part of his usual morning ritual? A result of biology rather than true interest or passion?

She licked her lips and tasted coffee and pure maleness. "Do you always kiss women you have just met like that?"

He considered her for a long moment. "No. Good morning, Miss Ross." He turned on his heel and walked away from her.

Lisette remained in the shadows until the flush on her cheeks disappeared and her heart rate returned to normal. She'd kissed a lot of men, but most of them never dared to take such liberties with her person as Lord Swanfield had. She was usually the one in control. Despite his lack of courtesy, he excited her more than any other man.

She sighed and went to find her cloak. There was no time to ponder the interesting matter of her attraction to such a man now. She needed to get ready for the day as her father's hostess.

Dare she turn up tomorrow for her riding lesson? It seemed likely that Lord Swanfield would want to continue his other, more sensual lessons as well. She shivered at the thought of him touching her again, and realized she had no choice. She'd be back in the morning whether it was safe or not.

3

Gabriel tried to concentrate on the sway of Miss Ross's body in the saddle as she trotted past him, but his treacherous imagination kept placing her in a different situation altogether; on top of him as she rose and fell, her naked breasts in his face, his fingers on her clit, stroking her to a climax.

"Was that better?" She pulled up alongside him.

"Hmm. Do it again."

She pouted as he sent her off around the field again, but it was that or pull her out of the saddle and shove his cock deep inside her. Briefly, Gabriel closed his eyes as his expanding cock kicked against his breeches. He hadn't felt like this about a woman for years, this driving need to possess, to own, and to dominate. He hadn't meant to kiss her yesterday either, but the chance to help her win her bet had given him the perfect excuse to tease her. He'd thought he'd never feel capable of wanting a woman like that again. Miss Ross had made a fool out of him, whether she realized it or not.

"My lord?"

"Canter now."

She sighed, but she obeyed him, her lithe body reacting perfectly to the change of pace and the lengthening of the horse's stride. She'd be ready to try that abomination of the sidesaddle tomorrow and all his good work would be ruined, but at least she'd have her confidence back. He turned toward the gate and opened it, waiting for her to catch him up. Her knee brushed his as they rode together up the narrow path, sending a jolt of pure lust straight to his cock.

She glanced up at him as the stable boy relieved them of their horses. "Are you going to kiss me again today?"

"Do you want me to?"

Her hazel eyes narrowed. "Not particularly."

He closed in on her, moving her back into the shadows of the huge medieval barn. "Liar." He sought her mouth, found it already waiting for him, and was engulfed in a fiery need that shocked him to the core. Without further thought his hands worked on the waistband of her borrowed breeches and dragged out the tails of her shirt.

She pulled his hair hard. "What are you doing?"

"Finding your breasts."

"I . . ." She stopped speaking and gasped instead as he shoved aside the linen binding her breasts and sucked her nipple into his mouth. He drew hard on her, used his fingers to bring her other nipple to a needy point and then sucked that one, too. She didn't push him away. She caught the rhythm of his suckling and moved her hips to it, offered herself to him, even if she didn't realize it. He shoved his knee between her legs until she rode his thigh, felt her fingers tighten and tighten in his hair until he no longer felt the sting of pain, until she climaxed with a muffled scream and buried her face in his shoulder.

Despite his protesting cock, he slowly pulled away and stared down at her. He'd learned the hard way to control his passions, never realizing that his painful experiences might aid him now.

"Are you sure that there isn't anything you want to ask me, Miss Ross?" He winced at the hoarseness of his own words, the northern burr he'd tried so hard to eliminate from his speech. It irked him that she'd made no effort to win her wager and coerce him into asking her for a dance at the upcoming ball. It irked him that he was attracted to her at all.

"Why do you keep asking me that?" She stuffed her shirt back into her breeches and fastened them. "Or is it your way of suggesting I take you up to my bedchamber and have my wicked way with you?"

God, he'd like that, like her stretched out naked on the sheets, her long legs open wide, his mouth sucking and licking at her wet, willing sex.

Her hazel eyes narrowed and he wondered what she'd seen on his face. "Do you think I'm the kind of woman who would take a lover before marriage?"

He blinked down at her, his salacious thoughts still cluttering his brain. "You let me kiss you."

"Kissing a man is not the same as bedding one!"

"Surely one thing leads to another?"

"Not always, Lord Swanfield."

He stepped back just in case. "And how am I supposed to know that?"

"From your long and no doubt varied career seducing women?"

He glared down at her. "I kissed you because I wanted to. If you don't want me to kiss you, perhaps you should show more restraint and not throw yourself at me and stick your tongue in my mouth."

His head snapped back as her bare palm met his cheek with a resounding crack. He waited to see if she would hit him again, and saw instead that tears glinted in her eyes. He couldn't bear that. He swallowed hard. "I apologize for my last remark. It was uncalled for."

She bit down on her lip. "No, it wasn't. You are quite right. No single woman should be kissing an eligible man behind the stables. I should be apologizing to you."

"I liked you kissing me."

Her smile was wry. "And I liked kissing you, but I'm forced to admit that you are right. It certainly isn't a very ladylike way to behave."

He shrugged, aware that all he wanted to do was kiss her again until she screamed his name and begged to take his cock inside her. He'd known she was an unusual woman, and her reaction to his kisses had proved it. But he still had his fences to mend, and for once he was willing to make the effort.

"I didn't mean to imply that you were a loose woman."

"Thank you—I think." She smoothed a hand over her disordered hair and glanced up at him. "My family circumstances make it imperative that my conduct is beyond reproach. Sometimes I find it hard to live up to society's expectations."

"Obviously you don't know much about my position in society," he said dryly. "I have many of the same restraints."

"Really?" She gave him a speculative look as they both turned to retrace their steps back to the house. "What did you do?"

He kept his gaze on the path. "It's a long story. I'm sure you'll find someone amongst your acquaintance to tell you all the juicy details."

"I'd much rather hear the truth from you."

He halted on the path and bowed, hoping his smile was as withering as his tone. "Then you'll have to wait a very long time. Good morning, Miss Ross. I'll see you tomorrow at five."

He strode away from her before she said something else to either infuriate or arouse him. How long was it since a woman had elicited such a response from him? He couldn't remember and didn't want to remember. What the devil was wrong with him? He'd been much happier just concentrating on his horses.

Yet again, Lisette found herself following after Lord Swanfield as he strode ahead of her. Sheer rage quickened her stride, then finally made her run after him and call his name.

"I wish you would stop walking away from me."

He didn't stop. "Our conversation is over."

"If you weren't implying that I should ask you to my bed, what *were* you expecting me to ask you?"

He stopped then but didn't turn around. Lisette struggled to control her ragged breathing as she waited for his response. When he said nothing, she forced herself to continue. "I assumed you kissed me because you wanted to, but perhaps there is more to it."

He looked over his shoulder at her, his expression inscrutable. "What more could there be?"

"Surely that is for you to tell me?"

"If you don't know, then there is nothing to say."

Lisette resisted the urge to stamp her booted foot or kick him in the shins. Was she angry because she'd realized that while she was unable to resist him, he was totally in control of his actions, aware of his affect on her, and able to pull back whenever he wanted to? She was usually the person who did that. She'd learned from her mother, a master of the erotic arts. Perhaps it was simply her hurt pride that urged her to question him.

"Never mind." She sighed. "I'll see you tomorrow."

"At five." He bowed. "I'll make sure Mr. Green uses the sidesaddle."

"Tomorrow will be our last lesson before the hunt."

"Then we should make sure to use the time wisely."

She glared at him. "Don't worry, my lord. If you can keep your hands to yourself, I'll keep my tongue in my mouth."

His mouth twitched up at the corner as if he was about to smile but he quickly suppressed it. "Indeed."

Lisette watched him leave and headed up the back stairs to her bedchamber. Morning sun stippled the rose-patterned carpet and glinted off the gold mirror outside her door.

"Been anywhere interesting, sister?"

Lisette stiffened as Christian strolled toward her. His cravat was untied and his coat lay over his arm; his hair was tousled as if he had just woken up.

"Just down to the stables."

"At this hour?" Christian leaned up against the doorjamb. "I thought you loathed riding."

"Which is why I'm trying to improve." She put her hand on the door handle. "Excuse me, I have to get changed."

Christian followed her into her room and shut the door behind him. He strolled across to a chair and sat down. "Did I mention that I saw Lord Swanfield creeping in as well?"

"Did you?"

"He, too, was dressed for riding."

"How interesting." Lisette took off her coat and fiddled with the cuffs of her shirt. "And where have you been? You scarcely look as if you are dressed for the day."

He smiled lasciviously. "I'm not."

She met his far from innocent hazel gaze. "And yet you have the gall to question me about my whereabouts."

His eyebrows rose. "My, my, we are defensive this morning. Are you worried I'll put two and two together and assume you clandestinely met Lord Swanfield in the stables?"

"I did meet him in the stables. He is a hard man to avoid." Lisette rang the bell for her maid and undid the fastening of her braid so that she could brush out her hair. She was all too aware of Christian watching her in the mirror.

"And?"

"And nothing." She turned to smile at him. "He really is the most infuriating man."

Christian stood up. "I don't believe you."

"That he is infuriating? Trust me, the man has the manners of a commoner and the morals of an elderly nun."

"And you know this because you've tried to flirt with him?"

"I've given up trying to flirt with him. I leave that to Emily."

Christian didn't look convinced. "I think I've seen him at the pleasure house."

"So?"

"So, don't trust him."

Lisette forced a laugh. "Really, Christian, if I mistrusted everyone who went to Maman's I wouldn't have any confidence in the vast majority of the aristocracy, the entire house of Lords, and quite a few members of Parliament."

Christian headed for the door. "If you don't want to listen to me, I'll leave you to dress."

Lisette stood up, too. "You haven't said anything worth listening to yet."

"I've suggested you keep away from Lord Swanfield. Isn't that enough?"

"You suggested nothing. You merely told me not to trust him. And I don't. I'm not stupid, Christian."

His smile was reluctant. "I know that." He studied his fingers. "But, God knows why, I get the sense that he is important to you."

"More important than you, perhaps?" Lisette tried to make a joke of it. "Are you jealous?"

Christian looked at her steadily. "Yes, I think I am. It's not like you to defend another man."

Lisette sighed. "Why are you making this so difficult? I haven't asked where you were last night. I haven't made assumptions about your choice of companion or commented on your morals."

"And you never do, do you?" His smile was rueful. "I've always tried to protect you from the worst of my excesses."

Lisette bit her lip. "I don't need protection from Lord Swanfield. He will be gone after the ball and I doubt I'll ever see him again."

"Let's hope that's true. You seem . . . different this time and that concerns me." Christian nodded as Lisette's maid entered the chamber. "I'll leave you to dress."

Lisette sat back down again, her thoughts in turmoil. She and Christian had always been close, some gossiped unnaturally so, and she was shaken by his questions. For the first time in her life she wasn't willing to share her feelings about another man, to hold him up for either Christian's ridicule or his approval. She wanted to keep her meetings with Lord Swanfield private. Was that so wrong?

She was almost twenty-two now and no longer a child. Had she finally reached a parting of ways with her brother? Perhaps it was time they grew apart. He had become increasingly distant over the last year anyway, his sexual activities a closely guarded secret; his friends, his adventures no longer shared with her.

Lisette listened to her maid's chatter and stared at her perturbed reflection in the mirror. If she managed to get through tomorrow's riding lesson without incident, perhaps her unsettling attraction to Lord Swanfield would disappear and all would be well between her and Christian again. She sighed. Or perhaps it was simply too late to return to how things had been and she should move on.

With a stifled curse she realized she couldn't trust herself to ride with Lord Swanfield. She craved his touch more than she craved peace with her twin and that was unacceptable. Despite her efforts to behave like a lady she'd allowed a man to make her climax in public! A wave of heat flooded her cheeks and she pressed her hands to her face. There was no excuse. She would have to renege on the arrangement and keep out of his way until he left.

* * *

"Let me be, man."

Gabriel scowled down at Keyes, his valet, who continued to fuss over the arrangement of his cravat and the positioning of the single jet pin to secure it.

"Just a minute, sir, and I'll be done. You want to look your best, don't you, sir?"

"Not particularly."

Keyes looked aghast. "You're going to a ball, sir. You have to impress the ladies."

"And if I don't want to impress them?" Gabriel moved irritably away from the mirror, hating the sight of his own face, the same face as the man who'd sired him for the most dishonorable of reasons. "In truth, I wish all women to the devil."

Miss Ross hadn't turned up for their riding lesson and she'd avoided him all day. Just to spite her, he'd asked Miss Emily to dance with him at the upcoming ball and endured her rapturous acceptance. But even that hadn't persuaded Miss Ross to seek him out, and now he was committed to attend the kind of social occasion he loathed. He could only hope he'd manage a moment alone with Miss Ross to set things straight between them, and then he'd leave, hunting be damned.

"You look very nice, sir."

Gabriel managed a smile. "Thank you, Keyes."

"Yes, sir."

His valet forgot his change of circumstances and saluted his employer as if they were both still in the army and Keyes was still his batman. Gabriel found himself returning the salute and then headed for the door. As he paused on the landing, he heard the faint sound of music playing and the gentle swell of conversation. Apparently, Lord Knowles's Hunt Ball was a much anticipated local event that drew in all the aristocratic families for miles around. Many of them stayed the night in order to be up bright and early for the hunt, which started the next day in front of the big house.

Gabriel took a deep breath. He hated crowds, but if he wanted to buy the horses, he had to do his duty to his host and not abuse his hospitality. He found himself still hesitating and looked down from the minstrel's gallery onto the crowds below. He spotted the younger Miss Ross and strained for a glimpse of the older. Ah, there she was, dressed in a pale blue gown that seemed to shimmer. He had no idea what the name of the fabric was, but he liked the way it clung to her long legs.

He wanted her. There was no logic behind the thought, just a deep instinct that terrified and excited him. He'd spent the last few nights, his cock in his hand, endlessly fantasizing about the sex they would have, endlessly coming, his cock now sore from the attention, but he wouldn't change anything. Her unusual directness appealed to him at a very basic level, as did her ability to both inhabit the polite world of the ton and yet revel in her deep sensuality. Perhaps she might be able to teach him the way of it. Despite himself, he'd begun to hope that maybe there was a way out of his current sexual dilemma, a way to overcome his past and move forward.

He put his thoughts into action and made his way down the stairs toward his host, who stood greeting his guests at the entrance to the ballroom. Gabriel bowed and received a welcoming smile in return. Lord Knowles liked a man who knew his horseflesh, and Gabriel had enjoyed sharing his knowledge with him.

"Ah, Lord Swanfield. I believe my younger daughter is expecting you to dance with her. Perhaps you would care to partner her for the opening set?"

"Of course, my lord." Gabriel forced a smile. "It will be my pleasure."

He waited patiently at Lord Knowles's side until Miss Emily

appeared, and took her hand and walked with her into the ballroom. Heat from the massed candles and the noisy conversation rolled over him like a suffocating wave. He realized she was speaking to him, but she spoke so quickly he could barely understand her. He smiled and nodded, hoping she didn't notice his struggle to overcome his sudden claustrophobia.

"Ooh, Lord Swanfield, this is so exciting!"

Gabriel had nothing to say to that and concentrated on getting her to the middle of the dance floor. The small orchestra struck an opening chord and he forced his feet to move through the intricate steps of the country dance. After a few moments, he realized that there was another couple on the floor, Lord Knowles and Miss Ross. In control of himself now, he tried not to look at her every time the dance brought them closer together, tried to focus his attention on charming Miss Emily and making her smile. Not that that was hard work; she seemed inclined to giggle at everything he said.

When the music ended, he remembered to bow and lead Miss Emily off the floor, but his attention was for Miss Ross, who seemed to have disappeared again. He ignored several comments from other guests and headed in the direction he'd last seen her. She was talking to another man, their fair heads close together, his fingers casually stroking the curve of her elbow.

Gabriel stopped walking and simply stared at the couple, aware that he was reacting far too strongly to another man holding her, touching her skin. At last, the man moved away and she was alone. She looked up, straight into Gabriel's eyes, and he bowed and walked toward her.

"Would you like to dance with me?"

"I'm already engaged for this dance, my lord."

He shrugged. "Then tell whomever it is you are sorry and let me get you some refreshments instead. It will be much easier to talk that way."

She raised her chin at him. "I don't require any refreshments, thank you."

He glared down at her. "Then you'll dance with me." He took her hand and marched her toward the dance floor, drew her into his arms, and started to move.

"This is very high-handed of you."

"You left me no choice."

"I didn't intend to give you a choice. I've been trying to avoid you."

"I know. I'm not stupid."

She sighed as he drew her closer. "You're far from stupid and I am far too attracted to you. There is no reason for it, either, because all you do is bully me."

"I do not bully you."

"What do you call this?"

"Gentle persuasion."

"You are an autocratic bully, and I refuse to be told what to do by such a man."

He found himself smiling. "Some women like to be told what to do."

"Well, I'm not one of them."

"Why didn't you come for your lesson this morning?"

"You know why."

"You were afraid I would 'bully' you into my bed?"

She looked him right in the eye. "No, I was afraid I'd let you."

He contemplated her response and allowed the simmering excitement in his belly to grow and consume him. "I didn't take you for a coward."

"What is that supposed to mean?"

"I wouldn't have allowed you to take me to bed."

Her steps faltered and he caught her tightly against him to stop her from stumbling, relished the press of her breasts against his waistcoat. He stepped off the dance floor and pulled her with him, right through the ballroom windows and onto the stone terrace outside.

She wrenched her hand out of his grasp and walked away from him, to a more secluded corner of the garden. She turned her back on him to study the dark parkland beyond the formal gardens. "Are you suggesting that even if I'd thrown myself at you, you would've resisted me?"

"Yes."

She swung slowly around, the thin skirts of her gown catching the slight breeze. "You haven't resisted me so far. In fact, you have been the aggressor in our encounters."

"You're a lady. I want you, but it's not socially acceptable to . . ."

"To bed me?"

"Aye, to bed you without offering marriage."

"And you're not *quite* enamored of me yet to offer to marry me."

"Exactly."

"Thank goodness for that." She shut her fan and slipped the band over her wrist. "What if I was married already?"

He shrugged. "Then you would be fair game, as long as your husband was the acquiescent and forgiving type."

"How nice for you." She glared at him. "If you were my husband, I would not look kindly on you straying like a tom cat."

"And I would not like that in a wife." He sighed. "I'm just trying to be honest with you about what I want."

"So that you can have an excuse to walk away from me again? Because I have shocked you with my unmaidenly desires?" Her lip curled. "You scarcely strike me as a man who expects to wait for marriage to experience all the pleasures of the flesh. Why should it be different for me?"

He took a step closer and then another. "You're right. There are other ways to give you pleasure, without bedding you."

She opened her eyes wide at him. "I know. I'm not stupid either."

He stepped in until there was no space left between them. "I want you naked, my mouth on you, my fingers buried deep inside you as you scream my name. I want my cock in your mouth, your hand wrapped around my shaft, and my cum all over you. Is that clear enough?"

She blinked at him and took a long, shuddering breath. "Do you always make such romantic speeches?"

He knew that most gently reared young ladies would've run away screaming by now, crying for their mothers. He had no idea why he'd known Miss Ross would hear him out, but he'd known it in his soul.

"Have I offended you?"

She turned her head away from him. "No."

He straightened and realized he'd almost kissed her. "What?"

"I'm not offended by your words."

He kissed her then, his tongue in her mouth, one hand flattened on the center of her back holding her close. She pulled away from him and pushed at his chest. "I have to go back now."

"Why?"

"Because I am my father's hostess."

"And that means more to you than taking your pleasure with me?"

"Yes." She curtsied, her back straight, her grace that of a queen. "I'll think about your interesting offer and let you know after the ball."

Unconsciously, Gabriel's hand went to comfort his now engorged cock. "I might not want you after the ball."

"And I probably won't want you either and will have thought better of it. Then we'll have nothing to say to each other after all, will we?"

Anger stirred in his stomach, curdling the lust. "Is this because I danced with your sister first?"

"What?"

"Are you toying with me because you lost your wager?"

"How did you know about that?" She turned back to him, her expression suddenly formidable.

"I overheard something to the effect quite by accident."

She stormed back toward him. "And you thought what? That I'd deliberately met you in the stables to coerce you into asking me to *dance*?"

"It was a possibility."

Her hazel eyes widened as she stared at him. "Is that why you kissed me? You kept asking me whether I had something I wanted to ask you. Was that it?"

"I wanted to give you the opportunity to win the wager."

"Because dancing with you is such an honor? I knew there was something wrong, I knew it." She swept him another curtsey. "If I'd wanted to win the wager, I would've won it. The whole idea was my sister's, and I simply went along with her."

"Easy for you to say now you've lost."

"Lord Swanfield, let me repeat myself. I'm not stupid. If I'd *wanted* to dance with you, I would have asked you. I've never needed to resort to deceit to make a man do *anything* for me."

He bowed. "Indeed. And as you've obviously decided to blow a trivial thing out of all proportion just so that you can run away from me, I'll wish you good night."

"Trivial thing?" She spared him another scathing glance. "Good night and good riddance, my lord. You conceited, arrogant presumptuous idiot!"

She stormed away from him, leaving him alone on the secluded terrace, his thoughts at war with his body's demands, his temper barely under control. Was he conceited? Surely not. Arrogant? Perhaps . . .

He sighed and headed for his room. He'd had enough of the

ball and of Miss Ross for one night. Her opinion of him certainly didn't matter; he hardly knew her. He paused on the edge of the ballroom, watched her smiling at her father. So why did he feel so damn wounded? She'd only behaved like the rest of her class. But that wasn't true, was it? She'd actually admitted to wanting him, and only his stupid insistence on mentioning the wager had spoiled the erotic possibility of a night in her arms.

He bit off a curse. Aye, daft and stupid, that was it. He'd managed to alienate the only woman who had interested him in years. Now all that was left was for him to leave with his dignity intact and try and forget her.

4

Lisette glanced up at her two smiling companions and tried to decide which one of them seemed most likely to aid her. It was the fashionable hour to be seen in the park and she knew she looked well in her new blue pelisse. Being accompanied by such handsome men only gave her an additional caché. It was hard to decide whom she preferred between the dashing Captain Merrival and the quietly amusing Lieutenant St. Clare. Both men were of a similar age to the irritating Lord Swanfield, and both of them had served in Spain with the army.

Lord Swanfield refused to leave her thoughts or her most heated dreams. Lisette had decided the best way to rid herself of him was to find out exactly what he had done to make himself such a pariah. Surely then he would lose his allure? She'd gleaned enough information to decide that he must have done something socially unacceptable, but most people seemed unsure exactly what.

She bestowed a dazzling smile on Captain Merrival. "Would you mind if I asked you something personal?"

The captain winked at her, his brown eyes full of interest. "It depends, Miss Ross. If you wish to know if I'm married, the answer is no."

"I'm fascinated to hear that, sir, but my question was more about the past and of a military nature."

"You are interested in the military, Miss Ross?" Captain Merrival found a vacant bench, brushed it with his handkerchief, and invited Lisette to sit, Lieutenant St. Clare by her side.

"I'm interested in a particular man from the military."

Captain Merrival clasped his hand to his heart and groaned. "Alas, I fear you don't mean me. Now all my hopes are dashed."

"Don't be ridiculous, Captain. I happen to know you are practically engaged to Miss Fenton, and, despite the gossip, I'm not the kind of woman who interferes in another woman's love life." She shifted on the seat so she could see both of their faces. "In truth, it is a rather delicate matter. I recently met a Major Lord Gabriel Swanfield. He was buying horses from my father."

"Ah, Major Swanfield."

Lisette waited hopefully to see if Captain Merrival was going to volunteer more information but his expression had taken on a closed look that didn't bode well.

She manufactured a little laugh. "Is it something too terrible to share with me?"

Captain Merrival frowned. "It is . . . complicated. I never quite believed Swanfield was capable of such behavior although the evidence against him . . . ."

"Major Swanfield was brought up before a military court in Spain on charges of supplying the enemy with military secrets," Lieutenant St. Clare said.

Lisette turned to look at him. "He was?"

"Yes, Miss Ross. The circumstances were unusual enough that rather than face a full court-martial, he was forced to leave Spain and return to England."

Lisette pictured Lord Swanfield's austere face, remembering

his claims to be honest and his bluntness. "I can't imagine him doing that."

Captain Merrival snorted. "With all due respect, you can never tell what a man will do under duress, especially during a war. The information he carried with him was certainly given to our enemies."

"But if you remember, Merrival, Swanfield was missing for almost a year. He and I spent most of that time in a French prison." Lieutenant St. Clare's voice was quiet but determined. "He claimed that the information must've been removed from him forcibly when they recovered his body from the rock slide ambush they'd set up."

"Or he gave it up under torture. He certainly returned in a state near death."

Lisette stared at both of the men, her gloved hand pressed to her chest. "He was missing for almost a *year*?"

"It happens sometimes in war, especially in the Spanish campaign amongst those treacherous mountains." Captain Merrival shrugged. "Prisoners are taken, exchanged, or released all the time."

"Yet he wasn't court-martialed."

"In truth, Miss Ross, he was in no state to stand trial and several of the men he commanded begged the commander in chief to allow him to leave quietly. Up until his disappearance, his record had been exemplary."

"And as a peer of the realm, the authorities were reluctant to pursue him as well," Lieutenant St. Clare finished unwillingly. "So he was allowed home, but there are many who still shun him because of what happened."

"Do you shun him?" Lisette asked, her stomach tied in knots as she contemplated the ruin of Lord Swanfield's reputation and the horrible certainty that such rumors and gossip made it impossible for him to set things right. She knew all about that, had suffered the full weight of society's condemnation herself in the past. And Lord Swanfield was scarcely the kind of man who would crave society's favor or fight for it. No wonder he had retreated and made himself almost invisible.

"I haven't seen him for years, Miss Ross," Captain Merrival said. "But I wouldn't refuse to shake his hand."

"Neither would I. I think the army made some grave mistakes in his trial."

"Really?" Lisette studied Lieutenant St. Clare's suddenly unsmiling face, and saw a depth of bitter experience that surprised her.

"Major Swanfield was too ill to defend himself properly, and the authorities refused to allow him time to recover before they held their investigation. They preferred to hurry things along and bury the truth out there in Spain. A longer investigation wasn't in their best interests. It was much easier to make Major Swanfield the scapegoat and send him home in disgrace."

"But that hardly seems fair."

"Not much fair about war, Miss Ross." Captain Merrival got to his feet and bowed. "Shall we continue our walk? I believe it is getting a little chilly."

Lisette rose to her feet and laid her hand on his proffered sleeve. She had much to think about and a burning desire to see Lord Swanfield again and ask him to explain himself. She knew she had no right to ask him anything, but perhaps she just wanted another opportunity to see him again. Yes. She really was that pathetic, wanting to see a man who had annoyed her so greatly she'd called him as many vile names as she could think of and walked away from him, denying herself the opportunity to experience his prowess in bed.

She tried to conceal her troubled thoughts and smiled at her two escorts. She had to think of a way to meet Lord Swanfield again and at least give him the opportunity to tell her his version of the truth. He might even relish the opportunity to tell someone who might be sympathetic toward him, but how would she find him in such a huge city?

Lisette suddenly thought of her father. He was always very careful about the people he sold his horses to and had a disconcerting habit of dropping in on them unannounced to see how his bloodstock was being treated. Lisette let out her breath. If anyone knew where Lord Swanfield was located, it would be him.

"Papa, do you have a London address for Lord Swanfield?"

Her father looked up from his newspaper and studied her across the breakfast table. "Now why would you want to know that?"

"Because I assumed you would wish to invite him to dine with us one evening here in Town, so that you could hear how your horses are settling in."

"You assumed all that—for me?" His smile was full of mischief. "Such a saintly daughter I have, only thinking of others and never of herself."

Lisette realized she was blushing and gave her father a serene look. "I only think of your well-being, Papa."

"Poppycock. Did you like him then, Lisette? He seemed remarkably closemouthed to me, except when he talked about horses."

"He talked to Lisette." Christian put down his cup and eyed his sister. "They spent some very happy moments together in the stables."

"That is pure speculation, Christian, and you know it."

"And the heat of your reply does nothing to change my opinion. You were attracted to him, Lis."

"And what does that have to do with you?"

"Children." Philip's voice broke through Lisette's fierce attention on her brother. "Not over the breakfast table, please, I have a delicate digestion." He nodded at Lisette. "I will ask my secretary to send him an invitation to dine with us, later this week."

Lisette ignored Christian's grinning face and smiled at her father. "Thank you, Papa. And if I am available, I would be glad to join you."

"That is very good of you, my dear. Now I must return to my desk. I have a whole morning of distributing the servants' quarterly wages ahead of me, and then I have to meet your mother."

"She is coming here?"

Philip paused in the act of rising. "Unfortunately, no. I am to meet her at the pleasure house." He sighed ruefully. "Helene is a very busy woman."

Lisette contemplated her plate of eggs and bacon as Philip left the room. She loved Helene, but sometimes she could tell that Philip felt neglected for the demands of the pleasure house. In truth, he was a most unusual husband in that he allowed Helene to live at another house and keep their marriage a virtual secret.

"So you get your wish to fawn over Lord Swanfield again."

Lisette's head jerked up as Christian spoke. She'd almost forgotten he was there. "I don't 'fawn' and what business is it of yours who Father invites to dinner?"

Christian raised his eyebrows. "What's the matter, Lisette? It's not like you to snap at me over a man."

"I'm not snapping at you!"

"Why is Lord Swanfield so important to you?"

Lisette sighed, defeated. "I'm not sure."

"Now, that's better. At least you've stopped denying you're interested in him."

"I just wish to find out the truth about his supposed infamy."

"Which is none of your business."

"I suppose it isn't." Lisette hesitated. "But you know me; I hate to see injustice done to anyone."

"I don't doubt that, sister mine. You always want everyone to be happy. But I have a suspicion that you want to see the man again because you want to." Christian held her gaze. "And I'm still worried because he might not be the right kind of man for you."

"Are you warning me off again?"

"I'm telling you that his particular sexual tastes are well suited to the pleasure house."

"You've already said that." Lisette stood up and planted her hands on the tabletop. "Either tell me everything, or don't interfere."

Christian leaned back in his chair until he could look up into her face. "I work for Maman, and I respect the privacy of our guests. I'm not going to tell you exactly what he does or doesn't do, and, in truth, I don't believe anyone has the right to judge another man's sexual tastes."

"Yet by bringing them to my attention, you are judging his."

"I'm simply preparing you for the notion that he isn't as straightforward as you might think. You haven't spent as much time at the pleasure house as I have; you have no idea of the complexities of some of the guests' sexual tastes."

"I've spent plenty of time there. I'm not some naive debutante." Lisette glared at her twin. "And I refuse to discuss this with you again."

Christian shrugged, his eyes narrowed, his expression cool. "Fine." He toasted her with his coffee cup. "Go ahead, make a fool of yourself."

Lisette realized she was trembling. For the first time in her life she was at complete odds with her brother and she had no intention of letting him persuade her otherwise. "Thank you, I will."

There was nothing left to do but exit the room and brood over her brother's strange behavior. A startling thought occurred to her. Was Christian attracted to Lord Swanfield himself? She had an idea that his sexual tastes were not restricted to women. Was this the reason he was so adamant that Lisette would not find happiness with the other man? Surely not . . .

Lisette almost turned back. Perhaps she should ask him outright and clear the matter up once and for all. But she sensed Christian wouldn't tell her even if it was true. The gap that had developed between them recently seemed as wide and deep as a chasm, and it hurt. She started walking again. She wasn't going to allow him to dictate to her. If Christian truly wanted Gabriel Swanfield, he'd have to deal with her first.

"Good evening, Lord Swanfield."

Lisette smiled sweetly as her prey turned away from her father and focused his intent gaze on her. He wore a superbly cut black coat and plain white linen that did nothing to diminish his height or fine physique. He was one of the few men who made Lisette feel small and feminine. She imagined his weight bearing her down on the bed, his arms wrapped around her, his mouth . . .

"Good evening, Miss Ross." His dark blue gaze was guarded, his expression bland enough to curdle milk. "I hope you are well."

Her father led the way into the small family dining room, where four places were laid at the table. The green damask curtains were drawn and soft candlelight illuminated the gleaming oak table and intricate crystal glasses. Lisette prayed that Christian wouldn't appear. He had the ability to destroy her evening if he chose to.

Lord Swanfield paused to pull her chair out and then retreated to the opposite side of the table so that he faced her. "Is Miss Emily joining us?"

"No. She is remaining at Knowles Hall for at least another week preparing for her debut," Lisette said. "The place is set for my brother, but he rarely dines with us."

"I'm not sure I've met your brother, Miss Ross."

Her father laughed. "Christian is adept at avoiding social activities. But he is hard to miss. He bears a striking likeness to Lisette. They are twins."

"Is that so?" Lord Swanfield's keen gaze considered her. "Come to think of it, I might have caught a glimpse of him at your ball."

Lisette's heart gave an uncomfortable thump. She could only assume he'd met Christian at some point at the pleasure house. She hoped his impression was vague and that he wasn't about to make a connection that would lead to trouble.

To her relief, the meal proceeded amicably enough, her father making most of the small talk as Lord Swanfield's replies tended to be short and to the point. She contributed her part as well, played the silly society woman to the hilt, a role she'd come to loathe, a reputation she wished she'd never encouraged.

"I have something for you, Swanfield," her father announced. "I found it in my study on my return from Knowles Hall. If you'll both excuse me for a minute, I'll go and fetch it for you." He winked at Lisette and retreated, taking the lone footman stationed at the door with him.

Lisette put her wineglass down and stared at the tablecloth. Having Lord Swanfield sitting across from her was quite overwhelming and she was at a loss for what to say. She didn't want him to see her as a chatty empty-headed twit, but all the conversational gambits that rose to her lips were stupid inanities and she didn't like that at all. Her attraction for him was far more visceral and base; she didn't want to talk to him, she wanted to touch him. She'd already noted he didn't use strong cologne; only the scent of cigarillo smoke, saddle leather, and lemon soap drifted across the table to tantalize her senses, to make her yearn to lean over and stroke his cheek.

"Miss Ross."

She looked up and he rose to his feet, reached across the table, and cupped her jaw in one of his hands. His mouth came down over hers, and she welcomed the fierce intimacy of his kiss, the savage heat of it, and even the implied possession. Before she could speak, he resumed his seat and her father returned with the footman bearing a small oil painting, which he presented to Lord Swanfield.

"Here you are, Swanfield. It's a portrait of Wellington as a foal with his sire."

Lisette was instantly forgotten as Lord Swanfield's attention switched to the painting and he smiled. "Thank you, sir, I will treasure it."

"You are welcome." Philip resumed his seat and beckoned to the footman to pour him another glass of brandy. "Perhaps you would care to take a turn in the garden with my daughter, my lord? She loves the evening air."

Lisette frowned repressively at her father, who simply continued to smile at her. "Perhaps Lord Swanfield would prefer to stay inside and discuss horses with you?"

"Oh no, a breath of fresh air would be very welcome, Miss Ross." Lord Swanfield pushed back his chair and stood up. He offered her his arm. "Shall we proceed?"

She moved around the table to stand next to him, and realized again how tall he was when she had to look up. Her father gestured at the French doors leading out of the dining room. "You can access the garden from here. I'll make sure the staff doesn't lock you out."

"Thank you, Father."

Lisette waited while the footman deftly unlocked the double doors and then she stepped outside into the fragrant garden. Spring flowers were in bloom and her kid slippers sunk into the soft green grass as if it were a Persian rug. They walked in silence for a moment until they were out of sight of the dining room windows.

"Am I forgiven then?"

Lisette looked up. "Why ever would you think that?"

"Because I am here, and because your father obviously approves of me."

"My father always takes a great interest in anyone who buys his horses. As his daughter, it is my duty to accept and welcome all his guests."

"So you're still sulking then."

Lisette stopped walking. "I am not sulking. I had a perfectly legitimate reason to consign you to the devil."

His smile was slow and screamed danger. "Yet here we are, together again, and I don't think you mind it that much." He reached forward and brushed his thumb over her lower lip. "You still taste the same. I still want you."

"And you are still arrogant."

He leaned into her and kissed her lightly on the lips. She fisted her hands at her sides to stop herself from sliding them into his thick black hair and holding him close. He kissed her again, the tip of his tongue outlining the seam of her lips, seeking access, something she wanted to give him more than she wanted to breathe.

He drew back and stared down at her. "Why are you being so stubborn?"

"Why do you make it sound so simple when it isn't simple at all? As we've already established, a young lady can't go around kissing every man she meets just because she wants him."

"I've heard you've kissed quite your fair share."

Lisette raised her chin. "Have you been listening to gossip about me, my lord?"

"Perhaps I have."

"And you believe I am a flirt?"

He considered her for a long moment. "So I've been told, but I've learned to my cost that gossip can often be wrong."

Lisette swallowed her outrage. "In this case, the gossip is true, I *am* a flirt. I *love* to bring men to their knees and then laugh and walk away from them."

"That won't happen with me."

The absolute confidence in his voice shook her. "It won't happen, my lord, because I refuse to flirt with you."

He grabbed her hand and pulled her hard against him. "I don't want you to flirt. I want you to be yourself, to admit that you want me and stop complicating something as straight-forward as lust with romantic womanly notions of love."

She struggled to pull her hand free from his chest, but he kissed her and somehow her hand ended up wrapped around his neck as she kissed him back. God, she could drown in his mouth, in the press of his hard body against hers, in his arms around her.

"Let me give you pleasure." His husky words were barely whispered into her ear. "Let me touch you. I burn for you, I'm hard for you all the time; I come thinking of you every night."

She sighed against his throat. "I wish you would stop saying things like that. It is so unfair."

He nipped her ear. "Because you like it?"

"Yes, and thus I increase my reputation as an incorrigible flirt."

He sank down onto a convenient bench and drew her into his lap, his arm encircling her waist, his mouth returning to hers. This time she let him in, her tongue tangling with his, as his hand inched up from her waist to cup and squeeze her breast, making it swell over the constriction of her bodice and corset.

"God . . ." His hoarse comment excited her further as his

mouth latched onto her nipple and sucked hard. She shivered and slid her hand around his neck to hold him close. His other hand was under her skirts, caressing her buttock and she wasn't about to stop him, not yet, not now, not until he. . . She gasped as one of his long fingers brushed her clit and discovered the thick wetness between her thighs.

"Touch me." His rough command and the way he grabbed her hand and pressed it to the front of his pantaloons made her feel victorious, that she wasn't the only one in danger of losing control.

She remembered this sensation of falling, of the notion that nothing existed beyond his hands, his mouth, and her willing body. She arched her back and shamelessly rubbed her mound against his wide, calloused palm, felt the tip of his finger penetrate her and moaned. "Please . . ."

He slid his finger a little deeper and she moved against it, didn't care what he thought of her, just wanted the pleasure she knew was close. He groaned as her fingernails cut into his skin. His thumb was on her clit, his finger working her to the rhythm of his suckling. She gripped his shaft as hard as she could and felt dampness and heat beneath her fingers as he shoved himself into her hand.

She climaxed and his mouth claimed hers, sealing in her cries of release and joining their breath. When she opened her eyes he was still holding her, his hands now on the outside of her clothing, his expression strained. She forced herself to climb off his lap, and noticed he hadn't come, that his cock still tented his pantaloons.

She cleared her throat and haphazardly straightened her gown. "May I help you with"—she waved vaguely in the direction of his groin—"that?"

He glanced down at himself and then at her. "Thank you, but no."

Even as she absorbed the implied rejection and felt it sting far more than she had anticipated, she tried to make a joke of it. "Surely you have realized by now that I am indeed a terrible flirt, and that even more shockingly, I enjoy touching and being touched by a man. You wouldn't be the first man that I've 'helped.'"

A muscle flicked in his cheek. "I can see that."

She took a step back feeling cold. "I invested a lot of energy in my 'fast' reputation and now I believe I regret it."

"Why?"

"Because I don't like the way you are looking at me."

He angled his head to one side. "How do I look?"

"Judgmental."

He shrugged. "I have no right to sit in judgment of you."

"No, you don't."

"But if you don't wish men to think you are a flirt, your behavior with me hardly helps."

"You are right. I don't know what came over me. I must be even worse than the gossips imagined!" She glared at him and gathered the ends of her shawl tightly in her fist. "What a feather in your crown; you are obviously irresistible."

He stood up slowly and studied her. "Don't put words into my mouth, Miss Ross. I'm quite happy to engage in a flirtation of this nature with you, but I refuse to share you with any other men."

"Gossip suggests I indulge in orgies, does it?" Her sexual warmth dissipated rapidly replaced by sheer anger.

"That's not what I meant. I . . ."

"Gossip is an insidious thing, isn't it? You must know that yourself. Your reputation is hardly stellar."

His shoulders stiffened and his faint smile disappeared. "You have been listening to gossip about me?"

"I asked after your army career, if that is what you mean."

Lisette drew her shawl over her breasts, aware of a sudden chill that emanated not from her surroundings but from the man in front of her.

"And did you enjoy hearing about my disgrace?"

She blinked at his suddenly arctic tone. "Of course not!"

"It is a remarkable tale, is it not? The lowly aristocrat showing his true colors by betraying everything and everyone who believed in him."

Lisette took a deep breath. "Lord Swanfield, you refused to answer me when I asked you to explain yourself. In truth, you told me to go to the devil. You can hardly complain if I try to find out the truth myself!"

He bowed. "Good evening, Miss Ross."

"Wait." Lisette caught at his arm. "Surely we are even? We both sought information about the other in the only way available to us. Why are you allowed to storm away in a huff and I'm not?"

"Because being labeled a flirt is far less damaging than being labeled a coward." He tried to shake her hand off his sleeve, but she refused to let go.

"Is that so? Of course, a man's reputation and honor is *so* much more important than a woman's, isn't it?"

He glowered down at her. "Yes, it is."

Lisette let go of him then and stepped back. "Sometimes I do not like you at all."

His bow was full of scathing magnificence. "And I do not like you very much either."

"Then we are done, sir, and all there is left to do is wish you a long and happy life."

"Indeed."

Lisette managed one last disdainful toss of her head before she picked up her skirts and headed back for the house. Of course he didn't follow her, and by the time she reached the dining room, the scent of one of his ridiculous cigarillos reached her. She tried not to breathe it in, aware of an ache in her heart and a more physical ache from her body. She touched her lips where he had kissed her and acknowledged a particularly exasperating fact. She might not like him at all, but she still wanted him and he had no intention of playing the game by her rules at all.

5

"Lisette, whatever are you doing here?"

Lisette jumped at the sound of her mother's amused voice and forced a smile. When she'd decided to slip in through the servants' entrance of the pleasure house, she hadn't expected to find Helene in the kitchen sharing a cup of chocolate with the cook. She blew a kiss at Madame Durand, who smiled and retreated to the far end of the kitchen. Lisette took off her cloak and bonnet and laid them carefully over the back of a chair, then slipped effortlessly into the colloquial French of her childhood.

"Nothing, *Maman*, I just decided to enjoy myself at the pleasure house this evening for a change."

"But I thought you'd decided to avoid the place in favor of supporting your half sister's debut." Helene, her mother and the owner of the pleasure house, studied her quizzically. She was dressed for the evening ahead in a gown of blue silk that matched her eyes and sapphire jewelry that Lisette knew had been a wedding gift from her father.

Lisette sighed. "I'm wondering if I made the right decision

about that. Christian believes I will do Emily more harm than good by being seen with her."

Helene's perfect eyebrows arched upward. "And you *agreed* with him?"

"My reputation is not exactly pristine."

Lisette sat opposite her mother in the quiet of the normally bustling kitchen. When she and Christian had first moved to England, it had become their favorite place in the house. Madame Durand was endlessly kind and they'd enjoyed sampling her wares, listening to the scandalous gossip from upstairs, and plotting ways to annoy their mother. Christian was never there now. He was far too busy dealing with the real business of the house in the main office upstairs.

"And your reputation matters to you now because . . . ?" Helene asked.

Lisette forced herself to meet her mother's blue eyes, and remembered her encounter with Lord Swanfield on the previous evening. "I just wish I hadn't been quite so . . ."

"Enthusiastic?"

"So keen to embrace the joys of the flesh." Lisette grimaced. "I made some bad choices, *Maman*, you know I did. I'm not even a virgin anymore."

Helene gave a dismissive snap of her fingers. "Any man who thinks less of you for *that* is not worth having. I've always hated such double standards."

"I'll remember that, *Maman*." Lisette thought of Lord Swanfield. He hadn't seemed shocked that she'd let him touch her so intimately; he'd just insisted that he wouldn't share her with anyone else. Her smile dimmed.

"Is there something in particular you wish to discuss with me, *ma petite*?" Helene asked gently.

"Not really, *Maman*. Do you remember how hard I tried to scandalize you?" Lisette had to smile then. "That is, until I learned you were completely unshockable."

"You were only eighteen when you first came to live with me, and, unfortunately, because of the nature of my business, I gave you more opportunities to explore your sexuality than most mothers would." Helene sighed. "And you quite rightly resented me for my long absence in your life. I'm not surprised you wanted to provoke me."

"You tried very hard to stop me even coming in here, but I refused to be put off," Lisette said quickly. "Please don't blame yourself."

Her mother's expression clouded. "I wasn't there for you as a mother for so many years. I regret that more than I can say."

Lisette rose to her feet and went to embrace her mother's petite form. Helene still didn't look old enough to be the mother of three children, including one, Marguerite, who was about to be married for the second time.

"I love you just the way you are, *Maman*, never doubt it. You made the best choices you could, and as Philip frequently reminds us, many young mothers simply abandon their bastards. They don't enroll them in expensive French nunnery schools and give them an education."

Helene winced. "Yes, I was able to take care of your material comfort; your emotional well-being is another matter." She gripped Lisette's hand. "Ah, but there is no point in regretting the past, is there? But I have always wondered if you and Christian would've been more . . . settled if I had been there for you."

Lisette mock-frowned at her mother. "*Maman*, you have given me a father and a family I'm proud to belong to. That is quite enough."

"Philip is a good man, isn't he? And he was so happy when he was able to give you his name and acknowledge you as his children." Helene half smiled. "Even if this ridiculously antiquated English law means that as we married long after your birth, Christian can't inherit the title."

"I don't think Christian cares about that, do you? He never even uses the 'Ross' name. He is far too busy enjoying his life to worry about all the responsibilities poor Richard will have to face."

Secretly Lisette wondered if that was still true. As Christian had withdrawn from her this past year, she had wondered whether he resented his position as the oldest son of a future earl, but not the legal heir to the title.

"That is true." Helene rose to her feet and smoothed down the front of her blue silk gown. "I have to go back to my office and finish my work. Why don't you run along and enjoy yourself, my dear?"

Lisette kissed her mother's soft cheek. "I think I will." It was the best revenge on Lord Swanfield she could think of. Not that she was thinking of him at all. "And don't worry, I'll wear a mask."

Helene laughed. "I'm sure your father and Emily will be grateful for that."

Lisette watched her mother leave and envied her grace and composure, even as her heart raced at the prospect of an illicit evening at the pleasure house. In her younger years, her mother's perfection had made her feel so inadequate. It was only as she'd learned to listen to what her mother was really trying to tell her about the horrors of her youth, her struggles with the pleasure house, her desolation when Philip had first left her, that she'd come to understand and love the complex woman who had given birth to her.

And just talking to her mother had emboldened her. Since her far too intimate encounter with Lord Swanfield, she needed to prove that he was not the only man who could make her forget her resolve to behave more appropriately. Perhaps she truly was a wanton woman and any man would do.

After an hour of searching out all the delights the pleasure house could offer on the first floor, she was at a loss. None of the men excited her, even those who had solicited her company. None of them seemed tall enough or elegant enough or had dark blue eyes. . . .

Lisette picked up her skirts and started determinedly up the stairs to the more intimate setting of the second floor, where the sexual games were both more explicit and performed in smaller settings. She'd deliberately chosen a brown satin dress more suited to a mature married woman and dressed her hair in a more severe braided style than her usual haphazard curls. With the half-mask over her face, she hoped her disguise was sufficient to fool most of the ton. A young, unmarried lady would be an unusual and unwelcome sight at the pleasure house.

Lisette headed toward the largest of the intimate salons and paused at the doorway to investigate. At first glance, nothing seemed too unusual: a fair number of women and some men were seated on the comfortable red couches watching a trio of naked performers entwined on the low stage at the front of the room. As they watched, a succession of half-naked men moved among them, serving drinks and small delicacies.

The masked servers wore tight white pantaloons that looked as if they had been stitched onto them, leaving the guests in no doubt as to the shape of each man's arse, the size of his cock, and exactly who was aroused.

A flurry of movement drew Lisette's gaze to the back of the room where a pair of women tried to attract the attention of one of the servers. Despite herself, Lisette's gaze was drawn to the broad, scarred back of the man who faced them. Something about the way he carried himself alerted all her senses. One of the women reached around to caress the man's buttock and pinched his arse through the satin as if testing the mettle of a horse.

The man sank to his knees and offered the tray of drinks to the women. They continued to talk to each other, one of them fondling the server's cock as if she were petting a lap dog. As the candlelight fell on the man's scarred profile, Lisette remained frozen in the doorway. Surely it couldn't be . . .

She drew back as the man stood up again and turned toward the center of the room. He was magnificently aroused now, his thick cock pushing at the satin as if threatening to tear its way out. His gaze was respectfully on the floor as a good servant's should be. Another man beckoned him over, pushed him against the wall and roughly handled his shaft. Lisette swallowed hard. Even though she couldn't see his eyes, she knew exactly who it was. With all the care she could manage, Lisette moved away from the doorway and back into the hall, her heart thumping, and her hand over her mouth.

It was not uncommon for an aristocrat to take on the role of a servant in the pleasure house. In truth, a lot of people enjoyed playing a subservient character and submitting themselves to the will or the whims of others. But she'd never expected Major Lord Gabriel Swanfield to be such a man.

She slowed down and had to stop because her breathing was so erratic. Christian had warned her, so it was ridiculous to feel so betrayed. Obviously Lord Swanfield's words about her being the only woman he wanted had been a lie. She'd been a fool to think he was different, that he'd wanted to be honest with her, that she would be able to be honest with him. . . .

She found her mother ensconced in her office with a large accounting book in front of her.

"*Maman*, can I ask you something?"

Helene removed her spectacles. "Anything, *ma petite*, you know that."

Lisette paced the worn rug in front of her mother's desk. "There *is* a man . . ."

"Does this have to do with your reasons for regretting your reputation?"

Lisette chose to ignore that question and concentrated on the scene she had just witnessed. "The servers in the large salon on the second level. Do they have sex with the other guests?"

"You know the rules, Lisette. Each person here is allowed to make their own decisions as to how far they are prepared to participate."

"So they can have sex, then?"

Helene's eyebrows rose. "Is there someone here tonight you wish to bed?"

"There is someone here who drives me to distraction, but I don't want to bed him, I just want to get even with him."

"Because he has wronged you?"

"Because . . ." Lisette smiled at her mother. "Just because."

Helene shuffled some papers on her desk and opened another book. "If you tell me which man you mean, I can find out what his sexual limits are. Would that help?"

"You don't have to do that, *Maman*. Perhaps, with your permission, I could talk to whoever is in charge of the servers on that floor and get her to help me?"

Helene shut the book. "You do not want me to know which man you are interested in."

"Not really, *Maman*." Lisette tried to keep her tone light. "He doesn't mean anything to me."

"Yet you still wish to punish him for his transgressions?"

"From what I've seen tonight, he obviously enjoys being servile. He'll probably enjoy himself more than I will."

Helene held her gaze. "Be very careful, Lisette."

"I will."

"Just remember that when sex is involved, people can behave very strangely."

"I know that."

Helene blew her a kiss. "Then go and talk to Marie-Claude. Tell her I said she should help you and good luck."

"Thank you, *Maman*."

Sometimes Lisette was so relieved to have a mother like Helene, a woman who allowed her to make her own sexual choices and didn't expect her to behave like a conventional naive miss. Thanks to her mother, she had the perfect opportunity to expose Lord Swanfield as the hypocrite he was.

Gabriel stepped back into the servants' hallway at the pleasure house and leaned against the wall. His cock ached like the devil tonight, and yet he'd refused all the offers to bring him release. He wasn't sure why. Perhaps he preferred the torture of blue balls to the loss of dignity required to allow some stranger to make him come. He kept imagining Miss Ross's expression if she could see him here, at his worst, at his most desperate.

"Monsieur?" He looked up and saw Marie-Claude beckoning imperiously to him. "Come along."

Without thinking, he followed her to the end of the hall and into one of the smaller, more private rooms that adjoined the salon. A woman dressed in brown silk sat in a chair beside the bed, a woman Gabriel had no chance of recognizing unless he ripped off her bonnet and heavy veils. Marie-Claude nodded at him.

"This lady wishes you to pull down your pantaloons."

For a moment, Gabriel balked at the calm request and wondered why the woman couldn't speak for herself. Inwardly, he shrugged. He needed to come, and this was as good a way as any. In the struggle to push the tight satin down over his shaft he might even embarrass himself and spill his seed. At least then it would be over and he could go home and sleep.

Slowly, he worked the two buttons loose, wincing as his cock pulsed and soaked the satin in pre-cum. He managed to lower the placket and shove down the sides of his pantaloons. His cock strained upward toward his stomach, the wetness at the tip catching the candlelight.

"Touch yourself," Marie-Claude said.

Gabriel was quite happy to oblige. He wrapped one hand around his thick shaft and worked his heated flesh through his fingers. God, he was so close, so close to coming. . . .

"Stop, monsieur."

His fingers stilled even as his mind screamed a denial and he forced himself to breathe slowly.

"Come closer." Marie-Claude murmured.

Still clasping his shaft he moved nearer, he focused his attention on the woman seated directly in front of him. He shuddered when she lifted one gloved hand and traced from the tip of his cock down to his balls with her index finger. She returned her finger to the crown of his cock and slowly circled the tiny weeping hole at the center. His hips jerked toward her touch, straining, wanting, and she obliged him, flicked and circled his aching tip until he almost started to come.

He groaned out loud as she expertly shifted her grip to the base of his cock and cut off his spasms, leaving him suspended somewhere between pleasure and pain.

"Please . . ." he whispered. She let him go and Marie-Claude spoke again.

"Finish yourself. Come for her."

He replaced his hand on his cock and with two savage jerks, he came hard, his cum pumping over his fingers to drench his fist and his stomach. He didn't watch himself, he watched her, the woman who had wanted to see him like this, half naked and willing to let himself be touched by anyone who wanted to.

"Thank you, monsieur. You may go now." Marie-Claude paused as the woman whispered in her ear. "Madame requests that you return to this room tomorrow night and meet her again."

Gabriel nodded and shoved his limp cock back into his pantaloons. It was time for him to go home and perhaps he would sleep for what remained of the night, his cock now sated, his unsavory appetites indulged. He bowed at the two women again and retreated through the servants' door. The mysterious woman had obviously enjoyed the show, and, to his shame, he had enjoyed it, too. Despite his self-disgust, he couldn't help but wonder what she would ask of him on the morrow.

Lisette waited for the door to shut behind Lord Swanfield before throwing back her veil and pulling off her gloves. Marie-Claude smiled at her.

"Did it go as you wish? He has a fine cock, *non?*"

"He does." Lisette could only agree, and she pictured Lord Swanfield coming in front of her, his face contorted in a grimace of pleasure as his cum released all over his fingers. She'd wanted to lean forward and lick it up, had almost done so before she'd remembered that would make it necessary for her to remove her veil.

"Does he have sex with the guests?"

Marie-Claude looked thoughtful. "Not full sex."

Lisette wondered why that made her feel a little better. "Does he service men?"

"Yes, but with his hands and mouth. I don't believe he enjoys male penetration either."

Lord Swanfield was proving to be more of an enigma than Lisette had expected. She frowned up at Marie-Claude. "Then why does he do this?"

"Play the role of a servant?"

"Yes, and allow himself to be fondled and touched by complete strangers."

Marie-Claude shrugged. "Perhaps it is the only way he can find sexual release, or the only way he *allows* himself to find sexual release."

Suddenly Lisette remembered Lord Swanfield's comments about not taking her to bed even if she'd wanted him to. "That might be true. Perhaps he really is saving himself for marriage or someone special after all. . . ."

"Do you know him then, Lisette?"

"I've certainly met him before."

"And you like him?"

Lisette stared at the older French woman. "I'm not sure."

Marie-Claude's brown eyes narrowed with amusement. "You like him. You were practically salivating when he revealed his cock."

"Weren't you?"

"I've seen so many." Marie-Claude winked. "Although I must admit he certainly is large. What do you plan to do with him tomorrow night?"

Lisette smiled properly for the first time that evening. Major Lord Gabriel Swanfield, finally in her hands and at her mercy. "That remains to be seen."

Gabriel spent much of the next evening searching for the woman in brown silk, not that any fashionable woman would wear the same dress twice; even he knew that. But he still hoped to seek her out. Something about the tilt of her head and her calm demeanor had seemed familiar. He hardly needed any of the guests to touch or stimulate his cock tonight. He'd been half erect since he arrived.

He endured the other guests' fondling and groping, but turned down all the offers for further exploration. Somehow, keeping himself in readiness for the unknown woman appealed to his perverted sexual desires and made him even more aroused. When the clock struck eleven, he found Marie-Claude in front of him again.

"Come along, monsieur. She is waiting."

Gabriel entered the room and saw the woman sitting, as before, in a high-back chair in front of the bed. Tonight she wore black, her bosom spilling over the top of her low-cut gown, her face still veiled beneath the high sweep of a Spanish mantilla and veil. Her gloved hands lay together in her lap, her fingers entwined. He nodded at her but she didn't offer him anything in return. He took up a stance in front of her, feet slightly apart and hands behind his back.

"The lady would like to see your cock."

Gabriel unbuttoned his pantaloons to display his shaft. He wasn't as desperate as he had been on the previous night, but knowing she watched him quickly dispelled any notion that he wouldn't come at her slightest touch.

"Touch yourself until you are almost ready to come."

Gabriel applied himself to the task, no hardship for a man who deliberately sought out this particular form of sexual torture at the pleasure house. The only sounds in the room were his ragged breathing and the slick, wet sound of his cock sliding between his fingers. He just remembered to stop before he came and waited to be told what to do next.

The woman removed one of her gloves and leaned forward to scoop a bead of pre-cum from the tip of his cock. Gabriel shivered as she sucked the finger into her mouth and beckoned him closer.

"The lady wishes you to put your hands behind your back and close your eyes."

Gabriel did what he was told and groaned as he felt her hand on his cock and then the unexpected coldness of metal. He opened his eyes and looked down. The woman was busy wrapping his cock and balls within a supple spiral of braided metallic wire. When she reached the tip she angled the metal coil over the slit of his cock.

"Monsieur, you were not supposed to look," Marie-Claude said. "Do you wish to punish him, ma'am?"

Gabriel's cock swelled at her words and his tender flesh pushed against the metal, hot against cold, yielding flesh and unresisting silver. He wanted her to touch him again so much it hurt to breathe. She shook her head and he tried to relax, found it impossible when she lowered her head and she blew a stream of air onto his beleaguered cock.

"Close your eyes, monsieur, and keep them closed this time or I will blindfold you," Marie-Claude said.

The threat of that was enough to make him obey. After the long months in the unlit cells of a French prison, he hated not being able to see properly. Even the mask he wore at the pleasure house was almost too constricting. He braced himself for what would happen next, groaned out loud when the unknown woman's tongue flicked over the silver constraints and delved deep to delight his flesh.

He squeezed his eyes shut as she continued to torment him with her tongue, and he fought the urge to slide his hands into her hair. What color was her hair? He was aware of his hips rocking gently with the rhythm of her licking, his buttocks flexing with the need to shove himself deep into her mouth and beg her to take his cock, to take all of his cum.

"Let me help you, ma'am," Marie-Claude murmured.

He flinched as he felt movement behind him and then realized it was Marie-Claude, pushing his pantaloons down further to expose his arse. Her warm hands cupped his arse cheeks and then he felt her fingers stroking the sensitive flesh between his arse hole and his balls.

God, he wanted to die, wanted the subtle torment to end, but never end, wanted it harder and rougher, wanted to come . . . but could he come within the restriction of the silver coils? It felt as though his cock would always be erect and trapped. The woman's tongue probed his slit, and he bit down hard on his lip, enjoyig the slight pain with the edge of pleasure.

She sucked him into her mouth, silver rings and all, and just held him there. Gabriel tensed as Marie-Claude's now-oiled finger circled the tight bud of his arse hole and then eased inside. He held his breath as she went deeper and deeper and then he forgot anything but the desperate need to come as pleasure narrowed to a point so clear and sharp that he felt as if he was about to fall.

Cocooned in the woman's warm mouth, his cock gave up the struggle and he started to come, each shuddering wave swallowed down her throat, his hands gripped together behind him, his nails digging deep into his own flesh. When he stopped shuddering, the woman had sat up and replaced her veil. Marie-Claude, however, still knelt on the floor. She glanced up at the woman and removed the silver bands. Gabriel sighed in relief until her heard her next question.

"Shall I make him hard for you again, ma'am, or have you seen enough tonight?"

The woman whispered something in French and Marie-Claude smiled. "Of course, ma'am." She looked up at Gabriel. "It seems as if my lady approves of you. Now keep still." She knelt up and cupped his balls in her hand. "I'm sure you can do even better than that."

Marie-Claude winked at Lisette as she sucked Lord Swanfield's cock for the second time. They'd played with him endlessly, licked him, sucked him, tormented him until his cock streamed with pre-cum and he was begging hoarsely for release. It was time to end the game now, and for that, she needed his full attention.

When Marie-Claude stood up, Lisette whispered in her ear, "This time we let him handle himself and when I nod, you will open the door so that we can make a quick exit."

"Agreed, Madame." Marie-Claude raised her voice. "Monsieur, you may pleasure yourself. We will watch."

His long elegant fingers dropped to cradle his balls and curve around his cock. He was careful with himself this time, obviously feeling sore and well used. Lisette nudged Marie-Claire and frowned. "Tell him to do it faster and when he comes I want him to look at me."

Marie-Claude relayed the message in flawless English and Lord Swanfield complied, his hands moving more quickly, his motions rougher. Lisette licked her lips and tasted him in her mouth, knew she wanted to taste him again at some basic uncomplicated level where he simply appealed to her most vital needs.

She watched his face through her veil, her hands ready, and waited for him to look up as he came. He started to pant, his hands gripping and releasing his thick, straining cock, and started to come, looked up at her as instructed. She raised her veil and let him see her, watching the horror and sexual high collide on his face as he realized exactly whom he had been performing for.

Before he even finished coming, Lisette blew him a kiss and left as fast as she could, making sure Marie-Claude locked the door behind her just in case Lord Swanfield tried to come after her. She wasn't ready to go home yet, so where should she go? Her heart was beating so hard she feared she might faint, and her body was screaming for release.

The solution was obvious. Her old room in the private part of the pleasure house was still available to her. She would take herself to bed and worry about exactly what Lord Swanfield would do on the morrow.

"Damnation!" Gabriel fell to his knees, his hands cradling his still-spurting cock, his teeth clenched against the onslaught of pleasure. He stayed down, his head bent, and tried to breathe properly, to collect his scattered thoughts and make sense of what had happened. But it was impossible. His two worlds had finally collided. What the devil was a well-brought-up young lady like Miss Ross doing in the pleasure house?

He gave a shuddering sigh and tried to pull up his pantaloons, aware that his cock was now sore and throbbing from overuse. Normally he liked the sensation, but this time there was only pain. There had always been a risk that someone he knew would recognize him. He'd seen several of his old army colleagues at the pleasure house, and none of them had seemed to know him, not even his cousins.

Miss Ross had not only known him but made sure he knew it, too. He groaned and strode toward the door. What would she do with that information? She hadn't struck him as the type of woman who enjoyed humiliating a man in public. But she had reason to believe he had deceived her, and that made any woman dangerous.

The door refused to open, and, after trying it several times, he slammed his fist into the wooden panel. She obviously didn't want him to follow her. And what would he do if he caught her anyway? Wring her neck or shove his cock deep inside her and finish what she had started. God, he still wanted to fuck her, wanted it even more than he had before. . . .

Shame washed over him, along with a sickening sense of his own stupidity. Why would she want him? With a groan, he retreated from the locked door and focused on washing himself clean and planning his next move. She couldn't avoid him forever. Even if she never came back to the pleasure house, he knew exactly where she lived.

6

"Good morning, Swanfield." Lisette's father smiled at Gabriel across the breakfast table where he sat conspicuously alone. "What brings you to my house so early in the morning?"

Gabriel bowed. "I apologize for disturbing you, sir, but I was hoping to invite Miss Ross to ride with me."

Philip Knowles looked surprised. "Lisette isn't known for her love of riding. She doesn't even have a horse in London. Are you sure you mean her?"

"I spent some time with her at Knowles House helping her regain her confidence. I thought she might like to continue our lessons."

"That is very thoughtful of you, Swanfield, but she isn't here. She spent the night at her mother's house."

It belatedly occurred to Gabriel that he had never met Lord Knowles's wife. Was there some scandal about their relationship he had missed?

"Her mother doesn't live here?" He cringed at his own words and braced himself for Lord Knowles's wrath.

Amusement glinted in Lord Knowles's eyes. "She lives here sometimes, but I don't want to bore you with our complicated domestic matters."

"Ah, exactly." Gabriel tried hard to think of what to say next. "Do you have Miss Ross's direction, sir?"

Philip's eyebrows rose. "You seem remarkably anxious to see her, Swanfield."

Gabriel met his gaze. "I am, sir."

"Then perhaps you might care to leave a message, which I will endeavor to deliver to her on her return."

It was said gently enough, but there was no mistaking the implacable note behind Lord Knowles's words. Gabriel sighed and realized he was beaten. If he kept pressing, Lord Knowles would grow suspicious and pass his concerns along to his daughter and that would lead to him being barred from the house.

"That is an excellent idea, sir. I'll ask her to ride with me on the morrow. I'll supply her with a horse."

Lord Knowles stood up and held out his hand. "There is paper and ink in my study. Please feel free to use them before you leave."

Gabriel shook the proffered hand and allowed the footman to lead him into Lord Knowles's study. He wrote an innocuously polite note, informing Miss Ross that he would call for her at eight in the morning unless he heard otherwise, and left it unsealed on Lord Knowles's desk. As he replaced the pen in the inkwell, he noticed a collection of miniature paintings on the polished wooden surface. He recognized Lisette instantly. The others eluded him, apart from a vaguely familiar blond woman, although he guessed they were pictures of Miss Emily and her brother when they were younger.

He nodded his thanks to the footman and was shown out the door. He put on his gloves and then his hat as he strolled down the steps. It was only after he mounted his horse that he remembered where he might have seen the other blond woman. Whoever she was, she also frequented the pleasure house. He clicked at his horse and started moving. Was that the connection between Miss Ross and the erotic club? Did she have an older sister or a mother who visited the place and thus had entry?

He had no idea, and could only hope that Miss Ross would be brave enough to face him tomorrow. There was little he could do to her while she was on horseback in the middle of a public park, although several scenarios involving dragging her out of the saddle and putting her over his knee had presented themselves to his fevered imagination. . . . His cock stirred protestingly and he shut down that line of thought. There would be time enough to gauge the state of their "relationship" tomorrow without inviting trouble.

"Swanfield!"

Gabriel looked to his left and saw an all-too-familiar figure waving at him. He guided his horse to the edge of the road, and looked down unsmilingly at his cousin Lieutenant Michael Granger. Michael was neither as tall nor dark-featured as he was, and his eyes were a pale gray. His older brother, William, was far more like Gabriel in looks and temperament.

"Good morning, Gabriel, and how are you?" Michael's smile seemed genuine enough, so Gabriel forced himself to respond.

"I'm well, thank you."

"Are you back in Town for good, then?" Michael swallowed hard. "I hadn't heard that you were opening up Swanfield House."

"I'm not."

Michael looked confused. "Why not?"

"Because it seems an unnecessary extravagance just for one person."

"But you're the earl and it's your home. People will expect you to live there."

Gabriel shrugged. "I've never felt that way about it, Michael. I've only been there twice."

"Well, at least you should go and see the old place. You might like it."

"I doubt that."

Michael sighed. "Still as cantankerous as ever, I see. One day you'll have to accept who you are and let the past go."

"Like your brother William has?"

Michael's cheeks flushed. "William is a fool and you know it."

Gabriel inclined his head. "It was nice to see you again, cousin."

Concern flashed across Michael's face. "Don't go yet. I have no idea how to contact you, or where you are living."

"Why would you want to contact me? I'm not exactly welcome in your family, am I? Seeing as I 'stole' the title from your brother."

"That's not true. We all . . . became accustomed to that disappointment years ago." Michael persisted, his expression pleading. "Perhaps we could meet at my club?"

Gabriel allowed his horse to back up two steps. "I don't frequent the clubs. I'm still considered a disgraced man, remember?"

"But we could help you with that, show some family solidarity for once, rebuild your reputation."

Gabriel almost smiled. Unlike his fiery brother William, Michael had always been a peacemaker. "I fear it is too late for that. Good-bye, cousin, and take care."

He moved off even as Michael continued to speak, and threaded his way back into the stream of traffic. The encounter had unsettled him. He preferred not to think of his father's relatives and the hopes he'd dashed by daring to be born. The Granger side of the family had treated him appallingly as a child and he'd never quite forgotten that. Even during the investigation in Spain, his cousins hadn't quite bestirred themselves to argue his case. He'd heard Michael tried, and as for William . . . Gabriel hadn't expected anything from him at all, and, from all reports, William hadn't surprised him.

Guilt stirred low in his gut. He might say that he wanted nothing to do with his father's family or the land and houses that now belonged to him, but he still took the income from the estates and used it. He wished he had the ability to throw it back in his solicitor's face, but he had nothing else to live on, and so he lived as frugally as he could, his only extravagance his horses.

Gabriel drew his horse up behind the house where he rented his lodgings and dismounted. Mather, his groom, came out to take the horse into the mews and they spent a few minutes discussing the new stock and made plans for Gabriel's ride in the morning. He had the perfect horse in mind for Miss Ross and his groom was in agreement.

Satisfied at least with the progress of his campaign to see Miss Ross again, Gabriel headed into the house. At the bottom of the stairs, Captain David Gray and his valet were just about to leave through the front door. Gabriel found them easy company and wasn't foolish enough to inquire too closely as to their relationship. He had a sense that the two men were far more than servant and master, had seen them together at the pleasure house.

Captain Gray saw him first and smiled. "Good morning, Swanfield. Lieutenant St. Clare was looking for you earlier."

"Good morning, Captain, Mr. Brown." Gabriel nodded to both men and paused on the first step. "Is he still here?"

"I believe he is, sir." Robert Brown, Captain Gray's softly spoken Welsh valet said. "I saw him going up the stairs to his rooms."

"Thank you." Gabriel watched the men leave, noticed their

ease with each other and the sense of closeness between them. Since enduring the hellish nature of captivity, he didn't begrudge anyone happiness, even if it was with another man.

He climbed past his extensive set of rooms on the second floor and went on to the more cramped quarters of the old attic level, where Lieutenant Paul St. Clare lived when not on duty. Gabriel knocked on the door and received an invitation to enter. He opened the door and recoiled at the smell of cabbage.

"Good God, man, whatever are you eating?"

Paul grinned at him. "It's soup. My aunt sent it over for me." He held up the spoon. "Would you like some?"

Gabriel shuddered. Since his captivity, he'd become a fastidious eater, his stomach no longer able to tolerate rich food, but the cabbage soup didn't appeal to him either. "Why don't you come down to my rooms and share some luncheon with me? Keyes was preparing something with beef, I believe."

"Thank you, I will. I wanted to talk to you anyway."

Gabriel turned back down the stairs and found his door key. "So Captain Gray said." He went to unlock the door, only to have Keyes sweep it open instead. "Well, come on in."

His space was in immaculate order. He liked it that way, everything in its place, no surprises, and no dark corners. Keyes bowed and led the way into the dining room.

"As soon as I heard the lieutenant was looking for you, sir, I made enough for two."

"Thank you, Keyes."

Gabriel sat down and surveyed the plates piled high with slices of beef and plain boiled potatoes. Despite his slender form, Paul usually ate enough for three men, so there should be plenty. Keyes poured them both some ale and left them be.

"What did you want to talk to me about, Paul?"

His companion paused to drink some ale and then put down his tankard. "Nothing too extraordinary, more of a coincidence, really. I've heard your name being bandied around rather a lot recently."

"Really? By whom?"

Paul chewed slowly on his beef and swallowed. "There have been a couple of questions asked about you in the officer's mess. One of your cousins was after your whereabouts, I believe. I didn't tell him anything."

Gabriel nodded. That might explain Michael's unexpected appearance and far too pleasant manner. Was there some family matter Michael was loathe to bring to his attention or was he simply sounding out his cousin for his own benefit? As a younger son, Michael was always short of ready funds.

"And who else was asking after me?"

For the first time, Paul looked uncomfortable. "I'm not sure who was seeking information about you in the gentlemen's clubs; I didn't run into any of those people personally, just heard the rumbles." He pushed his blond hair back off his face. "I did, however, share some information about you with a young lady of my acquaintance. I'm still not sure if I should've done so."

"Let me guess." Gabriel knew his smile wasn't pleasant. "Was the young lady called Miss Ross?"

"Ah, you know her then?" A relieved smile appeared on Paul's face. "I assumed you did, but after all the other inquiries as to your whereabouts, I became a little alarmed."

"I know her." Gabriel fought a shudder as he pictured her tongue probing the crown of his cock, her mouth drawing his shaft inside and letting him come down her throat. "I'd appreciate it if you didn't tell her anything else."

Paul paused, his knife halfway to his mouth. "You don't like her?"

"At this precise moment, I'd like to wring her neck."

"Then I can only apologize. I wanted her to hear the truth

about your unfairly gained reputation. She seemed shocked that you had been treated so badly."

"She did, did she?" Gabriel swallowed down more ale. "Don't worry, Paul. I'll take care of Miss Ross. She won't be a problem for much longer."

"I'm not sure I like the sound of that. She seems to be a very pleasant young lady."

"Aye, she does." Gabriel's thoughts dwelled lovingly on the image of Miss Ross over his knee, her skirts thrown up to her waist, and his hand as it connected with her bare arse. Paul's worried voice jerked him out of his daydream.

"Are you concerned about all this renewed gossip?"

"I'm not sure. As you know, I'd prefer to let matters lie and hope that eventually everything is forgotten, but I sense someone doesn't want me to succeed."

"That was my thought, too." Paul leaned forward, his hands clasped together on the table. "Are you certain that you don't wish to revive this matter with the military authorities? I have friends who could help us, could make sure that this time you receive a fair hearing."

Gabriel sighed. "We've been over this a thousand times. What's the point? I don't care what anyone thinks of me anymore. The people who really know me know I would never betray my country like that, so who gives a damn about the others?"

Paul sat back, his brown eyes troubled. "I was there for most of your captivity. I know what really happened and I would be honored to speak for you."

"I know that and I appreciate it, but there is no need."

Paul persisted. "But in the future, for the sake of your family name, for your heirs . . ."

"I don't intend to have any heirs. I've almost decided that the title should die with me and revert back to the Granger side of the family." Gabriel grimaced. "They'll be delighted."

"That's very generous of you."

Paul's dry tone made Gabriel look up and smile. "I thought so, too."

Paul reached across for another slice of beef and winked at Gabriel. He still ate like a man who never knew where his next meal would come from, a legacy of their shared captivity that Gabriel had fought hard to shake. "Perhaps you'll change your mind when you meet the right woman."

Gabriel didn't bother to reply. He feared he had already met the only woman who interested him, and the odds of Miss Ross agreeing to be his wife were too long for even the most optimistic of bookmakers to offer them. His amusement dimmed as he contemplated their meeting the next day. He suspected that escaping with any shred of dignity was the most he could hope for. Asking her to meet him again so that he could have her naked and writhing in his arms until they were both sated was a very distant possibility indeed.

Lisette studied the stark strokes of Lord Swanfield's handwriting. His note was as short as most of his spoken sentences and just as infuriating. He wanted her to ride with him on the morrow and he would arrive at her house at eight, presumably with an extra horse.

"Is there something wrong, Lisette?"

She glanced up from the note to find her father, who had just handed her the message, studying her. "No, Papa, everything is fine."

He gestured at the paper clenched in her hand. "Lord Swanfield seemed most insistent that he meet with you. Has he developed a tendre for you?"

"I doubt it." Lisette tried to laugh. "He probably wants to kill me. I can't see him."

"Whatever did you do to the poor man?"

Lisette frowned at her father as he took a seat behind his desk. "Don't you care that he might end my life?"

His smile was angelic. "Swanfield does not strike me as a man who takes offense very easily."

Lisette sighed and sat down. "I played a trick on him, and I thought I was being very clever. Now I just feel ashamed of myself."

"What kind of a trick?"

"The kind that is played at the pleasure house."

"Ah. No man enjoys being sexually manipulated."

"Or woman, Papa."

"He manipulated *you*?"

"He . . . misrepresented himself to me."

"And that made you angry enough to hurt him."

Lisette felt like squirming in her seat. "I'm not sure if I was angry or just hurt that he had deceived me as to his sexual tastes."

"So you saw him at the pleasure house and something about his sexual choices made you want to pay him back."

"Yes."

"Does he frequent the top floor?"

"Not as far as I know." She studied her hands twisted in her lap. "His tastes are not *unattractive* to me; they are simply not what I thought he would indulge in at all."

"Because he has such a strong personality in his normal life?" He smiled. "You might be surprised how some men and women crave the opposite in private. I've seen any number of aristocrats and members of Parliament who like nothing more than to be treated like naughty schoolboys or taken in hand by a strong woman."

Lisette looked up, surprised by his acumen, and then remembered that he, too, held a financial interest in the pleasure house and knew almost as much about the members' varied tastes as her mother.

Philip shrugged. "So you tricked him, and now he wants an explanation. I think you owe him one, don't you?"

"Papa . . ."

"If he has the ability to hurt you, Lisette, you have the ability to hurt him back. At least allow the man the opportunity to tell you how he feels."

Lisette bit her lip. "I thought you would support me, not tell me to do something so hard."

Philip sat back. "Having spent more years of my life than I care to remember not speaking my mind and building up resentments and hatred, I'm scarcely going to support your desire to hide from the consequences of your actions, am I?"

"I suppose not." Lisette got to her feet. "But if he strangles me and dumps my broken body in the Thames, I hope you'll be sorry."

"If that should happen, I'll cry buckets at your funeral, I promise."

"But you don't think it will, do you?"

Philip's smile was full of understanding. "Darling, he might be angry with you, but in order to feel angry he has to feel *something* and my guess is that he cares about your opinion of him."

"Don't say that. Now I feel even guiltier."

"Good, then meet him in the morning and I promise to send a search party after you if you haven't returned by midday."

Lisette paused at the doorway to study her father. "You are not exactly a conventional man, are you?"

His smile was slow. "I married your mother. How on earth could I be?"

She smiled back at him even as her courage faltered when she contemplated her meeting with Lord Swanfield. "Good night, Papa."

"Good night, my dear."

Lisette headed for bed, knowing that her chances of sleeping were miniscule but determined to try. She had much to think on before the morning and perhaps as she tossed and turned she might come up with something useful to say to a probably furious Lord Swanfield.

7

Gabriel barely had the opportunity to climb the steps of the Knowles townhouse before the door was flung open and Miss Ross appeared, attired in a dark green riding habit and brown boots. Either his previous remarks about her lack of punctuality had borne fruit or she wanted to get her meeting with him over with all speed. He bowed and took off his hat, but before he could utter a word, she swept past him onto the flagstone pavement.

Mather, his groom, greeted her cheerfully. "Good morning, miss. This is Lavender. She's a nice horse, and she won't give you any trouble."

"Thank you." Miss Ross smiled brightly and gathered the voluminous skirt of her riding habit. Before Mather could step forward to help her, Gabriel was at her side. He cupped his hands to form a step.

"May I help you, Miss Ross?"

She hesitated for only a second before placing her foot in his hands and allowing him to toss her into the saddle. While he fiddled with her stirrups and watched her settle into her seat, he didn't dare look up at her face. Not for the first time in his life he was uncertain how to proceed. He felt as callow as a school-boy and twice as awkward. She'd seen him half naked and pleading for release, and, despite his anger, he couldn't blame her for reacting the way she had. He deserved her contempt. God knew, he hated himself enough for both of them.

After ascertaining that all was well with Miss Ross, Gabriel mounted Wellington and they set off at a slow walk toward the not-too-distant park. Luckily, at this hour of the morning there was a lull between the activities of those rushing to provision the great houses of the upper-classes and the emergence of the fashionable from those houses.

Because of the trailing feathers on her hat and the angle of her head, he couldn't quite see Miss Ross's expression, but she seemed remarkably unperturbed. He couldn't decide if that was good or bad. Perhaps she was one of those women who smiled as she ripped out your heart or kicked you in the balls.

They reached the park, and he was pleased to note that despite the fine spring weather, there were very few people about. After a quick glance at Miss Ross, he encouraged his horse into a trot and she followed suit leaving Mather behind. When Gabriel pulled up, they were in a much quieter area of the extensive grounds, shaded by massive oak trees and grassy slopes. Gabriel took a deep breath and turned to Miss Ross. It occurred to him that he'd rather face a firing squad than her righteous disgust and disdain.

"Would you care to dismount and walk among the blue-bells, Miss Ross?"

"That would be delightful, sir."

With a quick prayer to a God he no longer quite believed in, Gabriel dismounted and tied Wellington's reins to a tree, then turned to help Miss Ross down. She moved easily into his arms, and, as he inhaled the glorious scent of her skin, he barely resisted the temptation to pull her close. He set her back on her feet as quickly as he could and moved away from her.

As she started to walk, her skirts stirred up the sharp, peppery scent of the bluebells. It reminded him of his home up north and his mother's smiling face as she gathered armfuls of the flowers to sell at the market.

"I owe you an apology, my lord."

Gabriel's head snapped up and he found himself staring into Miss Ross's hazel eyes. "I beg your pardon?"

She half grimaced. "No, sir, I am begging yours."

It took him a moment to find his voice. "Why?"

"Because what I did to you the other night was childish and unforgivable."

"Hardly childish, Miss Ross."

"I *reacted* like a child. I should have stopped and thought about my actions before I put you in that position."

He looked away from her, focused on one of the flower stems, and counted each individual bluebell trumpet. "I'm sure you noticed that I enjoyed being in that position. I came more than once."

"And I enjoyed watching you come."

He had to face her now, had to see if she was mocking him. "Then why are you apologizing? You achieved your aim: you made a fool of me and showed me up for the hypocrite I am."

She licked her lips, her eyes still fixed on his. "But you aren't a hypocrite, are you? You only allow the other guests the same pleasures you offered me."

He stared at her, almost unable to form a coherent sentence, shocked by her all-too-accurate assessment of what she had seen. "Why are you being so sympathetic?"

"Because I've had time to think things through, and to try and understand." She swiped at the bluebells with her riding crop. "I was so angry when I saw you there, letting anyone touch you, caress you, have you ... I felt betrayed, which is ridiculous, I know, because there is nothing truly between us and I'd already told you to leave me alone."

He took a step toward her. "Of course there is something between us. You must have known I would've sought you out again."

"Would you?" She sighed. "Then you are a braver man than I thought."

"I don't fuck anyone there." He had to be clear on that. She had to understand at least that. "And I don't let anyone fuck me."

"I know." She walked on another few paces, her skirts dragging on the ground and then stopped and looked back at him, her chin raised, her eyes calm. "Marie-Claude told me."

"Why were you there that first night?"

"Because I was trying to forget you."

God, he liked that, liked her honesty far more than he was prepared to admit to himself. "I haven't seen you before," he persisted, as he tried to puzzle out her motives.

"I haven't been there for a while and I rarely frequent the higher levels. As I told you, I've been trying to behave more appropriately because of Emily's imminent society debut."

He studied her for a long moment and she continued to stare back at him, her expression composed, her luscious mouth relaxed. Such a fascinating mix of sophistication and pure sensual woman. A challenge he craved and a prize he wanted to win. He realized he was clenching his fists and slowly relaxed his hands.

"If I did not disgust you, will you meet me there again?"

"Yes, if you like."

A lick of heat warmed his stomach and groin as he imagined undressing for her again, feeling her mouth on him, getting the chance to pleasure her in return. He bowed low. "I would be honored to serve you."

She smiled and swept him a curtsey. "I depend on it."

He walked toward her and took her gloved hand, turned it palm up, and kissed it. "You are an extraordinary woman."

"And you haven't apologized to me yet."

"I thought you said I didn't need to?"

She glared at him as they skirted the bluebell patch. "What were you intending to do if I hadn't surprised you like that?"

"If you wish to know the truth, I was still debating between telling you I was sorry and putting you over my knee and spanking you."

She stopped walking. "Spanking me?"

"I, too, was angry when you left me like that, still coming, unable to do anything but fall to my knees and gasp for air." He kept hold of her hand. "I spent several very happy hours imagining you over my knee begging my pardon and sobbing."

"I wouldn't have sobbed, and you are deliberately distracting me from my first point, which is the apology you owe me."

He drew her into his arms. "You would've sobbed and then I would've had to console you. I insist you would've enjoyed yourself in the end." He kissed her closed mouth, kissed her again. "And as I resisted the urge to spank you, surely that is apology enough?"

She pushed him away. "You are just like my brother, sir. He never apologizes to me either."

He tucked her hand into the crook of his arm and led her back toward the horses. He put her up into the saddle and then mounted himself. "There is one thing I don't quite understand, Miss Ross."

"If we intend to become so intimately connected, you may call me Lisette, my lord."

"Thank you." He hesitated, tried to think how to frame his next remark without offending her, and realized it was impossible. "It is unusual to see an unmarried woman at the pleasure house."

"That is true."

"Then how is it that you . . . ?"

She turned to look at him. "My mother took me there."

"Your *mother*?"

Her chin went up another notch. "Didn't you know? She owns the place. Her name is Helene Delornay." She stared out between her horse's ears as if she'd never met him before. "Perhaps that changes your decision to meet with me. She is not exactly considered a respectable person, despite the number of aristocrats who flock to her premises."

He pondered the slight defensiveness of her tone, and found it intriguing that he recognized it in his own voice when he spoke of his family. "Hardly. My mother was a scullery maid."

He caught a glimpse of her startled face and kicked his horse into a canter. Why had he said that? He never told anyone about his mother. But at least he'd escaped Miss Ross now. She would either increase her speed or follow him at her leisure. Either way, by the time they reached the exit to the park, the conversation would not be resumed or referred to by him even if she wished to pursue it. He'd much rather think about their next time together at the pleasure house than go over the past.

He waited for her by the gate and avoided her gaze. To his relief when he left her at her door, she said nothing except a cordial thank-you for the ride and an expression of interest in riding with him again. It wasn't until he rode away that he started to wonder whether her silence had been for his benefit or her own.

He hadn't exactly made any specific arrangements with her for their next sexual encounter either. But that appealed to him as well and perhaps she realized that. The anticipation of waiting for her to appear at the pleasure house and take him in hand was an erotic experience in itself. He patted his horse and started to grin. He wanted her—and to his utter amazement, and despite the complications, she wanted him back. He had never thought to start his day in such a perfect manner.

Lisette couldn't decide what to wear for her next meeting with Lord Swanfield, whom she noted had not asked her to call him Gabriel. She wanted something that was elegant and alluring and, even more important, accessible—without looking like she wished him to tear off her clothes.

Eventually she selected a pale yellow muslin frock with an overskirt of finely embroidered silver gauze and silver lace at the low-cut bosom. When she reached the pleasure house she took her usual route through the kitchen to wish Madame Durand a good evening and found Christian lounging by the door. He wore a brown coat and olive waistcoat that brought out the green in his eyes.

When he saw her, he straightened and ran an experienced eye over her outfit. "You look very nice, Lis. Who's the lucky man?"

"I should imagine you know that by now." Lisette answered as she patted at her flattened curls. His smiling face hadn't put her at ease at all. "You are as astute as Maman when it comes to understanding what goes on here."

Christian held out his hand and patted the bench next to the big pine table. "Lis . . . will you just stop for a moment and talk to me?"

"Why?"

"Because we are at odds, and it doesn't sit well with me. Please."

With some reluctance she went and sat opposite him at the table. "I know what you are going to say, Christian. That Lord Swanfield is not the right man for me, that I cannot meet his sexual needs, but I can. We have discussed it."

"You might think you understand him, Lis, but are you sure?"

Lisette struggled to find the right words. "Why can't you trust me to make my own choices? Why do you have to destroy any chance I have to find out my own limits and my own preferences?"

He grabbed her hand and squeezed hard. "Because I don't want you to get hurt. I want you to find a decent, simple, straightforward man who doesn't need to come to this damn place to find sexual gratification."

"But I'm not a straightforward woman, am I? I've already indulged in more sexual activities than almost any unmarried woman of the ton."

Irritation flickered on Christian's face. "You don't have to be like Maman, Lis."

"I don't want to be. Whatever gave you that idea?"

"You've always envied her, and I agree that she is remarkable, but you don't need to be her." He half smiled. "You wouldn't have gotten involved in that scandal-broth with Lord Nash if you hadn't been trying to emulate Maman's sexual reputation."

"That's not true. I thought I was in love with him."

Christian sighed. "You mean you were in lust with him. And my point still stands: you were trying to get Maman's attention. At that point in our existence, we both were."

Lisette bit back her hasty denial. Was Christian right? Had she romanticized her short relationship with Lord Nash because she couldn't face the fact that she'd simply been competing with her incomparable mother?

"That might have been true then, but I realized long ago that I could never have survived what our mother did in the Bastille, or single-handedly built a business such as this. I admire her enormously, but I'm not cut from the same cloth."

"But you still seek out men who are attracted to what she has built here."

"If you are referring to Lord Swanfield, I didn't seek him out. I was caught unawares when I found him here."

He shrugged. "I told you he was a member. In fact, I warned you to keep away from him. You're not stupid, sister. You came after him, admit it."

"I'd forgotten what you'd said. I came here to prove to myself that I could find another man who attracted me."

"I don't believe you."

Lisette stared at her twin. Was Christian right? Had she unconsciously sought out Lord Swanfield and then pretended to be shocked by what she'd seen? She covered Christian's hand with her own.

"I love you, Christian, but unless you are already in a sexual relationship with Lord Swanfield and wish to argue a prior claim to him, I refuse to discuss him any longer."

Christian pulled his hand away. "As far as I know, I haven't fucked him; does that make you feel better?"

"Not really, because we are still at odds, aren't we?" Lisette sighed. "I can't share this with you. It is too important to me."

He got to his feet. "Oui, I understand, but you must also understand that I might not necessarily have any sympathy for you when it all goes horribly wrong."

She looked up at him, her throat tight. "That is both unkind and unlike you."

He shrugged. "It's how I feel."

"Just because you are unhappy, I must be unhappy, too?"

He stiffened. "I'm not unhappy."

She met his gaze. "We are twins, I *know* you. I know in my heart that you are restless and dissatisfied and confused."

His smile was mocking and meant to hurt. "All that just from being my twin?"

She frowned at him. "Why are you being like this?"

He sauntered toward the door. "Perhaps you're right and

I'm simply jealous that you have finally found something you want more than me."

"But you replaced me in your thoughts long ago. You've pushed me away all year."

"Have I?" He nodded as if she made perfect sense. "Maybe we need this distance between us. Maybe it is for the best."

"Christian . . ."

"Good night, Lis, and take care."

He bowed and headed out of the kitchen, his expression so impenetrable that even she couldn't tell what he really felt. She clasped her hands together and stared down at the scarred table. Had he deliberately done this to unsettle her before she met Lord Swanfield? Had he wanted to remind her that she had once told him everything, and worshipped the very ground he walked on?

She let out a painful breath. Maybe he was right and there needed to be more distance between them, but it still hurt far more than she had anticipated.

8

Lisette sat in the cream and gold painted salon and watched Lord Swanfield serve the other guests. On the center stage, three women played with one naked man who was tied to a chair. Despite his gag, Lisette could still hear the man's moans as the women touched his cock and rubbed themselves against him.

Lord Swanfield was aware of her arrival, but so far she had done nothing to seek him out, preferring to watch him move around the space, his body graceful, his long legs and fine arse encased in the tightest satin. She doubted any of the men could sit comfortably in the pantaloons; they would probably tear. But then, they were not there to sit and chat, were they? They were there to offer sexual opportunities to the guests.

She realized she'd hardly touched him during their previous two encounters and she found she wanted to quite badly. See-ing other women brush against him and fondle him made her feel a strange combination of jealousy and arousal that was hard to deal with. Christian's warnings about her previous sexual encounters resonated in her mind and she forced herself to ignore them.

The next time Lord Swanfield turned in her direction; she raised her hand and beckoned him over. She saw the mingled excitement and reserve in his face and understood it completely. It seemed he was no more at ease in this public setting than she was. When he straightened from his bow, his groin was level with her face and she could see that he was already aroused. Was it for her or for all the women in the room?

She leaned forward and nipped at the taut satin covering his shaft and he shuddered. She did it again, harder and his hips jerked forward as if inviting her to take more of him, to bite, to lick, to devour. And God, she wanted to, wanted every person in that room to see how she affected him and how he was hers alone. She'd never thought of herself as a particularly possessive woman, but something about Lord Swanfield made her want to keep him all to herself.

She sat back and stared up at him. His dark blue eyes were narrowed with lust, and his lips moved in a silent curse.

"Come with me," she ordered.

He stepped back to allow her to stand and she led him to one of the intimate bedrooms close to the salon and locked the door behind him. She ripped off her mask and did the same to his. Still caught in the terrifying need to brand him, she knelt at his feet and continued her exploration of his cock and balls with her teeth, heard his breath hiss out, and licked away the wetness of his pre-cum seeping through the satin.

His cock grew even bigger and harder and yet he couldn't seem to stop himself from pushing into her, asking for more, taking every sharp nip and bite and never drawing back. She grasped his hips to hold him still as she tried to get her mouth around the head of his shaft, which was attempting to force its way out of the top of his pantaloons. She sucked in the glorious wetness of his arousal, the sheen of the satin and the sliver of the most sensitive skin at the tip of his cock, all jumbled together in her mouth, all needing to be caressed and licked and bitten.

"Christ . . ." His cum exploded from his cock and she didn't stop lapping at him, even when he leaned into her as if his legs could no longer support him, as if he wanted to fall to the ground despite still being wedged against the door.

Lisette sat back on her heels and wiped her fingers over her mouth, her whole body trembling with arousal from what she had just done. "Touch me. I want your mouth on me, I want . . ."

Before she could finish speaking, he brought her down to the floor, his mouth seeking hers, his tongue plunging deep as he kissed her with a ferocity she had never encountered before. His lips feathered down her throat and then settled between the hollow of her breasts. "Don't stop," she managed to gasp. "Don't . . . stop."

He shoved her puffed sleeve down from her shoulder and worked the buttons at the back of her bodice, loosened the laces of her corset as well. His mouth came down over her breast and he sucked her into the hot cavern of his mouth. She arched helplessly against him, moaned as his hand slid past her stocking to the top of her thigh and cupped her mound. She opened her legs for him and he slid his fingers over her clit and plunged them inside her. He pumped her hard to the rhythm of his suckling, his palm wedged against her swollen clit, demanding a response she was oh so willing to give him.

She screamed into his shoulder as she climaxed and he didn't stop moving, brought her to another peak and then another until she was so wet and needy that she wanted more, needed to be filled. She slid her fingers between them and found he was hard again, fought to open the soaked placket of his pantaloons and hold him in her hand.

"Come for me again, come with me."

He moved against her hand, his body hard and urgent, all finesse gone, the desire to come a rampant, unstoppable need they had to conquer together, to feed until there was nothing left to burn.

He climaxed with a groan into her hand and she came with him, enjoyed the way his weight fell on top of her, his fingers still buried between her thighs.

As she lay there, the busy sounds of the pleasure house infiltrated her sexual high. She'd behaved in a way that would shock society and amuse her mother. She didn't even dare contemplate what her father or Christian would say.

She opened her eyes. She had no idea what to say to Lord Swanfield either. He'd left all the talking to her, and she suspected he'd continue to do so. Should she thank him, or should she simply say good night and go on her way as if nothing had happened? What did people normally do in situations like this when they had just tried to bite off a man's cock?

Lord Swanfield rolled off her and seemed to be setting himself to rights. She turned her head to look at him. He caught her gaze and stopped what he was doing.

"Do you not want me to get dressed?" He gestured at his soaked pantaloons. "Do you want more?" He'd give her more if she wanted it. He'd give her anything after that last voracious coupling. She seemed to weigh her answer, her gaze fixed on the opening of his pantaloons. His cock responded to her interest even though he was sore as hell and he gritted his teeth.

"I'm . . . fine," she whispered.

She didn't sound fine. Gabriel concentrated on stuffing his rebellious cock back into his pantaloons and assumed the most neutral expression he could manage. If she wanted to treat him politely, he could do the same. All he had to do was pretend she was just another client from the salon, someone who would forget him in an instant when he had provided what she wanted.

But, God, he didn't feel like that. He was shaken by the intensity of his response to her, the way she'd made him feel so out of control.

Devil take it, he needed to go home. He got to his feet and bowed.

"If you don't require my services anymore, ma'am, I'll wish you good night." Good, that was formal enough and gave them the opportunity to part with at least some dignity.

"Are you going back to find another customer?"

He flinched both at the quiet question and the assumption behind it. "Do you imagine I 'perform' like this with all the guests?"

"I don't know. I've never seen you with anyone else, have I?"

He heard it clearly then, the hurt behind her words, her fear that she was just one of a crowd of faceless people whom he'd serviced. How strange that a woman who'd practically devoured his cock could be so unsure of her hold on him now. He knelt down beside her and took her hand, studying the luscious swollen curves of her trembling mouth.

"Thank you for letting me come." He kissed her fingers. "Will you let me attend to you tomorrow night?"

She looked into his eyes and he almost forgot all the well-thought-out reasons why he needed to leave her.

"Yes."

He kissed her then and just managed to pull away. She lay on the floor, her soft muslin skirts spread around her like a flower, one stockinged leg bent at the knee and out to one side. He licked his lips and yearned to follow the shadowed curve of her thigh to her sex and place his mouth over it. But, as her servant, he wasn't supposed to ask for anything, he was supposed to wait to be asked and then obey.

"Why aren't you leaving?" she asked softly.

Because he couldn't.

Without speaking, he leaned forward and dropped a kiss on

her bent knee, kissed a little higher and breathed in the thick scent of her arousal. She didn't stop him, and he felt the brush of her fingers in his hair as he inched ever closer to his goal. He paused to draw back her skirt and petticoat, exposing her cunt to his avid gaze. His tongue met her clit and he explored it slowly, flicked his way over and around it until it throbbed against his flesh. He widened his exploration to include her swollen lips and the hot wet center of her.

She gasped as he slid his tongue deep, used it as he wanted to use his cock on her, a constant thrust and retreat until she grabbed hold of his shoulders and urged him onward and upward. When she shuddered to a climax, he was glad that he'd had the sense to rebutton his placket. Otherwise he'd have been inside her as she came, felt her contract against his shaft, filled her with his seed.

With that last thought came sanity and he slowly moved away from her. He kissed her knee once more.

"Thank you. I have to go now. Will I see you tomorrow?"

She managed a nod and he got up and retreated to the door. He stepped into the hallway and took a deep calming breath. And it *was* a retreat, not yet a rout. He needed to get away from her to regroup and remind himself of all the reasons why he'd chosen the pleasure house for his sexual salvation.

Wanting to shove his cock into Lisette Ross was not part of his plan at all, but he knew he'd be back on the morrow, that it wasn't as simple as just walking away from her. He could still taste her in his mouth, and had a sneaking suspicion that he always would.

His mind in a whirl, he changed into his normal clothes and bade a smiling Marie-Claude a distracted good night. He felt more sexually sated than he ever had before and that was the most worrying thing of all. Tonight he knew he would be able to sleep without waking to either a nightmare or wanting sex.

He glanced up at the imposing façade of the pleasure house

and knew he'd be back, that he'd follow this through to the end. He had a suspicion that Lisette would either be the making of him or complete his utter destruction. He even managed a smile at his own dramatic imagery. Whatever happened, it was better than the way he'd been living, wasn't it?

"Are you all right, Lisette?"

Lisette saw Marie-Claude peeping through a crack in the door and feebly beckoned her to come in.

"I think so."

"But you are lying on the floor."

Lisette rolled onto her side and then managed to sit up. Her muscles protested the motion and she closed her eyes.

"Lisette." Marie-Claude shook her arm and she opened her eyes again. "I was worried about you. You disappeared about two hours ago."

With Marie-Claude's help, Lisette managed to sit in a chair. "I'm fine, I just forgot to get up."

Marie-Claude chuckled. "Was my Lord Swanfield that good?"

"Yes, he was." Lisette tried to smile but ended up having to bite her lip to stop it from trembling. "Did he . . . go off with someone else?"

"No. I saw him changing his clothes and then he left. He seemed somewhat lost in thought and now I realize why."

"I think I surprised him."

"Well, that is good, is it not? A man like that needs to be kept on his toes." Marie-Claude patted her shoulder. "Now why don't you join me in the kitchen for a cup of hot chocolate before you retire? You look as if you need something to restore you."

"Marie-Claude, I bit his cock, I forced him to come in his pantaloons."

"If you are that hungry, you should eat something more substantial. A nice pork sausage, perhaps?"

"It's not funny, Marie-Claude. I . . . behaved appallingly."

"And did monsieur protest?"

Lisette heard the echo of Lord Swanfield's passionate groans and the way he'd literally become weak at the knees. "No, he seemed to like it."

Marie-Claude's smile faded. "Lisette, when he comes here, he chooses to play the role of a servant. He obviously likes giving up sexual control to his partner, so why shouldn't that partner be you?"

"Because I am trying to behave in a more conventional and ladylike manner." Lisette headed toward the door and found her legs were still shaking. "It was humiliating. I simply didn't like seeing all those people touching him and I overreacted."

"I understand." Marie-Claude smoothed a comforting hand over her back as they descended the servants' stairs. "Perhaps we can do something about that."

Lisette stopped. "No, we can't interfere. He has to *choose* to be with me alone."

"You are right, of course." Marie-Claude held open the door that led into the kitchen. "I noticed that tonight, he seemed less inclined to seek out other people to arouse him. I assumed he was waiting for you."

"Really?" Lisette found herself able to smile again. She sat down on the kitchen bench and waited for Marie-Claude to join her with the hot chocolate that Madame Durand always kept simmering on the stove. She pictured Lord Swanfield's reverent expression as he had lifted her skirts and licked his way up to her sex. She'd wanted his cock inside her so badly at that moment and wondered if he had been tempted, too.

"I want him to make love to me."

"I thought you wanted to redeem your reputation?"

"I do!" Lisette stared at her laughing friend. "But I also want him." She covered her face with her hands. "Oh God, I don't know what I want anymore. As usual, I seem to be caught between my two worlds. Lord Swanfield has made me act like a dithering debutante with a nasty set of teeth."

"Hardly that." Marie-Claude sipped at her hot chocolate and sighed. "He's been a guest here for almost a year and I've never seen him have sex with anyone."

"There has to be some way to convince him to bed me." Lisette frowned in thought. "But I already know to my cost that he is a very stubborn man."

"Perhaps you could just ask him." Marie-Claude suggested, her brown eyes alight with mischief. "There has to be some good reason why he won't have sex."

"I'll ask him tomorrow. I'm supposed to be going riding with him." Lisette groaned as she noticed the time. "If I can get out of bed in five hours."

"You'll make it. Sleep is far less important than finding out what Lord Swanfield is up to, isn't it?"

"I suppose so." Lisette got to her feet and finished off the remains of her hot chocolate. She smiled down at Marie-Claude. "Thank you for listening to me."

Marie-Claude shrugged. "It was a pleasure."

"And thank you for not thinking I am fit only for the madhouse for biting a man I like."

"You are welcome." Marie-Claude rose, too. "I have to go back upstairs and finish out the night. I will see you tomorrow. Good night, my friend."

Lisette kissed her cheek. "Good night." She watched Marie-Claude leave and then turned toward the stairs that led up to the private part of the house where all her family had rooms. She hoped to God that Christian wasn't around. She really didn't want to face him at the moment. She managed to make it to her room and fell onto the bed fully dressed.

The next thing she knew, the birds were singing and one of her mother's maids was standing over her laughing at her for sleeping in her clothes. It was time to get up and face Lord

Swanfield again, and this time, as they were away from the pleasure house, she doubted he would be in quite such a conciliatory or servile mood.

She opened her eyes wide. Oh goodness. Lord Swanfield would assume she was at her father's house, and await her there. With a quiet curse she scrambled out of bed and asked the maid for some hot water. It was already half past seven, and if she had any chance of getting to the Knowles house before the impeccably punctual Lord Swanfield, she needed to move fast.

9

Gabriel checked his watch and looked expectantly up at the door of Knowles House.

"Maybe she ain't coming, guv," Mather said cheerfully. "You never know what nonsense females get into their heads these days."

"Thank you, Mather." Gabriel replaced his watch in his pocket. "Perhaps you might refrain from making witty remarks and go and ring the bell."

Undaunted by Gabriel's chilling tone, Mather grinned and bounded up the steps to the front door. Gabriel shivered as a gust of wind caught him unawares, and his horse, equally spooked, shied at nothing. Perhaps Miss Ross thought it too cold to go out this morning, although she hadn't struck him as that kind of overprotected woman.

"She's not here, sir." Mather volunteered loudly from the top step. "She's at her mother's."

Devil take it, he hadn't thought of that. She'd probably stayed at the pleasure house last night. He frowned as he considered his options. He didn't want to be seen loitering at the front of Madame Helene's and he certainly didn't want Miss Ross subjected to the kind of gossip her presence there with him might raise.

"Sir?"

He looked down at Mather who was now standing beside his horse. "Yes?"

"The butler gave me her direction. We'll find Miss Ross at One Barrington Square."

"*Barrington* Square?"

"Yes, sir, do you know where it is?"

"I'm not sure."

"I know it." Mather mounted up again and also took back the reins of the horse Gabriel had brought for Miss Ross.

Gabriel followed along behind and soon found himself in an all-too-familiar area of Mayfair. He glanced at Mather, but the man seemed quite at ease as he guided his horse one-handed through the busy streets. He pulled up in front of an unfamiliar white mansion on the corner of a treelined square

"Here you are, sir. I have a cousin who works at the house next door."

Gabriel stared at the long windows and thick drawn drapes of the house. Perhaps Madame Helene had more than one property in the city. And, in truth, this secluded square was very close to her other house, in fact. . . . The front door opened and Miss Ross emerged, one hand holding up the skirts of a black riding habit adorned with white lace.

Gabriel dismounted and went to meet her. "Good morning, Miss Ross. Your father's butler gave me your direction. I hope I didn't discommode you too much."

"Not at all, sir." She glanced up at him before reaching for her hat and ramming a pin back into her piled-up hair. "I was worried that you might leave without me."

He helped her mount. "I was tempted, Miss Ross. But once I realized it was hardly your fault that I had the wrong place, I decided to try this address."

She pressed her hand to her heart. "I confess I am quite overwhelmed by your forbearance, my lord. I can barely stand the stupendous honor of your company as it is, but this . . ."

He frowned at her as they overtook a grinning Mather and left him to follow discreetly behind. "Does the pleasure house back onto this property in Barrington Square?"

"How very astute of you, my lord. In truth, most of this house is part of the other. My family has their private quarters in the rest of it."

"Ah, that explains it, then." He lapsed into silence, suddenly aware that in his impatience to solve the riddle of her disappearance, he'd forgotten to be nervous about seeing Miss Ross again. Dressed in her military-style black riding habit, she seemed her usual acerbic self, which pleased him greatly. He relaxed a little in the saddle. Perhaps she would be wise enough to allow him to keep his private and personal lives as separate as he usually preferred.

"Lord Swanfield, may I ask you something?"

He checked his horse's longer stride to match hers and draw level again. "Of course, Miss Ross."

"Why don't you bed anyone properly?"

He swallowed hard as all his confident predictions of separation evaporated. "I hardly think that is any of your business, Miss Ross."

She kept looking at him, her quizzical expression unchanged. "I disagree."

"Are you suggesting that you *want* me to 'bed' you, Miss Ross?"

"That would be very forward of me indeed, my lord, wouldn't it? I'm just curious."

"And curiosity killed the cat, didn't it?"

She sighed. "I thought I'd give you the opportunity to answer my questions outside of the pleasure house. If I ask you again tonight, will you feel obliged to answer me?"

"That's hardly fair. And if we are being curious, why aren't you a virgin?"

She opened her eyes wide at him. "Now who is being forward? Perhaps we should agree to a trade. I'll answer your impertinent question if you answer mine."

"And if I choose not to answer you?"

She shrugged and returned her attention to the path ahead of them. "Then surely we have nothing more to say to each other."

Frustration rose and twisted in his gut. She had him now and she probably knew it. He wasn't sure that he liked being put in this position, but he was damned if he'd walk away from her again.

"All right. I agree." When they entered the park, he nodded at a more secluded path that meandered away from the main thoroughfare. "Shall we turn down here and then walk for a while?"

She followed his lead down an avenue of old elm trees that formed a tunnel over their heads and turned the flickering shadowed light to a green haze.

He dismounted and helped her down, even remembered to hobble the horses. She turned to face him, her fine features shadowed by the brim of her hat and the uncertain dancing light.

"Yes, my lord?"

He stared down at the immaculate polish of his boots. "Ladies first."

"Lord Swanfield . . ."

He looked up and contemplated her determined expression. "What exactly do you want to know?"

She sighed as if he was being difficult, which he supposed he was. "Why won't you bed anyone?"

"Because I believe that procreation belongs inside marriage."

"That makes no sense."

"Many worthy people would disagree with you. Why doesn't it make sense?"

"Because you are not that kind of man."

"Not worthy?" He smiled. "Well, that is certainly true, but you hardly know me, Miss Ross, so how can you judge what kind of man I am?"

Color tinted her cheeks. "Lord Swanfield, you love being touched. You let perfect strangers arouse you at the pleasure house!"

He shrugged and allowed his gaze to wander around the avenue of trees as if he didn't have a care in the world. "I admit I have needs. I just don't choose to express them in the way most men do. Having a child out of wedlock is not something I approve of."

She angled her head to one side to study him. "Is it because you already have too many bastards?"

"Good God, no."

"Then, why does it concern you so much? There are many ways to avoid making a child with a woman, my mother says. . . ."

He swung around to face her more fully. "And none of them are completely reliable, are they? I'm sure your mother has told you that."

She didn't back down. "If you were born a bastard like I was, I would understand your bitterness, but for you to inherit a title, you must have been a legitimate child."

She sounded more confused than annoyed, and that gave him the courage to continue. "I told you that my mother was a scullery maid."

"Yes."

He rested his gloved hand on one of the old trees and focused on the gnarled bark beneath his fingers. "She was thirteen when my sixty-year-old father, the late Earl of Swanfield, met her in the hallway and decided to rape her. She was fourteen when I was born."

The silence behind him grew until he wanted to reach out and punch the tree just to break the tension. "When he found out from the butler that she was pregnant and about to be dismissed, the earl married her in secret, and threatened to kill her if she told anyone."

He leaned back against the tree, glad of its solid warmth. "I continued to live on the estate, totally unaware of my mother's marriage, until the earl died when I was nine and all hell broke loose."

He forced himself to meet her gaze. "The rest of the family tried to break the marriage, but there was nothing they could do. The earl had tied everything up perfectly legally and I was his heir."

"And it did not sit well with you?"

He shrugged. "I grew up thinking I was the by-blow of a scullery maid, that I was lucky to be fed and even tolerated on the estate of such a great lord. I was an uneducated savage and when everything changed I had no idea how I was expected to behave."

"It sounds as if you would've preferred to have remained a bastard," Miss Ross said slowly. "In truth, I would think your objections would be *against* marrying to create a legitimate heir, not for it. And I would've expected you to have a thousand bastards to prove your point."

He stiffened. "You are suggesting that my mother should've remained unmarried and borne her shame alone?"

"No, of course I'm not. It sounds as if she was treated appallingly. But for you, the marriage was a blessing, wasn't it? So I don't understand . . ."

He scowled at her. "Understand this. When I marry, my wife will never have to worry about me committing adultery. I will remain true to my vows."

"And give her all your children?"

"Yes."

"And what if she doesn't want to be continually pregnant?" He blinked at her suddenly angry face. "What?"

"Has it ever occurred to you, as you so graciously offer to endow your poor wife with all your mighty seed, that repeated pregnancies can kill a woman?"

"My poor wife?" He struggled to recover from her unexpected broadside. "This conversation has gone on for quite long enough. You asked me why I won't fuck anyone and I've answered you."

"Despite your own experiences, you believe that it is better for a child to be legitimate and unhappy than for a child to be illegitimate and content."

"Yes."

"And you'd rather enjoy the sexual games at the pleasure house than have a real mistress who might get pregnant."

"*Yes.*" He glared at her composed face. "Are you done with me now?"

"I certainly understand you better." Lisette swallowed hard. "Did I tell you that I was brought up in France?"

"You mentioned it, but . . ."

"But you didn't realize why? My mother was busy running the pleasure house and my father was married to somebody else."

He let out his breath and gave her the courtesy of looking straight into her eyes. "I'm sorry, I didn't know . . ."

"My father formally acknowledged us three years ago and we bear his family name of Ross as well as our mother's." Her attempt at a smile fell short. "There is no need to feel sorry for me. I am quite happy with my life."

"Are you?"

"Yes, I am." She glared at him, hating the flatness of his response. She was not going to tell him that his stance on bastard children made her respect him a little more. How strange that they'd both had to fight the unusual circumstances of their birth to be recognized by society, to be accepted.

"If I fucked you," he said slowly, as if explaining something to a half-wit, "I could get you with child."

"I understand that."

He reached for her then, and placed his hands on her shoulders so that he could better glower down at her. "Dammit, Miss Ross, you would not want to bear my bastard. You of all people should understand that. Can't you just accept what I can give you, and be happy with that?"

She reached up to cup his scarred cheek. "As you've already noticed, I'm not a virgin, and my reputation is dubious to say the least. Why should I not be willing to take the risk and lie with you?"

His grip tightened. "Because if I got you with child, I would have to marry you."

"Whether I wanted you to marry me or not?"

"Yes." He kissed her slowly and then drew back. "And, in truth, I do not wish to marry at all. I've already decided to leave no heirs and let the rest of the family fight it out after my death." He kissed her nose, and she felt the humiliating burden of unshed tears gather in her eyes and throat. "Now tell me the name of the bastard who took your virginity."

She tried to pull away but he wouldn't let her. "I'm not going to tell you his name. It has nothing to do with you, and it was my fault anyway."

"How so?"

"I thought I was in love with him."

"And that he would marry you?"

"I suppose so." She managed to wiggle out of his arms. "Not only did he have no intention of marrying me, but I later found out that he had won a great deal of money thanks to a bet concerning the first man to seduce me placed at his club."

Anger flared in his dark blue eyes. My goodness, he was magnificent when he scowled. "Tell me his name."

"Don't look so fierce. It happened a long time ago and I am quite reconciled to my tarnished reputation."

"He *bragged* about having you?"

"Of course he did, otherwise how would he have claimed his money?"

His hand came to rest on his hip as if in search of the long cavalry sword that used to lie there. "Did no one avenge you?"

"Avenge me? And cause even a bigger scandal as to why I was at an exclusive pleasure house just asking to be compromised? It was hardly worth it." She shrugged. "I learned my lesson."

"Miss Ross . . ."

She couldn't allow him to feel sorry for her, or responsible for what had happened. It had been hard enough dealing with Christian's fury and concealing the whole sordid affair from her father. She *had* to redirect his thoughts into more practical matters.

"Will you still meet me at the pleasure house?" she asked. She held her breath as he studied her.

"If you will accept me for what I am, and for what I can give you."

"I'll do my best."

"You think you can change my mind, don't you?" he asked.

She started walking back toward the peacefully grazing horses. "Perhaps."

As she strolled away from him, a thrill of unexpected lust shot right to Gabriel's groin. He didn't want to fuck her, he *didn't*. His cock was just responding to a sexual challenge. He was strong enough to resist the lures of the flesh and had proved it many times. He took a slow step toward her and then another. Part of him wanted to bring her to the ground, pull up her skirts, and just have her until she screamed his name.

She waited for him by her horse, her taunting gaze dropping to the extremely inconvenient erection that now tented his breeches. He unconsciously smoothed a hand over his cock and fought a groan as it just made him feel worse.

"Perhaps we should walk the horses back rather than post." Her smile was full of sexual interest and he fought not to return it.

"Indeed." He mounted his horse and followed along behind her, watching her body sway in the saddle, and got even more aroused. Despite all the confidences they had shared and the startling glimpse of her past, he still wanted her. But was she right? Would he fall to her, and what in God's name would he do then?

10

Gabriel rode home deep in thought as he considered Miss Ross and her unsettling effect on him. They had far more in common than he had believed possible, although in many ways, they handled their respective issues completely differently. She flaunted her bad reputation and dared the ton to ignore her, whilst he tried to disappear into the background and hope that everything would blow over.

He sighed. She made him feel like an even worse coward than he already did, but he no longer had the stomach to fight. At least he knew the truth about himself. He handed Wellington over to Mather, thanked him, and headed up the stairs to his lodgings where Keyes was busy laying out his breakfast.

"Good morning, sir. Did you enjoy your ride?"

Gabriel chose to smile vaguely rather than reply. His rides with Miss Ross were always eventful and usually meant that his solitary journey back was accomplished with a set of aching balls and an erect cock. A knock on the door distracted him from thoughts of Miss Ross and he nodded at Keyes to open the door.

He stared at the three men who had entered and bowed. "Good morning, gentlemen, to what do I owe this honor?" He gestured at the table and took his seat, too hungry to delay breaking his fast and too familiar with at least two of the gentlemen to worry about offending them. Keyes bustled about bringing extra plates and coffee, and soon the other men were seated around him.

Captain David Gray was the first to speak. "Good morning, Swanfield." He gestured at the dark-haired man to his left. "I'm not sure if you've met Major Thomas Wesley."

"I don't believe I've had that pleasure, sir." Gabriel nodded pleasantly enough at the major. "But you are more than welcome."

"Major Wesley works at the War Office." Paul St. Clare, the third of his visitors, said, as he piled more ham on his plate.

"How interesting." Gabriel spared Wesley another glance. "And yet you have a look of a man who has carried out the majority of his soldiering in warmer climes."

"I spent almost two decades of my life in India. Family business drew me back to England and I decided to stay and work at the War Office."

"Major Wesley is interested in what happened to you in Spain, Swanfield," David said.

Gabriel put his fork down. "Surely there is nothing of interest in that."

"Ah, but there is, Lord Swanfield." Major Wesley leaned forward, his brown eyes steady on Gabriel's. "There have been several complaints against the officers in your regiment during that particular peninsular campaign and some concerns over the decisions made, particularly in your case."

"Major, I left my regiment with privileged information to pass on to my commander in chief. I returned almost a year later to find that the information had ended up in the hands of our enemies."

"And you were too sick to defend yourself at your make-shift trial and were shipped back home in disgrace without a proper hearing."

"Yes, and that's all there is to it."

"At the time, several people came forward to defend your military record and declare their support. Were you aware of that?"

Gabriel shrugged and slid a quelling glance at David and Paul, who were listening carefully. "I know of some. It is always pleasant to hear that one is not completely reviled."

"But don't you see, Swanfield," Paul intervened. "You could appeal your conviction and reinstate your good name."

"I wasn't formally tried and found guilty," Gabriel said flatly. "Restoring my reputation would be like trying to fight a ghost."

Major Wesley smiled. "Recently we've become aware of some new attempts to resurrect your case and formally try you."

"What?" Gabriel stared at the other man, a sick feeling in his gut. "Who in God's name started that up again?"

"I'm not sure, but we are bound to investigate such matters if they come from high enough up. It was when I reviewed your file that I realized you had been much maligned with very little real evidence."

"And now he wants to help you," David said. "And we've agreed to help him, too."

Gabriel nodded at each man. "It is very kind of you to take an interest in this matter, Major Wesley, but it all happened so long ago. Surely it's better just to let things lie?"

Major Wesley stood up. "I wish I could do that, sir, but unfortunately I have to investigate this matter. I would appreciate your cooperation."

Gabriel stood, too, and shook the proffered hand. "You have that, but I don't think it will make any difference."

Major Wesley sighed. "It might if I'm forced to drag you through an official military court-martial."

"You don't think it will come to that, do you?"

"I hope not." Major Wesley saluted and turned to the door. "Thank you for enduring my unexpected visit, sir, and I'll keep you informed."

"I'd appreciate that." Gabriel nodded as David got up, too, and headed after the major. "Good morning to you both."

Gabriel waited to sit down again until the door shut behind the two men. He contemplated the food on his plate and suddenly felt nauseous. It seemed that all the years of trying not to be seen, of deliberately cutting himself off from his peers, had been for naught.

Paul cleared his throat. "Are you angry?"

Gabriel picked at his now congealed scrambled eggs. "That Captain Gray brought Major Wesley around to see me? Not really. I'm grateful for the warning that someone is meddling in my business."

"Have you any idea who it might be?"

Gabriel's attempted smile was forced. "I've always been outspoken, you know that, and I certainly offended a few of the higher-ranking officers in my time."

"Because you got things done."

"Sometimes my sympathy definitely lay with the rank and file rather than my supposed peers. That was usually attributed to my lowly start in life and my complete lack of breeding."

Paul sighed. "You aren't happy about this at all, are you?"

Gabriel met his worried gaze. "No. I'm not, but you're probably the only man who'll know that." He shifted in his seat. "I'm also wondering if my family has got anything to do with this sudden interest in my past."

Paul's smile was wry. "I suppose it's possible. Your cousins have never been your friends, have they?"

Gabriel pushed his plate away. "Actually, I was once quite close to William, until he finally realized that I was going to inherit the title he'd assumed was his. He never liked me after that."

"Obviously. He didn't exactly rush to your defense during your time in Spain."

"Major Wesley seems like a fair man, though." Anxious to stop all references to his cousins, Gabriel stood up. "He also looked slightly familiar."

Paul was still eating, but he paused long enough to grin. "He visits the pleasure house; you might have seen him there."

"That's right. I've seen him with another man."

"That would probably be the notorious Lord Minshom, the terror of the top floor. Well, not so terrible now since he's connected with Wesley and become a father."

"Minshom has children?" Gabriel pictured the cold blue eyes of the man and remembered the lurid tales surrounding his legendary adventures in the pleasure house.

"Indeed, twin girls, if you can believe it. David knows both of the Minshoms quite well and corresponds regularly with Lady Minshom."

"Ah, that's right. Robert Brown used to be Lord Minshom's valet." Gabriel smiled. "What a small world we live in."

Paul swallowed down a gulp of ale. "Speaking of small worlds, I was wondering if you might do me a favor."

"Does it have to do with my horses?"

"No, it's rather more complex than that. My aunt is having a ball tonight for my eldest cousin, and she has invited me to attend."

"And?"

"And I was hoping you would go with me."

"Me? I'm certainly not considered good company or good *ton*. You'd be better off asking Captain Gray. He's both well-born and incredibly charming."

"But I want you to come. My aunt would like to meet you." Paul met Gabriel's skeptical gaze and color flooded his cheeks. "I would be honored if you would accept."

Inwardly, Gabriel cursed, but he knew he would go. The ties between him and Paul were too complex to ignore. "If I agree, you must promise to let me leave whenever I choose."

"As long as you get to meet my aunt and uncle, I'll be happy."

"Then I'll come with you."

A smile lit up Paul's face and he jumped to his feet. "Thank you. I'll be ready to leave about nine."

"That will be fine." Gabriel studied Paul's unkempt brown coat and breeches. "You do have some more formal clothing, don't you?"

"Of course, and if the worst comes to the worst, I can always wear my dress uniform and let the debutantes swoon over my medals."

"Indeed." Gabriel watched him leave, his smile dying as Paul closed the door behind him. He was deeply fond of the man, but sensed Paul still wanted more from him than friendship. During their imprisonment, they'd struck up an unlikely companionship. Gabriel had used his strength to defend the slighter man, and Paul had . . . Gabriel sighed at the memory. Paul had insisted on providing Gabriel with all the sex he wanted, whenever he wanted it. And to his shame, Gabriel had taken advantage of the other man, used him, enjoyed it even, found it arousing to feel another man under him taking his cock.

Perhaps it was time to have a serious conversation with Paul about his sexual needs. He suspected Paul would still be happy to lie down and let Gabriel fuck him even now, and that would never do. Gabriel abandoned his half-eaten breakfast and opened the newspaper. Perhaps he could sponsor Paul into full membership at the pleasure house?

That thought made him relax a little and find his usual solace in reading the paper. It also kept him from wondering what his reception would be like at the ball that evening. With his background he never felt quite at ease in social situations. He'd worked hard to overcome that, only to have his hard-earned skills ripped from him by the dual horrors of captivity and being considered a traitor.

"Keyes?"

His valet appeared. "Yes, sir?"

"Will you make sure my evening clothes are in good enough order for me to wear tonight?"

Keyes actually rubbed his hands together. "Yes, sir. You can wear your new blue coat."

Gabriel lowered the newspaper. "What new coat?"

"The one I picked up for you from your tailors while you were away at Knowles Hall, sir."

Gabriel sighed. Keyes was always trying to improve his wardrobe and he couldn't blame the man. "All right, put it out and I'll see if I like it."

"Yes, sir, it will be a pleasure, sir."

Keyes positively skipped away, his homely face shining, and Gabriel felt the beginnings of a reluctant grin. He'd do his best for Paul tonight and reward himself by seeing Miss Ross later. A man could only be virtuous for so long.

"Come in, Lisette."

Lisette smiled cautiously at her father as he beckoned her into his study. There was something about his expression that made her feel like a young girl about to be faced with a list of her transgression.

"Is something the matter, Papa?"

His smile widened. "Is there something you're afraid I've found out about, daughter?"

"Of course not." Lisette sat down and put her hands in her

lap. "Emily will be here soon. Does it have something to do with that?"

"Nothing has changed. She will be here at the end of the week. My second cousin's widow, Mrs. Horrocks-Smith, will join us as well and stay for the Season."

"Will she be a good chaperone for Emily? Is she kind?"

"Daphne is not only kind but experienced at managing the Season's intricacies. She managed to marry off four daughters and a couple of them, might I say, were not quite as pretty as they might have been."

"Well, that is good to know. I'm sure Emily will enjoy herself exceedingly."

"I'm sure she will." Philip hesitated. "I'm more concerned about you."

Lisette stiffened. "Have you been talking to Christian?"

"I try and talk to him almost every day."

"I meant about me and my effect on Emily's coming out."

Her father frowned. "What has Christian been saying to you?"

"You probably know already, but he thinks I'm not a suitable person to be around Emily. He fears my reputation will affect hers."

"Does he?" Philip's expression darkened.

"And he may have a point. I behaved rather stupidly in my youth—you know I did." Lisette hoped her father never knew quite how stupidly, but he'd probably seen enough to realize how wild she'd been. "I would hate to ruin Emily's chances of making a good match."

"You have been very kind to Emily, Lisette, and I appreciate that more than I can say." He sighed. "Considering the nature of your birth and upbringing, your wild years could've been so much worse."

"Now you sound just like Maman," Lisette said, and hastened to change the subject. "You didn't know she was pregnant when you left her. And when you did find out, you treated Christian and I just like your legitimate children. If anyone should have a problem, it should be Richard and Emily."

"Emily loves you both. I'm not so sure that Richard has reconciled himself to my lurid past." A flicker of pain crossed her father's face. "He avoids coming home."

"Richard is twenty, Papa, why would he want to come home? We hardly ever see Christian either."

"That is true. But I've almost forgotten what I wanted to say to you. I discussed the idea with your mother, and she told me to ask you."

"What idea?"

Philip sat forward. "You were never properly presented at court or to society. I've spoken to Mrs. Horrocks-Smith, and she is quite happy to chaperone you as well as Emily."

"That is very kind of her, and of you, but I don't wish to steal Emily's big moment and I'm quite happy as I am."

"Are you sure, my dear?" Philip hesitated. "Sometimes, forgive me, it seems as though you watch from the sidelines and don't feel able to join in with the younger ladies."

"That's because I don't fit in." She regarded him steadily. "I don't, Papa, and I never will. In truth, living that life would stifle me, and I have no wish for it." In essence that was true and she hoped he realized it. The fact that a small part of her would always yearn to be acknowledged and accepted simply for who she was would never go away. Was that how it felt for Lord Swanfield, too? That longing to be accepted and the fear that one never would?

"And what if your latest beau draws you into that world? Will you be able to do your duty to him then?"

"My latest beau?" For a moment Lisette was confused. "Oh, do you mean Lord Swanfield? He is scarcely that."

Philip smiled. "If you say so, my dear, but he does seem remarkably keen on you."

"Lord Swanfield eschews society even more than I do."

"So I've heard. Your mother thinks very highly of him."

Lisette sat up straight. "She does?"

"She knows everything that goes on in the pleasure house, Lisette, don't forget that."

Lisette's smile faded. "And after talking to my mother, what do you think of Lord Swanfield?"

"I think he is a complex man and I trust you to take care of yourself."

"Papa . . ."

"Lisette, I *trust* you." He held her gaze. "And if the bastard hurts you in any way, I'll make sure he lives to regret it."

"Thank you, I'll bear it in mind." Lisette made as if to rise from her seat. "If that was all you wanted to say to me?"

"Actually, there is one more thing. An old friend of mine is holding a ball tonight for his daughter who is of a similar age to Emily. I wondered if you would care to accompany me to the ball, and decide whether Emily would benefit from the acquaintance."

"I'd be happy to, Papa." It was the least she could do when he was so kind to her. Sometimes she felt that she didn't deserve his forbearance. He'd tried so hard with her and Christian, even when they'd attempted to disrupt his renewed relationship with their mother.

"Excellent. We can have dinner together and leave after that."

"Of course, Papa." Lisette blew him a kiss and hurried to her bedchamber, where she rang for her maid. If she was going to a ball on her father's arm, she needed to make some effort to appear as beautiful as possible. She could never match her mother's magnificence, but then very few women could.

Lisette smiled at the thought of her parents' stormy and unconventional relationship and realized there was probably very little she could do to shock her father either. He deserved her love. He deserved more from her than she could ever probably give him, but she hoped he'd never realize that.

Gabriel tugged irritably at the tight linen of his cravat and earned himself a smile from Paul St. Clare.

"Do you hate these occasions as much as I do?"

"Is it that obvious?" Gabriel replied, his gaze moving past the receiving line and around the already full ballroom.

"Only to me." Paul sighed. "My aunt and uncle have offered me a home, but I'm not ready to settle down yet. I need my freedom."

Gabriel knew that war affected some men that way, turned them into restless spirits who could never settle easily into the placid life of a peaceful nation, men who craved the horror of conflict even as they feared it.

"Ah, here is my aunt," Paul murmured, and stepped forward to greet a pleasant-faced older woman with faded blond hair. "Good evening, Aunt. May I present my friend and former commanding officer, the Earl of Swanfield?"

"A pleasure, ma'am."

Instinctively, Gabriel braced himself for the moment when she faced him. He'd become hardened to being given the cut direct, or, worse still, being greeted politely only to see the person whispering about him a second later. But for once, he wanted to make a good impression. He owed Paul that, at least.

To his surprise, she grasped one of his hands in hers and squeezed it tightly. "Lord Swanfield, it is such a pleasure to finally meet you." She drew him closer and turned to the distinguished man at her side. "Marcus, Lord Swanfield is here."

Gabriel found himself facing one of the most influential peers in the House of Lords. His hand was taken in a firm grip. "Swanfield, I want to thank you for what you did for my nephew."

"I did nothing any man would not have done in similar circumstances."

"Untrue, my lord. From what I've heard, you should've received a medal for bravery rather than a coward's dismissal."

Gabriel winced at the loudness of Lord Ashmolton's booming voice. Either he wanted everyone around him to hear exactly what he was saying, or he always spoke like that.

"I was only doing my duty, sir, and your nephew was courageous in his own right."

"Still." Lord Ashmolton's voice rose even louder. "You're a damned fine man and a hero in my book. I'd be proud to sponsor you into my club."

"That's very kind of you, sir, but . . ."

Again Gabriel found himself silenced as Lord Ashmolton rumbled on about how sick Paul had been on his return to England and that he'd only survived at all because of Gabriel's care. The people around them in the receiving line were starting to stare and whisper and he suddenly felt hemmed in.

He shook Lord Ashmolton's hand one last time and stepped back from the couple. "Thank you again for your welcome, sir, but I must not keep you."

Paul grinned as his uncle slapped him on the back and they were able to move along and pay their respects to Paul's cousin, Lucinda, whom the ball was in honor of. Lucinda seemed at ease with Paul, her brown eyes fixed on him, her pleasure in his company so obvious that Gabriel wondered whether Paul realized his fate yet.

Eventually they made their way down to the dance floor and Gabriel helped himself to a drink from one of the passing footmen.

"You should have told me that my welcome would be so effusive, and that your uncle was a duke."

"And then you wouldn't have come."

Paul glanced up at him. He looked far older in his evening clothes, his blond hair tamed, and his brown eyes alert and full of laughter. He was only two years younger than Gabriel but often seemed a mere boy. There was no sign of that youthfulness tonight, only a wariness that echoed Gabriel's.

"Your cousin seems very fond of you."

"Yes, she is a delightful girl." He shrugged. "They want me to marry her."

"She would make you a fine wife."

Paul's mouth quirked up at the corner. "Please, Major, you know my tastes do not run in that direction. It would be cruel to her."

They continued to circle the ballroom, both of them instinctively keeping their backs to the walls. Eventually they settled on a secluded corner near the large windows. "Have you ever been in a relationship with a woman, Paul?"

"Do you mean have I ever tried to conform?" Paul sighed. "I fear my tastes were formed at Eton, and nothing I have encountered since has changed my mind."

Gabriel stared out across the ballroom and caught sight of an all-too-familiar figure. Miss Ross hadn't mentioned her intentions to go to a ball, but then he hadn't either. She looked very nice in some sort of pale gauzy confection that made him want to unwrap her like a bonbon and sink his teeth into her. . . .

"Swanfield?"

He looked down at Paul. "I'm sorry, St. Clare, what did you say?"

"I was going to ask how you feel about women, and then I noticed you were ogling one."

Gabriel studied his friend's smiling face and saw the strain around his eyes. "I prefer women."

"Yet you've had both."

"But given a choice, I would always pick a woman." He

stared into Paul's eyes. "I know what you want from me, but I can't give it to you. I'm sorry."

"I understand. In truth, I understood that a long time ago."

"If I were that way inclined, I would choose you, Paul. You are an excellent lover."

His friend started to laugh and placed his hand on his heart. "Thank you, my lord. You . . . unman me."

Gabriel smiled. "You are all man, St. Clare, and there is no one I would rather have at my side in a fight."

"Or at your back."

"Preferably where I can see you."

St. Clare's smile faded. "I wish things were different between us. I would happily share your bed for the rest of my life."

For one ridiculous second Gabriel forgot where he was and wanted to reach out and curve his hand around St. Clare's head and simply hold him. "If I held you to that, it would be as cruel as you marrying Miss Lucinda. You deserve someone to love you for who and what you are."

"Yes, I see that." Paul turned away as someone approached them, but not before Gabriel had seen the pain in his eyes. "Ah, look, beauty awaits you." He bowed. "Good evening, sir, miss."

Gabriel stepped forward. "Lord Knowles, Miss Ross, may I introduce you to my friend Lieutenant St. Clare?"

Lord Knowles nodded at Gabriel. "Good evening, Swanfield. St. Clare, it is a pleasure to meet you."

Miss Ross smiled at them. "How are you this evening, Lieutenant? It is a while since I have seen you."

Gabriel's attention snapped back to Paul. He'd forgotten that his friend already knew Miss Ross and had admitted to telling her about some of Gabriel's past.

"I'm very well, Miss Ross, yourself?"

Miss Ross's glance strayed to Gabriel's face and he drank in the pure lines of her cheekbones, her intelligent expression, and the multitude of colors in her ever-changing eyes. She wasn't classically beautiful, but there was an animation and glow in her face that drew men toward her like bees to honey.

"Would you like to dance, Miss Ross?"

The words were out of his mouth before he had a chance to consider them. So much for his hope of remaining incognito at the dance and making a quick exit.

"If that is all right with you, Papa?"

She looked at her father, who released her hand from his and placed it carefully in Gabriel's. "Go ahead, my dear. I'll wait for you in the supper room."

Paul sighed. "I suppose I should go and do my duty to my cousin. She asked me particularly to dance with her." He bowed to Gabriel and Miss Ross. "It was a pleasure to see you again."

Gabriel led Miss Ross toward the dance floor and drew her into his arms. He could now see that the dress was pale yellow and displayed her bosom to advantage.

"You look very nice this evening, Miss Ross. Like a spring flower."

She looked up at him. "And you look nice, too. Is that a new coat?"

"I believe it is. My valet and Captain Gray chose it for me."

"Ah, Captain Gray always dresses well."

"So you know him, too?"

"I know several of the men who frequent the pleasure house. David is a particular friend."

"Ah, of course you do." He fell silent as they danced together, and simply enjoyed the feeling of her in his arms. It was usually difficult for him to tolerate this level of noise, let alone enjoy himself. Perhaps it was because Lisette knew more about him than any other woman he'd ever met. She seemed to accept both sides of his fragmented personality with an equilibrium that astounded him. In fact, she made him feel almost peaceful. . . . The music stopped far too quickly and he resisted the temptation to keep her close, to allow her to rest her head on his shoulder and simply surround her with his warmth.

"Lord Swanfield."

He looked down at her upturned face. "Yes, Miss Ross?"

"Are you going to take me back to my father?"

"Of course, Miss Ross." He led her back through the crowds of guests, stopping only when a man dressed in his old regiment's uniform stepped deliberately into his path.

"Cousin Gabriel."

"Captain Granger." Gabriel nodded his head. Behind William stood Michael, his face pale, his horrified expression indicating that he'd rather be in China than watching his brother confront their cousin. William was Gabriel's height and had his coloring; the only major difference between them was Gabriel's unusual eye color. "I hope you are well, sir?"

"As well as can be expected." William's gaze turned to Lisette, and Gabriel tensed. "I don't believe I've met your dance partner."

"Miss Ross, this is my cousin Captain William Granger."

"A pleasure to meet you, sir." Miss Ross bobbed his cousin a graceful curtsey.

"And you, too, Miss Ross." William's smile didn't even attempt to conceal his disdain for anybody or anything that willingly came into contact with Gabriel.

"If you will excuse us, I must get Miss Ross safely back to her father." Gabriel ushered Miss Ross past William, only to have his arm caught in a punishing grip.

"Have you been to Swanfield Hall recently?"

"You know I have not."

William's laugh was harsh, "Oh, aye, you have no sense of

duty to your name or to the estate, do you? But then who would expect you to? You were hardly born equipped for this role."

"A fact which you and your family have taken pains to remind me of all my life." Gabriel met his cousin's angry stare. "Is it any wonder that I don't want to visit a place that you and yours turned into a living hell for me?" He pulled out of William's grasp. "Good evening, sir."

"It's not that easy, Gabriel. You're a man now, not a child. Isn't it time you took responsibility for those who depend on you?"

Gabriel paused to look back. "Like you, you mean?"

William's face went white and Michael looked equally shocked. "What the devil is that supposed to mean?"

"I believe my estate paid for both you and Michael's commissions to the regiment and has continued to pay for your advancement ever since." Gabriel nodded at them both. "Perhaps you are right and I should take more interest in the finances of my estate. I'm sure your father would be more than happy to turn over all the records that my solicitor has requested for the last five years."

"Damn you, Gabriel, my father has done nothing but work himself to the bone for you, and this is how you repay him?"

"I think the question is how much should he be repaying me, don't you? Good evening, William, Michael, and good night."

Before William could say anything in reply, Miss Ross took Gabriel's hand and marched him away. She kept moving past the supper room and down a long dark hallway that led toward the back of the house and away from the gawkers and gossips who had gathered around to enjoy the angry confrontation.

"Gabriel, are you all right?"

He looked down at Lisette and let go of her hand. "I apologize, Miss Ross. I meant to take you to your father before I flounced off like a discarded mistress."

She reached up and touched his cheek, brushed a soft kiss over his skin. "It's all right. Your cousin was deliberately antagonizing you."

"He always does. I should be used to it by now." He stared up at the ceiling. "How the devil was I supposed to know how to run the estates when no one showed me? Even after I succeeded to the title they kept all the knowledge for William and Michael and shut me out."

"Do you really believe his father cheated you?"

He glared at her. "Questions like that are why I try and avoid airing my family's dirty linen at social gatherings."

"Don't tell me then. I was just trying to help." She made as if to whisk herself away from him and he couldn't bear that. He sighed and placed his hands on her shoulders.

"I've spent the last five years trying to wrest control of the estate away from the Granger family. William might not admit it, but ever since his father was declared my guardian, his family has bled me dry."

"That cannot be right."

"It isn't, but I've made it harder by refusing to visit my uncle in person and sort it out face-to-face, in a genteel, gentlemanly manner. Solicitors and lawyers make it a very slow process, but at least I don't have to look at him. I'm afraid I might try and kill him." Gabriel sighed. "And William does have a point. In my efforts to keep away from his family, I've stayed away from the people who depend on me for a living."

She stroked his cheek again as if trying to soothe him. "But you can change that. I know you can."

"Perhaps your faith in me is misplaced."

"Now you are just feeling sorry for yourself."

He blinked at her. "What?"

She poked him in the chest. "You are perfectly capable of taking control of your own destiny. I suspect your reluctance comes more from your not wanting to hurt the family that brought you up."

"Hurt them? They treated me like scum and they treated my mother . . ." He shut his mouth and struggled to breathe properly. "I don't feel sorry for them at all."

"Then you need to face them."

He glared down at her calm face. "Easy for you to say."

"That's true, but you'll have to do it eventually, so why not now?"

He considered her carefully, and tried to decide what to tell her and what to leave out. He didn't want her thinking he was any more of a coward than she obviously did. "Because someone is busy trying to blacken my reputation again and make the War Office reopen an investigation into my supposed traitorous crimes. If the Granger family wait a while and the evidence goes against me, all that I own might revert back to them."

"But you were imprisoned and almost died! How on earth do they think you were responsible for anything?"

He was shocked to see that she looked almost as angry as he felt. It made him feel curiously warm inside, as if she was still holding his hand. But this conversation couldn't go on. He needed to get away from the ballroom and the stares of his peers.

On impulse, he bent his head and kissed her. She started talking so he kissed her again, this time outlining the seam of her lips with the tip of his tongue. She made a low noise in her throat and opened her mouth to him. While he stroked his tongue inside, he captured her wrists and brought both her hands around to the small of her back and held them captive in one of his.

She sighed and leaned into him, melted into the kiss and let him possess and explore her mouth at will. God, he wanted her now, wanted to repel the shock of his cousin's appearance and bury himself inside her until he felt nothing but the need to fuck and burn. Her breasts pressed against his chest, and her belly against his cock.

He kept kissing her as he pressed her even closer until he suspected that the buttons of his waistcoat and the heat of his shaft would be imprinted on her skin forever.

"Miss Ross, will you meet me at the pleasure house tonight?"

She looked up at him, her lips swollen from his kisses, her hazel eyes so full of warmth that he feared he might drown in them.

"I can't."

He frowned, his sexual anticipation doused by her prosaic words. "Why not?"

"Because my father asked me to attend this ball with him, and I can hardly abandon him here."

"But I want you."

She moved away from him. "And tonight you will not have me."

"And what am I supposed to do about this?" He gestured at his thick erection.

She dipped him a curtsey. "You have a hand, don't you?"

"And you are an impudent baggage."

Her smile was full of anticipation. "That is true. Perhaps I will see you tomorrow night?"

"You aren't going to ride with me tomorrow morning either?"

"I have an appointment with my dressmaker."

"Perhaps I should simply go to the pleasure house by myself tonight after all."

Her smile dimmed at little but she still raised her chin at him before she started walking away. "What an excellent idea. Good night, my lord."

He caught up with her in two strides and took her hand. "I didn't mean that."

She wouldn't look at him. "You are a free man, my lord. What you choose to do is scarcely my concern, is it?"

"It is your concern if I choose to make it so."

"But you don't, do you? You are too scared to settle on one woman in case she wants things from you that you are not prepared to give."

He stared down at her as her words hit home, and he slowly released her hand. She deserved more than him. She deserved a man who would love her to distraction and give her as many children as she wanted. "Good night, Miss Ross."

"Good night, Lord Swanfield."

God, he couldn't let it go like this, he just couldn't. She'd gone halfway down the hallway before he found the courage to speak. "Miss Ross, if I was available just for you at the pleasure house, would that please you?"

She turned back slowly and studied him for a long moment across the distance. "Yes, it would."

"Then that is what I shall do." He bit his lip. "I'll wait in our room every night until you decide to favor me with your presence. I won't let anyone else bring me sexual release."

She inclined her head a regal inch and then turned and left him standing there, his heart thumping, his cock aching in an unsteady echo. After a few moments, he turned and made his own way back up the hall. To his relief, Paul St. Clare stood right by the entrance to the ballroom holding both their cloaks.

"Miss Ross said you might want to leave, my lord. I've already summoned a hackney."

Gabriel grabbed his cloak and hat and held them in front of his tented pantaloons as they edged their way around the ballroom. Whispers followed him like the lightest rainfall and he kept his face blank, looking neither for William nor for Miss Ross, and concentrated solely on getting out of the front door.

In the hackney cab, he collapsed on the seat and allowed Paul to direct the driver and then follow him inside. Gabriel closed his eyes and fought the sensation that his world was shifting out of his control again. He thought he'd learned patience and the fickle nature of life and death in the prison cell, but some part of him was shocked at the randomness of events.

He shuddered as he became aware of Paul's hand under his cloak lightly settling over his engorged cock.

"Do you need some help with that?"

"Paul . . ."

Paul immediately removed his hand. "I'm sorry, Gabriel, it was just so difficult to resist. If I got down on the floor and sucked you into my mouth, I'm sure I could have you all finished by the time we reached our lodgings."

Just for a moment, Gabriel let himself imagine the strong pull of Paul's clever mouth on his cock, the immense gratification of being able to come down the other man's throat in thick pulsing waves. . . .

"Thank you, but no."

Paul sighed, the sound loud in the smelly confines of the cab. "Then can I just watch you do it?"

Gabriel managed a smile. "No." He glanced down at his rebellious cock. "And stop talking about it. You're making it worse."

He'd wait until he found the privacy of his own bed before he touched himself, knew it wouldn't take long for him to come hard. With a groan he rearranged his stiff cock in his pantaloons, glad that they weren't as tight as the ones he wore at the pleasure house. Then he thought about Miss Ross and waiting for her to touch him and nearly came all over himself.

"Damnation!"

Paul laughed as Gabriel cursed. "It was much easier in the

prison cells, wasn't it? No one asked if you wanted a hand there. You usually had to fight them off." Paul's voice grew quiet. "Sometimes I miss that."

"I don't," Gabriel muttered. The carriage drew to a halt and Gabriel felt in his pocket for some coins and groaned again as his fingers brushed his cock. He promised himself that if he managed to get upstairs without coming in his pantaloons, he'd call the awful night a success after all.

11

"I want to surprise him," Lisette said firmly, her gaze fixed on Marie-Claude, who sat opposite her at the kitchen table in the pleasure house. "I want to make him my slave."

"He already is your slave. He's given up everyone else here just for you."

"I know, but . . ." Lisette frowned. "There must be something I can do to him tonight, something deliciously decadent."

"Like what?"

Lisette felt her cheeks heat up. "When I saw him with Lieutenant St. Clare last night at the ball, I wondered if perhaps Lord Swanfield enjoys a man's touch more than he has admitted."

"He certainly allows men to touch him, but I don't think he is naturally inclined that way." Marie-Claude put down her glass of wine with a businesslike thump and started to get up. "Do you wish me to find a man to help you?"

"No." Lisette smiled for the first time and Marie-Claude sat down again. "I think I'll play that part myself."

* * *

Gabriel paced the small bedchamber and watched the hands on the clock on the mantelpiece move slowly around the dial. It was past eleven now and there was no sign of Miss Ross. And in this place, he had no control over her tardiness and she knew it. He halted by the small fire. Was that what she wanted? For him to grow impatient with her and forget his place?

"Good evening, Gabriel."

He turned around and found Miss Ross in the doorway. She wore a simple pink muslin frock without adornment, and her long, fair hair was gathered at the nape of her neck with a single ribbon. She managed to look both as pure as an innocent debutante and as sensual as the most experienced woman he had ever met. His heart rate sped up and sent tremors of lust pulsing through his veins.

"Good evening, Miss Ross."

She nodded and crossed over to the bed, where she deposited a bulky silk bundle. "Please undress completely, Gabriel."

He complied, taking his time peeling off the obscenely tight pantaloons, stockings, and shoes. When he straightened, she was still watching him. She patted the black satin counterpane of the bed.

"Get on the bed and kneel up facing the headboard."

He walked toward her and climbed onto the bed, his breathing erratic as she surveyed him, her gaze cool, her hands remaining in her lap. He tensed as she moved behind him, urging him closer to the headboard, placing his hands flat on the wood and widening the gap between his knees. The tip of his erect cock grazed the wood and he flinched at the unexpected contact.

"Don't turn around."

He focused his gaze on the intricate grain of the mahogany as she fussed around behind him.

"Keep still."

He shivered as the scent of orange blossom invaded his nostrils and her oiled fingers caressed his shoulders and then his biceps. She continued oiling down his arms until her fingers laced with his and then withdrew, leaving a silky trace of warm oil all over his skin. She continued to massage his back, and then her arms slid around to his front and worked the oil into his furred chest.

His cock jammed against the headboard and stayed put, pulsing in time to the movements of Miss Ross's skilled fingers. She circled his nipples, pulled and drew on them until they were hard and he hissed a curse. Her hands moved lower and he sucked in a breath as she touched his flat belly and then his lower back and buttocks.

"Do you like this?" she murmured.

He managed to nod, too caught up in the experience to do more than curse or beg her never to stop.

"Good."

Her fingers moved between his legs to play with his balls and the soft skin behind them and he arched his back. He hardly cared when she slid one oiled finger into his arse and then a second.

"I should imagine you want me to touch your cock."

He set his jaw as she added a third finger and started to move them back and forth, pushing his already tortured cock harder against the wood. He wouldn't beg yet; he was much stronger than that.

"You don't want me to touch your cock? Perhaps I'm not doing this correctly."

Her right hand dropped away from his balls and he wanted to cry out.

"If my fingers aren't enough to make you beg, perhaps one of these will work better." Sounds of rustling and movement behind him made him wary and he shut his eyes. "Look down."

He opened his eyes and saw a variety of dildos laid out on the pillow below him. They were made of different substances—

leather, glass, jade—and were a variety of lengths and thicknesses.

"Which one would make you beg?"

He bit down on his lip. Did she mean to try them all on him? A flicker of dark excitement stirred low in his gut. There must be at least six of them. She leaned around him and the bones of her corset pressed against his back. He realized she must have taken off her dress. She touched each dildo and rearranged them from smallest to largest.

"You don't have a preference, Gabriel?"

He refused to reply, almost afraid to give away his complete slavish willingness to do whatever she wanted. She picked up the smallest dildo, which was made of glass and about seven inches long.

"Then I'll have to try them all."

Time blurred as she worked each dildo inside him in turn, narrowed to the sensation of the exquisite fullness, her soft voice, and what was happening to his beleaguered cock. He wanted to give in, wanted to beg, wanted to lie down and worship at her feet as she tormented him so pertly.

He shivered as her thumb brushed his lower lip.

"You've bitten this ragged. Is it so difficult to beg, then?" Helplessly he licked her thumb, drew it into his mouth, and tasted orange oil and his own blood. He felt more at peace than he ever had before. "What if I offered you another way to relieve your cock?"

He almost stopped breathing as she pressed the last and biggest dildo deep inside him and held it there. What did she mean? Damnation, he wouldn't fuck her, he wouldn't.

"What if you were able to slide your cock into my arse? Would you beg for that?"

He went still and tried to sort out what she offered him from what he'd thought she'd want. "Your arse?" he managed to whisper.

"Yes."

"God . . ." And it was suddenly too much. He climaxed with such a jolt that he groaned out loud as his cock spurted his seed all over the hardness of the headboard. He crumpled forward until his head met the wood with a thud and he struggled to breathe. He realized she had removed the thick dildo from his arse. Would she be annoyed that he had come? Her fingers curled around his limp shaft and he groaned.

"Gabriel . . ."

"Yes?" He asked hoarsely.

"I still want you to slide your cock into my arse. Will you make sure I'm ready for you?"

"Yes."

Lisette waited for him to turn around and really look at her. Watching his big, strong body convulse with the fierceness of his climax had made her wet and more than ready to have him inside her. Not that he would come inside her sex, she knew that, but at least she would get to feel him. And after seeing him come like that, she wanted it even more.

"I am sorry that I came, Miss Ross."

"Why? I enjoyed it."

He kept his gaze lowered to the bed. "Because you didn't give me permission."

"I'm not your master, Gabriel. If you wish to have a relationship like that I understand that there are several guests up on the third and fourth floors who would be more than happy to oblige you."

He looked at her then, his indigo eyes serious. "I don't want that."

She licked her lips. "Good, because I am not the sort of woman who likes wielding a whip. Will you undress me now?"

"Yes, Miss Ross."

"My name is Lisette."

He reached for her then, his large, calloused hands gentle on her skin as he undid laces and buttons and finally drew her corset and shift over her head. When she was naked, he simply stared at her, his mouth a hard line, his eyes almost black as his pupils dilated.

"I am not going to tell you what to do next, Gabriel. If that is what you want, I'm not the right person for you."

His mouth came down on hers and he lowered her to the bed, his kisses as urgent and unfettered as she could've wished, his hands caressing, measuring, possessing every inch of her skin.

She gasped as he nuzzled her breast and then drew it into the heat of his mouth, teased her other nipple with his fingers. She opened her legs to him without thought and his heavy thigh shoved them wider, her wetness rubbing against his muscle and coarse hair creating an urgency and friction all its own.

She came then, pushing her hips higher to squeeze his thigh and gain the maximum enjoyment from her release. With a growl, he changed positions, his wide shoulders taking the place of his thigh, his mouth now feasting on the wetness and need of her sex. His oiled skin moved against hers, creating a slickness that eased his movements and made them flow together like the sea.

His tongue flicked over her clit and he eased two oiled fingers into her arse. She bucked against the sudden pressure, but he was inexorable, pushing his fingers deep, distracting her by tonguing and nipping her swollen bud, making her come and come until he had all four fingers wedged inside her, stretching and molding her.

With a sudden motion, he withdrew his fingers and rolled her onto her front over a pile of pillows. He came down over her, his stiff shaft erect again and rubbing against her buttocks. She grabbed his wrist and dug her nails into his skin until he grunted in protest.

"Do you want this?" she asked.

"Lisette . . ." He groaned and moved his hips against her again as if he couldn't stop himself. "God, yes."

"Enough to beg?"

He went so still she could only hear her own breathing and the frantic thump of his heart. He lowered his head until his lips touched the back of her neck.

"Yes, damn you. I'll beg for this. I want to be inside you more than I want to breathe."

Lisette smiled and let go of his wrist and heard him exhale. Then there was no more time to enjoy her victory as he positioned the thick oiled head of his cock against the tight entrance to her arse. She tried not to tense up as he slowly pressed forward, but he felt so big. . . .

"It's all right." He nipped her ear and then licked it, nipped it again harder and gained another inch or two. "You'll take me, you want to." His hands roamed her body and his thumb settled over her clit and circled it hard. She came again and he thrust forward, until she felt the first dark stirring of need deep inside her and the urge to lift herself against him.

"More," she whispered. "Give me more of you."

Gabriel stuffed all four of his fingers into her wet sex and started to pump them back and forth. She reacted by opening up to him completely and the root of his shaft and his balls finally met her skin. He flexed his fingers and felt the answering pulse of his own cock lodged in her arse, massaged himself through the thin wall, until both of them gasped and then he was thrusting into her, each stroke as long and hard as he could make it. He forgot about caution, the need not to push her too hard, the need to obey, and simply fucked her arse the way he yearned to fuck her cunt and wouldn't allow himself to.

Not that she was protesting at all. She moved with him, lifted herself into each stroke and gave it back to him, her muscles squeezing his cock and his fingers until he thought he'd go crazy if he couldn't come, that he never wanted to come, that he wanted to stay inside her forever. . . .

She screamed his name and his fingers were almost crushed by the strength of her climax. His cock followed suit, pumping his hot seed deep inside her while he shook and trembled with the sheer basic force of it, the power of it and the primal need to fill her. For him, it felt far better than any man.

He rolled away and covered his eyes with his hand. His come was all over her and he liked the idea of that far too much. The way her scent mingled with his, the need to keep her filled with his seed so that every other man would know that she was taken, that she was his. . . .

But she couldn't be his.

He groaned and got off the bed and thoroughly washed himself before pulling on his pantaloons. He found a bowl and a clean washcloth and returned to the bed. Lisette now lay on her back, watching him. Without offering any explanation, he wet one of the cloths and used it to wipe her sex. He took his time, knew she was staring at him and simply let her.

"Are you cleaning your seed off me?" she asked, her voice husky.

"Yes."

"Because you don't like to see me like this?"

He winced. "I like it too much." He gave himself another cursory wipe and threw the cloth into the bowl.

"But not enough to simply enjoy it and lie here with me instead of leaping up like a housemaid and cleaning up. But, of course, your primary concern is to make sure I'm not pregnant."

What the hell was he supposed to say to that? "Miss Ross . . ."

Lisette sat up and her hair tumbled down around her shoulders. "It's all right, I understand." She reached across to grab hold of her shift and struggled into it. "Can you find my gown?"

She knew she shouldn't care that he'd washed her. At some

deep level, she couldn't help it. Her plan to get him to notice her had succeeded perfectly, but had only left her feeling more confused and frustrated than before. Because she did want him. She wanted all of him—his cock, his seed—and she wanted him to want that, too.

She picked up her corset and rolled it up as best she could, feeling unwanted tears prick the back of her eyelids. Would she ever be good enough for anyone? Would she always be second best? She jumped as Gabriel's hand touched her knee.

"Miss Ross . . ."

She glared down at him, knew her rage was totally unfair and hated him anyway. "What?"

"I have your dress. Would you like me to help you put it on?"

"No, thank you. I can manage perfectly well." She snatched the muslin gown out of his grasp and tossed it over her head, struggled to find the sleeves, and suddenly felt trapped.

"Let me help."

She had to suffer the indignity of his hands moving competently over her like a nurse setting a child to rights. God, could this night become any more embarrassing? She'd made a fool of herself by wanting something that had clearly not been offered to her. And now she just wanted her own bed and the opportunity to weep alone.

"There, that's better."

His tentative smile as the filmy muslin settled into place made her feel even worse. She slid off the bed and hurriedly straightened her crumpled skirt.

"Good night, Lord Swanfield."

He caught her arm before she could escape through the door.

"Miss Ross, it's not safe for you to wander these hallways in a state of undress. Your motives for being here could be questioned. I'll escort you back to your quarters."

She turned on him and glared. "Perhaps I *want* to be taken advantage of. Perhaps I want a man to want me back."

Frustration clouded his face and he stepped away from her. "That's not fair. I told you what I was prepared to go along with and what I wasn't."

"I *know*!"

She started walking again, heard him bite off a curse and follow after her. She reached the servants' door and wrenched it open, staring down the stairs and through the narrowing passageways of the basement. His voice echoed behind her.

"Miss Ross, I hate to see you upset."

"My name is Lisette!"

"Lisette, will you at least stop and have this out with me?"

She stopped walking and spun around to face him. His hair was rumpled and his muscled chest still gleamed with the oil she'd massaged into his skin. She wanted to lick him clean. "I am not upset. I am furious with myself for still wanting you. It is humiliating and embarrassing and I just want to hide under my bedcovers and forget that you ever existed."

"Just because I wouldn't have sex with you?"

"Yes!" she hissed at him and he actually recoiled. "And no, because that's not all it's about, is it?"

"Isn't it?" He responded more warily now, as if finally convinced she'd gone mad.

She sighed, turned back around, and kept walking until she found herself outside the door to her bedchamber, Lord Swanfield still at her elbow. "Good night, sir." She pushed open her door and tried to go inside, only to be brought up short by his arm across the doorway. "What are you doing?"

"Making sure you are safe."

He marched her into the bedchamber and slammed the door shut behind them, then set about lighting a candle and adding coal to the fire. He pulled back the bedclothes and plumped the pillows. His expression was not reassuring as he finally turned to face her.

"Get in."

She raised her chin at him. "You intend to complete my humiliating evening by ordering me around like a child?"

He stepped so close that his nose almost touched hers. "I want you to get into that bed!"

"Why, so that you can pat me on the head and blow out the candle before you leave?"

He clamped his teeth together so hard that she heard the click. "No, so that I can hold you, damn you, so that if you want to cry, you can cry all over me until you drown me in tears. Hell, I know I deserve it."

"I am not crying over you!"

He picked her up and dumped her on the bed, followed her down, and stripped off her gown with ruthless efficiency.

"But I don't want you here," she whispered as he blew out the candle and pulled her into his arms.

"That's a shame, because I'm staying." He smoothed one hand over her tangled hair and pressed her cheek into his shoulder. "Now go to sleep."

She didn't want to go to sleep. With a sigh, she turned her face into the curve of his throat and sobbed her heart out.

Gabriel let Lisette cry as he tried to make sense of her impassioned words and even stranger behavior. He'd done everything she'd asked him to, even begged for her, and somehow he was still at fault. He would never understand the way a female mind worked, especially a woman like Lisette. Did women become as sexually frustrated as men? That was the only explanation that presented itself to him and he would be damned if he'd start asking her about that. He sighed into her tangled hair.

He still wanted her, and holding her in his arms was simply adding to his own frustration.

But it wouldn't be fair to fuck her. At least he knew that. What could he offer her, especially now with the threat of military legal proceedings hanging over him? He kissed the top of her head as she finally stopped crying and went limp against his shoulder. He wished he could sleep so easily, had always needed sex or alcohol to achieve unconsciousness, and he'd given up drinking excessively as it was killing him.

Lisette stirred again and cuddled even closer, one knee drawn up over his hip, the glories of her sex pressed against his stomach and shaft. His eyelids felt heavy and he yawned. Could he sleep like this? Could he find peace in her arms? God, he hoped so, or he was destined for a night of pure frustration. He let out his breath and allowed his eyes to close. He couldn't even remember the last time he'd willingly slept with a woman. . . .

12

Light exploded through the darkness and the windowpanes behind her head rattled fit to wake the dead. Lisette sat up with a gasp and stared outside, her heart thumping so hard she could scarcely breathe. A second roar reverberated through the glass and another burst of light, this time a golden one, which illuminated the indigo night sky and the rooftops of the other houses in the square.

Lisette let out a shaky breath as she realized she was only watching a fireworks display and not the end of the world as she had first feared. She frowned as she tried to remember what the fireworks were for. Was there a particular royal event being celebrated, or was the new King George merely being his usual extravagant self?

A stifled sound from the floor made her tense up again. She crawled toward the far side of the bed and peered into the shadows. Another flash of silvered light revealed the shape of a man crouched against the wall. Lisette put on her nightgown, got out of bed, and inched her way toward the hunched figure.

Gabriel sat with his back against the wall, his knees drawn

up to his chin, and his arms wrapped around his head as if protecting himself. Lisette paused to study him, noticing he was trembling and that his breathing sounded as ragged as hers when she had first awoken.

"Gabriel?" she whispered, but he didn't seem to hear her. His fear flowed over her, and the sense that he held himself together by the merest fragile thread. The fireworks boomed and he shook even harder, his fingers a stark white as he tried to protect himself. But from what? From her? From the noise?

She reached out and patted his cold bare foot. "Gabriel, it's all right. It's just the fireworks."

He didn't respond and she frowned into the murky darkness. He was obviously in the grip of a nightmare or enmeshed in a physical reaction to some deep-rooted fear. She got up and drew the thick curtains, which at least shut out the light, and deadened the worst effects of the noise. On her way back, she lit a single candle from the embers of the fire and placed it on the bedside table so that at least some light fell on him.

She knelt down again and touched his arms, smoothed her palms over his freezing cold skin as if he were a frightened colt. "Gabriel, it's all right. You're safe."

He exhaled and some of the tension leeched out of his body. Lisette continued to touch him. She'd heard stories about men who returned from war and suffered terrible consequences. Men who reacted to the sound of a champagne cork popping as if they were still under fire, whose dreams were so full of violence and the unfolding of their particular horrors that they even feared sleep.

Although she knew little of Gabriel's particular war experiences, it was hardly surprising he might be suffering now. Lisette bit her lip. She could climb back into bed and leave him there. He'd probably be mortified if he knew she'd seen him like this. She smoothed a hand over his thick hair, which was now damp with sweat.

But Gabriel had held her while she cried and let her sleep in his arms. If he'd left her alone, he wouldn't be here with her now struggling with his demons. How could she abandon him?

"Gabriel." She knelt up and wrapped her arms around as much of him as she could. "I'm here, it's all right." He shuddered so hard she thought he might throw her off. She tightened her grip on him, kissed his ear, his brow, the bridge of his autocratic nose, anything she could reach in an instinctive need to help him.

She had no idea how long she held him like that, only that the fireworks had long stopped and her knees were aching from kneeling on the hard wooden floor. Tension eased from him and she managed to prise his arms away from his face so that she could finally look at him.

"Gabriel? ¿Cómo estás?"

He muttered something in the same language, but she couldn't understand him. His eyes were closed, his color ashen. She framed his face with her hands and kissed his tightly closed lips, tasted his blood and still kissed him. She took one of his hands and brought it to her shoulder. "Touch me, Gabriel; let me know you are all right."

With a sudden harsh movement, he put his hands around her waist and drew her into his lap, so that she straddled him. His mouth opened under hers and he kissed her with a blunt, desperate savagery that took her breath away. One of his hands shoved into her hair as if he was determined to keep her exactly where he wanted her. Lisette didn't protest, just allowed him in, responded with all her strength, and yet let him have his way.

He groaned into her mouth and she caressed his tense muscled shoulders and back, felt his hand on her bottom, his fingers biting into her skin. The kiss went on and on until she was drowning in it, couldn't remember what it felt like not to have him sharing her every breath. Her breasts rubbed against the hair on his chest, her nipples hard and aching.

"Lisette." Without further warning, he lifted her over his cock and brought her down on him. She gasped at the sudden fullness, the shock, the sensation of being impaled. He wouldn't let her escape his mouth. His tongue settled into the same driving rhythm as his hips as he lifted and lowered her onto his thick shaft until she was gasping and fighting to stop herself from biting him with the intensity of the pleasure.

"*Dios*, Lisette . . ." he whispered, as she felt him come, the heat of his seed deep inside her as he shuddered and shook with the force of it. She tried not to climax so that she could experience him to the fullest, but she couldn't stop herself and sank her teeth into his lower lip as pleasure flowed over her.

He finally released her mouth and leaned back against the wall, his arms wrapped around her, his body still chained to hers. Lisette could only follow him down, her head on his chest, the solid beat of his heart beneath her cheek.

She realized she was scared to move, to have to look up and deal with his reaction to the enormity of what they had done together. Somehow she sensed that whatever happened, he wouldn't be pleased. He was not a man who easily relinquished control, except within the confines of the pleasure house. She gasped as his hands cupped her bottom and he stood up and brought her over to the bed. He laid her carefully on the counterpane and leaned over her, one hand on either side of her head, their bodies still joined at the loins.

She had to look at him now. She refused to be a coward any longer. To her surprise, his eyes were closed, and his expression remote as if he still wasn't sure if he was dreaming. She reached up and brushed his hair away from his face. He cursed in Spanish and started to pull away from her, groaning as her body fought to keep him inside.

"Lisette, I can't . . ." Before he even finished speaking he was driving into her again, his restoration so fast that it took her by surprise. At least he knew it was her and not some nameless dream woman he had to conquer. She curled her feet up and around his buttocks and held on, the force of his thrusts pressing her deep into the mattress. It was easier this time, now that she was so wet and stretched and, God, so desperate to feel him again.

She closed her eyes and allowed her body to take over, to simply enjoy the motion of his hips, the strength of his arms, his frantic breathing as he moved over her. Even within such bliss, she sensed this might be her only chance to experience him like this, the only time he would allow himself to break through the constraints that bound him and truly express his needs.

She climaxed and he choked out a cry and followed her, each pulse so long that she thought he'd never stop coming, that she'd always be pinned to the bed as he shuddered and shook over her. This time when he pulled away, he slumped down to the floor and she was too dazed to move. She lay on the bed and fought to breathe normally, knew with an aching sadness that he'd given her a sexual experience she would never forget. She also knew that the pleasure was unlikely to be repeated. She closed her eyes and curled onto her side.

"Miss Ross?"

She opened her eyes to find Gabriel on his knees beside her. She flinched at the desolation in his eyes.

"I'll speak to your father later this morning."

She blinked at him. "About what?"

He stood up and headed for the door. "About our marriage."

She managed to sit up and clutched the bedclothes to her chest. "What marriage?"

Her only answer was the sound of the door clicking shut behind her reluctant lover. Lisette struggled to get out of bed, but by the time she gained the hallway, Gabriel was gone. She stared down the stairs and fought an absurd desire to cry. He'd decided to *marry* her now? She went back inside and slammed the door behind her, her fingers trembling as she tried to pull off her nightgown. She had to make herself presentable and make sure she got to Gabriel before he had any chance to speak to her father.

Gabriel hesitated as the door of the Knowles townhouse opened before he'd even had a chance to knock. He'd gone home and dressed in his best black coat and breeches and then forced himself back out of the door and to Lord Knowles's house before he had time to think. After the event of the previous night, he couldn't think properly anyway, his memories far too raw and confused to make sense.

"Good morning, Lord Swanfield."

He barely remembered to acknowledge the butler. "Good morning. Is Lord Knowles available?"

"I believe he is, sir, let me go and inquire." The butler bowed and opened a door to his left. "Perhaps you'd prefer to wait in here, sir, where it's warmer."

"Thank you."

Gabriel unconsciously followed the butler's guidance and found himself in a small, pleasant morning room with a blazing fire. As the door shut behind him, he realized he wasn't alone and started to retreat. Miss Ross rose from one of the chairs and came toward him, her hands clasped in front of her, her gaze steady. She looked nothing like the woman he'd held in his arms earlier, the wanton who'd taken everything he had to give her and paid him back with a passion of her own that had blinded and enthralled him.

"What do you mean; you're *going* to marry me?"

He forced himself to meet her gaze, but kept his mouth shut as he became aware of a torrent of emotions he no longer had any control over, lust, remorse, desire, shame . . .

He resorted to being as businesslike as he could. "I would

assume you'd worked that out for yourself. I spent the night in your bed."

"But that doesn't mean you have to marry me."

"Yes, it does." He glanced at the sleek fall of her brown silk gown. "You might be carrying my child."

Her hand came up to rest just below her breasts. "And as I've already told you, that's a risk I'm prepared to take. Unlike most families, I am fairly convinced that mine will never throw me out simply because I bear a man's bastard."

He took a step toward her. "You know how I feel, and yet you chose to take me to your bed. We will be married."

"I scarcely *chose* to take you to bed, sir."

He tried to think back over the events of the previous night and couldn't pinpoint the exact moment when he'd found himself buried deep inside her, loving every erotic moment of it. Suddenly he felt sick. Was he as bad as his father? Had his true breeding finally shown itself?

"Are you suggesting I *forced* you? God, Lisette, I would never . . ."

She held his gaze. "There was no force involved; I came to you willingly enough, you know that. Yet it was hardly planned, was it? Neither of us set out to seduce the other, so neither of us is to blame."

He turned away from her to pace the carpet, hating the reasonable nature of her voice and her calm demeanor. "Then we will marry."

"Lord Swanfield, there is no need. We can continue to be lovers if you want, I'm quite happy to . . ."

He swung around to face her. "But I am not!"

Her face lost all expression and he felt it like a slap. Was she finding it as hard as he was not to show her feelings or was she simply not interested? She raised her chin. "Then perhaps you should just go."

Gabriel struggled to find even a modicum of control. "I can't do that. You might carry my child."

She sighed. "May I suggest a compromise? If I discover I'm carrying your child, I will let you know, and we can discuss the matter further."

"That isn't good enough!" Gabriel realized he was shouting as his temper finally shattered, only to spin around as the door opened behind him. Lord Knowles stood framed in the doorway, his expression lethal.

"Is there something I can help you with, Swanfield? Something that doesn't involve you terrifying my daughter?"

Gabriel bowed low as Lord Knowles came into the room, shut the door, and went to stand beside Lisette. "Good morning, my lord. I am not trying to frighten her at all; I merely wish to ask you for her hand in marriage."

"Is that true, Lisette?"

"Indeed it is, Papa. I have just been trying to explain to Lord Swanfield that we wouldn't suit."

Frustration laced with fear beat in Gabriel's chest and he wanted to choke on it. "I beg to differ, Miss Ross. In truth, we need to be married as soon as possible."

"Why is that, Swanfield?" Lord Knowles asked.

Lisette answered for him, her voice clear and hard. "Because Lord Swanfield is worried I might be carrying his child."

"Is that a possibility?"

"Of course it is," Gabriel interjected. "Otherwise why would I be here?"

Lord Knowles looked at him as though he were a mud fly. "Because you love her and wish to marry her for her many amazing attributes? This reluctant and grudging admission of having to marry to pay for your sins is hardly the kind of proposal any woman wishes to hear, Swanfield."

Gabriel swallowed hard and studied Lisette's composed face. Lord Knowle's words made him feel like a cad. "You're right, my lord. I wish to beg Miss Ross's pardon. She is indeed a wonderful woman."

Miss Ross glared at him. "He is only saying that because he has this old-fashioned notion that any child of his must be born in wedlock."

Lord Knowles looked at them both. "In truth, Lisette, for a man of his rank in this day and age, I think that is quite admirable."

"Papa . . ."

Gabriel pressed the small advantage. "Then you agree that we should be married, sir?"

"Hold on a moment, Swanfield." Lord Knowles addressed his daughter. "Are you carrying his child, Lisette?"

"How would I know? He only bedded me last night."

"That's not the point," Gabriel said urgently. "I don't wish for anyone to doubt my child's parentage."

"Are you so certain you are that potent?" Lisette asked. "What happens if you force me to marry you and then I never get pregnant?"

Gabriel sighed. "Then we will be married and I will do my duty by you regardless. What else do you want me to say?"

"Your *duty*?"

Lord Knowles cleared his throat. "Lord Swanfield, perhaps it would be best if you waited to find out if Lisette does indeed carry your child before sacrificing yourself to the institution of matrimony."

"But I don't want to wait."

"And I don't want to marry you."

He met her eyes and read the determination and strength in them, hoping she saw the same in his gaze. "I can see that any further discussion on this subject will not get me anywhere this morning." He nodded at Lord Philip. "Perhaps you might help Miss Ross come to a better decision without my presence."

"I'll certainly discuss the matter with her, Swanfield, but be aware that I'll support whatever decision she makes, without question."

Gabriel bowed low. "I understand that, sir. All I ask is that you keep me informed." He turned to Lisette who was regarding him most suspiciously. "Good morning, Miss Ross."

"Are you leaving? Just like that?"

He shrugged. "What else would you have me do? I can scarcely throw you over my shoulder with your father watching me."

He turned and left the room, nodded at the butler, and made his way down the stone steps into the freedom of the morning. He might not be able to drag Lisette off when her father was watching her, but there were other ways to achieve his aims. His steps slowed. If he wanted to win, being the perfect gentleman wasn't necessarily the best way to go about it. And he wanted to win very badly indeed.

Lisette gazed after Gabriel, her mouth open. "I can't believe he gave up so easily."

"Do you feel insulted?"

"No, not like that." Lisette paused, uncertain of how much of Gabriel's personal business to divulge. "Lord Swanfield's birth was not well managed and he feels it deeply."

Her father gave her a sidelong glance as he strolled toward the door. "Are you defending him now? You should've thought about whether he was a man of his word before you took him to your bed."

She sighed. "What occurred between us last night wasn't planned at all. It just happened."

"And he is a man who stands by his responsibilities and his convictions."

"I know that. It is one of the things I've always liked about him."

Philip opened the door to the breakfast room and held out a

chair for her. When she was seated he sat in the seat closest to hers and took her hand. "Would he really make such an objectionable husband? He has principles, wealth, a title . . ."

"A cloudy reputation, an inflated opinion of his own worth, and an extremely bad temper."

"Yet you went to bed with him."

"Yes, I did." Lisette sighed. "And I would do so again."

Philip patted her hand. "Perhaps after you break your fast, you should go and talk this through with your mother. She is invaluable in matters of the heart."

"That's excellent advice, Papa." Lisette withdrew her hand and poured herself some coffee. If anyone could see a way out of her dilemma, it would be Helene, a woman no man, save her father, had ever managed to master or successfully deceive.

13

Gabriel looked up as Paul St. Clare came into the dining room of his lodgings. He was wearing his patched coat, and from the look of his whiskers, he hadn't shaved for a few days either. "Ah, Paul, I need your help."

Paul sat opposite him at the table, his brown eyes alight with interest. He picked an apple from the fruit bowl and polished it on his shirtsleeve. "With what, exactly?"

"I'm planning an elopement."

"I beg your pardon?"

Gabriel smiled grimly. "You heard me."

"And what part am I to play in this charade? The damsel in distress?"

"No, you are going to be the bait. You know the damsel I have in mind, and I need you to lure her into my trap."

Paul sat back and regarded him steadily. "Have you gone completely mad?"

"No."

"Are you sure?"

"Yes."

"Then of course I'll help you. Although I find it difficult to understand why you can't simply ask the woman to marry you in church in front of her family like any other gentleman."

"I've already asked her." Gabriel gathered up the maps and documentation in front of him and stuffed them into a leather wallet.

"And she refused you?"

"She did."

"So you are going to abduct her." Paul cleared his throat. "And you don't care that this might finally destroy your already rickety social reputation, let alone the reputation of the woman who is stuck being married to you?"

Gabriel smiled slowly. "I'm sure everything will work out perfectly." He rose to his feet and nodded at Paul. "Be ready to help me on Thursday around noon. I have a few errands to run today to make sure that everything is settled."

"I'm sure you do," Paul muttered as Gabriel walked past him.

"And keep this to yourself," Gabriel added, slapping Paul's shoulder. "It's complicated enough as it is without all my friends being aware of it."

"Don't worry, I'll keep quiet." Paul winked and sank his teeth into the polished green skin of the apple. "As long as you tell me all the gory details on your return."

"There won't be any gory details. If things proceed as planned, we'll all have nothing to worry about."

"As long as you don't get shot by her enraged father."

Gabriel ignored Paul's last comment and headed out to the stables. Admittedly, his plan had some flaws, depending as it did on the cooperation of some of the most unlikely allies he could think of. But it had to work. His future with Lisette and the fate of his potential child was too important to contemplate failure.

He glanced at his pocket watch and groaned. He had a meeting at his solicitor's office in fifteen minutes, and he hated to be late. It seemed that at long last some progress had been made with the Granger family.

As he mounted up, it also occurred to him that his solicitor might like to know he was getting married and that he'd need to draw up a new will reversing his decision about the Grangers inheriting directly. Ah, but he was getting too far ahead of himself. His bride was scarcely in his trap yet. . . .

Lisette gave her brother a cool glance. "I would prefer to talk to Maman by myself."

On her father's advice, she'd come back to the pleasure house to speak to Helene, only to find Christian ensconced in her mother's office as well.

"I know that, but I'd like to stay."

"Why? So that you can tell me that I deserve everything that has happened to me?"

Christian sighed. "Lis, I know we're not getting along at the moment, but you are my twin and I care about you. If I promise not to interfere in the conversation unless I feel it is absolutely necessary, will you let me stay?"

Lisette glanced at her mother, who nodded encouragingly. "All right, then, but please let me tell you everything before either of you say a word."

Briefly Lisette outlined what had happened that morning at Philip's house, Lord Swanfield's insistence of marrying her, and her reluctance to agree. Helene listened quietly, her expression calm, her hands folded together on the desk in front of her.

"So what do you think I should do, Maman?"

"You are considering his proposal then?"

Lisette felt herself flush. "I am trying to consider all my options."

"You know that even if you are pregnant, your father and I will always support you?"

"Yes."

"Then obviously, at least on your side, you feel there is more to this proposal from Lord Swanfield than just duty."

Lisette shifted uncomfortably in her chair. "Lord Swanfield has some very deep personal reasons for wishing any child of his to be born in wedlock."

"And you agree with his reasons?"

Lisette bit her lip. "I'm not sure if I agree with them, but I certainly *understand* them."

"Would he be willing to wait to see if you really are pregnant before pursuing his suit?"

"I suggested that and he didn't take it very well." Lisette tried to smile. "Even when I mentioned that neither of us might be capable of having children, he wouldn't be shaken off."

Helene rose from her chair and paced the carpet, her brow crinkled in thought. Then she stopped, sat opposite Lisette, and took her hand. "But if he married you, and you proved to be barren, he'd have no heir."

"He told me once that he didn't want an heir, that he hoped the title would die out with him or pass to another branch of the family."

"And yet he wants to marry you."

Lisette looked into her mother's sympathetic eyes. "You know why he comes here, Maman, and you know what he does to avoid having a full sexual relationship with a woman."

"But he *now* has that relationship with *you*."

Lisette shrugged. "There were reasons for his behavior last night; he wasn't quite himself. . . ."

"Are you making excuses for him *raping* you?" Christian asked softly, his tone so full of menace that both Helene and Lisette spun around to stare at him. "Have you started to believe that is all you deserve from a man?"

"Lord Swanfield didn't rape me. I was more than happy to

be his bed partner. In truth, I'm the one who is responsible for him being anywhere *near* my bed last night."

"So *you* raped *him*?"

Lisette smiled reluctantly at her brother. "No, it was a mutual decision."

"Well, that's good then, or else I'd have to be paying him a visit this afternoon."

Helene reclaimed Lisette's attention by placing a hand on her arm. "It sounds as if you are in an impossible situation, but I'm sure there's hope. We can help you disappear for a couple of months until you know whether you really are pregnant. Then you will have the freedom to make your decision without Lord Swanfield glowering at you."

"I suppose that is the best thing I can do." Lisette sighed. "Lord Swanfield is not the sort of man who would sit back and wait for me to make my choice. I suspect even if I moved in here he'd be haunting the place demanding an answer every hour."

"Don't worry, love, between us, your father and I will keep you safe."

"I know, but it also means that I'll have to miss Emily's entrance into society." Lisette grimaced. She didn't want to run to her parents for help again, but it seemed she had no choice. "I suppose it can't be helped, unless you can miraculously find another woman for Lord Swanfield to bed and marry?"

At the thought of Gabriel with another woman, Lisette's smile faded. She'd hate to see that, to see all Gabriel Swanfield's prime male attention focused on another woman.

The clock on the mantelpiece chimed the half hour and Helene jumped to her feet. "Lisette, I'm so sorry, but I have to consult with Madame Durand. Will you wait with Christian until I come back?"

"Of course, Maman, and thank you for your help."

Helene kissed her cheek and hugged her tightly. "We will sort this out, my love, don't ever doubt it."

After Helene left, Lisette glanced at Christian, who was regarding her lazily from his chair. "You can say what you want, now. I'm quite prepared for you to tell me I'm a fool."

"I don't think you are a fool. I think you got exactly what you wanted all along."

"What is that supposed to mean?"

Christian uncurled himself from his seat with all the grace and poise of a cat. "I think you want Swanfield, Lis."

"I do want him. I'm not ashamed to admit it. He is the best lover I've ever had." He shook his head as if she was being stupid and her temper sparked. "You think I wanted him to marry me all along?"

"Not all along, but I think somewhere inside you, the fact that he is *willing* to marry you agrees with you."

"Because I want to be married so badly?"

He came across the room and sat opposite her, his hazel gaze locked with hers.

"Yes, because deep down that's what we both want, isn't it? Someone who will stay with us. And it's not surprising, really, when we were abandoned before we were even born. The fact that Swanfield is prepared to marry you simply on the off chance that you might carry his child is very appealing to you."

"I don't resent our parents for not marrying, I don't."

"Hell, I do. Father marches off in a huff and marries someone else within three weeks of fucking our mother, and our mother doesn't bother to tell him we even exist for eighteen years? It bloody bothers me."

She searched his eyes, saw the lack of forgiveness burning there that he normally hid so well. "They did the best they could in the circumstances."

Christian exhaled hard. "I know that, and as an adult I even understand it, but it doesn't change how I feel inside." He leaned forward and took her hand. "If a woman came to me and said she carried my child, I'd do exactly what Swanfield wants to do. I'd marry her in a heartbeat."

He wiped at her cheek and she realized she was crying. "If you want him, Lis, have him. I'm certain he will do everything in his power to keep you safe."

"Now you've just confused me even more, *and* you've made me cry," Lisette whispered.

"Don't I always?" His wry smile was full of love. "Marry him tomorrow; don't wait until you know if you carry his child. The way you feel about him shows on your face and makes you look even more beautiful than usual." He kissed her nose. "I see it in you, twin. I only wish that one day I could find someone to put that look on my face."

"You will."

"I doubt it." He sighed.

"Christian? What if it *is* just duty for Lord Swanfield and he is incapable of loving me?"

"As Maman so wisely pointed out, when a man who insists he will never have sex or marry breaks all his own rules, he must do so knowingly, whether he realizes it at the time or not."

"Is that what Maman said?"

Christian sat back in his seat and smiled. "That was what she meant. Lord Swanfield has made his own bed, so to speak, and I would wager he is quite happy to lie in it."

Lisette got up and regarded her brother. "I thought he took his dismissal this morning far too lightly."

"Then I would be careful, my sweet. A man like that who served under the great Duke of Wellington is unlikely to see an orderly retreat as a complete disaster. He's probably just regrouping his forces for a fresh attack."

"Thank you, Christian." Lisette blew her brother a kiss. "I have a lot to think about."

He came across and embraced her fiercely. "Good-bye, love, and I wish you much happiness."

She scowled at him. "I haven't decided to marry him yet."

"Good for you, make him beg."

Lisette's smile died. "I already did that and look where I ended up."

"Where you wanted to be," he reminded her gently. She found she had nothing else to say and decided to escape down to the kitchen where the comforts of Madame Durand's cooking would help her forget her cares for at least an hour or so. Or, at least, she hoped it would.

Gabriel entered his solicitor's office with a smile that rapidly faded when he saw who else was sitting by the fire.

"Ah, good morning, my lord," Mr. Brecon said cheerily, his round face flushed as red as his balding head. "I hope you are well."

Gabriel removed his hat and gloves and shook Mr. Brecon's hand. "Quite well, sir."

William Granger shot to his feet and bowed. He wore his uniform and highly polished boots as if he had just come off parade. "I'm sure you wish me to the devil, cousin, but I thought you might at least hear me out in this more neutral setting."

Gabriel took a seat and gestured for the other men to do the same. "It depends on what you have to say."

William took a deep breath. "I'm sure you won't believe this, but until you told me, I had no idea that my military commission had been paid for by your estate."

Gabriel shrugged. "Why would you? Your father controls the money, not you."

William cleared his throat. "What I'm trying to say is that my father hasn't always been very . . . clear about how he differentiates between your money and his own."

Gabriel looked hard at William. For his cousin to say such a negative thing about his father's management of the Swanfield estates was unheard of. "I know that, too. This is why I've been trying to gain full control over my estate for the past five years."

"He is getting old and I fear his reasoning is not quite as astute as it once was." William grimaced. "Now I sound as if I'm trying to make excuses for him, and I'm not. He took on a lot of responsibility for you when the old earl died."

"And I am more than willing to take that load from his shoulders. The problem is, he seems loathe to relinquish it."

William looked up and his gaze met Gabriel's properly for the first time. "If I endeavor to persuade him to give up the estate books to you, will you promise not to ruin him?"

"You think the situation is that bad?"

"I'm not sure, but I know you have many reasons to be vindictive."

"You recognize that now, do you? The fact that I was sent away to an inferior school for 'difficult boys' while you and Michael enjoyed Harrow? That I wasn't even allowed home during the holidays? That my mother . . ."

Abruptly Gabriel stopped speaking. This was no time to air his grievances. The chance to take complete ownership of the Swanfield estates was far too big a prize to let slip through his grasp.

"I will not ruin him."

William visibly exhaled. "Thank you. Then I will do everything in my power to persuade him to hand over the books."

Gabriel sat back and studied his cousin. "Why the sudden change of heart, William?"

His cousin stood up and bowed stiffly. "Because the estate

needs someone to run it, and if my father is no longer capable, then it will have to be you."

"It still galls you that I succeeded to the title, doesn't it?"

"Of course it does, but not perhaps for the reasons you might believe. I was raised to run a large estate and trained to think of myself as the caretaker for future generations. It *galls* me to see the estate go to ruin under bad or indifferent management." He glared at Gabriel. "If you do take the reins, cousin, I will expect you to fulfill your obligations to the people who depend on you."

Gabriel looked up at his cousin's obstinate face. For once, he actually believed William meant every word. He could even understand his passion for the land and his heritage. Guilt eased into his gut and he tried to fight it off.

"When I'm in control, I will endeavor to be a good manager of the estate."

"You will visit there regularly?"

Gabriel raised his eyebrows. "I'll do what I have to. You have my word on it." William stuck out his hand and Gabriel shook it. "Get me the financial records for the estate and at least I'll know where I stand."

"Thank you."

William headed for the door and Gabriel stood up. "No, thank you, for being brave enough to bring this matter to my attention and for your willingness to do what's right for the people on the estate who have no voice."

William shrugged, his color heightened. "Don't make me out to be some kind of hero, Gabriel. I still don't like you."

"The feeling is mutual. I might be away for the next week or two, so if you have anything new to tell me, please communicate through Mr. Brecon."

"Of course, cousin." William saluted and then was gone, his booted feet clomping down the narrow wooden staircase.

Gabriel smiled at Mr. Brecon. "Let's hope that Captain Granger will be able to assist us."

"Let's hope so indeed, sir." Mr. Brecon positively beamed with good cheer. "Now, is there anything else we need to discuss?"

Gabriel nodded. "I'm planning on getting married, so I need to revise my will and any other documents you see fit."

"Married, sir? You? May I be the first to offer you my congratulations?"

"Indeed." Gabriel nodded. "It is obviously a day for surprises. If there are any messages for me in the next week, please leave them with Mr. Keyes at my lodgings."

"Yes, sir. And will you be reopening Swanfield House for your lady wife?"

Gabriel picked up his hat and gloves. "I hadn't thought about it. I'll let you know on my return."

"Excellent, sir. I'll look out the spare keys for the property and make a list of the new staff you will require."

"Thank you," Gabriel said and turned to leave. Thoughts about the estate and the reluctant truce between him and William filled his mind. To finally control his heritage was something he'd dreamed about for years. After his return from Spain, he'd allowed ill health and his reluctance to provoke further scandal to scupper his attempts to establish himself. The Grangers believed him to be weak and unstable, but devil take it, William was right, the estate was in his trust. He finally had the power to rewrite the past. . . .

Gabriel put on his hat and contemplated the leaden skies. He could only hope that the luck from his first meeting would carry him throughout the day. He had a suspicion that his next encounter might be a lot more difficult. With sudden resolve, he turned his horse back toward Mayfair.

By the time he reached the discreet mews at the back of the house, it had started to rain steadily. He handed his horse over to a groom and took stock of his bearings. If he remembered correctly, the kitchens and basement that connected the two buildings were accessed from behind the mews. Without waiting for direction, Gabriel headed toward the servants' door, moving through a cluttered passageway and into the warm, scented kitchen. He halted at the entranceway until a large woman he assumed was the cook questioned him in French.

As he started to reply, another voice cut him off. He turned to see a tall, fair-haired man regarding him coldly.

"Lord Swanfield, I presume."

"Indeed." Gabriel inclined his head a deliberate inch. "And who are you?"

"I'm Christian Delornay-Ross. Although I don't use the Ross surname." A flicker of amusement crossed the other man's face. "Don't you remember the people you've had sex with here?"

Gabriel managed to hold onto his temper. "I would certainly remember you."

"And you don't, which is all well and good, seeing as you are currently involved with my twin." Delornay came closer, his expression still far from friendly. "Did you come here today to relieve your frustration because my sister is proving difficult?"

Gabriel set his jaw. "I came to see Madame Delornay."

"She isn't here." Delornay closed the gap between them and studied Gabriel. "But I'm glad you're here. I thought I was going to have to come to your lodgings."

"You wished to speak to me?"

Delornay's smile was not meant to reassure. "Didn't I just mention that you are in a relationship with my twin? Don't you think I take an interest in the men she sleeps with?"

"I'm not going to abandon her like that other bastard did, if that's what you mean."

"Good, because I'd hate to have to take another man out and beat him senseless."

Gabriel smiled slowly. "I doubt you'd beat me."

Hazel eyes that reminded Gabriel of Lisette met and clashed with his. Christian smiled back. "That, my lord, remains to be seen. Now, if there is something you wished to say to my mother, perhaps you'll consider unburdening yourself to me instead."

14

Lisette tied the blue ribbons of her new lutestring bonnet and studied her reflection critically in the mirror. She looked far too pale for her liking, so she pinched her cheeks and added some rose lip paint her mother had given her. She heaved a sigh and buttoned herself into the matching lutestring pelisse.

The weather looked as changeable as her mood, but she decided that the invitation for a walk in the park with an intimate friend of Lord Swanfield was definitely worth the chance of a soaking. It had been two days since she had last seen or heard from him, and his silence was becoming ominous. She gathered up her reticule and gloves and made her way downstairs. Her father was stationed in the hall as if waiting for her to descend.

"Ah, there you are, my dear. Are you going out?"

"Lieutenant St. Clare asked me to go for a walk in the park with him and his cousin, Lucinda, the young lady we met at the ball. I thought I might ask her to visit us when Emily is in residence."

"That's an excellent idea." Philip smiled and kissed her cheek, kissed her again and patted her shoulder.

"I was just trying to help, Papa." Lisette eyed him uncertainly. "It's not as if she's the heir to the throne or anything."

Philip's smile was warm. "Just enjoy your walk, my dear, and give Lieutenant St. Clare my best."

"I will." Lisette headed for the front door just as the butler opened it to reveal a smiling Lieutenant St. Clare. "Good-bye, Papa."

"And good morning, Miss Ross." The lieutenant swept her a low bow and stepped aside to reveal his smaller companion. "Miss Ross, may I present my cousin, Lady Lucinda Haymore?"

Lisette held out her hand. "It is a pleasure to see you again, my lady."

"Oh please, call me Lucinda, everyone does." Lady Lucinda's smile was warm and a little shy. "Well, apart from Paul, who calls me 'Lucky.' "

Lieutenant St. Clare offered them both an arm and headed down the steps toward the flagstone pavement. "I promise I won't call you that during your grand Season."

"Thank you, I think." The bashful glance Lady Lucinda shot at the lieutenant was full of awe. "It would be nice if it remained just between ourselves."

Lisette wondered if Paul St. Clare knew that his cousin was a little in love with him. Was he the sort of man who would marry simply to avoid any scandal about his sexual preferences— or would he be brave and stay a bachelor? Lisette sensed that he wouldn't want to hurt his cousin, who obviously held him in high affection.

Wind gusted around the corner and Lisette let go of Lieutenant St. Clare's arm to grab at the brim of her bonnet. It wasn't raining, but the sky was turning an unpleasant pewter gray, which threatened to obscure even the meager sunlight. They turned onto the main thoroughfare, and Lisette saw the green shimmer of the park up ahead.

A carriage and four horses rumbled slowly up the street behind them and Lieutenant St. Clare glanced back and maneuvered his cousin away from the curb. Lisette moved away by herself and was surprised when the lieutenant took her arm in a firm grip.

For a moment he stared down at her. "I'm sorry, Miss Ross."

Before she could answer him, he picked her up. As she started to struggle, the carriage door flew open and a pair of gloved hands reached out and took her weight, bringing her inside the carriage. The door shut again and she tried to straighten, only to be brought back down to the floor and have a thick shawl thrown over her head. While she struggled to free herself, the carriage picked up speed and headed back down toward the river.

A heavy weight settled on her back, effectively pinning her to the floor. Was that his boot? Lisette set her teeth and counted the minutes until he would have to set her free. Her fingernails curled into her palms until they hurt, but not as much as they would hurt him when she launched herself at his face.

Time moved on, and she focused on steadying her breath and easing her position to avoid cramping her muscles. Eventually the carriage slowed, and she was lifted up and set on the seat. As soon as the shawl was plucked from her head, she went for him, claws at the ready, anger and fright bonded together into a rage she had never experienced before.

"*Salaud*! You *charogne* . . ."

Lord Swanfield fended her off far too easily and held her trapped in his grasp. She gave up trying to scratch out his eyes and tried to bite and kick instead. When her booted foot connected with his shin and he hissed out a curse, she felt a surge of pure joy.

"Lisette, stop it."

"Why should I? You worm, you despicable rake, you . . ."

"I am all those things." He agreed far too easily and yet he wasn't laughing at her. "I am behaving appallingly."

"Then take me home!" She wrenched herself free of his grasp and sat back with a thump on the seat opposite him, her breathing harsh and her mind in turmoil. How dare he snatch her from the street in broad daylight? And how quickly would someone raise the alarm and come and rescue her?

She raised her chin. "Where are we going?"

"To Scotland." His gaze was steady, his hands linked together between his thighs. "We can marry there."

"I am not going to marry you."

He shrugged. But before she could say another word, he held up his hand. "Please, I'd rather wait until we stop for the night to have this out properly, wouldn't you?"

She glared at him as he sat back and appeared to relax in his corner. The carriage was moving swiftly now, so she guessed they were on the main North Road. There would be little chance of escaping while they were traveling—or even when they were stopped. She recalled with dismay that Lord Swanfield moved rather fast for such a tall, indolent man.

With a sigh, she took off her mangled bonnet, angled her body into the corner of the seat, and glared at him. He appeared to be going to sleep, but she sensed it wouldn't take much to wake him. She would spend the rest of their journey together imagining every horrible way she might torture him and had hoped he could see it in her eyes.

She awoke with a start to find herself being carried into an inn, her head again swathed in the black shawl, the rest of her held firmly in Lord Swanfield's arms. She heard jovial voices and learned that they had been expected and that their rooms were ready. She clutched at Lord Swanfield's shoulder as he adjusted his grip and started climbing the stairs. The landlord went ahead of him, sharing details of the dinner he would bring up and his hopes for the lady's swift recovery.

"Thank you, Hodges, my wife suffers from carriage sickness. She will be perfectly fine after a bite to eat."

"Thank you, my lord. Your dinner will be up shortly."

The door shut behind the landlord and the black shawl was eased away from Lisette's face. She allowed her head to fall onto Lord Swanfield's shoulder and cuddled close.

"Ah, Lisette," he murmured. "That's better."

She bit down hard on his earlobe and he dropped her so fast that she bounced on the bed before he came down over her, his expression extremely unfriendly.

"That hurt."

"It was supposed to. Now let me up."

His eyes narrowed. "I don't think I will. You're just going to go for me again."

"So? What did you expect? A kiss?"

"Why not?" He fitted his mouth over hers and she nipped at his lip. He drew back and glared down at her. "If you want to sit up and eat your dinner like a civilized person, you have to promise not to hurt me anymore."

"I'm not promising anything."

"Then I'll tie you to the bed, draw the covers over you, and feed you myself!"

She stared at him for a long moment. If he was willing to talk to her, there was still a chance she could make him change his mind. She wasn't above using some female tricks of her own to get what she wanted.

"All right. Let's call a truce until after we've eaten."

He let out his breath and climbed off her, allowing her to sit up. Her hands went to her hair. "How am I supposed to make myself look civilized when you have treated me like a sack of potatoes?"

He indicated a small dressing table in the corner of the room and a discreet screen. "There are brushes on the table and warm water in the jug, as well as the necessary. Please help yourself."

"While you watch?"

A smile flickered on his face. "As long as you don't try and jump out of the window, I'm not going to stand over you while you relieve yourself, if that is what you mean."

She shuffled off the bed. Her left knee was aching badly and she stumbled. He caught her in an instant.

"What's wrong?"

She bit her lip. "When you flung me onto the floor of the carriage I banged my knee. I'm sure it will be fine shortly."

"Let me see."

He sat down on the bed, put her on his lap, and pulled up her skirts and petticoats. Lisette tried to slap his hand away as it closed over her ruined stocking and pulled that down, too. "Lord Swanfield!"

He ignored her, his fingers gentle as he discovered the rapidly blackening bruise on her knee. He bent his head and kissed it. "God, I'm sorry, Lisette. I never meant to hurt you."

She shoved at his shoulder and slid out of his lap. "Then you shouldn't have abducted me, should you?"

He stayed on the bed as she hobbled over toward the dressing table. With another forbidding glance over her shoulder, she went behind the screen to do what was necessary and then returned to wash her hands and face and contemplate the ruin of her hairstyle in the faded, rust-spotted mirror.

With a sigh, she started unpinning her hair and then set about brushing it using the silver-backed brush and comb set out on the dressing table. Her head was aching, so rather than attempt an elaborate style without the aid of her maid, she twisted her hair back into a simple knot at the back of her neck and pinned it deftly into place.

By the time she finished, there was the distinct sound of activity in the hallway and the aroma of cooked food wafted under the door. Lisette realized she had no idea what time it was, only that she hadn't eaten since breakfast time and it was now dark outside. A knock on the door signaled the arrival of dinner and Lisette waited as two maids brought in the food and laid it out on the small table beside the fire.

"We'll bring up some tea in a while, my lady," the younger of the two women said shyly.

Lisette smiled. "Thank you, I would appreciate that, and also anything you might have to ease my headache."

Lord Swanfield frowned. "You are still unwell?"

Lisette ignored him and concentrated her attention on the serving maids, who were whispering together.

"Mrs. Hodges has a tisane she brews herself, my lady. Would you like to try that?"

"Yes, please, but there is no hurry, bring it up with the tea."

"Yes, my lady." The maids curtsied and left them alone.

Lord Swanfield stood up and bowed. "My lady?" He held out a chair for her.

"I am not your lady."

He sighed and took his seat. "I thought we weren't going to fight until after we'd eaten."

"No, I said I wouldn't *injure* you. Verbal sparring is perfectly acceptable."

"May I serve you some beef?"

"No, thank you."

He applied himself to the meal, heaping his own plate with the pigeon pie, cold beef, and roasted potatoes. Without comment, he poured two glasses of the red wine and slid one across to Lisette. She was too hungry to object and settled to eating without complaint, finishing her meal with some stewed apples and clotted cream.

A knock on the door heralded the arrival of one of the serving maids with coffee, a pot of tea, and another mug containing a pale green herbal brew.

"Mrs. Hodges says drink it while it's hot."

"I will and please thank her for me," Lisette replied. She

picked up the earthenware mug and inhaled the scent of chamomile and willow bark. She sipped cautiously at the brew, found it sweetened with honey, and took another swallow.

Lord Swanfield helped himself to coffee and then sat watching her as he drank it. Lisette closed her eyes and allowed the aroma of chamomile to soothe her disordered senses.

"Are you all right, Miss Ross?"

"For a man who has just brutally abducted me, you sound remarkably concerned."

He sighed. "I never meant to hurt you. You must know that."

She opened her eyes. "And my original answer still stands: then don't kidnap me."

He looked remarkably unrepentant. "But it was the only way I could have you."

She put the mug down. "I already told you that if I am pregnant, I'll let you know and we can take up our discussion again."

"But what if you aren't sure for four or five months? Some women aren't. My mother was so ignorant she had no idea she was with child until the butler noticed the size of her belly." He leaned forward and stared down at his linked fingers. "What if you are pregnant and we don't marry until you are that far along? Everyone will know that our child was conceived out of wedlock."

"So what?"

He reached for her hand and held it between his. "Lisette, we both know how it feels to be gossiped about. Would you really want to inflict that on our child?"

She thought back to the insults of the other children at the orphanage, the fights she and Christian had gotten into, the subtle dislike of the nuns and the snubs from the cream of English society . . . "But I might not be pregnant."

"I know. It is a difficult decision, isn't it?"

He sounded so reasonable and sympathetic she found herself tempted to agree with him. And there was something to be said for a man who stood by his responsibilities. . . .

But he *had* abducted her. She forced a sigh. "It is hard to be wanted for only one reason."

"What do you mean?"

She pulled out of his grasp. "You only asked to marry me because you feared I carried your child."

"Yes, but—"

"But *nothing*. My father was right. No woman wants to feel that she is merely a brood mare."

"I don't think of you in those terms, in fact—"

"And what happens when you have your heir? Will I be forced to give you a dozen other children as well?"

His blue eyes narrowed and a sense of satisfaction blossomed within her as his voice rose.

"Miss Ross. I swore never to marry and never to have a child and the fact that I am contemplating doing *both* says more about how I feel about you than you could ever imagine!"

She looked at him through her eyelashes. "I don't believe you."

He shot to his feet, reached across the table and picked her up, marched over to the bed, and dropped her on it. She pretended to struggle while he rucked up her skirts and wedged his wide shoulders between her thighs.

"Believe this."

His mouth descended over her sex and he licked at her clit, his tongue swirling and stabbing between her folds until she was wet and arching up against him. He drew back, his mouth wet with her juices, his eyes intent. "I want to lick your cunt every day, slide my fingers deep, and make you come so hard you scream my name and beg for my cock. Does that sound like I am marrying you for your breeding capabilities?"

She gasped as he slid two fingers inside her and worked them back and forth. His intent gaze flicked between her face and his fingers. She tried to reach for him, to dig her nails into his skin so that he would feel what he was doing to her. He added two more fingers and used the palm of his hand to torment her clit as he slammed into her.

"Gabriel . . ." She moaned.

He stopped, his fingers embedded deep and his palm cupping her mound. "Tell me you believe me now. Tell me this is what you want."

His mouth returned to add to her torment and she could no longer stop her climax flooding through her. He held himself still as she arched against his hand, waited for her to go still, and then licked her clit again.

She tried to pull away from his tongue but there was nowhere for her to go. Without removing his fingers from inside her, he unbuttoned his breeches with his left hand and climbed carefully onto the bed. He straddled her so that his head was parallel with hers. She grabbed at his hair and pulled it hard.

"Marriage isn't just about sex either, though, is it? Just because we do this well together doesn't mean we should get married."

He gazed down at her. "You can do without this?" He reached down to grasp his cock and knelt up until he was able to brush the swollen wet crown against her lips. "You think another man can make you feel like this?"

She clung to his arm. "I don't know! It's possible."

His eyes widened and he bent to kiss her, his mouth possessing hers so completely that she could do nothing but accept him and kiss him back. When he pulled away she was shaking and so was he.

"I can't do without that, Lisette. I can't think of anyone but you. I want it all."

She studied him carefully and tried to control her ragged breathing. "I'm not eloping with you."

He sucked in a breath and then stared at her until all traces of emotion were removed from his face. "What do you want me to do?"

"I want you to take me back to London."

He rolled away from her and rebuttoned his breeches, walked across to the abandoned dinner table, and poured himself another glass of red wine. What was he supposed to do now? Abandon his plan or allow it to unfold as he'd wanted it to, without the surety of her marrying him at the end of it?

He had no choice. In truth, there was already the sound of a commotion in the hall below. He walked across to the fireplace and turned to face the door as it flew open to reveal Christian Delornay, a pistol in his hand and a murderous expression on his face.

"Swanfield, you bastard."

"Ah, Mr. Delornay-Ross. Please come in and shut the door."

An explosion of petticoats on the bed meant that Lisette had righted herself.

"Christian, what on earth are you doing here?"

"Rescuing you, I believe." Christian nodded at his twin. "After I've taken care of this blaggard, of course."

Gabriel scowled. "I'm not fighting you."

Christian uncocked the pistol. "That's all right, because you're not enough of a gentleman to waste a bullet on. I'd rather just shoot you in the back like the coward you are."

"I'm no coward either. Unlike you, I'm simply concerned for your sister's reputation. Fighting a duel over her will scarcely help."

"Strange how you've suddenly thought about that," Christian sneered. "Now that you've been caught abducting her."

Gabriel took a step toward Delornay. "I want to marry her, not ruin her. Can't the pair of you get that into your thick heads?"

Lisette moved past him to stand beside her twin. "We are not stupid, sir!"

He met her gaze and held it. "I know that." He bowed to Christian and forced out the words. "She wants to go home. Perhaps it would be better if you took her."

"It would be my pleasure, sir." Christian jerked his chin at Lisette. "Gather your belongings, twin."

Gabriel tensed as Lisette stepped between them. "Will you excuse us for a moment, Lord Swanfield?"

"Of course. I'll be down in the taproom if you need me." It took all his courage to walk away from her, to leave her to make her choice, to trust that somehow she'd choose him despite his clumsy handling of the whole affair.

Lisette watched Gabriel leave, his expression bleak, his eyes so sad than she wanted to cry. She swallowed hard as Christian smiled at her.

"Shall we go?"

She studied his face. "How did you know that I was here?"

He shrugged. "By a process of elimination. After you disappeared, I talked to everyone who knew Lord Swanfield, including his groom, and discovered his plans. Then I borrowed one of Father's best horses and set off after you."

"Then how am I supposed to go back with you?"

"We'll take Lord Swanfield's coach and leave him my horse." Christian looked around the room. "Do you have anything at all to bring?"

Lisette shook her head. "I'm not coming."

Christian halted by the door. "What?"

"I'd just decided to marry him after all. I was in the middle of making him declare his feelings to me when you walked in." She swallowed hard. "And now he's being all ridiculously noble and offering to let me go with you because he thinks I meant what I said."

Christian frowned. "Lis, he's a man. If you told him you didn't want him, of course he'll believe you."

"But it's supposed to be part of the game."

"What game?"

"The game of love."

Christian looked disgusted. "God, I'll never understand women and their stupid games. If you want him, stay with him. If you don't, come home with me, now."

"I think I'll stay then."

Christian sighed. "Are you sure?"

"Yes." She smiled tremulously at him. "I am."

He drew her into a hug and kissed her cheek. "Make very sure you mean it this time, because I don't think Swanfield is a man to play too many games with, do you?"

"I'm sure." She kissed his forehead. "Now go home and tell everyone that everything will be all right."

He bowed. "I'm not telling anyone anything. This is one scandal I'll try to forget. Take care, Lis."

She watched him leave and sat down on the bed. After half an hour ticked by and her anticipation turned to irritation, a huge yawn shook through her. She stripped off her clothes and went to bed. She didn't have the energy to wait for Gabriel to return—if he ever did. Perhaps she should simply go to sleep and await his reaction to her presence in the morning.

15

Gabriel sat outside the inn and slowly smoked his second cigarillo. It was far too cold to be out, but he'd lived through far worse in Spain. He blew out a cloud of smoke and watched the wind whip it away across the barren fields. A tankard of ale sat at his elbow, and he forced himself to drink it coughing when he realized the helpful landlord had added a tot of brandy.

He'd like to get drunk now, to submerge himself in misery and try and forget what a fool he'd been. But he wasn't a pleasant drunk; he became far too violent, as if the alcohol unleashed the most secret of his fears and horrors and made him see them in other innocent faces. So he wouldn't drink any more than the tankard of ale and then he'd go to bed.

Alone.

With a sigh, he stubbed out his cigarillo on the stone wall and headed back up the stairs. At least Lisette and her obnoxious twin should be halfway back to London by now.

The inn was quieter as well, the taproom deserted, the fire banked for the night with peat. He'd almost expected Hodges to come and inquire as to what was going on, but the landlord had proved remarkably discreet, no doubt in hope of a suitable financial addition to his bill.

Gabriel opened the door to his bedchamber and breathed in the subtle scent of Lisette's rose perfume. The candles had been extinguished, so he undressed in front of the fire and headed for bed. It wasn't until he tried to pull back the covers that he discovered it was already occupied.

With all the care he could muster, he eased between the sheets and gently rolled Lisette onto her back. He could barely make out the shape of her features, so he bent his head and traced the outline of her nose with his finger, his heart beating so hard he thought it might burst.

He felt the brush of her eyelashes against the back of his hand as she opened her eyes. He kissed her forehead.

"You stayed."

Her fingers drifted across his unshaven cheek and settled by his jaw. "Yes, but only for tonight."

"What does that mean?" he whispered. He was almost too afraid to speak in case he broke the spell of her presence and found he was dreaming.

"I still want you to take me back to London."

He sighed against her throat, felt her swallow. "Then why not go with your brother?"

"Because I want you to take me."

"So that your father can shoot me in cold blood?"

"No, so that you can ask for my hand in marriage properly and we can organize a small wedding with my family around me."

He went still as her words sunk in. "You will marry me?"

She tugged at his hair. "Didn't I just say so?"

He drew her into his arms and simply held her as a series of totally unacceptable emotions threatened to overwhelm him.

He swallowed convulsively and buried his face into the crook of her neck. Her hand settled over his head and she stroked his hair.

After a long while, he kissed her throat, her face, her lips, savoring each inch of satiny skin, tasting and tempting her to respond to him. She opened her mouth and let his tongue inside to lazily stroke hers. His hands roamed over her body, stopping to appreciate the smallness of her waist, the curve of her hip, the tight buds of her nipples as he sucked them into his mouth.

She moved restlessly beneath him, her hips lifting into each ragged pull of his mouth on her breasts. Her hands settled on his upper arms, her fingernails biting into his muscled flesh. He lifted himself off her long enough to change their positions and slide his legs between hers. His cock slid against her belly, a thick, urgent reminder of his desire for her. But he was in no hurry. He slid his hand between her thighs and discovered her sex, already open to him, already wet and willing to take him deep inside.

"Gabriel . . ." She moaned his name as he touched her slick folds and circled her clit. "Please . . ."

He positioned the head of his cock at her entrance and felt himself being swallowed by her cunt, gave her more and then more until he was tightly sheathed within her. With a groan, he slid his hands under her buttocks and drew her into each stroke, her legs and feet wrapped around him like a vine and holding him even closer.

He kept his thrusts even and steady, wanting to feel her passion build, wanting to watch her come for him while he was buried deep inside. She moved with him as if they'd been lovers for all eternity, as if there was no other man for her but him. And he wanted that more than he wanted to breathe. She shifted against him and the angle of his cock changed, making her feel even tighter.

She started to walk her feet up the sides of his body, and his cock reacted, making him piston his hips even harder as the vise of her sex narrowed and narrowed until he could only fuck and breathe and feel her, only keep doing it even though the pleasure was edged with the fear that if he lost himself inside her he would never be able to be alone again. She climaxed with a scream and he hung on as his cock was squeezed so hard he thought it was screaming alongside her.

When he was finally able to come, his pulses were forced out, each so exquisitely painful he felt every one like a jolt. He rolled onto his back, bringing Lisette with him, unwilling to lose the connection and the sense of completeness. His need for her defeated his fear of the dark and the terror of his dreams. Would he ever be able to let her go?

He opened his eyes and stared out into the darkness as coldness formed in his gut. This was exactly why he'd chosen to leash his passions and use the pleasure house only for physical release. The thought of contaminating anyone with the darkness within him appalled him. Lisette sighed and relaxed against him, one palm splayed over his heart.

He forced himself to think of the possible child, reminded himself that he was getting married primarily for that reason and that he was at peace with his decision. His cock finally slid free of Lisette. Gabriel held her in his arms and prepared himself for another sleepless night. There was nothing he could do but carry on. His ability to walk away from her had been lost long ago. All that was left was to protect her, not only from society's critical gaze but from himself.

The next morning, Lisette awoke to find Gabriel already dressed and sitting by the window contemplating the grayness of the morning sky. She stretched and yawned, felt the unaccustomed ache of her muscles and the tenderness between her legs where Gabriel had penetrated her. She turned on her side to observe his profile and wondered why he didn't look more pleased with himself.

"Is something wrong?"

He turned fully to face her. "Good morning, Miss Ross. I hope you slept well?"

She sat up and clutched the covers to her chest. "I am Miss Ross now? Is something wrong?"

"Nothing at all, Miss Ross. I was just contemplating the awfulness of the weather."

She studied him for a long moment. "You don't seem very pleased to see me."

His guarded expression softened slightly. "Trust me, I am pleased. I thought I'd ruined my chances with you."

She raised her eyebrows. "Really? You don't strike me as a man who takes defeat lightly. I expect you are as tenacious as a bull when you don't get your own way. I assumed you'd just try something else."

He walked across to the table and held out a chair. "Will you join me for breakfast?"

Lisette wrapped the sheet around herself and waddled across to the table. "You are being remarkably polite this morning."

"I thought you might appreciate being treated with the courtesy and respect you deserve as my future wife."

She peered at him suspiciously, but there was no trace of sarcasm in his voice or on his face. "You agree to take me back to London and marry me in a proper church then?"

He inclined his head. "I would be honored to do so."

"You wouldn't prefer to continue on to Scotland?"

"As you have agreed to marry me, the least I can do is let you decide the details."

Lisette ate a piece of bacon and chewed it thoroughly. Lord Swanfield was saying all the right things, but somehow he seemed different. She put down her knife. "Why are you being like this?"

He stared at her. "Like what?"

"So . . . nice."

His smile widened. "You would prefer me to shout and rage at you?"

"At least then I know your passions are engaged."

"That is certainly an unusual way to look at it." He continued to eat his breakfast.

Determined to match his calm demeanor, Lisette buttered some toast and added marmalade. "Perhaps I should be the angry one."

"Why?" His attention instantly refocused on her. "You are not thinking of changing your mind again, are you?"

She smiled at him sweetly. "My brother says that men do not appreciate the games women play, is that true?"

"It depends what games they are."

"Have you not noticed that women often say the opposite of what they mean?"

He frowned. "You mean like you saying you didn't want to marry me?"

"I didn't want to marry you."

His smile this time was a challenge and full of male smugness. "Yes, you did."

"Not in the beginning."

"That's true." He finished his coffee and put his cup down. "We'll set off in about an hour if that is convenient for you. I sent your clothes down to the kitchen to be pressed. They'll bring them up with your bathwater." He stood up and bowed. "I'm going down to the stables to check that the horses are all fit for the return journey. I'll be back in a while."

Lisette looked up at him. If women were infuriating for playing games, men were far worse for ignoring them. She managed a smile. "You're not going to leave in a huff without me then?"

"Of course not."

"Because maybe I have it wrong and it is you who is having doubts about marrying me." She bit her lip. "Sometimes when a man gets what he wants, it is no longer of value to him."

He came around the table and knelt at her feet, took both of her hands in his strong grasp. This close, his eyes looked very blue. "I'm not going to change my mind; I'm not the sort of man who would bed you and then abandon you like that other sorry bastard. Once I've given my word, I honor it." He brought her hands to his lips and lightly kissed them. "We will marry as soon as I can arrange it."

She watched him leave, but the knot of doubt inside her refused to untangle. She knew he meant what he said and that he would keep his promises to her. But what of the passion they had shared the night before? Where did that figure in his talk of duty and honor? She always sensed a struggle in him between his strong physical desires and his need to behave like the perfect gentleman. It was a struggle she'd seen firsthand at the pleasure house.

A knock at the door made her sit up and conjure a smile as her bathwater was delivered to the hip bath Gabriel had already used by the fire. There was nothing more she could do now other than get ready for her trip back to London. Once she was reunited with her family, she would surely be able to make sense of her muddled feelings.

She sighed as one of the maids helped her pile her hair up on top of her head to keep it out of the way of the water. It would take far too long to dry if they were leaving in an hour. She stepped into the bath and sank into its warm, rose-scented depths and closed her eyes, willing her uncomfortable feelings away. Whatever happened next, she was going home, and if she changed her mind, even Lord Swanfield would fail against the combined might of her mother and father's support.

She smiled to herself as she began washing her arms with the sea sponge the maid had handed her. If she married Gabriel, she would be a countess and would take precedence over her older sister, Marguerite, who was about to marry the younger son of a marquis. The thought made her want to giggle—not that Marguerite would care, of course; she wasn't like that. Now all they needed was for Christian to marry a duchess and their family would *have* to be treated with respect.

Lisette's gaze fell on the towel warming by the fire and her newly pressed clothes. If she was to be ready to leave in less than an hour, and face her future, she needed to stop daydreaming and get dressed.

"We're almost there, Miss Ross."

Gabriel's soft voice woke Lisette from her sleep. Somehow during the long drive she had ended up sitting on his lap, her head nestled comfortably against his broad shoulder, his arm anchoring her at the waist.

"Good," she murmured.

"We are going to your father's house. I hope that is acceptable?"

She opened her eyes then and he allowed her to sit up. "Of course. What day is it?"

"It is Saturday."

"Then Emily must already have arrived."

"Your sister, Emily?"

"Yes." She frowned at him. "You made me miss her arrival."

"If I hadn't listened to you and turned around, you would be missing a lot more than one day of her visit. Scotland is a long way."

"I know." She repressed a shiver. "And a lot colder."

His lips brushed her ear and her shiver turned into something else entirely. "I would keep you warm."

She disentangled herself from his arms and moved across to the other seat. He looked his usual composed self, his black hair unruffled, not a crease in his clothing and no signs of fatigue on his face. In contrast, Lisette felt like a wet rag. Her hair was a mess, her new dress covered in marks she feared would never come out, and her half boots scuffed.

He raised his eyebrows. "What is wrong now?"

"Why should anything be wrong?"

"You are scowling at me."

"Because you look as neat as a pin, and I look like one of the women who ply their trade down at the docks."

"Hardly that." His gaze moved over her. "But I have seen you look better."

"Maybe I'd look better if you hadn't dragged me into your carriage and held me down on the floor with your *booted foot*."

He reached forward and patted her knee, caught her hand in his. "I've said I'm sorry for that. Just because you are nervous about your reception from your parents, there is no need to snipe at me."

"I am not nervous!"

"Of course you are. I'm nervous myself."

She snatched her hands back. "You should be. You abducted me."

"That is true." He agreed far too amicably for Lisette's liking. Getting Lord Swanfield to show his feelings could be quite exhausting sometimes.

She fixed him with her most quelling stare. "I hope my father does shoot you."

He ignored that comment and looked out of the window, then rose to his feet as the carriage slowed down and unlocked his door. Lisette waited until the carriage stopped completely and found herself unable to move any farther. Had she done the right thing? What would her parents think about her choice to marry? She suspected they would both consider her too young, too unsure of what she really wanted, too inadequate . . .

She jumped as the door opened and Lord Swanfield loomed over her. He held out his hand, his gaze steady on hers. "Miss Ross?"

Somehow, seeing him standing there waiting for her quieted her nerves and allowed her to get down from the carriage and into the hall of her father's house. Then there was all the bustle of arrival, her father kissing her cheek and trying to send her upstairs to bed, Lord Swanfield being lost to her as Emily hugged her and refused to let go.

She surrendered herself to Emily, too tired to do anything except listen to the stream of chatter pouring out of her sister. As she mounted the stairs, she tried to look for Gabriel, but her father was already leading him down the hallway to his study. She stared after him, her desire to be by his side when he dealt with her father at odds with her own reluctance to be judged and found wanting.

"Miss Ross."

She looked right into his eyes and he nodded slightly as if he understood her dilemma and wanted her to know that everything would be all right. It was so typical of him that she wanted to smile. With a sigh, she continued up the stairs, her arm linked with Emily's, her thoughts full of confusion.

Gabriel watched Lisette disappear up the stairs, aware that she was still anxious, but unable to do much to reassure her. He planned to restate his case to Lord Knowles, ask Lisette to marry him properly this time, and pray that on the morrow everything would go as planned.

Lord Knowles handed him a brandy and Gabriel pretended to sip it as the older man settled behind his desk. He felt like a young, inexperienced officer about to be bawled at in front of his men by his sergeant major.

"I understand from my son, Christian, that my daughter now wishes to marry you after all." Lord Knowles paused. "Which is lucky for you, seeing as if she hadn't, you and I might not be having quite such a harmonious meeting."

"Yes, my lord."

"From the state of the carriage you just drove up in, it appears that you and my daughter have been traveling."

Gabriel set his jaw. "Yes, sir. I originally intended to take Lisette to Scotland."

"*Scotland?*" Lord Knowles's stare was now glacial. "I'm not sure I agree with your methods of persuasion, Swanfield. If I'd known exactly what you intended to do to my daughter, I would not have been quite so eager to help you."

"I can understand that, sir. I can only state that if I'd believed any other method would've worked, I would've tried it. Your daughter is a remarkably tenacious woman."

"I know that," Lord Knowles snapped. "I also know that if there is the slightest suspicion you have threatened, blackmailed, or coerced her into making this decision, I will not let any union between you stand."

Gabriel shifted uncomfortably in his seat. "I have made no physical threats against her person, sir. In truth, when she told me she wanted to come home, I instantly complied."

"Yes, I've been wondering about that." Lord Knowles studied him intently. "Why go to all that effort to abduct her and then turn around the moment you get the opportunity?"

"I don't know what you mean, sir."

Lord Knowles didn't blink. "You know damn well what I mean, Swanfield, and you're going to tell me right now."

Briefly, Gabriel considered his options and then realized he had no choice. He took a deep breath. "Well, my lord, it was like this . . ."

16

When Lisette first woke up, she was confused as to exactly where she was. The presence of a green silk canopy above her head reassured her that she was in her own bed, and Emily was sleeping beside her. For a moment, she had imagined that she was still being held in Lord Swanfield's strong arms. Lisette hid a smile behind her hand. She hoped she hadn't done anything untoward to her half sister during the night.

Her door opened and Molly, her maid, appeared, face flushed with excitement as she tiptoed toward the bed.

"It's all right. I'm awake, Molly."

"Good morning, miss. I've already ordered your bath. It's very late."

"Really?"

"About eleven, miss."

Lisette subsided back onto the pillows. "That is late. I was tired after my travels."

"I'm sure, and her ladyship said to let you sleep as long as you wanted."

Lisette sat up again properly. "My mother is here?"

"Oh yes, indeed she is. And Mr. Delornay as well."

Lisette digested that information as Emily slept on and Molly bustled around the room bringing clothes out of the wardrobe and chests. Either they'd all arrived to see if she was well or they'd called to see Emily. She hoped it was Emily.

"Did Lord Swanfield leave?"

"Oh yes, miss, and what a lovely man he is, too."

"I wouldn't exactly call him lovely," Lisette muttered as she swung her feet over the side of the bed and headed for her dressing room, where she could hear the sound of the bath being filled. Molly's reply was drowned out as the door swung shut behind her. At last she could wash her hair and feel a bit more the thing.

As she inhaled the rose-scented bathwater, she remembered that the bath she'd taken at the inn had been similarly perfumed. Had Lord Swanfield arranged that? It seemed far too romantic a gesture for him to make, but it was unlikely that the inn would've offered such an expensive scent.

She bathed and Molly helped her with her hair, rinsing the dirt and dust of the road away until Lisette felt much better. When she returned to her bedroom, Emily had gone and the bed had been made. She sat down at her dressing table and looked for her silver-backed brushes. Molly picked one up and began the long process of untangling and drying Lisette's hair.

While Molly brushed and chatted, Lisette thought about the brushes she'd found waiting for her at the inn. She could almost imagine they'd been the same as hers. . . . Her head jerked as Molly encountered a tangle. Yet another example of Lord Swanfield's care for her? If he'd planned to go all the way to Scotland, she imagined he would have to provide her with some of the basic comforts.

Molly left Lisette drying her hair in front of the fire and laid out her clothes on the bed. Lisette's attention was caught by the elaborate stitching on the white corset.

"That isn't mine, is it?"

Molly flushed. "Lady Knowles told me to put these particular clothes out for you, miss."

Lisette walked over to the bed and studied the corset, the gossamer-thin petticoats, and the new dress, which was pale green silver lamé edged with fine blond lace over a green satin slip.

"It's very beautiful, but I don't remember ordering it."

"I believe it might be a gift, miss."

Lisette stroked the fine fabric. "Someone has been very generous. I can't wait to wear it, although it looks a little fine to be going down to a family luncheon in."

"You'll look lovely in it." Molly picked up the corset and advanced on Lisette. "Now put on your shift and I'll lace you into everything."

By the time Molly had finished with her hair, Lisette felt as if she should be attending court rather than simply meeting her mother and father. She tried to voice her objections, but Molly wouldn't listen and positively bullied her out of the room and down the stairs.

To Lisette's surprise, Emily was waiting for her in the hall-way, wearing her cloak and an expectant expression. "Oh, there you are at last, Lisette! I was beginning to wonder if I was going to have to come and get you."

"For what?" Lisette allowed Emily to take her hand and lead her toward the front door where a carriage bearing her father's coat of arms stood waiting for them before she balked. "Where are we going?"

Emily gave her a brilliant smile. "To find everyone else. Come *on*."

Still befuddled and now deeply suspicious, Lisette got into the carriage. Was her father about to engage Lord Swanfield in a duel in public or was something else wrong?

"What is going on, Emily?"

"You'll see."

"And will I like what I see?"

Emily looked positively shocked. "Of course you will."

Lisette sighed and settled back against the seat. She suspected that if she continued to ask questions, Emily would eventually give her the answers, but perhaps for once she would simply wait and see. For all she knew, it might have nothing to do with her at all and be all for Emily's benefit.

When the carriage drew to a stop, she waited for the door to open and was surprised to find herself being handed down by her father, who looked very smart in his best brown coat.

"Good morning, my dear." He took her hand, helped Emily down, and then marched Lisette forward into the gloom of a series of stone archways and up to a small oak door set deep into the wall. "Emily?"

"Yes, Papa?"

"Do you have your sister's flowers?"

Emily handed Lisette a small posy of pale pink roses tied with a darker pink ribbon. Lisette frowned at the door and inhaled the strange odor of musty stone, damp wood, and incense. "Why are we at a church?"

"So that you can marry Lord Swanfield, of course, silly," Emily said cheerfully.

"Today? Now?" Lisette stared at her father. "But . . ."

He held onto her hand and turned her to face him. "If Swanfield has forced this decision upon you, tell me now, and I'll never allow him to become your husband. Or, if you no longer wish to marry him, I'll happily take you home with me."

Lisette pointed a shaking finger at the door. "Are you saying that Lord Swanfield is waiting for me in there?"

"Yes, he is."

"But how could he have arranged this so quickly?"

"You'll have to ask him that." Philip smiled encouragingly at her. "Well, what's it to be?"

Lisette stared at the forbidding oak door. In some ways, she wasn't surprised at all by Lord Swanfield's ability to surprise her and attempt to sweep her off her feet. But was it too fast and too controlling of him? Did she really want to start her married life like this?

"I want to talk to him."

"To Swanfield?" Her father looked startled. "Now?"

She raised her chin. "Yes."

"Why? I thought you'd already decided to marry him."

"I have, but this . . ." She waved her posy of roses in the direction of the chapel. "It seems a little fast." She gazed at her father. "Do you want me to marry him?"

His smile was sweet. "I want you to be happy, love. Does he make you happy?"

"He makes me feel alive."

"And if you walk away now, do you think you would live to regret it?" He shrugged. "When I walked away from your mother I regretted it for every moment of my life, until I saw her again, and realized I had the chance to make things right between us."

Lisette slowly let out her breath, which condensed in the frigid air. She tried to imagine her life without the interesting presence of Gabriel Swanfield in it and found it surprisingly difficult. He'd become as necessary to her as breathing. He'd brought her home the instant she'd asked him to, and agreed to be married in front of her family. Was she prepared to take the risk and marry him?

She nodded at her father. "I'm going to marry him."

"You're sure, now?"

"Yes." Lisette smiled up at him and rested her right hand on the sleeve of his coat. "Let's go in."

Gabriel set his jaw as his teeth tried to chatter in the coldness of the damp chapel. How many hours had he been here? He couldn't even check the time without looking as if he was worried that his bride wouldn't arrive. And he was worried. He never quite knew how Lisette would react to his bold decision making.

Paul St. Clare nudged him and whispered. "Stop fidgeting."

"I'm not, I'm just freezing to death. Do you think she's here yet?"

Paul looked at him. "Why do you sound so unsure?"

"Because . . ." Behind them, the arched oak door creaked open and a blast of even more freezing air, spiced with the scent of roses, hurtled up the aisle. Gabriel stiffened and stared straight ahead at the clergyman who had magically appeared at the altar.

"She's here," Paul whispered.

Gabriel still didn't turn his head. He felt like one of the mortals in the fairy tales his mother had told him as a child who would forever forfeit his faerie prey if he dared to look back.

The vicar raised his hands and smiled as Lisette drew up alongside Gabriel on the arm of her father. Gabriel glanced down at her then, but she was staring at the vicar. The moment when Lord Knowles passed Lisette's hand over to him was so affecting that he wanted to pull her tightly into his arms and never let go.

The ceremony continued and he realized that he couldn't stop trembling, that the words were a blur, and that the only reality was the woman standing next to him. As the vicar bound them together for life, he vowed that he would keep her safe, even kill for her, be killed if it meant she stayed with him.

And then it was done and she was his. He bent his head and kissed her cold lips, saw the warmth in her eyes and managed to smile. No doubt she would have a few choice words for him when she realized quite how complex his plans to ensnare her had been, but he'd survive. In truth, he had no other choice.

* * *

Lisette allowed her family to surround her. Helene was weeping beautifully and even Christian's smile was less guarded than usual. Marguerite and her fiancé, Lord Anthony Sokorvsky, was also there, offering their felicitations and joking about the suddenness of her wedding compared to the long, drawn-out saga of their own.

She glanced across at Gabriel and realized he had no family around him, only his two friends, Paul St. Clare and Captain David Gray. She moved across and touched his arm. "Have you met my other half sister, Lady Justin Lockwood, the soon to be Lady Anthony Sokorvsky?"

Her older sister laughed. "As Lord Swanfield has just become part of our family, he might just prefer to call me Marguerite." She stood on tiptoe and kissed Gabriel on the cheek. "Welcome, sir."

Lisette watched as Anthony offered his hand to Gabriel and spoke a few kind words. This was better, seeing Gabriel being accepted into her family, who, despite their annoying ways, brought charm and their unique warmth to any occasion. She glanced down at the gold ring on her finger and studied it. It fitted perfectly. How on earth had Gabriel known so much about her? Her gaze settled on her mother, who was busy clapping her hands and inviting everyone back to Knowles House for the wedding breakfast. They were having a wedding breakfast?

Lisette allowed Gabriel to take her hand and lead her into the first of the carriages. Christian and Emily climbed in with them, so there was no opportunity for her to question anyone, or, indeed, to be able to speak at all because of Emily's chattering.

When they reached the house, in the bustle of removing cloaks and bonnets, Lisette managed to avoid Gabriel and find her mother.

"Maman, may I ask you something?"

206 / Kate Pearce

"What is it, *cherie*?" her mother asked distractedly. "Surely you are not worried about your wedding night?" She patted Lisette's hand. "I'm sure it will be wonderful."

Lisette managed a smile. "Thank you, Maman, I'm sure it will, but I wanted to ask you about something else. Did you know that Gabriel was planning to marry me today?"

Helene sighed. "I knew you'd notice. I told them, but would they listen to me?"

Someone called her mother's name from the doorway, and Helene started moving away. "Ask your father, darling. I have to consult with the staff about the food."

Lisette took the glass of white wine offered to her by a smiling footman and set off again to find her father. He was standing by the fireplace with Christian and Gabriel, which suited her perfectly. As she approached she delicately cleared her throat to make sure she had everyone's attention.

"Did you know that Gabriel intended to marry me today?"

Her father tried to look apologetic. "Well, yes, my dear, otherwise how would he have organized it all while he was busy with you?"

"Busy abducting me, you mean? Did you tell him to do that, too?"

"Of course not." Philip looked insulted. "I didn't know his intentions until you returned."

"Lisette," Gabriel broke into the conversation. "That was my idea. Please don't blame your father. He simply helped organize the arrangements, the marriage license, the vicar, the church."

"That was kind of him." Lisette looked steadily at her father. "So everything you said to me earlier about making up my own mind was a lie. You'd already decided I should marry Lord Swanfield."

"That's not true. I was merely trying to make sure that if

you *did* want to marry him, there would be no barriers to prevent it from happening quickly."

"Because you wanted me out of the way." Lisette bit down on her lip.

"What on earth is that supposed to mean?" Lord Knowles asked, his voice rising, his expression incredulous.

Gabriel took her hand. "Please excuse us, Lord Knowles. Lisette, come with me."

She allowed him to walk her out of the main drawing room and down the hall to a small parlor meant for the lady of the house, which her mother never used. He shut the door and walked over to the fireplace, his expression neutral and his arms folded over his chest

"If you want to blame someone, blame me. I asked for your father's help because I wanted to make sure he knew I meant what I said. I was trying to ensure that I married you in front of your family as you requested."

Lisette swallowed hard. "He's probably just glad I'm off his hands, and he can focus on Emily without worrying that I'll ruin her debut with my notorious reputation."

Gabriel took her into his arms and held her close. "Ah, no, love. It's not like that at all. The man loves you dearly."

She turned her face into his chest and let him hold her, aware of his strength and warmth surrounding her. After a while she raised her head to look up at him. "You put rose-scented oil in my bath."

He looked distinctly uncomfortable. "You always smell like roses."

"Did you ask my mother to pack my belongings?"

"No, I didn't ask your mother. Why would you think that?"

"Because I'm almost certain those were my hairbrushes at the inn as well." She eased out of his arms. "And if they were my things, then someone from my family knew you planned to elope with me all along."

He sighed. "Lisette . . ."

She ignored him as she began pacing the small room. "Then if it wasn't my mother, and my father insists he only helped with the wedding part of it, who helped you?" She stopped moving and stared at him. "You asked *Christian*?"

Gabriel held out his hand. "Not quite, he . . ." But she was already half out of the door and intent on finding her twin. He was drinking champagne and joking with Emily by the window. His expression cooled when he saw her marching toward him and he moved away from Emily to intercept her head-on.

"What can I do for you, sister mine?"

"Why did you help Gabriel abduct me?"

"Because it seemed like the right thing to do."

"To meddle in my life?"

"Perhaps, but only because I wanted you to make up your mind and decide what you really wanted."

"So you concocted this plan with Gabriel and pretended to come and save me." Lisette was aware that everyone around them was listening to her conversation with her brother, but for once she didn't care what they thought.

"No, I merely offered my services to your new husband to make sure he truly wanted you."

Gabriel's light touch on Lisette's shoulder made her jump. "I went to the pleasure house to ask for your mother's help. I met Delornay instead and he agreed to help me. I was determined to marry you, but I also wanted you to make a choice. When you chose to stay with me at the inn rather than return with Christian, I was delighted."

Lisette ignored Gabriel's interruption and glared at Christian. "Do you not understand that by allying yourself with Lord Swanfield you betrayed *me*? Do you all believe that I am incapable of making my own decisions?" She let her gaze swing around the assembled guests until she found her parents. "I always thought we were loyal to each other, but I was obviously wrong." She looked up at Gabriel. "Will you take me home?"

"Of course. I'll get your cloak."

She walked out after him, ignoring her mother's plea for her to wait and her father's hasty step toward her. When Gabriel handed her into his coach, she stared out of the small window until the view became obscured by her own tears. She felt manipulated, and although Gabriel had been part of that, she almost expected it from him, had known he'd try anything to keep her. But her family's connivance? That hurt far more than she could've imagined. The sense of always being left out, of not being judged worthy, flooded through her and escaped in her tears.

A large clean handkerchief appeared under her nose and she took it gratefully without saying a thing. She'd survive this, she'd survive anything, and if Gabriel Swanfield thought she'd allied herself with him, he had better beware. She still had a few questions to ask him. At the moment, luckily for him, he was simply the lesser of two evils.

17

Gabriel glanced uncertainly down at Lisette as he shut the front door of his lodgings behind him.

"This is only temporary, of course. I assumed we'd be spending our wedding night at your father's house...." He stopped talking as she started to walk around the suite of rooms, her fingers trailing over the worn, comfortable chairs by the fire, the small dining table, and the well-filled book-shelves. "I gave my staff the week off."

She shrugged and put down the hood of her cloak. He took a step toward her, worried by the absent look in her hazel eyes. "Lisette..."

"Do you have any brandy?" She sat in one of the chairs and drew her cloak around her. He hurried to set light to the kindling in the fireplace, hoping the coal would catch quickly and warm the place up.

"Yes, would you like some?"

She nodded and he went to pour her a small glass of brandy, decided not to indulge himself, and instead went on a search for some blankets. He found a couple in a chest by his bed and brought them back to the living area, tucked one around Lisette's shoulders and the other over her lap. She sighed and cuddled into the soft wool.

He took the seat opposite her and stretched out his feet to the small fire. This wasn't quite how he had anticipated starting married life, but in some ways he preferred it. Just Lisette and him together. No one else to bother about. If only she wasn't so distressed. A wedge of guilt lodged in his throat.

"I owe you another apology, don't I?"

She regarded him steadily over the top of the blanket but didn't reply.

"I thought that by involving your family, I would gain their trust. But in doing so, it appears I have committed a greater sin and lost yours."

"I'm not sure I trusted you anyway."

He tried not to flinch at that. He certainly deserved it. "But you did trust your family."

She nodded and he caught the glint of tears in her eyes. "They were all I had."

He contemplated the toes of his boots. "I don't understand families. I've never really had one. It didn't occur to me that you might feel betrayed by them."

"Why would it?"

He raised his gaze to hers. "I intended to have the opposite effect. I hoped that if you saw your family was willing to help me, you'd like me better." He cleared his throat. "That was selfish. I wanted to marry you so badly that I was prepared to do anything to get you to that church."

"I understand that, and I knew you would try your best to have me. I just didn't expect my family to join in quite so enthusiastically to get rid of me."

"Why do you think they are getting rid of you?" he asked gently. "I didn't sense that at all."

She frowned at him. "They are not your family. How would you know how it felt?"

Gabriel chose not to answer that. He could only hope that the Delornay-Ross clan would be able to regroup and make sure Lisette understood what she meant to them.

"They took away my choice, Gabriel," she whispered. "They handed me to you like a neatly wrapped package, and they didn't need to interfere. I was going to marry you anyway."

"They didn't know that, though, did they?"

"But they *should've* known. They should've trusted me to make the right decision." She swallowed hard. "I've spent almost three years trying to keep them all talking to each other, to stop Christian's excesses, to help Philip see more of my mother, and what thanks do I get? They band together against me, and, at the first opportunity, they try and get rid of me."

"You forget that I was the one who instigated and planned the whole affair. I organized the abduction because it was the only way I could think of to make you choose whether to marry me or not."

"Are you defending my family now?"

"No, I'm just trying to put their minor role in this into perspective."

She held his gaze. "You gave me a choice, Gabriel. If I'd decided to leave with Christian, you would've let me go, wouldn't you?"

"Yes."

"Even though you wanted me to stay?"

"Yes. That was the whole point of the exercise."

She stood up, the blankets clutched in her hands, and he instinctively came to his feet as well.

"Then you achieved your aim, didn't you? Are you happy now?"

"I would be a lot happier if I didn't feel so damn guilty."

She finally looked at him and he took a hasty step toward her only to pull up short when she turned away.

"Would you mind if I wanted to be alone for a while?"

God, he minded. He minded so much it hurt. "No, of course not." He gestured at the short hallway. "My bedroom—I mean, our bedroom—is down there. Please make yourself at home."

She nodded at him and walked away, the blankets catching on the floor behind her. He stayed on his feet until the bedroom door closed with a firm click and then he sat down to contemplate the fire. She said she didn't blame him and that she blamed her family, but that wasn't quite true. And he blamed himself for lacking the knowledge to understand her, to realize that the tactics he used to break a military siege were not always appropriate when handling delicate relationships.

"My lord?"

He looked up and saw Keyes in the doorway, his expression one of complete disbelief.

"Good afternoon, Keyes."

"Is everything all right, sir?"

"Yes, indeed, it is." Gabriel glanced down the hallway and lowered his voice. "I need you to keep everyone away from my lodgings for the next few days, but I also require sufficient provisions for me and my wife."

"Her ladyship is here?" Keyes hissed.

"She is and she'll remain here for as long as she likes. I also want you to go to Knowles House, tell them she is perfectly fine, but not receiving visitors yet, and pick up some clothes for her."

"Yes, sir, of course, sir." Keyes bowed. "Will you be requiring supper, sir?"

"That is an excellent idea, some soup perhaps or something light."

"I'll sort that out immediately, sir."

"I'd rather you dealt with the Knowles family first and then came back."

Keyes backed toward the door. "Whatever you want, sir, and may I be the first to wish you happy, sir?"

"Thank you." Gabriel smiled and realized that despite all the theatrics he was actually happy. His wife lay in his bed, he was a married man, and his children would be legitimate.

After Keyes left, he reached across and picked up Lisette's discarded brandy and drank it down in one gulp. The morning paper lay on the table, so he unfolded it and started to read. He'd give her the time she needed to come to terms with everything that had happened to her. She deserved that. Devil take it, she *needed* that. Betrayal, whether presumed or real, was hardly something to sneer at; he of all men understood that perfectly.

But, God help him, he wouldn't let her wallow in it. And she'd know that. She'd know he'd be after her again, that he would not allow her to hide from him. A reluctant smile curled his lips. They were married now, and, whether she liked it or not, they would face their enemies and vanquish them together.

Lisette woke up from her unhappy doze and found herself stretched out on her stomach in a strange bed again. Although this bed didn't feel quite so strange, because it smelled of Gabriel and the lemon soap he used. She rolled onto her back and inhaled the starchy scent of freshly laundered linen and twisted her wedding ring around her finger.

She was married. That was a fact she couldn't ignore. And she wanted Gabriel. That was another. She sighed as she thought of her family and the way they'd looked when she'd made Gabriel take her away from her own wedding breakfast.

She'd tried to pretend that her relationship with her parents was perfect and that she was important to them.

Was Christian right and she'd tried too hard to ignore the scars left by eighteen years of no parental care? It seemed her hurt was even closer to the surface than Christian's, and at least he allowed himself to be angry about it. Maybe by repressing her feelings, she'd simply created a wound that wouldn't heal. Perhaps Gabriel was also right and her reaction to their interference in his plans was a little extreme.

She frowned up at the dark-beamed ceiling. She hated having to admit that anyone else might be right, particularly Christian and Gabriel.

There was a tap on the door and then it opened to reveal Gabriel carrying a large tray. He'd taken off his coat and cravat, and his shirtsleeves were rolled up to the elbow. She didn't bother to sit up, just watched him ease the tray down onto the small writing desk by the window and then close the door. She inhaled the scent of chicken soup and her mouth watered.

"I thought you might be hungry," Gabriel said.

"I am."

He nodded at the small desk. "Do you want to sit here and eat, or shall I bring you something over?"

"Over here, please."

He removed some of the items from the tray and brought the rest to her: a bowl of the soup, a plate of crusty bread, some fruit, and a glass of red wine.

"This looks nice. Did you cook it yourself?"

He regarded the soup critically. "I asked my man Keyes to do it for me. My cooking skills are limited to incinerating anything over a campfire that might possibly be edible."

She picked up her spoon and then glanced at him. "Aren't you going to eat?"

"If I may." He settled himself on the chair by the desk, tore off a chunk of bread, and dipped it into his soup. "I wasn't sure if you would be awake enough to want company."

"You mean, you wondered if I was still in the mood to throw the soup at your head."

His smile flicked out. "There was that."

"I'm quite composed now."

"That's good." He continued to eat, addressing his food with a thoroughness that Lisette had noticed before, as if he feared to miss something. She started on her soup and soon finished the whole bowl, all the bread, and the fruit. "Keyes collected your bags from Knowles House. I'll bring them in to you later."

"My bags?"

He regarded her steadily. "I assumed you would want a change of clothing. The dress you have on is very nice, but rather crumpled."

"Did you buy this gown for me, too?"

"I told your mother the color I would prefer to see you in, but the end result was all her idea, thank God. I'm not very knowledgeable about lady's clothing."

Lisette sighed. "You are being very nice to me."

He shrugged. "You've had a difficult day."

"So have you."

He put down his spoon and turned to face her. "And as you mentioned, I've achieved exactly what I wanted. You, however, feel manipulated and lied to."

"I . . . I'm still glad that we were married."

He rose to his feet and came over to the bed, took the tray from her knees. "I'm pleased to hear that. Now let me take this back to the kitchen. I'll bring you some coffee and your bags and leave you to change."

"As I have no maid, you'll have to unbutton my dress for me."

"I'm sure I can manage that." He filled the tray with both their plates and headed for the door. "I'll be back in a moment."

Lisette stared after him, aware that she'd been unconsciously bracing herself for his disapproval and anger. Yet he'd behaved as if she was the wounded party and required understanding and care. He hadn't even berated her for ruining their wedding day, and she had ruined it. She wasn't stupid enough to deny that.

Gabriel returned with her bags and she got off the bed to examine what was in them. His fingers brushed her shoulder and she went still as he started to unbutton her bodice. His warm breath feathered the back of her neck as he worked each small pearl button free to reveal her corset, stockings, and shift.

"Shall I leave your corset laced?"

She swallowed as he breathed his question into her ear. It wasn't fair that he could make her knees tremble just by standing so close to her. "You might as well loosen it. I'm not planning on putting on another gown."

His fingers returned to their work, each gentle tug and subtle touch making Lisette's breathing falter. She had the absurd desire to turn around and simply bury her face in his chest and stay there forever.

"I'll leave you to change." He dropped a kiss on the top of her head. "Good night."

She heard him shut the door and clutched at her corset and the bodice of her dress to stop them falling down. He'd said good night. Did that mean he planned to stay away from his own bed on his wedding night? She stared at the large four-poster bed with its now rumpled covers. There was nothing left to do except put away her belongings, wash her face, and put on her nightgown.

A long while later, she was ready for bed. She'd even managed to remove all the pins from her hair and brush out the tangles. Her worry over Gabriel's whereabouts and his intentions hadn't receded. In truth, she'd reached a point where she was no longer prepared to be ignored. She grabbed her woolen shawl from the bed and headed back down the hall.

Gabriel sat by the fire, his stockinged feet propped up on the table, a glass of brandy beside him, and a cigarillo in one hand. He looked supremely comfortable and completely at home. When she came more fully into the room his head snapped up and he attempted to get to his feet. She waved him back down.

"What are you doing?"

"Reading the paper."

"Are you intending to read the paper all night?"

"Probably."

"And what about me?"

He looked faintly puzzled. "Is there something you need?"

"Have you forgotten that this is supposed to be our wedding night?"

He carefully stubbed out his cigarillo, folded the paper, and rested it on his knee. "I haven't forgotten."

"And yet you intend to sit here and read the paper."

"Yes."

"Without even inquiring as to whether I might perhaps *want* you to behave like a man who can't wait to bed his new bride?"

"I wasn't going to read the paper all night."

"What else were you planning on doing?"

"Playing cards, drinking brandy . . ."

She stalked across the room until she was standing right over him. "You wanted me to come out here and have to ask, didn't you?"

He looked up at her, his dark blue eyes serious. "Actually, yes."

She caught her breath as he reached out and shoved his hand into her hair and brought her face down to meet his. His kiss was as hot and passionate as she could have wanted. And she responded to him with all the enthusiasm she could muster.

When he finally relaxed his grip, she stepped away from him. "Good night, then."

His hands closed around her waist and he lifted her onto his lap. "I haven't finished yet. Stop wiggling." His mouth descended again and she was soon lost in his textures and his taste. Her hands slid into his hair and around his neck to keep him close.

He drew her back over his arm, exposing her throat and the curve of her breasts. His hands followed his gaze, owning her inch by inch, touching, teasing, demanding a response from her. She gasped as his lips closed over her nipple and suckled through her thin muslin nightgown.

"Gabriel . . ."

His teeth tugged at her nipple and his hands seemed to be everywhere, rucking up her nightgown, squeezing her buttocks, and molding her closer and closer to the heat of his erection. He groaned as she undulated her hips and pressed her mound into the swell of his shaft. His fingers slid between them to play with her clit and delve inside her slick folds.

She wasn't sure how he managed to open his breeches but suddenly she felt his cock against her belly, the heat and wetness making her writhe and moan his name. He lifted her over him and she took him deep, felt him shudder and shake and groan as her tight muscles gripped him hard. She braced her hands on his shoulders and his muscles flexed as her fingernails dug in.

"Bedroom," he whispered—the sound the merest thread.

"Why not here?" Lisette asked.

He was already lifting her. "Don't want an audience. Keyes might come back." She wrapped her legs around his waist and he lurched unsteadily toward the bedroom. They'd barely made the turn into the hallway when he backed her up against the wall, and, as if unable to contain himself for a moment longer, started thrusting.

Lisette held onto him and was almost disappointed when he managed to move again and make it the rest of the way down the hall and into the bedroom. He shut the door with his foot and bore her down to the bed, his weight fully on her, his cock still pumping hard as if he never intended to stop.

She climaxed and he thrust even faster, bringing her to a new level of pleasure so intense that she tightened her grip on him. She dared him to leave her now that he had taken her this far, incited him to take her even higher through her fear and into the exquisite pleasure she sensed beyond.

He groaned with each long stroke, slid his hands under her buttocks to raise her even higher, and sent her screaming into another wave of bliss so intense it was almost painful. She managed to open her eyes and look up at him; his gaze was focused on her, on his cock as it disappeared into her body, on her face. She touched his cheek and he turned his head to kiss her fingers, never letting up on each long powerful stroke or losing his rhythm as he pounded into her.

"Come for me again."

"I can't." She gasped as he reached between them, found her already sensitive clit and set his thumb on it. She started to convulse around him and scream his name. His thrusts became shorter and more desperate and she felt him gather himself to come, that moment of stillness over her, that moment of weakness when he climaxed and there was nothing he could do to stop it.

He collapsed over her, his breathing chaotic, his hand buried deep in her hair. She didn't protest his weight, even liked the idea of his long, elegant length covering and protecting her.

After a long while, he rolled off her and got out of bed to check that the fire was banked and to light a single candle.

When he got back in the bed, he took off what remained of his clothes. Lisette watched his body emerge with a profound sense of enjoyment. He was hers now. All that rippling muscle and strong frame hers, to have and to touch. She sighed and he looked across at her, deliberately cupped his cock and balls and stroked his thumb along his shaft.

"Aren't you glad you came to find me?"

She raised her eyebrows. "That's what you wanted me to do, wasn't it? You wanted me to have a choice."

He crawled toward her on all fours until he straddled her again and pulled her nightgown off over her head. "And are you happy with your choice?"

She looked up at him as he leaned over her and she lightly ran her finger down his muscled chest and belly and then along his cock. He shuddered and his shaft jerked against her fingers. "Yes, I'm happy," she said. "Are you?"

His smile was full of sexual intent. "Not quite, I haven't heard you beg yet."

She smiled back at him. "And you never will."

He moved closer until the crown of his half-erect cock brushed against her mouth. "We'll see about that, now suck my cock."

"I won't be able to scream your name and beg if your cock is in my mouth."

He eased the first two inches of his shaft inside her mouth. "I can wait. It's a long time until dawn."

Lisette gave up trying to convince him and concentrated on sucking his cock. Perhaps if she did it really well, he'd be the one begging.

Much later, Gabriel drew Lisette close against his body and wrapped his arms around her. She sighed and kissed his chest, her body so relaxed it felt as if he was covered in a silk blanket.

"I'll take you to see your new home tomorrow."

She didn't reply. He wasn't even sure if she was still awake.

As his wife, she deserved the best and that meant he needed to confront his past. By the end of the week, he hoped to have her established in her proper setting: the house that was his by birth. A house he had never been allowed to claim because of his damnable relatives. Surely it was time to reclaim what was his by right?

18

"Is this your home?" Lisette glanced uncertainly at Gabriel as they stared up at the large mansion on Portman Square. It was early evening and the house was lit up and obviously occupied.

"It is my family's London house. I've never lived here."

"But it appears that someone is. Maybe your solicitor let the house for the Season?"

"Not to my knowledge." He took her hand in a hard grip as trepidation flooded through his body. "Perhaps we should go in and find out exactly who it is."

Lisette hurried up the steps beside him and waited while he banged on the knocker. After what seemed like a long while, the door opened a crack and an elderly man peered around the gap.

"Good evening, sir, ma'am. May I help you?"

Ah, so he'd been right all along. Gabriel's smile wasn't sweet. "Is the family at home?"

"Yes, sir, everyone is home except the master. But they are just gathering for an early dinner. I doubt they will wish to be disturbed."

"That's a shame, because I'm coming in anyway." Gabriel shoved his hand against the door and pushed it open, drawing Lisette along with him into the spacious white and black tiled entrance hall. A large portrait of an all-too-familiar figure stared down at him from the largest wall. Anger replaced his fear and he fought a ridiculously juvenile urge to hurl himself at the mocking face in the picture and rip it to shreds.

The butler rocked back on his heels and held out his hand. "Sir, how dare you force your way in here. Have you no decency?"

"Do *I* have any decency? More than the people living in *my* damn house have."

"*Your* house, sir? Are you mad?" The butler readjusted his spectacles and stared up at Gabriel until his mouth dropped open. "Oh, good lord, you are the spit of the old earl."

Gabriel was already scanning the doorways peeling off from the main lobby. "So I've been told. Now tell me where the family is."

The butler pointed a shaking finger down the longest corridor. "The third door on the left, sir."

"Thank you, Bridge."

"You know my name, sir?"

Gabriel paused long enough to look back at the butler. When he spoke, even Lisette cringed at the cold fury in his voice. "Of course I do. You were the man who told the old earl my mother was pregnant. The man who treated me like a piece of misbegotten filth, even though you witnessed the secret wedding that made me the earl's legitimate heir. I suppose I should be grateful to you for my title and estate."

Bridge's face paled. "Gabriel Swanfield," he whispered. "Lord have mercy."

"Yes, that's right." Gabriel nodded. "But it's Lord Swanfield to you now, and don't you ever forget it."

He turned on his heel and marched down the hall, Lisette

following. When they reached the third set of double doors, he went in without knocking. The four people in the ornate room stared at Gabriel as if they had seen a ghost.

He bowed into the sudden, stricken silence. "Good evening, Mrs. Granger, Cousin Michael, Cousin Elizabeth, and Great Aunt Hortense."

The tallest of the three females present stepped forward, one hand clasped to her expansive bosom. "Is that really you, Gabriel?"

"Indeed it is, Mrs. Granger." Gabriel inclined his head a glacial inch. "Didn't Michael mention that he'd seen me around Town? With his clever tongue, he almost succeeded in making me not want to visit my own house."

"No, he . . ."

"It's a shame that he didn't succeed, because then you might have had a chance to find somewhere else to live before I discovered you inhabiting my property."

Mrs. Granger flushed. "This house belongs to the *family*. We have always used it when we've come up to Town."

"No, this house belongs to the *Swanfield family*, and, as I'm the current Earl of Swanfield, you are trespassing."

Michael stepped forward. "There's no need to cut up at my mother, Gabriel. She's right; we've always used this house. She's a Swanfield by birth, so it's a bit of a tradition for her, actually." He smiled engagingly. "You told me you weren't interested in living here, so why shouldn't we?"

Gabriel stiffened at Michael's terribly reasonable tone. "Because the house belongs to me, and, now that I am married, I feel I should heed your advice and take possession of my property."

He glanced at Lisette and she smiled at him encouragingly. He took her hand and drew her forward. "May I present my wife, the new Countess of Swanfield?"

"When did you marry?" His aunt gasped and Michael's smile

disappeared. "There has been no mention of an engagement in the papers, let alone a marriage."

"Yesterday." His gaze swept them all. "So I'm sure you'll understand why I want you out by the end of the week."

Mrs. Granger gave a strangled cry and collapsed against Michael's shoulder. "He is turning us out onto the streets! I always knew he would come back and destroy us one day. Bad blood will always out."

Gabriel shrugged. "Hardly the streets, ma'am. If I remember correctly, you own a perfectly good house on Half Moon Street. I suggest you kick out your tenants and take possession of that." He glanced at the clock on the mantelpiece as it chimed the hour. "I won't add the back rent to what you already owe me, but I will send my solicitor over to check that none of the items belonging to this house, or to the earldom, are accidentally added to your bags."

"Now he is treating us like thieves!" Mrs. Granger wailed. "What is to become of us?"

"I have no idea, ma'am, and, to be perfectly frank, I can't say that I care." Gabriel nodded at them all. "Good evening. Enjoy your dinner."

He walked out and through the vast echoing hallway. He didn't pause or draw a breath until his feet hit the flagged paving stones of the street and then he kept going.

"Gabriel?"

He stopped so suddenly that Lisette crashed into him and grabbed his arm for support. He stared down at her worried face and tried to breathe normally. She tucked her hand into the crook of his arm. "Shall we stroll for a while? I don't think it is going to rain yet."

He nodded and resumed walking, slowing his pace to match hers and simply concentrating on getting around the corner onto Baker Street. They walked right past the stables of the king's Life Guards Regiment before he felt able to speak again.

"You probably thought me harsh."

"Not at all." She looked up at him, her hazel eyes fierce. "I'm surprised you didn't pick them up by their hair and throw the lot of them into the gutter."

It took him a moment to realize she was angry *for* him and not *at* him. "I thought you told me once that I should make a better attempt to understand my family."

She snorted. "That was before I saw them all staring at you as if you were the devil incarnate. And living in your house, rent free, while they are at odds with you? That smacks of arrogance."

Gabriel maneuvered around a beggar's outstretched legs and dropped some coins into his battered cup. "I promised my older cousin William I wouldn't ruin them."

Lisette shivered. "If William is the man who confronted you at the ball, he seemed just as bad as the rest of them."

"He came to see me at my solicitor's afterward, and offered to help resolve the issues with his father." Gabriel walked a few more steps before continuing. "He believes his father is no longer capable of managing the estate."

"Perhaps William simply wants to absolve himself of blame when the whole shady business comes crashing down on his family."

Gabriel cast Lisette an appreciative smile. "That's what I originally thought, but he convinced me that his motives went far deeper than that. He truly loves the estate. Remember, he was brought up thinking it would be his until I appeared. I confess I have some sympathy for him."

"Maybe he's angling for the position of estate manager when you finally take the reins."

"I think he'd hate that. He has no love for me. I do believe he has a point about the estate deserving someone willing to serve and protect the people who depend on it. William wouldn't say this, but I suspect there are more problems under his father's stewardship than I might have imagined."

Lisette stopped and patted his arm. "Then the sooner you gain control of the earldom, the better."

"Easy for you to say, Lady Swanfield, but not quite so easy to put into practice." He sighed. "My uncle has many friends at Court and in the government. He was able to gain complete legal control over the estate because of that. Many still consider him a far better administrator than I'll ever be. The suspicion I fell under in the last few months of the peninsular campaign didn't help my reputation either."

He felt a drop of rain on his cheek and realized it was time to turn around and walk back toward Portman Square and their waiting carriage. He kissed Lisette's gloved hand. "Don't worry, love. I truly believe that with William's help I'll be able to regain my estate completely."

They walked for a while in silence, although Gabriel took comfort in Lisette's presence at his side. He suspected he'd never have been able to get through the "visit" with his family if she hadn't been there.

"Is your uncle not in good health?"

Gabriel grimaced. "Apparently not. I haven't seen him for years."

"Why not? I doubt he could hurt you now."

He stopped walking. "I know that, but . . ."

He glanced down at her tranquil expression, aware that he'd been spilling out his feelings like a small child and she hadn't seemed to mind at all.

She studied his face. "When I first met my mother, I could hardly believe we were related. She looked like a fairy princess, far too young and delicate to have ever given birth to a child, let alone three of them."

"She certainly looks younger than she is."

"But when I started to get to know her, I realized that she

had made choices she deeply regretted and that she was only human after all." She looked up at him. "Perhaps if you could stop seeing your uncle as the personification of evil, you might see him for what he really is: a sad old man who is dying, a man who made mistakes."

"The man you just told me to throw out of my house."

Lisette sighed. "Don't be difficult, Gabriel. You know what I mean."

"And if I don't choose to forgive him?"

"Then who do you hurt most? Him or you?"

He started walking again, this time without reclaiming her hand. "Don't try and tangle me up in all this emotional womanly thinking. I don't like him, I don't want to understand him, and I certainly don't want to forgive him."

"And that's it, is it?"

Their carriage came into view on the corner of Baker Street and Gabriel increased his pace. "Yes."

He opened the door of the carriage, helped Lisette inside, then climbed in himself.

"I can see why you don't get on with each other." Her smile was full of false commiseration.

"Why is that?"

"Because you are both too stubborn to admit a fault."

"I am not at fault. I was a child. He took everything I valued away from me, kept me from my home, my heritage, my family." He glowered at her. "*He* is at fault."

"And now you are in your prime and he is an old man."

"Yes."

"And?"

"And nothing! He deserves everything that happens to him. I don't give a damn whether he lives or dies."

She sat forward, her smile gone. "And what exactly do you give a damn about, Gabriel?"

"You?"

She sighed. "Now you are trying to change the subject." She looked out of the window. "Do you really wish to live at Swanfield House?"

He shrugged. "It is my family home and is certainly more suitable for you than my lodgings."

"I don't mind them. In fact I find them quite charming."

"You'll change your mind when you hear the rest of the tenants carousing or running races up and down the stairs while in their cups."

"You forget, I spent rather a lot of my time at the pleasure house. It was rarely quiet there."

Unbidden, an image of her playing with his cock in his tight pantaloons flashed through his brain and he was instantly aroused. He forced his thoughts into less dangerous waters. He was a married man now and his responsibilities had changed considerably. Lisette would be in his bed and in his arms every night.

He cleared his throat. "Do you wish to go and visit your parents today?"

She grimaced. "I don't think so. I'm still not quite ready to see them yet."

"And you think I'm stubborn," he muttered under his breath but she still heard him.

"At least I'm thinking about it. Compared to the sins of your family, mine do seem rather mild." She considered him, her head angled to one side. "Did you say your uncle sent you away to school?"

"He did. It was the sort of school for boys whose parents didn't care to see them much and didn't want to know what happened to them while they were at the school." He grimaced. "I wasn't allowed home at all for seven years. Eventually, I escaped and joined the army, which seemed quite pleasant after my school experiences."

"You enlisted?"

"Yes. When I was sixteen. Unfortunately, I was discovered by my uncle, and, due to my 'rank,' and because he couldn't afford to lose face, I was forced to train as an officer."

"I was sent away to school as well."

"Yes, I believe you said you were educated in France."

"Mother sent me and Christian away when we reached our first birthday."

Gabriel sat up. "I didn't realize you were that young."

"She couldn't really keep us and start her business. She had no husband, and she needed the money to survive and to pay for our care." She sighed. "And then, of course, after the war started it was almost impossible for her to either visit us or bring us home." She met his gaze. "Maman was imprisoned during the Revolution and barely escaped with her life. She was terrified that it would happen to her again if she tried to reclaim us."

He found himself frowning on her behalf. She made it all sound like an amusing lark and he suspected it had been anything but. "How old were you when she finally came for you?"

"Actually, Christian and I found out exactly what she did and where she lived and came to find her." She smiled. "She was not terribly pleased to see us at first, and we didn't exactly make it easy for her, hence my appalling reputation."

"I can see that."

"You can?"

"All too well. When I escaped from school and went into the army, I tried every vice available to me. I'm not quite sure how I survived the first year."

"You can imagine how it was for me then, coming from seventeen years in a convent-run school to my mother's pleasure house. She tried to keep Christian and me away from everything, but we constantly defied her. I think I was trying to shock her, but she and Father appeared to be quite unmoved by anything I did, so eventually I stopped."

She smiled at him and he smiled back, aware that he understood her better than he had understood any other woman, and that she understood him, too. A fact that was not only refreshing but quite outside his experience.

"When we reclaim Swanfield House, you may redecorate as much as you want."

"That will be interesting. I've never decorated anything bigger than a bonnet before." She frowned. "I'll probably need some help."

"Yet another reason why you should reconcile yourself with your mother as soon as possible."

She smiled at him, her hazel eyes alight. "Wretch."

"Hoyden."

"Bully."

"Nag."

She raised her chin at him. "Nag?"

He shrugged. "All women nag." She opened her mouth to say something else and he leaned over and kissed her. "Shall we go and visit my solicitor to give him the good news about my intended occupation of Swanfield House?"

"Why not?"

"And then perhaps we could go back home and retire to bed. You are probably tired after all these outings."

Her smile this time was full of rich sensual promise. She faked a yawn and covered her mouth. "I believe I am a little tired after all."

19

"The first thing I want you to do, Keyes, is take down that damn portrait and burn it."

"Burn it, sir?"

Lisette followed Gabriel into the entrance hall of Swanfield House and stared up at the massive portrait of a bewigged gentleman who bore a startling resemblance to her husband. She deduced from Gabriel's disgusted expression that it was the previous Earl of Swanfield in his youth and could quite understand his need to be rid of it.

Keyes sighed. "It will probably leave a lot of marks on the paneling when we take it down, sir."

"I don't care. Just do it."

Lisette followed Gabriel as he mounted the wide staircase and headed down the hallway, leaving all the doors open in his wake. It was just over a week since the Grangers had departed. He stopped near the end of the passageway and walked into one of the rooms.

"In here, Lisette."

She followed him into a large bedchamber complete with a huge oak four-poster bed draped in shades of blue and gold.

"I understand from the plans Mr. Brecon gave me that this is the Countess's suite of rooms." He strode toward a set of double doors and flung them open. "There is a dressing room between us." He looked back over his shoulder at her. "If you plan to start redecorating, you might want to start here."

Lisette stared doubtfully at the heavy oak furniture and the thick velvet drapes that obscured most of the long windows and kept out the light. "Are you sure you don't mind if I change it?"

"It's your room. You can do what you damn well like to it." He grasped one of the posts of the bed and tried to move it. "I assume this bed was built in here, but if you want another one, just ask Keyes to take care of it."

"But it might be a family heirloom."

Gabriel's mouth settled into a firm obstinate line. "I don't care if Queen Elizabeth slept in here. If you don't want it, you don't have to have it."

"That is very generous of you." Lisette studied the other pieces of furniture. "It is a little heavy for my taste."

"Then do what you want with it." He walked back toward the double doors into the dressing room. "I'm thinking about getting a bath put in here."

Lisette let him talk as she contemplated the coat of arms of the Swanfield family that was embroidered onto almost everything possible in the room, its ancient Latin motto *Fidelitas* mocked the most recent residents of the house, but epitomized her husband. He would never have betrayed any secrets to the French or the allies. That was one thing she was certain of.

Deep in thought, she went back down the stairs and headed toward the kitchens, where Keyes had assembled the female staff for her to meet and approve. Her mother and father were very well connected with the Royal Court and Parliament.

Perhaps with their help, the matter about Gabriel's supposed treachery could be properly investigated and he would finally be vindicated.

But then she'd have to make her peace with her parents and she was still avoiding them two weeks after her wedding. . . . Lisette walked into the kitchen and became aware of more than a dozen apprehensive faces staring back at her. She nodded at Keyes and smiled.

"Good morning, everyone, I'm Lady Swanfield. Would you like to introduce yourselves to me?"

Later that night she glanced over at the huge bed and shivered. She'd replaced all the linen with her own and taken down as many of the heavy velvet curtains as she and the staff could manage, but the room still felt oppressive. She glanced at the dressing room doors, but they were firmly closed. She hadn't seen Gabriel since dinnertime, when he had disappeared with Keyes into the wine cellar. After meeting all the staff and confirming their appointments, she was exhausted. She'd never considered how much work managing a big house and staff might be, and she didn't have to do anything but make the most basic of decisions.

With a sigh, she rose to her feet and headed for bed. She suddenly felt unsure of herself and her abilities. Perhaps her parents were right to be concerned about her choices. She'd never planned to marry at such a young age, had in truth thought she'd never marry after her encounter with Lord Nash. Publicly losing one's virginity had a way of narrowing a woman's choices.

She shook her head. No, she would not allow herself to think like that anymore. If Gabriel was willing to change his life and take on his responsibilities, the least she could do was support him. There was much to do on the morrow, and, despite Gabriel's absence, she might as well get some sleep.

* * *

"It's a beautiful room, sir. Perfect for a man of your rank and standing," Keyes said as he folded Gabriel's clothes over his arm.

"I hate it." Gabriel said irritably. "In fact I'm thinking about getting out my old camp bed and sleeping in the dressing room."

"But what's wrong with it, sir?"

"It reeks of my uncle and my father."

Keyes gave a loud sniff. "I can't smell anything but old leather, Bay Rum, and pipe smoke."

"Exactly." Gabriel glared at the monstrosity of the bed, which was complete with a crowned gilded swan, wings spread as if ready to take off into the night. "I think I'll have nightmares."

"I've changed the sheets and the eiderdown to your own ones and replaced all the pillows. There's not much else I can do tonight. I've already spoken to an old acquaintance of mine who is managing the bankruptcy sale for one of his clients. I believe I'll be able to pick up some almost-new furnishings from him until you can choose something for yourself."

"I understand that." Gabriel turned to face his valet. "And I appreciate everything you've done for me today. You have been magnificent."

"Thank you, sir." Keyes saluted, his face flushed with pride. "I've enjoyed seeing you claim your rightful place, sir."

Gabriel's smile died as Keyes left him alone in the horror of the earl's bedroom. He glanced at the clock and saw it was past twelve. Had Lisette gone to sleep in her new quarters or was she as unsettled as he was? He hadn't thought the matter through properly. If he'd had any sense he would've had the place gutted and refurnished to their specifications before they'd moved in.

As the day had passed by, a strange sense of duty had weighed on him as he discovered the portraits of his ancestors, their possessions, their treasures—a heritage that had been denied him until now. He had a noble name and Lisette deserved an orderly, secure life. He would do his best to provide her with one.

At the thought of Lisette, his cock thickened and he wondered anew if she was sleeping. He shrugged on his dressing gown and slipped through the dressing room, paused at her door and saw no light, but kept going anyway. She was sleeping on the very edge of the enormous bed, curled up rather more like a lap dog than the lady of the house. He leaned over her and stroked her hair.

"Gabriel?"

"Who else?"

She wrapped a hand around his neck. "Come to bed."

Somehow it was easier to obey her than to resist. Her room smelled of stale perfume and old dog rather than old earl. He could just about tolerate that. She murmured his name again as he slid into the bed beside her and drew her into his arms. She nestled against him, her cheek coming to rest on his chest as if she had always been there.

His cock hardened even more and he rocked his hips against her. In this bed, and in this house, he was the master; he could ask her for anything he wanted. He drew her hand down over his stomach and clasped it around his shaft. "Touch me . . . please."

She grasped his cock and he began to move his hand, bringing hers with him, adding to his urgency and arousal.

"Where have you been?"

He tried to word a reply, his thoughts too firmly interested in what was happening to his cock to use his brain. "I was in my bedchamber."

"Alone?"

"No, with Keyes."

"You have to sleep in your own bedchamber now?"

"It's common among the aristocracy, I believe," he managed to murmur. "It allows a married couple some privacy."

"Oh."

Her hand went still under his and he stopped moving as well, aware of a pulse in his cock thudding almost as loudly as the one in his heart. He released his grip on her hand, offering her the opportunity to move away from him, but she remained where she was, her fingers lightly stroking him now as if she was pondering something.

He swallowed hard. "Will you stop that?"

"Touching you?"

"No, thinking too much."

She squeezed his cock so hard he gasped. "It just seems strange to me, to want to sleep apart." She pushed the covers down and reared over him, her long hair sweeping across his stomach like a curtain of silk. "My parents always sleep together when they can."

He remained on his back where she had pushed him; his stiff cock trapped within her grip, and waited to see what she would do next. She bent her head and licked his crown.

"Turn around," he whispered. "Straddle me so that I can get my tongue inside you while you suck me."

"If you don't sleep together, how would you know when the other person wanted you like this?"

He stared helplessly up at her. "I don't know, but please, don't let that stop you from sucking me."

He sensed rather than saw her frown and decided it was time to take action. He sat up and rolled her underneath him, spreading her legs wide with his. He eased the first inch of his wet cock inside her, aware that she wasn't yet ready for him, but more than happy to tease and torment her until she could take him deep.

"I understand from my friends that when a gentleman visits his lady wife in her bed, he first makes an appointment with her, probably to make sure he doesn't bump into her lover." He gripped his shaft at the base and rubbed the head of his cock up and down her sex, spreading his pre-cum over her, paying special attention to the tight bundle of nerves that formed her clit.

"If the lady is agreeable to his visit, he waits until she is in bed with all the candles snuffed out, because God forbid he might actually see her naked, and then he joins her." He angled his cock back inside her and felt her give way to his hardness until he was three inches deep. Then he withdrew again and continued to rub himself against her now swollen bud, until she started to lift her hips into each slow, slick caress.

"Then he folds up her nightgown, lowers himself between her legs, and shoves his cock deep." He suited his actions to his words and she gasped his name. He held still over her until she stopped shuddering and relaxed again. "He fucks her hard until he comes, making sure that he is as quick as he can be, because no lady wants a man reveling in such an unpleasant business, does she? And then he climbs off her, bids her good night, and returns to his own bed."

She pulled his hair and he fought a gasp. "And what about his wife? How does she gain her pleasure?"

He stared down at her indignant face. "With her hand or with her lover, I suppose."

"I don't like the sound of that at all, Gabriel." She lifted her hips off the mattress and he settled even deeper inside her. "I don't want to be the sort of woman who is used solely to provide an heir."

He kissed her mouth, kissed her again until she was kissing him back, and began to move slowly over her, each stroke long and even and deep. She sighed into his mouth and her hands moved over his skin, delighting him with her touch and soon urging him on, as her fingers became small sharp claws digging into his back, making him take them both over the edge into pleasure.

He lay heavily on top of her, his head on the pillow beside hers, his arms wrapped around her.

"I like you sleeping in my bed, Gabriel."

He sighed. "I like it, too. I sleep better when you are with me."

"Really?" She nuzzled his neck. "That is good to know."

"I thought I might disturb you with my nightmares, but when I'm with you, they seem to disappear."

She kissed his ear. "Then why bother to go back to your own lonely bed? Stay here with me tonight. Stay with me every night."

He groaned and rolled onto his side, bringing her with him. "I don't believe I have the energy to move anywhere at this moment, so I think you'll have to put up with me, at least for tonight."

"I think I might go and see my father tomorrow."

He opened his eyes to study her face and found her steady gaze fixed on his. "Good."

"Is that all you have to say?"

"Yes." He closed his eyes again and heaved a sigh.

"I don't expect you to come with me."

"Are you sure?"

"Yes."

"I'm more than willing to. . . ."

She pressed a finger to his lips. "I know, but as I caused this problem, I think I'm the one who needs to resolve it, don't you? I'm tired of everyone thinking they have to protect me from everything."

Gabriel ignored his twinge of guilt about his plans to provide her with everything a society wife desired. "Absolutely." He kissed her finger. "I'm sure he'll be delighted to see you."

"I hope so." Lisette leaned into him and buried her face in his shoulder. "I've missed them."

Gabriel stroked her hair and listened as her breathing slowed and she fell asleep. He didn't miss his family at all; felt nothing except delight that he had finally evicted them from his house and soon from his estates. Was he unnatural or had life taught him much harsher lessons than it had Lisette? Sometimes he found her insistence that she bore no grudge against her parents for the circumstances of her birth and upbringing somewhat unbelievable. Not that he doubted that she loved them, but underlying her words he sensed a desperate need for security and normality that resonated with him.

He contemplated his meeting with William at his solicitor's on the morrow and hoped yet again for a successful outcome. Perhaps being deprived of his London "home" would finally bring his uncle to his senses and make him realize that Gabriel was no longer a child to be manipulated and ignored.

He smiled into the darkness. There was nothing else his uncle could do to him now. He'd tried to destroy him and hadn't succeeded. Gabriel was still alive and ready to set matters right. He had a wife now, a wife who needed a respectable home to live in and a family name to be proud of. He knew what Lisette needed better than she did herself, and he would make damn sure that she got it.

20

_____

Lisette cleared her throat. "Good morning, Papa."

Her father looked over his morning paper and slowly put it down on the breakfast table. His hazel eyes, the image of her own, were cool and slightly guarded. "Good morning, Lisette."

She gestured at the table. "May I sit down?"

"Of course. Would you like something to eat, some coffee perhaps?"

"No, thank you, I've already eaten." Lisette studied her hands on the tablecloth. "I came to apologize." He didn't say anything so she had to look at him again and swallowed hard when she realized he wasn't smiling. "I think I overreacted a little on my wedding day."

"A little?"

She felt herself blush. "I believed you and Maman were interfering in my relationship with Gabriel."

"We are your parents; we only wanted what was best for you."

"And you decided Gabriel was the best thing for me?"

"You married him, Lisette," he said gently.

"I married him because I wanted to, not because you or Christian or Maman decided I needed another keeper."

He frowned. "I never thought that."

She held his gaze. "Are you sure?"

"Obviously, I can't speak for your mother, but I wanted you to be happy. When Christian assured us that you wanted to marry Swanfield, I was pleased to help him speed up the arrangements." He hesitated. "If that was wrong of me, I apologize."

"You probably think I am being ridiculous now. That I got what I wanted and that I should be happy about it." Lisette clasped her hands together until her fingers hurt. "But I felt as if everyone had conspired behind my back, as if you didn't trust me to make my own decisions."

Philip covered her hands with one of his own. "Darling, you have to admit you've made some remarkably dubious decisions in the past."

She glared at him. "As if anyone will ever allow me to forget them."

"But then you must understand why we worry about you."

"I've grown up. I've learned from my mistakes!"

He smiled at her. "I'm sure you have, but for us, you will always be our little girl."

Lisette slowly stood up. "But I wasn't your little girl, was I? I was growing up in a French orphanage with Christian without any parents. Your only 'little girl' was Emily." She pushed in her chair. "Thank you for seeing me, Papa, and please, you are welcome to visit us at Swanfield House whenever you like."

Philip stood up. "Lisette, don't do this again."

As she walked out she realized she was close to tears. Why on earth had she said that? Where had all that anger come from? And did her father really believe he had a right to dictate her life choices after being absent from it for eighteen years?

"Lis?"

She bumped into something solid and found herself staring helplessly at her twin. He took her by the hand and then glanced over his shoulder, where she sensed her father had just appeared.

"It's all right, Philip. I'll take care of this." Before she had a chance to do anything but gape at him, Christian marched her up the stairs and into the suite he occasionally occupied. He guided her into a chair and knelt in front of her.

"What's wrong, twin?" He lapsed into the colloquial Breton French only they understood.

Her eyes filled with tears and she shook her head. He handed her a handkerchief and waited while she cried. When she regained control, he was still there, waiting for her to look at him, waiting for her to share her problems with him, just like he had at the orphanage and during their first terrible year in London.

"I came to apologize and I lost my temper with Papa."

"But at least you apologized."

She winced. "Don't try and make this into something amusing, something you can laugh about and walk away from."

He frowned. "I was just trying to cheer you up. Of course I want to listen to you. What happened after you apologized?"

"Papa tried to explain why he had acted as he had, and I found myself getting angry." She hesitated. "He suggested he had a right to care about me because I would always be his little girl. But he never knew me then, Christian, and neither did Maman."

"Ah, I understand now." He squeezed her knee. "*I* knew you."

"You are the only one who did," she whispered. "You are the only one who understands and yet you conspired with Gabriel to deceive me, too."

"I know I did, love, and I would do it again." When she opened her mouth to argue he held up his hand. "I'm your twin. I wanted you to have the choice of marrying Swanfield without Maman and Philip being involved. *That's* why I agreed to help him, and that's why I agreed to pretend to come after you, so that if you did change your mind, you could, and only Swanfield and I would ever know about it."

Lisette stared at him. "You're suggesting you tried to protect me from *them* and not from Gabriel?"

"Of course." He shrugged. "After you sent me away, I came back and assured our parents that all was well. If I'd returned with you, I wouldn't have gone near them and nothing else would've happened."

Lisette studied his face and saw only sincerity. She groaned. "Then perhaps I should go and apologize to Papa again."

Christian stood up and brushed at the knees of his breeches. "Not necessarily."

"What do you mean?"

"It doesn't hurt our revered father and mother to have to think about you in a new light."

"Are you suggesting I let them come to me?"

He shrugged. "Yes. Let them see you in your new home, with your new husband and social rank."

Lisette shivered. "And what if I make a mull of this as well?"

"That's Swanfield's problem, isn't it? Not theirs, and he seems more than happy to take you on." His wicked grin flashed out. "And you won't make a mess of it; I think you'll surprise everyone."

She stood up and hugged him hard. "Thank you, Christian."

He folded her into his arms. "You're welcome. And am I forgiven, too?"

She smiled up at him. "I think so."

He kissed her forehead. "Good. Now set a date and invite everyone around to dinner at your new house. I'll make sure that they all turn up."

*   *   *

Gabriel followed Mr. Brecon up the stairs and into his office and found William already there standing in front of the meager fire. He wore his army uniform, the buttons on his coat as brightly polished as his boots. His expression, however, was distinctly unfriendly.

"Good morning, Cousin," William said. "Did you enjoy throwing my family out of your house?"

Inwardly, Gabriel groaned, even as he arranged his features into a polite expression. "I didn't exactly throw them out. They had almost a week to leave. And by the way, I was glad to see that you weren't living there with them."

Mr. Brecon cleared his throat. "As to that, my lord, I can only apologize for not being aware that the house was inhabited . . ." Gabriel waved away the apology and focused his attention on William. William sat down heavily in the nearest chair. "I'm not quite that stupid. I told my father it was a bad idea when things were so unpleasant between us, but he refused to listen to me."

Gabriel took the chair opposite William, leaving Mr. Brecon to scuttle behind his desk. "I understand that your parents have taken up residence in Half Moon Street."

"Indeed they have." William hesitated. "I didn't realize you were to be married. My mother was quite shocked."

Gabriel shrugged. "It was something of a surprise to me, too."

William sat forward in his seat. "May I be so bold as to ask whom you married?"

"Miss Ross. You met her briefly at the St. Clares' ball."

"Ah . . . I wondered if that was who it was."

Gabriel tensed as William drew in a breath. "Is there something wrong, cousin?"

William met his gaze. "You know what I'm like, Gabriel, my mouth tends to run away with me, so I apologize if I give offense. Are you aware of who Miss Ross really is?"

"I'm well aware of her parentage, William," Gabriel said repressively.

William cleared his throat. "She is not exactly considered respectable. Last night at the officer's club someone repeated some very unpleasant gossip about her and Lord Nash."

Gabriel locked gazes with his cousin. "She is my wife and the new Countess of Swanfield. If you hear anyone else gossiping about her, please refer them to me. I would be delighted to disabuse them of any notions that she is not completely and utterly respectable."

William turned pale. "Absolutely, cousin. I'll be sure to do that. And may I wish you happy?"

Gabriel smiled. "You may. Now have you made any progress with your father?"

William patted his face with his handkerchief and stuffed it back into his pocket. "I believe I have. Mr. Sturges, the land steward who manages the Swanfield estates, is coming up to Town this week. I'll arrange for you to meet him. He is very concerned about my father's state of health."

"That would be excellent, and as, strictly speaking, he is *my* land steward, no one can possibly object."

"That's true." William sighed. "I asked him to bring the last three years' accounts with him."

"Even better." Gabriel held out his hand. "I know this is hard for you, William, but I appreciate it."

William stood up and shook his hand. "As I said, I'm a fool who often says far more than he should, but I can't abide dishonesty. Even though my own father is involved, I can no longer stand by and condone his behavior."

"Thank you." Gabriel turned to Mr. Brecon. "You will let me know when Mr. Sturges arrives so that we can all meet?"

"Of course, my lord." Mr. Brecon smiled and bowed.

Gabriel turned back to William. "Which club do you frequent these days, cousin?"

William looked resigned. "The Old Peninsular, of course." He bowed. "Good morning, cousin."

"Good morning, William." Gabriel watched his cousin leave. "A club where I'm probably still not welcome. How convenient." Gabriel sighed and knew he'd have to brazen it out anyway. There was no other option if he wanted to hear the gossip that had conveniently started up about his wife and maybe even ascertain the whereabouts of a certain Lord Nash.

Gabriel smiled at Lisette across the dinner table and finished the last of his wine.

"I have to go out this evening, do you mind?"

She contemplated him through the candlelight, her hazel eyes narrowed. "Where exactly are you going?"

"To visit some old army comrades of mine."

"I thought you avoided those people."

"Some of them. Others I still enjoy seeing."

"You aren't going to the pleasure house without me, are you?"

He quashed the peculiar thrill the thought of the pleasure house gave him and shook his head. "Not at all, why do you ask?"

She sighed and rested her chin on her hand. "Because I haven't quite made up with my mother yet. And she might wonder why you are there without me."

"I thought you were set on apologizing to your family today?"

"I got as far as my father and something he said made me angry so I ended up walking out again."

He put down his glass. "What did he say?"

"It sounds absurd now, but he made some reference to my childhood and I found myself getting annoyed."

"Because he wasn't really involved with your life then, was he? I'd say you had a right to be angry about that." He nodded at her. "About time, too, I'd say."

"You make it sound as if you approve of what I did."

"I do."

"Because I got angry?"

"Yes."

"But I don't get angry. I leave that to Christian. I completely understand why my parents couldn't be with me."

He shrugged. "Maybe you do now, but when you were a child? I don't think you ever forgive your parents for forsaking you."

"Just because you haven't, you mean?"

He stood up. "What?"

She looked up at him, her face composed. "You haven't forgiven your father for creating you in such an appalling manner, have you? And what about your mother? You never even talk about her."

He shoved back his chair. "Good night, wife."

"Where are you going? We haven't finished our conversation yet."

He strode toward the door. "I'll see you tomorrow at breakfast. Sleep well."

"Gabriel Swanfield . . ."

He ignored her, collected his hat, cloak, and gloves from Keyes at the front door, and stepped out into the night. He was quite happy to discuss Lisette's parents with her, but God help her if she wanted to discuss his. He was aware he was being unfair, but he didn't care. Rage and shame coalesced in his stomach and he fought them down. Better to preserve his energy for the potential confrontation ahead.

He mounted Wellington and nodded at Mather to fall in behind him. Paul St. Clare was waiting for him at his old lodgings. They would brave the horrors of the Old Peninsular club together.

Paul hesitated as they approached the double stained-glass doors of the club and turned to Gabriel. "Are you sure you want to do this?"

"Unfortunately, I have no choice. I refuse to have my wife's name bandied about in any club, let alone this one."

"All right then." Paul sighed. "But don't blame me if someone takes offense at your presence. I'm not the best man to have beside you in a fight."

Gabriel smiled. "I don't know, Paul. You learned to fight well enough in that prison cell we occupied."

"But, alas, not quite like a gentleman."

"We're alive, aren't we? Many of our fellow inmates weren't so lucky."

Paul's expression darkened. "That's true. I remember that first night when they brought you in all bloody and beaten."

"And I remember the way those bastards descended on me and stripped me clean before you and a couple of the other men saved my neck."

"And your arse," Paul added.

Gabriel shuddered. "And that—although by the time I recovered from my fever, I was willing to trade anything just for some clothes and water."

Paul opened the door into the club and nodded at the doorman. "As you said, we survived. Let's hope we can survive this far more civilized form of torture."

When they entered the main oak-paneled room, a sudden hush fell over the thirty or so occupants. Paul smiled in a general way and walked over to the far corner of the main salon, where they would get the best view of who came in and out.

Gabriel felt as if a hundred pairs of eyes were staring at him accusingly and wanted to turn tail. He'd deliberately chosen not to confront his ex-army comrades in the past, but now he had no choice. Lisette's honor was far more important than his cowardice. He refused to have her name sullied.

"Is that you, Swanfield?"

He looked up to see an older, shorter man with a bushy mustache staring down at him. "Good evening, Walsh."

Walsh looked around the room and deliberately raised his voice. "I'm surprised you dared show your face in here."

"Really? Why is that?"

"Because there are probably men here who lost comrades and even family because of your perfidy."

Paul cleared his throat. "Nothing was ever proven against Lord Swanfield."

"Only because he was too damn important to stand trial."

A small group gathered around their table and Gabriel felt suffocated. Lieutenant Walsh had never liked him, so it was hardly surprising he was the first to attack. Gabriel maintained his pleasant expression. "I offered to stand trial, but I was refused the chance. Someone decided I should be sent home."

"That's not what I heard." Walsh scoffed. "A close friend of yours told me that you faked your injuries and your illness simply to avoid being shot."

Gabriel slowly stood up so that everyone could see the scars on his face. "I faked nothing. I spent several months in a French prison and barely escaped with my life."

Paul rose, too, and faced the growing crowd. "And I can personally vouch for Lord Swanfield, seeing as we spent those months in the same godforsaken hole."

Walsh's color rose and he started to bluster. "You still shouldn't be here."

"I think he should." Walsh fell silent as another man pushed his way through the crowd. His prematurely white hair gleamed in the candlelight. His eyes were the pale silver of a wolf.

Gabriel found himself saluting. "Sir."

His immediate superior officer, Lieutenant Colonel Constantine Delinsky, nodded at him. "It's good to see you again, Swanfield."

"It's good to see you, too, sir."

"I had hoped to meet you before this, but on your return from Spain, you seemed to disappear."

"I was . . . unwell for a long time, sir."

"So I should imagine." Delinsky turned to face the other men. His slight Russian accent was soft but still commanded the attention of everyone. "It might interest you to know that my younger brother, Francis, was imprisoned with Major Swanfield and Lieutenant St. Clare."

His thoughtful gaze raked over Walsh. "My brother told me that during his time in the prison, Swanfield stopped his fellow prisoners behaving like animals, forced them to share their rations and water, and reminded them that they were still representing their King and Country." He paused for a long moment. "That does not sound to me like the kind of man who would betray his fellow officers."

Silence fell around them and Gabriel met Delinsky's silver gaze. "Your brother was an example to the other men, sir. He never despaired and was, in truth, one of the men responsible for our successful escape."

"That is correct. A breakout that nearly succeeded in bringing about your death, Swanfield, as I understand you insisted on bringing up the rear and making sure that everyone, including the wounded, got out."

Walsh cleared his throat and glanced around at his supporters. "With all due respect, Delinsky. If this were true, how is it that nothing was known about it at the time?"

"Oh, it was known about. The authorities simply chose not to believe it." Delinsky's idle gaze scanned the assembled company. "A matter which I have fought to have put right for many years."

He held out his hand. "I, for one, am delighted to welcome Swanfield as a member of this club. If anyone disagrees, please feel free to express your concerns directly to me. I don't wish to disturb Swanfield's evening any longer."

The gathering dispersed, leaving Gabriel still standing, one hand clenched at his side, the other just touching the edge of the table simply to feel something solid and real. Constantine Delinsky sat down and gestured for Gabriel and Peter to do the same. He leaned back to allow a waiter to pour them all a brandy.

"If you are established in Town now, Swanfield, may I bring my mother and brother to pay their respects?"

"Of course, sir." Gabriel responded instinctively, his nerves jangling, the desire to leave still pulsing through his veins. "I'm at Swanfield House on Portman Square."

"I know it well. I have an aunt who lives on the same square." Delinsky sat forward. "What made you decide to finally breach these potentially unforgiving walls?"

Gabriel stared into his former commanding officer's eyes and saw nothing but interest and the desire to help. "In truth, not for my own benefit. I have recently married and I've heard that gossip about my reputation, or lack of it, is being superseded by gossip about my wife."

"Ah. Would that be the former Miss Delornay-Ross?"

Gabriel sat up straight. "Yes."

"I know both her parents quite well, and I met Miss Ross during her, um, 'wilder' days." Delinsky smiled and Gabriel wanted to bare his teeth and growl. "Like you, in my opinion, her reputation was greatly exaggerated. I found her charming, but utterly devoted to that preening idiot Lord Nash."

Gabriel let out his breath. He would've hated to have to punch Delinsky after all the good work he'd done for him that night, but Lisette was his wife.

Delinsky frowned. "If someone *is* gossiping about Miss Ross it probably has something to do with Nash. He's never learned to keep his damn mouth shut." He nodded at Swanfield and got to his feet. "I'll let you know if I hear anything."

Gabriel stood, too. "Thank you, sir. Thank you for everything."

Delinsky paused to look back at him. "I did nothing but tell the truth. If you'd come and found me after I returned to England, I would've been glad to have offered you my help."

"I didn't think I needed it—until now, sir. But I thank you all the same." Gabriel hesitated. "Do you know a Major Lord Thomas Wesley?"

"I believe I've heard of him." Delinsky considered Gabriel for a long moment. "Should I know him?"

Paul answered for Gabriel. "He is investigating the allegations about Major Swanfield's conduct in Spain, sir. I'm sure he'd be delighted to hear from you and your brother."

Delinsky turned to Paul and saluted before nodding at Gabriel. "Thank you for the information, and I hope to see you both again soon."

"Thank you, sir," Gabriel said and sat down rather abruptly as Delinsky turned away. Paul shoved his brandy glass back into his hand.

"I think we'll be all right here now. Delinsky is one of the founding members of this club. If he offers you membership, I doubt anyone else will disagree with him."

"That's good, I think." Gabriel tried to gather his scattered wits. "Does *everyone* know Lisette?"

Paul grinned. "She is rather memorable, Gabriel."

"So it seems."

"I didn't mean that in a negative way at all," Paul said hastily. "She is very charming."

"I know." Gabriel grimaced and finished off his brandy in one swallow. "Now how can I stop the gossip about her without further damaging her reputation?"

"The best thing to do would be to track down the cause of the gossip and shut it off at its source. Lord Nash seems to be the obvious person to pursue."

"Indeed. Perhaps we should concentrate on meeting him in

private to convince him to keep his lurid speculations to himself?"

"We?" Paul asked.

"You aren't going to come with me?"

Paul sighed. "You make it damn difficult for me to refuse."

"I'm not being fair, am I?" Gabriel asked abruptly. "I've told you repeatedly that I'm not interested in having a relationship with you, yet I still expect you to jump every time I snap my fingers."

Paul's mouth twitched. "I'm not quite that desperate, Gabriel. I do have some self-respect, you know."

"Paul . . ."

His friend grinned at him. "I'm only joking. Now if you were to get down on your knees and start begging me, I might be persuaded to believe you cared."

Gabriel chose to say nothing, signaled the waiter to bring them more brandy, and settled back in his seat to watch the door. He'd enjoyed being on his knees to both men and women at the pleasure house and knew he'd still enjoy watching Paul come for him. His cock twitched and thickened in his breeches. God, would his perverse desires never leave him? He'd assumed that by finding the perfect woman he would be able to forget such strange aberrations, but the thought of Paul aroused him. . . .

"I think it's time to go home."

"Are you sure? We've hardly been here an hour."

Gabriel shrugged. "After all the excitement tonight, I doubt our prey will appear, do you? We'll come back another night."

Paul stretched and yawned. "You're probably right. Let's go. I'll let you know when I find a good time and place to talk to Lord Nash."

"That would be excellent." Gabriel threw some coins onto the table for the brandy and headed for the door. He didn't want Paul too close to him at this moment. His friend knew all his moods far too intimately not to notice the swelling in Gabriel's breeches and possibly realize he was the cause of it. And that would never do. Those days were long behind him.

He settled his hat on his head and mounted Wellington. His wife was at home and he knew that she would be more than willing to indulge his most outrageous sexual requests. An image of Paul sucking his cock while he licked Lisette's sex seared through his mind and made him tighten the reins until Wellington bucked in protest.

Where in God's name had that come from? Gabriel stared blindly into the night sky, willing both his imagination and his erection to the devil. He'd never share Lisette with anyone. He kicked the horse into a fast trot and headed for home, even as an even more insidious thought invaded his consciousness. He might not be willing to share Lisette, but would she be willing to share him?

21

"What are you doing in here?"

Lisette opened her eyes to find Gabriel looming over her and the fire beside her almost out. She yawned delicately behind her hand and drew her thick wool shawl closer to her breasts.

"Waiting for you."

"Here?" Gabriel flung out his hand in a disdainful gesture that included the whole of his gloomy bedchamber.

"I was bored and it occurred to me that I hadn't seen this room, so I came in and chatted with Keyes while he set things to rights."

"And you didn't leave." Gabriel discarded his coat and waistcoat and tugged at his cravat until he could slip the still-tied knot over his head.

Lisette frowned up at him as he dropped his clothes onto the floor. "I'll leave now if you are going to be so unwelcoming."

He took off his boots, unbuttoned his breeches, and pulled his shirt free. "I thought you would be asleep."

"You were home earlier than I anticipated." She studied him carefully. "Is something wrong?"

He sat down on the side of the bed to push down his breeches and underthings and she couldn't help but notice he was erect.

"Where did you say you were going?"

"To a gentleman's club that Lieutenant St. Clare belongs to."

Lisette sat up and allowed the shawl to slip down to her waist. "And how *was* Paul?"

"He was well. Why do you ask?"

Lisette raised her eyebrows and stared at his groin until he wrapped a hand around his shaft as if to protect himself from her gaze.

"What?"

"Lieutenant St. Clare is very fond of you, isn't he?"

"Aye, we were held captive together in Spain."

"All men together and no women."

He shot her a wary glance. "That's what prisons are usually like. Occasionally one of us was brought out and cleaned up so that the ladies and gents of the town could experience what it was like to fuck or abuse an Englishman secured to a bed in chains." His mouth curled in disgust. "But that was an exception. Most of the men were too sick or repulsive to be seen above ground."

"But you were used like that?"

"Yes."

"And you didn't mind?"

"Anything that meant a break from the horrors of that damn cesspit we inhabited was welcome."

Lisette shivered at the darkness of his expression. "But generally you were stuck in the cell with other men and principally Paul St. Clare."

"He saved my life the first night I was there, and I protected him in return." A muscle flicked on his cheek as he continued to contemplate the floorboards. "A bond like that is hard to break."

"I'm sure it is." Lisette considered him. "Exactly how close were you?"

Gabriel slowly raised his head and met her gaze, his blue eyes full of memories. "Close."

Lisette got up and strolled across to Gabriel, watched him slowly straighten as she stopped in front of him. "Close enough to be lovers?"

"Yes."

"And he still wants you."

Gabriel shrugged. "That is none of your business."

"That is true." She leaned in and ran her fingers over the curve of his hip and down toward his half-erect cock and balls. "What is my business, however, is whether you still want him."

He swallowed hard, his voice husky. "Why would you think that?"

She flicked the hard wet tip of his cock with her fingertip. "Because of this?"

He caught her hand and brought it to his lips. "I told you once that when we married I would never stray."

"I assumed you meant with a woman."

He nipped at the soft pad of flesh just beneath her thumb, then licked the pain away. "I don't need anyone but you."

She drew her hand out of his grasp. "You don't sound very sure. Would you like it if I allowed you to have male lovers?"

He sighed. "That's not fair, Lisette."

"Not fair of me to offer you what you want?"

He caught her hands and brought her hard against him. "I want you, I want this marriage, and I want our children." His mouth met hers and suddenly there was no breath left in her lungs for speaking. She wrapped her arms around his neck and stepped between his legs, felt the thick heat of his shaft rub and catch against the linen of her nightgown.

Before he could stop her, she dropped down onto her knees, drew his cock deep into her mouth, and sucked him hard. He started to groan, one hand fisted in her hair as she worked him. Even as his hips bucked and he ground himself against her, she couldn't help wondering if he was thinking of Paul St. Clare doing this to him. Would a man feel different? Would his strength make it harder for Gabriel to resist the need to come?

She opened her eyes and looked up at him. His expression was one of pure lust, his features locked and straining, his lower lip caught between his teeth as she sucked him. She slid her left hand over his buttock and delved between his legs, stroking the tender skin between his balls and his arse until he groaned her name. With her right hand she gripped the base of his cock and slowly withdrew her mouth from him.

"Do you wish Paul was here kneeling in my place?"

His eyes flew open and he stared down at her. "What?"

She circled the puckered bud of his arse hole and inserted the tip of her wet finger inside him. "Do you wish I was Paul?"

"No, damn you, I . . ."

She worked his cock through the tight grip of her fingers until his pre-cum ran over her fingers, and she shoved the finger in his arse deeper. "Are you sure?" She kissed his cock, let him see her tongue circle the crown and probe the slit. He tried to thrust upward, but she held him captive. "How about both of us?"

"God . . ." His pupils dilated so widely that almost all the blue in his eyes disappeared and he came all over her hand. She watched him climax feeling strangely detached and removed her hands from him.

"Good night, my lord."

He reached for her. "Don't go, not like this, not when I haven't explained. . . ."

She kept moving. It was her own fault after all; she'd asked him and he'd only told her the truth. He caught her as she reached the door and held onto her upper arms.

"Listen to me," he said urgently. "What I used to want and what I want now are two different things. You caught me at a vulnerable moment, but I'm a changed man. I promise you that you have nothing to worry about. I'll be in your bed and your bed alone."

She made herself look up at him. "I'm not sure I believe you."

"Why not?"

She sighed. "It's not that simple, Gabriel, is it? We can't change who we are or what we want."

He glared down at her. "Yes, we can."

"So we are going to become the perfect society couple who make an appointment to have sex and don't enjoy it at all?"

"It doesn't have to be quite like that, Lisette, but we will certainly be more conventional."

"Oh."

He kissed her nose. "I know you want that."

"To be more conventional?"

"Of course you do. After your upbringing I'm beginning to understand that a solid, unadventurous marriage and a respectable husband are exactly what you need and exactly what I am going to provide for you."

She stepped out of his arms. "Do you realize how pompous and arrogant that makes you sound?"

"Why?" He shrugged, his muscled skin gleaming in the soft candlelight. "I know you, Lisette. I know what you want."

"Strange that, when I'm not even sure if *I* know what I want."

"You want me."

She studied him as she backed up toward the door. "I'm married to you."

"What the hell is that supposed to mean?" Gabriel roared.

She slipped through the door of the dressing room, picked up her nightgown, and ran for the other door that led into her bedroom. Of course he followed her. She must know him well enough to realize he was hardly going to walk away from a challenge like that. She gasped as he tugged her nightgown over her head and brought her against his naked body, his hands

262 / Kate Pearce

roaming her flesh, cupping her buttocks, bringing her up on her toes to crush her against his rapidly expanding cock.

"You think our marriage bed will be boring?" He kissed her mouth, her throat, the curve of her ear; felt her breath catch as he lifted her and deposited her onto the bed on her hands and knees. He bent over her, his teeth grazing her shoulder as he rubbed his now erect cock against her buttocks. "You think this will ever be boring?"

He thrust inside her, one arm wrapped around her hips to keep her where he wanted her and the other on the mattress to take his weight. He dragged his hand lower and spread his fingers wide, slid the longest up and down over her swollen clit until she was writhing and bucking under him and coming all around his cock.

He kept thrusting, fingering her clit until she was begging him for release, until she was so slippery and wet that he could barely find her bud. He held still as she climaxed again, looking down at his cock embedded in her cunt and picturing it elsewhere.

God, he wanted to fuck her arse, knew she liked it, wanted it so much he almost came thinking about it. He tried to breathe more slowly. "Do you have oil, Lisette?"

"What?" Her voice was muffled by the pillows. "In the drawer by my bed. My mother gave it to me."

Gabriel reached out his right hand and connected with the bedside table, then fumbled his way down to the drawer and managed to open it. He retrieved the small glass vial of oil and poured some on his fingers. Lisette trembled when he stroked her puckered skin just above his cock and slowly inserted one well-oiled finger.

He kept his cock still and deep inside her as he worked her arse, adding more oiled fingers until he was moving four in and out of her. He bent to kiss her neck. "I want my cock in here, too. I want my cum all over you."

He pulled out of her cunt and slowly eased his cock inside her arse, bracing his oiled fingers against the sheets. "Is this boring? Are you bored?"

She moaned his name as he began to move, loving the different, more unforgiving tightness of her arse. After ten strokes he was no longer being quite so careful. By twenty he was slamming into her and groaning with every thrust, fighting off his climax with every fiber of his being until he was simply focused on coming.

He grabbed her hand, settled it over her mound, and encouraged her to finger fuck herself while he fucked her arse. She moved with him, her breathing as ragged as his own, her body tightening and fighting around him as he strained for completion, lost all rhythm, and simply exploded into her, all his passion, all his ridiculous longing for Paul, all his love for Lisette combined in the shuddering wave of his release.

He sank down on her and held her tight, whispered into her ear, "Not boring. Not boring at all, love." He didn't hear her reply as he fell into a deep dreamless sleep.

Eventually Lisette managed to wiggle out from under Gabriel's weight and claim a space in the bed for her own. She hadn't been bored, but she was far more worried than she had been before. Everything seemed wrong. Her parents were acting as if she was some foolish seventeen-year-old debutante who needed to be protected from her own folly and Gabriel. . . .

Gabriel was trying to turn them and their marriage into something they were not. She swallowed down an unacceptable desire to cry. What had happened to his oft-expressed opinion that she deserved to have choices? And what about the choices he was trying to make for himself just to keep her happy? None of it made sense and she wasn't quite sure how to deal with it.

One thing was certain: she was no longer obliged to play by anybody's rules but her own. She wasn't a child and she wasn't

Gabriel's perfect wife either. Now all she had to do was decide exactly what she wanted and how to achieve her own happiness. It was the only way to convince everyone that she was capable of choosing her own destiny and creating her own life. Whatever happened, she was determined not to be told what to do by anyone ever again.

22

"Don't forget that we have been invited to Emily's ball to-morrow night."

Gabriel had to look up as Lisette waved the invitation under his nose.

"I assume you want to go."

She sighed and perched on the corner of his desk, her expression thoughtful, her hazel eyes shadowed. "I want to go for Emily's sake, of course, but I'm not sure if I want to see my parents."

He put down his pen. "I thought we'd already discussed this and that you were determined to make amends."

"Actually, I decided to let them apologize to me." She swung her slippered foot back and forth, making her skirts rustle.

"For what?"

"For interfering, and for treating me as though I was incapable of making my own decisions."

Something about her airy tone made all his senses come to attention. "So you intend to continue the argument."

"Not exactly, because then they could say I'm acting like a child and that they were right all along."

He pinched the bridge of his nose. "I don't understand."

"I've decided to be gracious and well behaved and to pretend that everything is forgotten and forgiven." She brushed at his sleeve as if removing a piece of lint. "I would think you'd like that: me behaving like a proper married woman."

He leaned back to study her carefully. "Now why am I feeling concerned?"

She slid off the desk and smiled sweetly at him. "I have no idea."

"So are we going to the ball or not?"

"I rather think we should, don't you?" She walked toward the door. "Oh, and we are invited to dinner beforehand as well."

He regarded her suspiciously as she blew him a kiss and drifted away. Ever since he'd suggested that she would appreciate a more conventional marriage and husband, she'd been behaving strangely. He frowned at the now empty doorway. Well, not strangely perhaps, but far too properly.

He picked up his pen and stared down at the letter from Paul St. Clare's uncle he had been trying to read. Lisette still welcomed him into her bed and seemed to enjoy his lovemaking, but she didn't initiate anything or seek him out when he didn't come to her. He sighed. But that was what he'd wanted, wasn't it? An opportunity to leave the sexual excesses of the pleasure house behind him. He tried to focus on the letter and realized he hadn't understood a single word.

He threw down his pen and stood up. There was no point trying to work while he was in this mood. He'd go down to the stables and spend some time with his horses. That had always soothed him in the past.

Lisette had always been good at expressing her sexual needs before. . . . Gabriel paused to remember her mastering him at the pleasure house and immediately got hard. In truth, that was one of the things he appreciated most about her: her ability to shock him out of hiding, to force him to own up to his feelings and his desires. Had he taken that from her with his demands that she play the part of his wife? And by doing so, had he also denied himself?

With a curse, he headed down to the mews. Perhaps if Lisette resolved her issues with her family, he might find both a way to reach her and a way out of the tangle he had created. And he had created this mess; he knew that in his very soul.

Gabriel settled Lisette into the carriage and walked around to get in the other side. She was wearing what he assumed was a new gown made of rich cream-colored fabric with a low bodice sewn with pearls, which suited her perfectly. He'd prefer to keep the lush curves of her bosom for his own personal viewing, but even he knew that fashion allowed a married woman to display more of herself than a debutante.

There were pearls at her throat and in her hair as well, ropes of them entwined with the intricate braids that framed her face. He liked her hair down around her shoulders, but that delight, at least, was for him alone. . . .

"I'm not pregnant, Gabriel."

Drawn abruptly from his pleasant thoughts, he could only blink at her. "I beg your pardon?"

"I said, I'm not pregnant."

He studied her carefully, aware that beneath her subtle face paint she was paler than usual, her lips tight, her hands clenched on her lap. Inside him, something not yet fully realized shifted, broke, died, but he couldn't attend to it now, he had to pay attention to his wife.

"What would you like me to say?"

She shrugged. "I don't know."

"Then why fling the words at me like an accusation?"

She looked away from him. "If you'd agreed to my original

plan and waited for three more weeks, you could've avoided being married at all."

"I thought I'd already made it clear that I didn't marry you for your breeding ability." Why was speaking suddenly so hard? It felt like someone had punched him in the guts. He tensed as the carriage slowed and came to a stop. Damnation, he'd agreed to pick Paul St. Clare up and now he was regretting it like the devil. "Can we discuss this after the ball?"

"What is there to discuss?"

"Why you are so angry with me."

"Isn't it obvious?"

He heard Paul's jovial voice talking to the coachman as he approached the carriage and glared at his wife. "No, it isn't obvious, but then I've never been known for my quick wits. Perhaps you're angry because you are the one who is no longer free."

She opened her mouth to reply, but the carriage door was wrenched open and Paul appeared. His warm smile faded as he looked from Gabriel to Lisette. "Good evening, my lady, my lord. Shall I find another form of transport to the ball?"

Lisette smiled at him. "Of course not. We are more than happy to share our carriage with you, sir."

Paul sat down beside Gabriel. "That is very gracious of you, considering that the last time I accompanied you anywhere, I literally threw you into the arms of your husband here."

Lisette laughed and only Gabriel heard the strain behind it. Paul continued to talk as if nothing was wrong until they reached Knowles House. He jumped down to offer a hand to Lisette and winked at Gabriel.

"At least she's forgiven me for manhandling her."

Gabriel couldn't even raise a smile. "I wish she'd damn well forgive me."

Paul looked startled. "She married you. Doesn't that count for something?"

"You'd be surprised what it counts for," Gabriel muttered as he went on ahead to take Lisette's hand and lead her into the house. He glanced at the big clock in the hallway, which was about to strike eight. If they could just get through the formal dinner and the ball, he might stand a chance of speaking to her in the privacy of their own house—in about six hours' time.

Lisette glanced across at Gabriel as he smiled slightly at something her father said to him. His manners were impeccable as usual. She was probably the only person—apart from Paul St. Clare—who knew her husband was not pleased with her. She placed her hand on her heated cheek and sighed.

"Are you all right, Lisette?"

With great reluctance she turned toward her mother, who was studying her with obvious concern.

"I'm just a little overheated, thank you, *Maman.*"

Helene's blue eyes flashed and she took Lisette's hand. "I am tired of this, Lisette. Come with me."

Lisette rose with ill grace and followed her mother out of the elaborately decorated dining room and into the coolness of her father's study. Gabriel didn't even glance up at her as she left, but she knew he was as aware of her as ever, that he would come and find her if he thought she'd been gone too long.

Helene shut the door with a definite bang. "Are you going to treat me like this for the whole evening?"

"Like what?" Lisette stared at her mother.

"As if we are strangers?"

"*Maman* . . ."

Helene held up her hand. "I understand that you are annoyed with us for interfering but . . ." She stopped speaking. "Lisette, what is it?"

Lisette bit down on her lip and felt the sting of tears on her cheeks. "I'm not pregnant, *Maman.*"

"Oh, my love." Lisette was enfolded in her mother's arms

and held tightly, rocked as if she were an infant herself. "I'm so sorry."

"And I didn't think I cared until I found out this morning that I wasn't . . . and then I cried and cried." She shook her head. "It makes no sense at all."

"Sometimes, when we feel something very deeply, common sense has nothing to do with how we react." Helene hugged her hard. "It's all right, my love, it's all right to cry."

It took quite a while before she was capable of sitting beside her mother and speaking coherently again.

"When I told Gabriel, he just sat there like an unfeeling block of stone and accused me of shouting at him."

"Did you shout?"

"Of course not!" Lisette blew her nose in the lace handkerchief her mother handed her. "And *then* he suggested that the reason I was angry was because *I* still wanted to be free."

"I've found that many men have difficulty expressing their feelings properly. You probably took him by surprise, and he reacted by going on the offensive. That's a very male thing to do, especially when emotions are involved." Helene held Lisette's gaze. "And was he right?"

"About whether I want to be free of him? That's hardly the point, is it? I'm married to him now."

Helene looked thoughtful. "There might be something we can do about that. I'll talk to your father."

"What on earth do you mean?" Lisette looked up as there was a gentle tap on the door behind Helene and Gabriel came in.

Helene half-turned and raised her voice as if to include Gabriel in the conversation. "Just that we might be able to arrange it so that your marriage never happened."

Lisette jumped to her feet as Gabriel flinched and went still. She was aware that she must look guilty; knew from the unimpressed look on his face that he believed she'd sought her mother's help to escape him. He ignored her and bowed to Helene.

"May I speak to Lisette alone, please, my lady?"

"Of course you may," Helene said. "And if you do decide that you no longer wish to be married, please let me know."

After her mother left, Gabriel leaned against the door and studied her. "You wish to be free of me then."

"That's not what I said. My mother was merely . . ."

He interrupted her. "Marriage comes in many forms, Lisette. We don't have to do anything together if you don't wish to, but we will remain married."

She took a hasty step toward him. "Don't you care now that I'm not carrying your child?"

He looked away from her. "That is hardly fair."

"But this has all worked out perfectly for you, hasn't it? You have all the respectability a man in your position could desire, and, if you choose to avoid my bed from now on, you also have the opportunity never to have a child, which is what you wanted all along."

She wrapped her arms around herself. God, she hurt. She hurt so much, he had to see it, had to know, had to tell her that he understood. . . .

He sighed. "If you truly can't bear to be married to me, perhaps your mother can help you get out of it. I'm prepared to listen to anything she has to say." He hesitated. "I'm trying to offer you a choice, Lisette."

"You offer me no choice at all." Her voice trembled, but she kept speaking. Couldn't he see that she didn't want a choice? That she wanted him to tell her that it didn't matter, that he wanted her, that he loved her. . . . "In truth, you offer me nothing more than the sham of a marriage where all the power is in your hands."

He came away from the wall so fast she backed away from

him. "Damn you for twisting my words and for being pleased that you don't carry my child." He slammed his hand onto her father's desk. "And damn you for not believing I wanted you and that child of *ours* with every fiber of my being."

He stood his ground, his eyes burning, his voice shaken. "Damn you to hell, wife."

Before Lisette could say a word, he turned on his heel and walked out. She sunk down onto the nearest chair and buried her face in her hands. The sound of his contempt still rang in her ears. God, what a disaster. Why wasn't she in his arms now sharing her disappointment and seeking his strength?

She slowly raised her head and faced a bitter truth. Because she'd been a fool. He'd told her how he felt but with anger instead of love and she could only blame herself for pushing him into it. She'd allowed her fears of being abandoned to undermine her. She wiped at her swollen eyes. Was there any way to redeem herself or had she lost him forever?

Gabriel emerged into the hallway of Knowles House and stopped abruptly. He couldn't walk out. If he was to help restore Lisette's reputation, he could hardly refuse to attend her sister's ball at her side. He wanted to laugh at the irony of his situation. She didn't want him; she didn't want their marriage, yet he was bound to her in so many ways. . . .

"Gabriel? Are you all right?"

He turned to find Paul watching him from the doorway to the dining room. "I'm . . ."

Paul came toward him, his expression full of concern. "Can I help at all?"

Gabriel stared at his friend. "Not this time."

"Then why don't you come back and finish your dinner?"

Gabriel drew in a long breath. "I suppose I have no choice."

With Paul's gallant help, he managed to get through the excruciating meal. He even kept his seat when Lisette returned with her mother, her shock at seeing him still there evident in her eyes as she sat down. Had she no respect for him at all? Did she truly believe herself so unnecessary to his comfort that he would abandon her?

After the meal, they moved straight into the ballroom. Gabriel couldn't quite bring himself to take Lisette's arm but he followed along behind her as she chatted with a highly excited Emily.

Lord Knowles patted his shoulder. "We'd appreciate it if you and Lisette stood in the receiving line with us tonight."

"Of course." Gabriel nodded. At least it gave him a further excuse not to look directly at Lisette or attempt to converse with her until he'd decided what the devil to do next.

"Gabriel."

He almost turned his back on her when she touched his hand. He managed to stand his ground, but speech was beyond him. She drew him away from the rest of the family and behind some of the large potted plants that adorned the ballroom.

"I didn't ask my mother to arrange for our marriage to end."

He managed a shrug, but she stepped even closer and put her hand flat on his chest. Tears glinted in her eyes and he swallowed hard.

"Aren't you going to say anything?"

"What is there to say?"

She held his gaze. "That you care about me? That you want to stay married?"

Frustration laced with anger rose in his throat and for the first time in his life, he had no idea how to stop it. "What is the point? You obviously don't listen to a damn word I say."

"What is that supposed to mean?"

"I wanted to marry you. You are the one who refuses to believe that I meant it. You are the one who keeps assuming I'll walk away."

She shook her head. "I didn't mean . . ."

"Christ, Lisette, you fling words at me like honeyed traps, like tests that you want me to fail. How the devil am I supposed to react when you never tell me exactly how you feel or what you want? How many times will you push me away just to see if I'll come back? And what happens when I grow weary of always having to prove myself to you and do walk away? Will you feel vindicated then? That you were right and that ultimately you are unlovable?"

"I don't think that." She was pale now, lower lip caught between her teeth as if to stop it from trembling. "I don't try to trap you."

Wearily, he shook his head. "Yes, you do. You're doing it now. Half of me wants to toss you over my shoulder and take you to bed and make love to you until that's all you can think of, all you can crave. At least there I know you want me. The other half of me wants to walk away now before you pick me apart and spit out the pieces."

Anger finally sparked in her eyes and she lifted her chin. "And you're good at that, aren't you?"

"What the hell is that supposed to mean?"

"Walking away. You walked away from the problems in Spain and never tried to proclaim your innocence and you walked away from your responsibilities as an earl because you refused to confront your uncle face-to-face."

He set his teeth. "I was *carried* out of Spain on a litter because I was barely alive."

"That might be true but you've never tried to restore your reputation, have you?"

He stared at her, his breathing as labored as hers. "Why should I bother to defend myself when I'm already condemned?"

"Because many see your silence as a confirmation of your guilt."

"The men who fought with me, the prisoners in that French prison, *they* know me, *they* know I'd never betray my country." He leaned closer. "Perhaps I'm not like you. I don't need everyone to think that I'm perfect."

She flinched at that. "I don't . . ."

Shaken, he cupped her cheek. "I didn't mean that, Lisette. God, I . . ."

She stepped out of his reach. "You might not have meant it, but it's probably true." She glanced over her shoulder. "I think my father is calling us."

"Don't walk away from me now," he said urgently, quietly. "Not like this."

"You don't have to stay." She swallowed hard.

"Of course I'm staying. We're married and this is a perfect opportunity for me to stand by you and help restore our battered reputations." He bowed. "You're right about one thing. I can't keep running away from everything."

23

Lisette smiled at the next guest in the line, allowed her hand to be kissed, and answered a question about her recent marriage, all without really registering who she was talking to or what she actually said in reply. She just wanted the ball to end so she could stop pretending everything was fine. Hadn't she done that her whole life? Tried to keep her family together with her boundless optimism and refusal to dwell on the past?

Just to make matters worse, Gabriel stood by her side, his faint smile in evidence, the tension coursing through him at being trapped in the receiving line evident in every taut line of his body. He thought she didn't want him, thought she played games with his emotions. . . .

"Lisette, why don't you and Gabriel go and mingle with the guests, now?" her mother asked quietly. "I've asked Marguerite and Anthony to do the same."

Gabriel took her hand and led her into the ballroom, his grasp firm, his presence beside her both a sanctuary and a hell.

"May I get you something to drink, my dear?"

She glanced up at him and realized he wasn't looking at her at all. "Yes, please, that would be lovely."

He placed her gloved hand on his sleeve and walked through the assembled guests, nodding occasionally at acquaintances but not stopping to speak to anyone. She'd forgotten how much he hated crowds. Spending the evening by her side would cost him a restless night. She sensed the strain in him already.

"Thank you."

"For what?"

She took a deep steadying breath. "For staying with me despite everything."

The small orchestra started tuning their instruments and the chatter around them grew more animated until it was difficult to hear. "I mean it, Gabriel. What I said to you earlier about always running away from things—you've already proved me wrong by standing up with me tonight."

"You are my wife. What else would I do?" He inclined his head, found her a seat, and walked across to the buffet table to get them something to drink.

She waited until he took the seat opposite her and plucked up her courage. "I do not want to stay here for very long myself this evening."

"Why is that?"

"Because I'm not feeling very well."

"Ah. I suppose that is understandable." He drank his lemonade. "We'll stay for a few dances and then we can leave."

"Are you ever going to look at me again?" she whispered. He was silent for so long that she had to glance up at him.

"Is this another of your games?" He sounded as weary and defeated as she felt.

"No, I just hate it when you are angry with me."

"That's because you want everyone to like you and be happy around you."

"Not everyone. Just you." She took a deep breath. "I wanted that baby, too. I cried all afternoon. I want to be married to you, Gabriel."

He looked at her then. "But . . . ?"

"But nothing." She held his gaze. "I just want to be married to you."

"Excuse me, Swanfield, but there is something you need to know."

Gabriel looked up at Paul St. Clare and sighed. From the determined expression on his friend's face he guessed Paul wouldn't leave until he'd spoken to him.

"Paul, can't you see that I am busy?"

Paul lowered his head and whispered, "Lord Nash is in the card room and he's already making trouble."

Gabriel stood up. "I'm sorry, my dear. There is something I need to attend to for your father. Will you excuse me for a moment?"

Lisette barely nodded, and he cursed Paul's timing, knew that he would probably regret not staying with her, but realized he had no choice. He followed Paul toward the rear of the ballroom where two rooms had been set aside for cards and gaming.

He didn't need to ask which room Lord Nash occupied; the sound of raucous laughter was enough to guide him. He entered the room as quietly as he could and worked his way around the edge of the small crowd that had gathered around a handsome blond man.

He noticed Christian approaching from the other doorway and managed to catch his eye, made sure that his new brother-in-law understood that if anyone was taking Nash on, it would be him.

A couple of the men standing next to him seemed to recognize who he was and stepped aside, until eventually there was a substantial gap in front of Nash, which Gabriel adroitly filled.

He smiled gently at his victim.

"Good evening. Would I be addressing Lord Nash?"

"Indeed you would, sir." Lord Nash bowed and toasted Gabriel with his glass. "I regret I cannot return the salutation, sir, as I do not have the pleasure of your acquaintance."

Gabriel continued to smile and several more of the men gathered around Nash quietly dispersed. From the corner of his eye, Gabriel saw that Christian had been joined by Paul and Lieutenant Colonel Constantine Delinsky and that they were ushering everyone out of the card room. "Apparently you are acquainted with my wife."

Nash's smile disappeared. "Your wife?" He laughed nervously. "I doubt that, sir, seeing as I'm not the sort of man who likes to dabble with married women."

"Oh, she wasn't married when you 'dabbled' with her."

Nash glanced sideways at the door. "I have no idea what you are referring to, sir, perhaps you have mistaken me for someone else. Will you please excuse me?"

Gabriel moved slightly to bar his way. "I'm the Earl of Swanfield."

"Swanfield?" Nash swallowed loudly.

"Do you recall my wife now?"

"Are you referring to Miss Delornay-Ross? I was just talking about her sudden rise in fortunes." Nash forced a smile. "You can hardly blame me for repeating the truth, sir. Your wife wasn't exactly a saint in her youth."

"My wife was a young woman who believed she was in love. The fact that she believed she was in love with *you* is perhaps baffling, but she wasn't experienced enough to know what a complete bastard you were, was she?"

"I say, my lord, that is . . ."

Gabriel stepped even closer so that his face was half an inch from Nash's. "She also had no idea that you were pursuing her simply to win a bet."

"I didn't need to pursue her, Swanfield. She was quite willing to bed me." He sniggered. "As willing as she was to bed her own twin, or so I've been told."

Rage seared through Gabriel's veins as Nash continued to preen for his audience. "She was in love with you. She believed you meant to marry her."

"Ah, is that what she told you, Swanfield?" Nash asked, as if they were the best of friends. "Did she pretend to be a virgin to ensnare you? I can understand that you might be a trifle annoyed about that, but it is scarcely my fault, is it?"

Gabriel wrapped his hand around Nash's neck and squeezed until the man's eyes bulged. "She pretended nothing, and you are a pathetic excuse for a gentleman."

Someone cleared his throat beside him. "Gabriel? Don't kill him. He's not worth dying for."

He realized that Paul was speaking to him and he managed to lessen his grip and refocus on Lord Nash.

"As far as I am concerned, whatever my wife did before our marriage is irrelevant. I suggest that you forget you ever knew her, because if I ever hear a single whisper that you have been gossiping about her, I will find you and kill you. Do you understand?"

He released his grip and Lord Nash staggered backward, his cheeks flushed a hectic red. He glanced at Paul, Christian, and Constantine, straightened his cravat, and managed a sneer.

"I should have known a man with your lack of class wouldn't bother with the formality of a duel. And perhaps you and Miss Delornay-Ross deserve each other. I understand from your cousin that your mother and your wife's mother are well matched as both of them are lower-class whores."

Before Gabriel could react, Christian had a knife at Nash's

throat and drew it across his skin. Blood trickled down from a small puncture wound just behind his ear to mar the whiteness of Nash's intricately folded cravat. "What did you say?"

"Nothing! I said nothing." Nash whimpered.

Christian laughed. "The only coward I see here is you, Nash, a man afraid of a little blood, especially when it's his own."

Gabriel touched Christian's shoulder. "Leave it, Delornay. He doesn't merit either your attention or your anger."

Christian let Nash go and stepped back. "You can thank my brother-in-law for your life by remaining silent about my sister." He pocketed the knife. "But if you say another word about my family, I will come after you as well, and my methods of silencing you will not only be painful but terminal."

Lord Nash staggered backward and met Gabriel's stare; his mouth worked but no words came out of it. Gabriel nodded at the door. "Get out and let's hope you've learned your lesson."

They watched Lord Nash leave, escorted by Delinsky and Paul. Christian turned to Gabriel, his normally cool eyes full of rage and anguish. He reminded Gabriel of himself in his younger days. "He insulted my family and yours. Don't you care?"

"Of course I care, but murdering the fool in cold blood at your sister's coming-out ball would hardly help matters, would it?"

Christian sat down with a thump. "I suppose not, but I doubt he'll remain silent, do you? He seemed rather put out that we disagreed with him at all."

"He's a fool," Gabriel said abruptly. "If we have to, we'll deal with him in private. There are many ways to make his life very uncomfortable without actually killing him."

"But none of them are quite so satisfying," Christian muttered.

Gabriel tasted bile and swallowed hard. "Maybe for you, but I've seen enough bloodshed to last me a lifetime."

When Christian told Lisette what had happened, would she think Gabriel a coward? Would she assume he'd turned his back on a fight because that was his nature? He got to his feet. "I have to find Lisette."

"Before the gossips do."

"Something like that." He nodded at Christian. "I appreciate your help."

"Even though I damn near killed the man?"

Gabriel shrugged. "You did what you thought was right." He looked over at the door where the previously evacuated card players were now returning. "I'll see you later."

While she waited for Gabriel to return, Lisette listlessly plied her fan and watched the other guests promenade around the ballroom waiting for the first dance to start. A dance she would miss if Gabriel didn't return soon. Had he arranged for Paul to interrupt him if he saw Lisette was making his life difficult? Or was Paul simply so in tune with Gabriel that he'd sensed the conflict and acted by himself?

She sighed and took a sip of the champagne Gabriel had brought her. Emily walked by with their father, her face alight with happiness, and Lisette had to smile. Whatever her parents' motives in hastening her marriage, Lisette couldn't deny that Emily would benefit from it. At least she'd have the opportunity to find a man she loved without the specter of a ruined reputation behind her.

"Lady Swanfield?"

"Yes?"

She turned to find an elderly man at her elbow. His skin was the color of yellowed parchment, and he walked with the aid of a cane. Without asking for permission, he took the seat that Gabriel had vacated.

"So you're Gabriel's wife."

Lisette studied the old man cautiously. "I am. Might I ask your name, sir?"

"I'm Mr. Reginald Granger. Your husband's uncle and trustee."

Lisette stiffened. "Good manners dictate that I should be pleased to meet you, sir, but I find myself unable to agree."

Mr. Granger smiled to reveal small, rotting teeth. "I assume Gabriel has told you his twisted version of events. That boy has no respect for the years I toiled away for him, no respect at all."

"He is scarcely a boy, sir, and perfectly able to handle his own affairs."

His laughter was meant to belittle, to hurt. "You didn't see him when he returned from Spain, did you? I had no problem convincing the highest court in this land that he was incapable of managing his estates."

"As far as I understand it, sir, my husband was far too ill to defend himself from any assault on his estates or his person."

"Told you that, did he?" Mr. Granger gave a bark of laughter. "Did he forget to mention that he signed everything over to me again?"

Lisette slowly shut her fan and tried not to let her surprise show on her face. She looked away from the old man and straight into Gabriel's stormy blue eyes. With all the care she could muster, she rose to her feet.

"Your uncle just introduced himself to me."

Gabriel inclined his head. "I can see that."

"He really is a most unpleasant individual, isn't he?"

Gabriel's gaze flicked to his uncle and remained there as if he couldn't bear to look away. "Aye, he is."

Mr. Granger didn't bother to rise. "I was just telling your wife why you'll never get your estates back from me."

"He insists you signed them over to him on your return from Spain."

Gabriel's expression stilled. "Is that so?" Lisette stepped

closer to him as his gaze locked with his uncle and his whole body tensed as if for battle. "Good night, Uncle."

He took Lisette's hand and started for the door. When they reached the landing and stepped into the crowds milling on the stairs, he froze as if he had no idea what to do next. Lisette tugged on his hand.

"Come this way. It's a lot quieter."

She guided him through the servants' door and along the narrow passageways to her old bedchamber. He walked across to the unlit fire and sank into one of the chairs, his head in his hands. Lisette didn't say anything as she took the chair opposite him.

After a long while, he raised his head. "I suppose you want to know if it is true."

"That you signed over the estate to him?"

His mouth twisted. "He's right. I did."

She studied him carefully as he shoved a hand through his hair.

"Aren't you going to crow?"

"Why would I do that?"

He looked up at her. "Doesn't this confirm your suspicions that I walk away from damn near *everything*?"

Lisette took a careful breath. Here was her opportunity to make things right, to show him that she could understand his problems and help him face them, that she didn't want to pretend that everything was perfect anymore. "Despite great provocation, you haven't walked away from me, so I must assume that whatever your uncle did to make you sign away your rights was heinous indeed."

He held her gaze, his expression arrested. "You believe me?"

She opened her eyes wide. "We are married. Surely I have to believe in you?"

A muscle twitched in his cheek. "I did it for my mother."

"Your *mother*?"

"He always used her to keep me under control. He swore he'd kill her if I didn't allow him to manage the estate until I was well again."

"And you *believed* him?"

He shrugged. "Of course I did. He'd kept her from me since I was nine years old, why wouldn't he stoop to murder to retain the Swanfield wealth?" He got to his feet and started to pace the carpet. "And what could I do? I was so broken when I returned from Spain. I had no friends, no reputation, no ability to even get out of my damn bed and strangle the man. I had to agree to his terms. I've been fighting to reverse them ever since."

"Because you no longer believe that he can kill your mother?"

He turned to face her and the grief in his eyes made her want to cry out. "No, because she has completely disappeared."

"What do you mean?"

Gabriel sat back down. "Mr. Granger wrote to me a few years ago and suggested that I stop my attempts to regain my birthright or he would be forced to discuss my mother. By this point, I was unwilling to leave things to chance or to believe a word my uncle said, so I arranged for a man of mine to visit the Swanfield estate in Cheshire."

He sighed. "He could find no trace of my mother at the house or in the grounds, and no one would speak of her. I had to assume my uncle had carried through on his threat and murdered her."

"Why didn't you confront him with his deeds?"

He met her eyes. "Because, as you so rightly pointed out, I am a coward. I'd had my fill of violence and imprisonment, and I knew that if I saw him at that point, I would kill him."

"I don't think you are a coward, Gabriel."

His smile was guarded. "You will when you hear what else I did this evening. I met your old lover, Lord Nash, at the ball."

Lisette's hand pressed to her throat. "He was here? He must have arrived after we left the receiving line."

286 / Kate Pearce

"Aye, and he was already busy spreading lies about you in your own home. I had a few words with him, refused to fight him, and let Christian convince him that he had better leave." He looked away from her. "You should thank your brother really. He was the one who held a knife to Nash's throat and finally convinced him to shut up."

She studied him carefully. "Did you think I'd *want* you to fight a duel for me?"

"Most women would expect it."

"But if you'd fought him here, you would've ruined Emily's ball."

"That's exactly what I told your brother." He nodded at her. "I don't think you'll have to worry about Lord Nash in the future. Between us, I think we have him convinced to keep his mouth shut."

It was Lisette's turn to sigh. "I wish I'd never met him or fallen in love with him. I was such a fool."

"You were very young."

"And very wild and stupid." Lisette swiped at a tear on her cheek. "You haven't even asked me why I slept with him, or condemned me for being such a fool."

"I'm hardly in a position to do that, am I?"

"Why not? You're my husband. Surely you of all men have a right to ask me anything."

He leaned forward, his hands clasped together between his thighs. "Lisette, can't you see that it doesn't matter to me? I didn't marry you because you were perfect. I married you because . . ."

"Because you thought I carried your child."

"Because I wanted to." He stood up and unpinned his cravat. "Please don't start that again."

"And what if I wanted to be perfect for you?" she whispered. "What if I wanted you to have been the only man I ever bedded?"

He walked back over to the fire and crouched in front of her, his hard expression softening. "We can't change the past, can we? You told me recently that we can't change our true natures either. But we can choose what we do with our future together; we can decide to live happily ever after with the past buried behind us and nothing but goodwill and love on both sides to see us through."

She touched his cheek. "Do you truly believe that?"

"Of course."

"You think we can stay together and succeed?"

"Absolutely, if we both play our parts."

"But what are those 'parts'? The polite society marriage you think I deserve, or the marriage we want to build together?"

He let out a frustrated breath. "I told you I wanted you and that I would be content with you. Can you not believe me?"

She stared at him. "But we also need to be true to ourselves."

"Does that mean you want something else?" He swallowed hard. "You want other men?"

"I want you."

"You have me."

He looked at her as if he didn't understand what she was trying to say. How could she explain that she wanted him to be the same sexually complex man she had married, that she didn't want him to change just because he thought it was more socially acceptable? And what about love amongst all his talk of duty? "I don't want you to change too much."

"Ah." He looked away from her and slowly got to his feet. He took off his coat and concentrated on unbuttoning his waistcoat. Lisette watched him carefully, but realized he had nothing more to say. She needed to think about it, too, so she let her mind turn back to the other matter that concerned her.

"What are you going to do about your mother?"

"I've decided I have to keep going and dispossess my uncle; otherwise I'll never know what happened to her, will I?"

"That is an excellent reason," Lisette said softly. "And you are no coward."

"Having you by my side has made me stronger." He held her gaze. "Do you understand that?"

She could only nod. If he had the courage to face his demons and deal with his uncle, the least she could do was come to terms with her own problems. Gabriel might not like her solution to their issues, but she had to find the courage to offer him a way back to his true self. She loved him and he didn't seem to understand that yet. It was her responsibility to be brave and show him the truth. If it meant that she destroyed a few of his illusions about her and their future together, maybe that was just as well.

24

"Mr. Brecon sent this for you, sir."

"Thank you, Keyes." Gabriel slit open the sealed paper and read the short message. "It appears that Mr. Sturges, the estate manager from Swanfield Manor, will be here on Friday. I am looking forward to meeting him."

"I'm sure you are, sir." Keyes deftly removed the empty teacup and saucer from beneath Gabriel's elbow and backed away toward the door. "Her ladyship was asking for you at breakfast, sir. Shall I tell her you have returned from your ride?"

Gabriel nodded. "If you see her, please assure her that I'm in my study and at her disposal if she needs me."

"Yes, sir, I will."

Keyes left and Gabriel stared at the back of the closed door. Since the night of the ball, he and Lisette had achieved an uneasy peace, but things still weren't right. He hoped that after his meeting with Sturges he would be able to apply his mind to the question of his marriage and make sure that Lisette was happy, because that was important to him. Keeping her happy was more important than anything. He frowned down at his desk. He had to talk to her.

With sudden resolve, he headed out of his study and up the stairs to Lisette's rooms. He paused at the doorway, instantly aware that she wasn't there. The only reminder of her presence was the faint scent of roses and her discarded dressing gown draped over the bed.

"Are you looking for her ladyship, sir?"

He smiled at the maid who had just emerged from the dressing room, an armful of petticoats over her arm. "Indeed I am, Molly."

"She went out for a walk with Miss Emily, Lieutenant St. Clare, and his cousin, Lady Lucinda, my lord. I should imagine she'll be back in time to take tea with you."

"I'm sure she will. Thank you for telling me."

The maid bobbed a curtsey. "You're welcome, sir."

Gabriel's smile faded as he turned and went back down the stairs. He supposed he should get on with some work rather than moping around the house like a child deprived of his favorite toy. It wasn't as if he had nothing to do. Preparing to take back his estates wasn't an easy task.

He settled himself behind his desk and stared at the mountain of paperwork Mr. Brecon had sent him the previous week. Somewhere buried under all that paper was a letter from Paul's uncle that should at least be acknowledged—if he could ever find it or remember exactly what the old man had wanted. With a sigh, he reached for the first piece of correspondence and settled down for a long afternoon.

Lisette smiled at Paul St. Clare as the two younger girls walked ahead of them and chattered together. Their heads were close together and they laughed and talked at the same time without appearing to pause for breath.

"Your cousin is delightful."

"As is your sister. They are certainly well matched, aren't they?"

"I'm just glad Emily has found a friend to enjoy the exigencies of her London Season with."

Paul winked. "I'm just pleased that Lucky's found someone to chatter with other than me."

"I don't think I was ever that carefree," Lisette said. "At the orphanage laughing too loudly or giggling meant more hours spent on your knees in the chapel saying the rosary."

"It sounds as unpleasant as Eton, although whenever I was on my knees there it was for an entirely different and far more enjoyable reason."

Lisette found herself laughing and had to wave aside the girls' concern when they looked back at her.

"That's better," Paul said. "Both you and Gabriel are far too serious these days."

"That's because we're married."

"Gabriel takes his responsibilities very seriously."

"I know." Lisette sighed. "He is determined to make us the most fashionable and boring married couple of the Season."

"And you don't want that?"

"I just want to be married to him, not held up for society's approval. I've finally realized that being happy is far more important than seeking the approval of a group of snobs." She looked away from Paul's far too interested face and back at his cousin, Lucinda. "She's fond of you, isn't she?"

"Yes." Paul lowered his voice. "Her parents would like me to offer for her, but I won't."

"Because you don't wish to marry."

He glanced sideways at her, his eyes for once serious. "That is true. It would be . . . unfair."

"When you care about someone else."

"Is it that obvious?" He sighed and found them a seat to occupy, while the young ladies continued to promenade around the lake. "I thought I hid it rather well."

"Not from me." Lisette closed her parasol with a snap.

"But then, you love him, too, don't you?" Paul asked.

"Of course I do." Lisette took a deep breath. "And that's why I might need your help."

After one of the most boring but deeply satisfying days of his life, Gabriel retired to his rooms to find Keyes laying out his evening clothes on the bed.

"Am I supposed to be going out?" He groaned. Despite his best intentions, he'd managed to miss Lisette at tea and dinner.

"I believe so, sir. Her ladyship asked me to tell you that she would meet you at the Harcourts' ball."

"The Harcourts? Do I even know them?"

"That's not the point, sir. Her ladyship requires your presence at her side, and you will be more than happy to oblige her, won't you?"

"Turncoat." Gabriel muttered as Keyes continued his preparations to shave him. "Just because she remembers to inquire about your rheumatism and the health of your wife."

Keyes lathered up Gabriel's chin. "And let's not forget, sir, that she makes you happy."

"She does, doesn't she?" Gabriel mused about that as Keyes deftly shaved him. Even though things were strained between them at the moment—and wasn't that to be expected during the first few weeks of marriage—he was still happier being with her than being apart. In fact, she'd become necessary to him.

He loved her.

Had loved her right from the start. Loved her even more now that he'd discovered the real woman behind the polished, flirtatious shell. She'd brought him back to life; given him hope, and helped him make the decisions he had been putting off for years. He sat up so suddenly that Keyes had to step back.

"Are you all right, my lord?"

"Yes." Gabriel stared into the mirror and absently dabbed at the remaining spots of soap on his chin with the warm towel Keyes handed him. Had he ever told Lisette that he loved her, or had he been so busy ranting on about responsibility and children that he'd forgotten to say the most important thing? No wonder she didn't believe he cared about her. . . . He was a complete fool.

"I'll leave you to your bath, sir, and return to help you on with your coat," Keyes said.

"Yes . . . thank you."

Gabriel waved his valet away and stood up. He needed to go to the Harcourts' ball and that required a bath and clean clothing.

He bathed with a speed he had formerly reserved for a dip in an icy Spanish stream in winter, and vigorously rubbed his hair dry. On top of the pile of clothes he noticed a flat box that looked as if it might contain jewelry. He looked around for Keyes and then remembered his valet had already gone downstairs.

Curiosity compelled him to open the satin-lined box and view both the contents and the note written in Lisette's handwriting. Set in the white satin were three items that made him swallow hard: a thin silver collar, a long chain, and a matching cock ring.

His fingers trembled as he opened Lisette's note and read the words aloud. "Wear these for me tonight and meet me at the pleasure house in our room after the ball."

His heart rate increased and his cock thickened. Gabriel continued to stare at the erotic collection of items. Could he dare wear them under the stiff formality of his evening clothes, and, more important, did he want to?

His cock kicked against the drying cloth wrapped around his waist. God, why was he even trying to pretend there was a choice to make? He wanted to do this for her more than anything in the world—wanted to do it for himself as well. But if he did, what would happen to his desire to give Lisette the marriage he thought she deserved?

But this is her choice....

He picked up the thin silver collar. The metal felt cold against his fingers. He imagined it round his neck, what it implied, where Lisette would be able to lead him.... He loved her. What better way to show her that than by embracing the darker side of his sexuality and letting her experience it, too?

With sudden decision, he clasped the collar around his throat and settled it so that the chain hung down and brushed his half-erect cock. If he wanted any chance of getting the cock ring around his shaft, he had to do it now.

He pushed his balls through the two smaller rings and then settled the much thicker silver band around the base of his cock. It wasn't that tight now, but if things went as he expected, he'd feel the constraints of the metal before the night was over.

His fingers were shaking so hard that it was difficult for him to attach the chain to the silver ring, but he managed it at last and made himself look in the mirror. God, he liked the way the chain met the cock ring, wondered what it would feel like if she pulled it....

With a stifled curse, Gabriel drew his shirt over his head and carefully stepped into his tight pantaloons. Underthings would just complicate his evening, so he decided to do without them. He studied his now-covered groin in the mirror. Was it only he who would see the rigid lines of the metal rings, the engorged state of his cock?

Lisette would see them. She'd know what he'd done. He drew on a black waistcoat and somehow managed to knot his cravat and pin it into place. When Keyes reappeared he seemed unperturbed by either Gabriel's appearance or his distracted manner and quickly had him ready to leave the house.

His coachman seemed to know where Harcourt House was, so Gabriel was able to settle back in the carriage and await his arrival. Eventually, from the small steamed-up window of the coach, he saw a blaze of light and a throng of people moving up the steps to a large double-fronted mansion, which he assumed was also his destination.

For a moment, as he pushed his way up the stairs to the ballroom, he contemplated bolting. He hated the crowds, but for once, his desire to see Lisette prevented him from worrying too much. Etiquette demanded he join the end of the receiving line to meet his unknown hosts, but he chose not to. Time was of the essence. He needed to find his wife and see her reaction to him.

He spotted her at the far side of the vast gold and white ballroom with Emily and her father. Her light brown hair was piled high on top of her head with just a few curls allowed to brush her cheeks. She wore the green dress he'd chosen for her and emeralds glinted at her throat. He swallowed hard. Why hadn't he given her any jewels? What sort of a husband was he?

When he finally reached her, she turned to greet him, her hazel eyes cool, her expression neutral. His cock jerked and for the first time he felt the pull of the silver around the base. Her gaze flicked over him, settled on his pantaloons, and then moved back to his face.

"Good evening, my lord."

He bowed. "My lady, Miss Emily, Lord Knowles. I trust you are enjoying your evening?"

"Indeed we are." Emily, of course, answered for everyone, her eyes wide, her excitement barely contained. "Isn't it wonderful?"

He smiled at her as the orchestra struck up again behind them. "Would you like to dance?"

Her face fell. "Oh, I'm sorry, Gabriel. I'm already engaged to someone for this dance, and for the rest of the evening."

He pretended to sigh. "I suppose I'd better dance with my wife, then."

Emily giggled behind her gloved fingers. "I know you don't mean it like that, Gabriel. You'd probably much rather be dancing with her than with silly old me."

Gabriel turned to Lisette. "I hope my wife will understand if I refuse to answer that dangerous question. Do you have a dance left for me, my dear?"

She curtsied and slid the loop of her fan over her wrist. "Of course I do."

She placed her hand lightly on his sleeve and he walked them onto the already crowded dance floor. When he took her into his arms he could hardly breathe. He looked down at the top of her head.

"Sometimes it is hard to believe that you are only three years older than Emily."

"Almost four years, actually. My birthday is next week."

"Still . . ."

She tilted up her face to look at him. "She seems young to me, but that is how most English girls are. Even though I grew up in an orphanage, I'm far more worldly than she is."

"And of course, you added to your experience at the pleasure house."

She sighed as he promenaded with her around a corner. "I certainly learned how to sexually please a man. I thought I was trying to make up for my lack of knowledge, but now I realize I was just rebelling against my mother."

He squeezed her hand. "We all make mistakes."

"Even you?"

"Even me." They danced on for a while in perfect harmony until the music came to a close. "Would you like to go back to your father now, or shall we get some refreshments?"

"A glass of lemonade would be nice."

He led her toward the refreshment room, keeping a close eye out for Lord Nash, in case he suddenly decided to appear. Just before they reached the doorway, Lisette tugged on his hand and drew him farther into the depths of the house. His breathing quickened as she gently backed him up against the nearest wall.

She undid the first three buttons of his waistcoat and slid her hand through the opening to the neck of his shirt. He held his breath as her fingers moved over his chest, settled on the silver chain, and pulled hard. He closed his eyes as his cock was jerked upward and then up again until it felt like it might come off.

"God, Lisette . . ."

She let go of the chain, but traced its path up to his neck, found the silver collar, and paused to stroke it. He jumped as her other hand cupped his balls through his pantaloons. She thumbed the base of his shaft until the metal bit into his hot, needy flesh. His hips jerked forward seeking the pleasure and pain of her hands.

"I'm glad you wore this for me," she whispered and kissed his chin, then redid the buttons of his waistcoat. "I'll enjoy seeing you like this at the pleasure house."

Before he could reply, she walked away from him. He stayed where he was, aware that he couldn't hide what she'd done to him—that she'd made him fully erect in less than a minute. He took slow, deep breaths until he could at least walk without wanting to come with every step, and slowly headed back to the ballroom.

Lisette waved at him from the refreshment room and he had to go to her, had to sit down and make polite conversation, watch the hands that had so recently touched his skin hold a glass of wine instead. He danced with her again, too, and shivered every time she deliberately touched him, enjoyed every damn second of it so much he wanted to fall onto his knees and kiss her feet.

Toward the end of the ball, she met him in the overcrowded hallway and stood close. Her fingers stroking the taut satin covering his cock, her teeth a hairbreadth away from his ear. "Why don't you go on ahead? I'll say good-bye to Emily and my father for you and take our coach instead."

He could only nod helplessly and walk out into the night. The sky was a clear black tinged with a hint of gray. Although it was cold, he decided to walk to Madame's house rather than call a cab, as it was only around the corner. It would take forever for Lisette to extricate the coach from the melee in front of Harcourt House, so he had plenty of time to prepare himself.

Oblivious to the warning shouts of the footmen and the rumbling coaches around him, he stopped dead in the middle of the street. He wanted this. Had realized how much he'd missed the excitement as soon as he'd seen the collar and the rings. He let himself in through the back entrance of the pleasure house with the key Lisette had slipped into his hand, and made his way upstairs to the room on the second floor they had occupied before.

A fire had been lit in the grate and the curtains were closed, giving the space an intimacy and warmth he appreciated. He sat down on the side of the bed and wondered if he should remove his clothes. Anticipation curled low in his gut. Better to wait for Lisette. She probably had very definite ideas about what she wanted from him next.

25

Lisette entered the room and saw Gabriel sitting on the bed, his hands in his lap, his eyes cast down as if he was studying the polish of his shoes. Part of her was simply relieved that he was here. She hadn't been sure if he would respond to her bold invitation; had, in truth, worried that she might destroy his regard for her forever.

But he was here and he was wearing the gift she'd left for him under his clothes. Surely that meant something? Did he understand that sharing themselves like this would make them both happier? Her body stirred at the thought of that, that she alone knew how he felt, how he was constrained and adorned for her sexual pleasure. She took the chair opposite the bed and settled her skirts around her.

"I want you to strip for me. But do it slowly."

He stood up and faced her, his blue eyes lowered, and shrugged out of his tight-fitting black coat, his cravat, and finally his waistcoat. She found herself leaning forward as he carefully unbuttoned the placket of his pantaloons. He hissed as he gathered the hem of his long white shirt and pulled it over his head to reveal the collar around his neck and the chain hanging down that disappeared into his open pantaloons.

He kicked off his shoes and lowered his pantaloons and stockings in one slow careful motion. Lisette licked her lips as he straightened to reveal his erect cock and the glint of silver around his balls and shaft.

She got up and walked toward him. He stared straight ahead, his hands fisted at his sides as she reached out a finger to stroke the silver collar.

"I think I'll have my name engraved on this. Would you like that?"

He nodded, and she bent to lick the metal. She followed a hot, wet, salacious line around his throat and down the taut chain until she reached his stomach and stopped. His cock strained upward toward her mouth, the purple crown already dripping pre-cum, the solid length of him more swollen and thick than she had ever seen it before.

She flicked his crown with her fingertip and sucked the wetness into her mouth. "I wish you had a proper ring set in here." She plucked at the taut foreskin of his cock. "So that I could attach a chain to you." She squeezed one of his nipples hard. "And maybe here as well."

He groaned her name, and wetness slid from the slit at the tip of his cock to coat her fingers. "Would you like that? Your body pierced and chained for my pleasure?" She tugged on the chain. "Answer me."

"I would like whatever you want, my lady," he said hoarsely, his northern accent emerging more strongly as it did in times of great emotion.

She fingered the chain again, then his cock and his nipple, her fingers wet, her sex now wet for him as well. "I could lead you around the pleasure house by your cock." He shivered and she bent to lick him again. "Do you want to come?"

"Not unless you want me to, my lady."

She sat back down and looked up at him. "I don't want you to come for a long time. Do you understand?"

"Yes, my lady."

She went across to one of the chests of drawers and came back with a black mask. "Put this on."

She waited until he did what she told him and then put on her own mask. "Come on." She walked across to the door and looked back at him. "Put your hands behind your back and do not touch or talk to anyone unless I give you permission."

She waited breathlessly to see if he would balk at her request, but he merely licked his lips and continued to stare at the ground. She snapped her fingers. "Come on. Do I need to put a leash on you?"

She suspected he'd quite like that. In truth, she would like it herself. She opened the door and walked into the hallway. The sound of laughter and music echoed off the walls, and Lisette turned toward it. She paused at the doorway of the smaller of the two more public salons to ensure that Gabriel was following her and then went in.

The salon was full of people and Lisette had to take her time weaving through all the groups. She kept an eye on Gabriel, watched how he reacted to being naked in front of the other guests, to them touching him and his erect cock, to the noise levels he hated. At the large buffet table, she stopped and waited for Gabriel to catch up.

His skin now gleamed faintly with sweat, and his cock was a stiff, unyielding presence constrained by the rings and the chain. Lisette broke off a grape and popped it into Gabriel's mouth, waited until he swallowed, and then fed him another. She held up a glass of red wine to allow him to drink and caught the bloodred stain on his lips with her tongue before it dripped down to mar the perfection of his muscled skin.

302 / Kate Pearce

"Your pet is very nice, Madame. Is he for anyone's use?"

Lisette smiled graciously at the unknown young couple who were eagerly assessing Gabriel. "Alas, no. He isn't well trained enough yet to participate in any sexual games."

"That's such a shame, because he seems so . . . so well endowed." The woman giggled and clutched at her husband's arm.

"He is, isn't he?" Lisette stroked her index finger down the length of Gabriel's cock and felt his instant response. "Perhaps next time."

The couple retreated and Lisette finished her wine before turning back to Gabriel. "Follow me."

She went back into the hall and took him into the second and smaller of the two salons where there were fewer people and more extreme sexual acts being performed. She found herself a seat near the raised stage and directed Gabriel to kneel at her feet. She'd asked her mother to arrange this particular show for her tonight. It was really for Gabriel, but she hoped they'd both enjoy it.

Two men dressed only in their shirts and breeches came to stand on the stage. The darker-haired man stood behind the blond man and cupped his groin before smiling at the audience. "Good evening, my friends. My name is Jennings. Shall I make Maxwell nice and hard?"

"Yes!" shouted back several enthusiastic voices from the audience.

Jennings smiled and began to rub and fondle Maxwell's cock until it became obvious, even through the wool of his breeches, that the fair-haired man was erect.

"Shall I unbutton his breeches?"

Again there were several shouts to encourage him, so Jennings shoved his hand inside the blond man's breeches and kept working the other man's cock. Maxwell started to groan with every rough jerk on his shaft, his head pressed back against Jennings's shoulder, his face turned up as if he was seeking the other man's kiss.

"Show us his cock!" a drunken voice shouted.

The dark-haired man shoved down Maxwell's breeches and pulled his shirt out of the way to display his hand wrapped around the blond man's big thick thrusting cock. Lisette looked down at Gabriel and saw his attention was fixed on the stage, his breathing unsteady, his own cock wet in sympathy.

She reached down and traced his collar and his breathing hitched. On the stage now, at the suggestion of the audience, Jennings had the blond on his knees and was feeding his cock into the man's willing mouth. He looked around the room.

"Shall I let him play with his cock while he makes me come, or should I tell him to put his hands behind his back?"

"Make him wait!" someone shouted to a chorus of good-natured agreement.

The dark-haired man smiled and murmured something to the blond man, who immediately locked his hands together in the small of his back. He kept sucking, though, the wet sounds of his mouth clearly audible above the subdued chatter in the room.

Lisette twirled a loop of Gabriel's chain around her index finger, felt him instinctively try and rise from the floor to relieve the tug on the cock ring. She kept the chain taut, flicking it with her finger and sending the vibrations down to his shaft.

She smiled and returned her attention to the stage, where Jennings, the darker-haired man, was ordering his partner to kneel on all fours. He again turned to the crowd. "Shall I oil his arse or have him like this?"

"Oil," Lisette said clearly, and several of the men, probably those who knew exactly how a thick cock up an ungreased arse felt, took up her answer. She sat back and watched as Jennings oiled his cock and then Maxwell's arse and sank his shaft deep.

"Fuck him hard," someone suggested. "Work his cock while you do it."

Lisette stood up and motioned for Gabriel to follow her. If he wasn't aroused by now, there was nothing she could do about it. She led him back to the bedchamber and waited for him to face her.

"Did you like watching those men fuck?"

"Yes."

"Did it make you want to come?"

"Yes."

Lisette nodded at him. "I want you to keep the mask on and kneel on the bed."

She watched him climb onto the satin counterpane, his movements slow and careful, as if the slightest motion might make him come. She couldn't help but admire the long, scarred line of his spine, the tight muscles of his buttocks, and the long, endless elegance of his legs.

She picked up the black silk scarf she had draped over the chair earlier and walked across to the bed. "I'm going to tie your hands behind your back. Keep still."

He didn't protest as she wound the scarf around his wrists and made a knot and then a bow. She'd wondered about that, whether his time in captivity would make him uncomfortable being bound. But he didn't seem to object. With a sense of relief, she turned as the door opened a crack and smiled as Paul St. Clare appeared.

On the bed, Gabriel tensed, but she knew he was unable to ascertain who had come in. She handed Paul a vial of oil and nodded at Gabriel. Paul winked and strolled toward the end of the bed where Gabriel still couldn't see him. Lisette moved as well, climbing onto the pillows right in front of Gabriel.

She slowly eased up her thin silk skirts to reveal her stockinged legs and the allure of her naked sex beyond. Gabriel inhaled sharply and leaned toward her. God, she had missed this; her power over him, her ability to drive him wild and to make him submit to her alone.

"Would you like to lick me?"

He nodded, his wariness apparent in every gleaming inch of his quivering, muscled skin.

"There are conditions."

Gabriel tried to look up at her then, although the mask and his lower position made it difficult. He also sensed a presence behind him and that made him nervous.

"You mustn't come until we say so."

He waited to hear what else she had to say, knew that wouldn't be all.

"And you must let yourself be oiled."

Gabriel went still as he tried to puzzle out her meaning. There was obviously someone else in the room with them. Was it Marie-Claude or someone he didn't know? Had she asked one of the men who had performed in the salon to come and fuck him? He realized he didn't care, that he had to trust Lisette, and he knew he loved her enough to allow her to do anything she wanted with him.

He nodded and gasped when he felt strong, oiled hands curl over his shoulders and start massaging his flesh. Not Marie-Claude then, someone much bigger and probably male. His cock twitched at that salacious thought and he had to breathe slowly to prevent himself from coming.

"Lick me, then," Lisette whispered.

He groaned as she slowly opened her legs to reveal the slick wet heat of her sex and he bent his head. He tasted her with the tip of his tongue first, curled it around the bud of her swollen clit, felt the pulse of desire throbbing through her. She sighed his name and inched closer so that he could lick all of her, stab his tongue into the very center of her need, suck her nether lips into his mouth, and swallow her juices down his very willing throat.

He groaned against her flesh as the man massaging his skin skimmed his hands over his buttocks and thighs and then came back to attend to his tight nipples and the ridged planes of his stomach. He tensed as Lisette cried out, her hand fisting in his hair as she climaxed, tensed even more as an oiled finger slid into his arse. The silver band bit into his swollen cock, making his balls ache and tighten. God, he was going to come if he received any more stimulation. But could he come with such constriction on his shaft? Would he have to stay erect regardless of what Lisette did to him?

She moved out of his reach and he remained where he was, head down, heart thumping fit to burst, his cock and balls on fire, his arse . . . he arched his back as more fingers stretched him wider.

"Gabriel. I want to suck your cock."

He tried to look up, tried to answer her and only succeeded in driving the other man's fingers deeper.

"Gabriel?"

"Whatever you want." He forced the words out through his clenched teeth.

"And while I suck your cock, you'll be fucked."

He closed his eyes, remembered his most erotic dreams, and nodded.

"Do you want to be fucked?"

He tried to concentrate, aware that the fingers had disappeared and that something wetter and thicker now probed his arse hole. Did he want this for her, or for himself, or was it simply what they both wanted?

"I want it." God, it was so hard to say the words, but so rewarding as Lisette bent to take his shaft in her mouth and the man behind him eased the first inch of his cock inside him.

Gabriel forgot to think after that. He just concentrated on the sensation of being sucked and fucked, of being held between the two other bodies and given the most extreme sexual pleasure of his life. Lisette was careful with his overstimulated cock, licked him gently, held him in her mouth while the man worked his cock into Gabriel and set about thrusting hard, the forward motion allowing Gabriel to simply let his cock move within the tight confines of Lisette's mouth.

"You may come now, Gabriel." The man behind him started to groan and thrust faster, his hands hard on Gabriel's hips. Gabriel inhaled an all-too-familiar scent of rosemary soap and male sweat and knew exactly who was behind him—knew it, and then forgot everything except climaxing.

When he regained his breath, he sat up and looked over his shoulder, smiling into the extremely satisfied face of Paul St. Clare. "Thank you."

Paul shrugged. "It was all your wife's idea. She had some strange notion that you needed to have some sense fucked into you."

"She was right." Gabriel turned back to Lisette, who sat with her back against the headboard and her legs curled up under her. He bent to kiss her stockinged toes. "Thank you."

"For giving you Paul?"

"For giving me everything I desire."

Lisette swallowed hard. "You aren't angry with me?"

"For knowing me better than I know myself? For understanding what we both need and being brave enough to ask for it?" He shook his head. "How could I be angry about that?"

She bit down on her lip. "I don't want to be a conventional wife, Gabriel."

"I know that now."

"And I don't want you to be a conventional husband either."

He smiled at her, trying to put everything he wanted to say into that smile. "I was a fool to even think I could forgo all this, to think I could force either of us to change our sexual tastes." His wide gesture included the bed, the walls of the pleasure house, and Paul. "I was a fool not to tell you how much I love you as well."

Her hazel eyes widened and she put a hand to her throat. He regarded her carefully for a long moment, but it seemed she had nothing to say. Just as he was about to turn away and look at Paul, she launched herself at him and wrapped her arms around his neck.

"I love you, Gabriel. I love you more than anything in the entire world."

Gabriel let out his breath and held her tight. He had to swallow hard and his eyes blurred. "I want you to be happy, Lisette, and I'll do anything you want to keep you satisfied in bed."

Paul cleared his throat. "And I think that is my cue to leave." He patted Gabriel's shoulder. "I'll see you tomorrow at your solicitor's. I understand you have some business with my uncle."

Gabriel tore his gaze away from Lisette's and looked at Paul. "You don't have to go, Paul." Gabriel hesitated and Lisette nodded encouragingly at him. "I've been an idiot. I've denied my feelings for you for years."

"No, you haven't. I've *always* known how you felt about me." Paul's smile was full of wry compassion. "There are many different kinds of love, and I know you love me in your own way, and that you always will." He smoothed the crumpled sheets. "I did this so that you would be able to move *on*, not to try and rekindle our relationship."

"What do you mean?"

Paul held his gaze. "Seeing you with Lisette has finally made me understand what you meant when you said I deserved more than you were willing to give me." He shrugged. "You were right. I want more. I deserve to be loved completely."

"Are you sure?"

Paul grinned. "Not that I wouldn't welcome the opportunity to practice my skills in your bed with either of you until the love of my life comes along."

Gabriel put his hand on Paul's shoulder and drew him into a fierce, tight embrace. "You are always welcome to share our bed, Paul, for as long as you want."

Paul kissed the top of his head, kissed Lisette and climbed off the bed. "Then all is well."

"Are you certain, Paul?"

Paul looked back, his expression serene, his mouth curved in a wicked smile. "Yes, now stop worrying about me and go back to convincing your wife that you love her."

"Thank you," Gabriel whispered.

"And I thank you, too, Paul," Lisette added.

Paul waved a hand in airy dismissal and left the room, still naked and still smiling.

Gabriel barely noticed either Paul's exit or his lack of clothes. He was too intent on lowering his wife onto the bed and kissing her senseless. Her fingers brushed the silver rings and she slid them off his balls and rapidly expanding cock. She sighed his name and he continued to kiss her until he slid inside her as easily as if they were made for each other. And maybe that was true; perhaps he had finally found the place that made him feel safe forever.

He fucked her as sweetly and gently as he could and fell asleep in her arms; woke later without conscious thought and had to have her again. This was love, this sharing of themselves in the darkness. The horrors of his past couldn't compete with the joy of his future.

Tomorrow he had to face the final hurdle to regaining his inheritance and he would face it and win. He had everything to play for now.

26

Gabriel frowned as the crowd assembling in Mr. Brecon's small office grew even larger. Lisette had insisted on coming with him, but he'd expected that. He hadn't expected Paul to appear with his uncle, Lord Ashmolton, who'd apparently arranged the meeting in the letter Gabriel had failed to find and read a few days previously.

"Don't you have a bigger office, Mr. Brecon?"

His solicitor looked up from the mass of papers on his desk and shook his head. "I'm sorry, my lord. I didn't realize, until about an hour ago, that you had arranged to meet with Lord Ashmolton and Major Wesley today as well."

"Neither did I," Gabriel muttered. "Major Wesley is coming, too? If Mr. Sturges arrives, perhaps you can entertain him elsewhere until I've finished up here."

"Of course, my lord." Mr. Brecon turned toward the door. "Ah, here comes Major Wesley. Now we can begin."

Gabriel stood up to acknowledge Major Wesley's arrival and then resumed his seat beside Lisette and looked askance at

Lord Ashmolton. "What can I help you with today, gentlemen?"

Major Wesley smiled. "It's more about what we can tell you." He produced a large file of papers from a battered leather box. "I'm sure you'll be pleased to hear that my committee has absolved you of any wrongdoing over the loss of that information you carried in Spain."

Lord Ashmolton cleared his throat meaningfully. "I told the Prime Minister *and* the Minister for War that the charges were ridiculous. I'm glad they had the sense to listen to me, and to your committee, Major."

Gabriel nodded at the older man. "That was very good of you, sir, and most unexpected."

"Lord Ashmolton wasn't the only man who wished to speak on your behalf either." Major Wesley showed Gabriel a thick sheaf of papers. "All these testimonials are from former soldiers in your regiment or those still serving, including Lieutenant Colonel Delinsky and your cousin William Granger."

Gabriel took the bundle of letters with a hand that shook. "I find it hard to believe that all these men took the time to come to my defense."

"You were one of the best officers we had, Gabriel," Paul said quietly. "No true soldier would ever forget that."

Gabriel looked helplessly at Lisette. "At first I thought it was William who had raised this matter again, but obviously I was wrong."

Major Wesley placed the rest of the substantial file on the desk with a thump. "I'll leave this with you for a day or two, Swanfield, so that you can go through all the evidence against you and see my notes. I'm sure you'll find it interesting reading." He glanced at Gabriel. "It seems that your uncle, a Mr. Granger, has been the most vocal advocate for your court-martial."

"That doesn't surprise me at all."

"Mr. Granger's influence is waning though, Swanfield," Lord

Ashmolton said. "I doubt he'll be able to retain his stranglehold on your estates when word of this gets out. And word will get out and pressure will be mounted, you can depend on that." He snorted, "From what Wesley, here, has been telling me, Granger has been squandering vast sums of money trying to buy people to testify against you, but with little success."

"Other than beggaring my estate," Gabriel muttered. He felt curiously distanced now from the threat of more public condemnation and disgrace. "My uncle has a lot to answer for."

Lord Ashmolton stood up and stuck out his hand. "I apologize, but I have to leave now. I'm due at the House. I just wanted to be here when Wesley passed on the good news and to assure you that I will be doing everything in my power to make sure you regain both your reputation and your estates."

Gabriel shook the older man's hand. "As I said before, sir: You didn't have to do this for me, but I appreciate it more than I can say."

"Nonsense, young man!" Lord Ashmolton's voice boomed off the low-beamed ceiling, making Gabriel wince. "You brought our nephew out of that damn prison, saved his life! The St. Clare family always helps those who help them."

Gabriel decided to keep his mouth shut and just smile and acknowledge the assistance. It was still difficult for him to accept that he had friends and comrades who cared enough about him to stand by his side. He glanced down at Lisette, who was laughing at something Major Wesley was saying to her. If he hadn't met her, would he ever have restored his reputation? Somehow he doubted it. She'd given him the necessary courage to move forward and change his world. He found himself grinning like a fool. Perhaps his mother had been right, and a man's deeds did indeed come back to haunt him.

Gabriel looked at the bundle of letters in his hands, saw the one bearing William's name, and frowned. He looked through the rest and raised his head.

"I've just remembered something. Originally I thought it was William who was gossiping about me and stirring up the past, but I believe I was wrong."

Major Wesley paused to look at him. "You have another cousin who is in the military, don't you?"

"Yes, my cousin Michael." Gabriel grimaced. "He was always so pleasant to my face. Are you suggesting that he was working with his father all this time?"

"Read the file." Major Wesley tapped the pile of paperwork. "From all accounts he wasn't too happy about you *or* his older brother inheriting the earldom. He seemed to think it should be his."

"I wonder if he was also responsible for stirring up Lord Nash? They used to be quite close." Gabriel groaned. "Sometimes I hate families."

"You and me both." Major Wesley smiled. "Mine are after me to marry and produce an heir within the next twelve months and will not take no for an answer."

He saluted the assembled company and then turned to shake Gabriel's hand. "A pleasure meeting you again, Swanfield. I hope to renew our acquaintance at the Old Peninsular Club. Delinsky speaks very highly of you."

After Major Wesley departed with Lord Ashmolton and Paul, Gabriel sat back down and accepted a glass of sherry from Mr. Brecon. In truth, he was more nervous about this second meeting with Mr. Sturges than he'd been for the first. He vaguely remembered a Sturges family that had lived on the Swanfield estate when he was a boy, although he didn't know them well. If Sturges was a long time tenant of the previous earl and indebted to Mr. Granger, he was unlikely to be well disposed toward Gabriel.

He stood as a somberly dressed man of about Lord Ashmolton's age came into the office. He had thinning hair that might once have been red, and the slight build of a jockey.

"Lord Swanfield?"

Gabriel put out his hand. "Mr. Sturges. It is a pleasure to meet you, sir."

Mr. Sturges regarded him for a long moment over his wire-rimmed spectacles before he proffered his own hand. "We've met before. When you were a boy, you enjoyed stealing apples from the trees in my orchard."

Behind him, Gabriel was aware of Lisette's skirts rustling as if she'd sat forward to hear better. He studied the older man more carefully.

"Did you ever catch me?"

"Unfortunately not. You were always the first one back over the wall."

"I can only apologize for the loss of your apples, sir. At the time, I suspect they formed a large part of my diet."

Mr. Sturges met his gaze squarely. "I am more than aware that the previous earl treated you and yours shamefully, my lord. It is surprising that you didn't die from starvation or neglect."

Gabriel shrugged. "In truth, it was excellent preparation for the hardships of war. I was able to endure conditions my peers were unable to." He gestured at the empty chair beside Lisette. "Would you like to sit down, Mr. Sturges? And may I introduce you to my wife, the new Countess of Swanfield."

Mr. Sturges took Lisette's gloved hand and bowed low over it. "A pleasure to meet you, my lady. I read about the marriage in the *Times* on the journey down to London."

He settled himself in his chair and turned back to Gabriel. His forthright accent reminded Gabriel of his home, of his mother. . . . "I expect you'll be wanting to see the account books I brought with me."

Gabriel blinked at him. "The books you brought to show Mr. Granger?"

Mr. Sturges sighed. "With all due respect, my lord, Mr.

Granger has proved . . . very difficult to work with over the last few years. He's been attempting to wring money out of the estate that is simply not there. And unlike a lot of land agents, I refuse to evict perfectly decent families just to add to his revenues."

"I appreciate that." Gabriel let out his breath. "It would make matters a lot easier if you could simply hand the books over to me and Mr. Brecon, so that Mr. Granger doesn't even get to see them. Legally, the estate is mine. All I have to do is get my uncle to see that as well and renounce his claims. He can no longer claim I am unable to manage the estate and his threats no longer work."

"I'd be happy to do that. I was planning on handing in my resignation the next time I saw Mr. Granger."

"I'd much prefer it if you would stay on and help me run the estate properly."

Mr. Sturges stared at him as if sizing him up for market and then slowly nodded. "I believe I would like that. As long as you promise to come back and show your face. There are people there who would like to see you again, sir."

Gabriel swallowed hard and studied the floorboards. "That will be difficult for me, Mr. Sturges, because the one person I loved the most is no longer there."

Mr. Sturges took off his glasses, polished them on his handkerchief, and put them back on again. "Are you referring to your mother, my lord?"

Gabriel nodded and Lisette took his hand and squeezed it. "My uncle threatened to kill her if I did not obey him. I assume he carried out his threat."

"No, sir, he didn't."

Gabriel looked up at the other man. "I beg your pardon?"

"Your mother is very well." Mr. Sturges took off his glasses again. "In truth, she consented to become my wife several years ago."

Gabriel stared at him and wondered distantly if his mouth was open wide like a village idiot's. "She is your *wife*?"

"Indeed. After you were sent to school, I was ordered to keep her safe and secure. As the years went by, I grew very fond of her and refused to believe that she was a threat either to you or the earldom as Mr. Granger insisted." His voice hardened. "When Mr. Granger told me to lock her up and leave her to starve, I pretended I'd done what he'd asked. Then I, and the rest of the tenants, made a vow to keep her hidden from him and his agents whenever they turned up."

"You are my *stepfather*?"

Mr. Sturges sighed. "Yes, for my sins, I suppose I am."

"Then you have to forgive me those apples from your orchard."

Mr. Sturges smiled. "If I forgave you then, I can certainly forgive you now, seeing as everything on the estate, including my apples, belongs to you anyway." He frowned. "I only hope you can forgive me for going along with Mr. Granger for so many years. Your mother insisted I stay on and help the people who lived there. She said that my leaving would only create more hardship for those left behind, and I fear she was right. She was convinced you would come back to her one day."

Gabriel covered his face with his hands and tried to picture his mother the last time he'd seen her. She'd been screaming his name and trying to escape one of the Grangers' burly footmen to run after the carriage that was taking him away to school. A separation that neither of them realized would last over twenty years.

"My lord?"

Gabriel managed to look up and found a small miniature painting being pressed into his palm.

"This is how Rose looks now. I thought you might like to see it." Mr. Sturges hesitated. "She wanted to write to you, but she is still ashamed of her handwriting. I told her that you wouldn't care, but she assumes you are some high and mighty nobleman these days who wants nothing to do with her."

Gabriel stared down at the brown-haired woman smiling mischievously back at him, her blue eyes as startling as his own. Yes, she looked a little older, but her spirit was still there, the spirit that had survived rape and separation from her child and found happiness.

He struggled to speak. "I wanted to go back to her so badly but . . . my uncle said if I tried to contact her he would kill her. . . . I was too afraid. . . ."

Lisette touched his hand. "You can tell her that when you see her. I'm sure she'll understand."

"God, I hope so," he whispered. "I'd hate her to believe I'd simply abandoned her."

Mr. Sturges stood up. "I'll leave the books I brought with Mr. Brecon, and I'll speak to the Grangers' London agent. I'm sure he'll have some information for you, too."

"This will break him, won't it?" Gabriel looked up at his new stepfather. "This will finally bring him down."

"I hope so, sir. You deserve to succeed."

Gabriel stood up and held out his hand. Mr. Sturges shook it. "Good morning, my lord. It was a pleasure to meet you."

"Come to dinner with us tonight." Gabriel said, "We'll see you at seven."

For the first time, Mr. Sturges looked a little uncertain. "Are you sure? I'm hardly of a social standing that merits a dinner invitation. Perhaps I could call on you tomorrow morning instead?"

Lisette stood up and kissed him on the cheek. "You are the Earl of Swanfield's stepfather. You are welcome in our house at any time, isn't he, Gabriel?"

Gabriel could only look at her and nod. His life was about to change in so many ways, and he owed it all to his stubborn, argumentative, beautiful, adorable wife who had taught him what courage really meant.

He got up and patted Mr. Sturges on the shoulder. "Yes, indeed. It's about time I started paying you back for all those apples I stole. And when you meet the rest of the family, you will realize that you and my mother will fit in very well, very well indeed."

This time, Mr. Sturges's smile was far more genuine. "Then I'll gladly accept your invitation, my lord, as long as you don't mind if I bring another guest."

"Bring anyone you like, Mr. Sturges," Gabriel said jovially. "We'll welcome them for your sake."

By the time Mr. Brecon escorted Mr. Sturges down the stairs, Gabriel was glad to be alone with Lisette. His smile died as he looked at his wife.

"I have to go and see my uncle, don't I?"

She met his gaze. "You don't *have* to, Gabriel, but I think it might be a good idea, don't you?"

He sighed, rose to his feet, and held out his hand. "Will you come with me?"

She placed her gloved hand in his and smiled. "Of course. I wouldn't miss it for the world."

"You are a bloodthirsty wench, aren't you?" he murmured as they proceeded down the narrow staircase and out into the busy street. "I promise you I'm not going to lay a finger on him."

Their carriage rolled up and Gabriel gave the coachman the address of his uncle's club and then helped Lisette inside.

27

Gabriel took a deep steadying breath as he studied the imposing door to his uncle's club. He took Lisette's hand and walked
up the steps toward the doorman.

"Good morning. We wish to see Mr. Granger. Is he available?"

The doorman looked Gabriel up and down as if he was a
street vender hawking his wares. "Are you a member here, sir?"

"Obviously not."

"Then you can't go in, sir."

"I'm sure you have a morning room for callers tucked away
somewhere in this monstrous building?"

"We do, sir, but . . ."

Gabriel took off his hat and pulled off his gloves. "Then
we'll wait for Mr. Granger in there." He kept walking even as
the doorman tried to bar his way. "You'd better show me
where it is, or else I'll simply barge upstairs and start looking
for Mr. Granger myself."

"The waiting room is through here, sir." The doorman
sounded flustered as he darted around Gabriel to fling open a

door at the end of a dingy hallway. "Whom shall I say is asking for him, sir?"

"The Earl and Countess of Swanfield."

"Yes, sir."

Despite his age, the man disappeared from view with the speed of a greyhound. Gabriel grimaced at the cold dreary oak-paneled room and mourned the lack of a fire. Lisette tucked her hands into her fur muff and started pacing the floorboards, as if she was too cold or too nervous to sit down. Gabriel concentrated on calming his breathing and watching the door.

After a considerable wait, he heard voices in the corridor and straightened up. The door opened to admit his uncle, who was using a cane to walk with. Even in the dim light, Gabriel could see the yellowish, waxen tone of his uncle's skin, and the lines of pain etched into his face. Mr. Granger ignored Lisette and turned to Gabriel.

"I understand you wish to see me, Swanfield."

Gabriel inclined his head a frigid inch. "Indeed. I wanted to inform you that your stewardship of my estates is at an end. I've taken the final steps to regain control of my finances and separate them entirely from yours."

"Is that so?" Mr. Granger eased himself into a chair by the fireside and looked up at Gabriel, his expression inscrutable. "And what of the powers you so willingly relinquished to me on your return from Spain?"

Gabriel met his gaze without flinching. "I'm no longer *willing* to give you any control over me at all. According to my solicitor, the letter I signed when I was ill isn't legally binding. I have also gained the backing of some of the most influential men at court and in the government. Your day is done, uncle."

"My day *is* almost done, nephew, but that is between me and my God." Mr. Granger straightened painfully in his chair. "Do you intend to continue to extract vengeance from me for my 'imagined' wrongdoing?"

Gabriel tried to relax his clenched fists. "I'm not like you, uncle. Once my affairs are free of your interference I'm willing to let things stay in the past."

An expression of intense distaste flickered across Mr. Granger's face. "For a moment I thought you'd discovered your balls, nephew, and intended to act in a manner befitting your sire."

"You would prefer it if I ruined you? Why would I wish to do that, when I find nothing to admire or respect in the previous earl's conduct? I'd much rather move forward."

Anger flashed in Mr. Granger's faded brown eyes. "If he was here to witness your sniveling cowardice, your father would wish he'd smothered you at birth."

"No doubt he would." Gabriel found himself smiling at the impotent fury on the other man's face. There was nothing his uncle could do to hurt him anymore. *Nothing.* He had a whole new life to embark upon. His estate was safe, his mother was alive, and, best of all, he had Lisette beside him. For a moment, he almost felt sorry for his uncle, but not quite.

Mr. Granger glanced at Lisette. "Have you thought through all the ramifications of your choices, nephew? You are newly married. Is your wife ready to share in your continuing disgrace when a military court finds you guilty of cowardice?"

Lisette raised her chin and looked first at Gabriel and then at his uncle. "I'm ready to share in all aspects of my husband's life, sir. Surely that is what family is for?"

Gabriel fought a smile as she sat down. "I received news this morning from Major Wesley that I've been cleared of all charges," Gabriel said calmly. "I'm sure it will be in all the papers tomorrow. Please don't forget to tell Michael. I'm sure he'll be mortified to hear that his efforts to discredit me on your behalf have amounted to nothing."

Gabriel held out his hand and Lisette came to join him. He withdrew a letter from the inside of his coat and handed it to his uncle. "I've written down the terms of our legal separation.

I expect you to reply to my solicitor by the end of the week and agree to them."

"Why would I do that?"

Gabriel shrugged. "Because if you don't, I *will* drag you through the courts and beggar you. You might not be long for this world, but your family will suffer in your stead. I'm sure you wouldn't want that."

Spittle glistened on Mr. Granger's chin as he bared his teeth. "I've always said bad breeding will out. You are indeed the devil's spawn."

"Aye, and as I said, I have no wish to be like my father." Gabriel bowed. "Good-bye, uncle, and I hope I never have to see you again."

He turned to the door and escorted Lisette out. His desire to lambaste his uncle for every slight, grievance, and hurt had completely disappeared. It simply wasn't worth it. He waited for his composure to dissolve and for his body to start shaking in reaction to facing down his enemy, but nothing happened. He simply kept walking, his head held high and his past finally behind him.

Much later that evening, as Gabriel waited for Lisette to join him in the small family dining room at the rear of the immense house, he realized that he felt different. It was as if he'd sloughed off a skin and emerged into the light again. The small brass clock on the mantelpiece struck seven, and the door opened to admit his wife dressed in pale green and cream.

"Am I late?"

Gabriel smiled at her and noticed her heightened color and the small bruise on her throat where he'd nipped her skin during their recent lovemaking. "Not at all, my dear. In fact, I think our guests have just arrived."

Lisette came to stand by his side and he placed her gloved hand on his sleeve. He could hear the sound of voices approaching and the deep burr of Mr. Sturges's northern accent echoing in the marble hallway.

"Mr. Sturges, welcome to our . . ." He stopped speaking as Mr. Sturges ushered a diminutive woman into the room, a protective hand on her shoulder. She wore a modest, blue high-necked muslin gown and a soft white cap. Gabriel swallowed hard. "Ma'am?"

The woman lifted her head and smiled tremulously at him. "Gabriel?"

He wasn't aware of stepping forward, but suddenly she was in his arms and he was holding her and babbling incoherent nonsense in her ear. The familiar scent of lavender engulfed his senses. He couldn't let her go, he just *couldn't*.

"I never thought I'd see you again, I thought he'd killed you, I . . ."

She stroked his hair and rocked him until tears flowed from his eyes. "Ah, my little lamb, I know, I know . . ."

After some time, he found himself sitting next to his mother on the couch, still clutching her hand like the nine-year-old boy who'd never wanted to let her go in the first place. His emotions were in pieces, his vaunted control destroyed, and yet he didn't care at all. He looked up to find Lisette and Mr. Sturges smiling at him and managed to smile back.

"You didn't tell me that you'd brought my mother to London with you, sir."

His mother patted his hand. "He didn't bring me, lad. I insisted on coming. I figured Mr. Granger could no longer hurt me." She sighed. "I wasn't expecting you to want to see me. I thought I might get a glimpse of you in passing, just to make sure that you were all right."

He squeezed her hand. "How could you think I wouldn't want to see you?"

She grimaced, her vivid blue eyes fixed on his. "I'm still a scullery maid at heart, love. I wouldn't want to shame you in front of all your new, high-class friends."

Gabriel brought her work-roughened hand to his lips. "You could never shame me."

Mr. Sturges cleared his throat loudly. "I told you so, my dear. I told you he was a good, decent man despite his sire."

Lisette came to kneel at his side and looked up at his mother. "Of course Gabriel is a good man. He *is* your son after all." She nodded reassuringly at his mother. "Ma'am, Gabriel and I have both learned that listening to society's opinions is a very bad thing indeed. We are quite happy to walk our own path." Her smile was bright and full of love. "My family isn't exactly what you might consider *conventional* either."

Gabriel studied the faces of the two women he loved most in the world. His past and his future irrevocably intertwined, his life made whole, his ability to love mended and renewed. Whatever the future held, he knew he would face it with confidence, because he really didn't have a choice. Between them, his wife and his mother would never let him be alone again.